THE LIVING EDGE

CHAINS
BOOK 2

CHERISE SINCLAIR

VanScoy Publishing Group

TO MY READERS:

It's been over a decade since I wrote The Dom's Dungeon. (Eeks, time got away from me). But Drake wanted his story. So... I'm ignoring the long interval and setting The Living Edge in the current year; however in the *story* timeline, only a year or so has passed since The Dom's Dungeon. I'm sorry it took so long to bring you this story!

The Living Edge

Copyright © 2025 by Cherise Sinclair All rights reserved
ISBN: 978-1-947219-61-8
Published by VanScoy Publishing Group
Cover design by April McMillan
Cover Photographer: Golden Czermak FuriousFotog
Cover Model: Brian Naranjo

This book is a work of fiction. The names, characters, places, and incidents are products of the writer's imagination or are used fictitiously. Any resemblance to persons, living or dead, actual events or locales is entirely coincidental.

All rights reserved. This copy is intended for the original purchaser of this book only. No part of this text may be used, including but not limited to the training or use by artificial intelligence (AI), or reproduced, transmitted, down-loaded, decompiled, reverse engineered, or distributed in any manner whatsoever without express written permission from the author.

Warning: This book contains sexually explicit scenes and adult language and may be considered offensive to some readers. This book is for sale to adults only, as defined by the laws of the country in which you made your purchase.

Disclaimer: Please do not try any new sexual practice, without the guidance of an experienced practitioner. Neither the publisher nor the author will be responsible for any loss, harm, injury, or death resulting from use of the information contained in this book.

This book is licensed for your personal enjoyment only. This book may not be re-sold or given away to other people. If you would like to share this book with another person, please purchase an additional copy for each recipient. If you're reading this book and did not purchase it, or it was not purchased for your use only, please purchase your own copy.

Thank you for respecting the hard work of this author.

ACKNOWLEDGMENTS

Heaps of gratitude go to Bianca Sommerland of I'm No Angel who edited the content amid juggling a thousand other things.

A big shout-out to the intrepid copy-editing and proof-reading team of Red Quill Editing: Ekatarina Sayanova, Tracy Damron-Roelle, and Rebecca Cartee always manage to catch bloopers and comma splices and idiotic author errors whilst leaving comments that crack me up.

A bazillion hugs to wonderful Monette Michaels for hand-holding and cover art help. And then to critique the blurb? That's truly the mark of a bestie.

My alpha and beta readers: y'all have stuck with me for years now, and my gratitude grows stronger with each book. Thank you, JJ Foster, Lisa White, Marian Shulman, and Barb Jack. Y'all are the best!

Leagh Christensen and Lisa Simo-Kinzer, what can I say? To admin a readers group requires an inexhaustible supply of patience and tact...and when those readers are Shadowkittens? Well, you two magnificent women leave me in awe. Thank you.

My Shadowkittens—you'll never know how much your support means to me, especially this year when my dearheart and I were laid low with health issues and when the flow of words stuttered to a halt. But instead of the recriminations I feared due to the long wait between books, you have poured out all the loving support and cheerful encouragement any author could ask for. I love you all.

- *Cherise*

PROLOGUE

"C'mon, you stinking piece of dead metal," Aralia Lanigan whispered.

From behind her came the sounds of jiggling, like Sticks needed to piss—or was as scared as she was. "Fuck's sake, stop talking an' hurry up," he muttered.

Hey, picking a lock wasn't something she could hurry. Forcing her fingers to stay steady, she inserted her piece of metal into the keyhole and applied pressure, then worked her makeshift pick in to lift the pins. *Work, damn you.*

Back when Pa added locksmithing to his handyman business, she'd gotten really good at picking locks. But proper tools made the difference.

She raked the pick over the pins again.

Metal hardware is so lame.

Not like wood. Wood was *alive*. She loved everything about it, from choosing the perfect grain and density, to cutting and fitting and sanding it smooth of any tiny imperfection. And scents like cedarwood or cherry or pine made her smile every time.

Metal or not, her stupid lockpicks better get the job done fast. She *needed* a place to stay, even if she'd have to share it with dumbass Sticks who'd spotted the overcrowded mailbox and newspapers on the porch and known the owners were on vacation.

"Speed it *up*, Ray," Sticks hissed. Rail-thin under baggy clothes.

"Doing my best." She gritted her teeth to keep from yelling at him and lifted another pin.

Why'd you have to die, Pa?

No, shouldn't blame him, even if it was so freaking unfair. He'd been tearing out planking in a fire-damaged house, and the entire floor gave way, and he'd landed real bad in the cement basement.

He never woke up. Not even to say goodbye.

Tears blurred her eyes. He'd loved her, mostly, but they hadn't got along so great. He'd wanted a quiet daughter.

I tried to be what you wanted, Pa. She'd tried so, so hard.

Now he was gone, and her whole life was screwed up.

Like being dumped into a group home to wait for a long-term foster home or adoption. Only no one wanted sixteen-year-old girls.

No one except three older boys who'd kept pushing her for "favors."

Last week, it'd all gone bad.

So she stole baggy clothes from one dipshit's room and ditched school after attendance. Tight-wrapped her boobs, chopped off her hair, streaked her face with dirt.

Funny how a boy on the streets was safer than a girl in a group home. Being stinky and filthy helped—even the pissbuckets who went after young boys didn't give her a second look. Some kids in an old warehouse let her sleep in a corner.

This house would be better.

"Got it yet?"

"Nearly." Feeling Stick's breath on her neck, she bit her lip and carefully tried the next pin. *Almost...almost...*

Behind her, a car door thudded.

Sticks spun. "Shit, we're busted!" He shoved her so hard, she fell on her ass, then he leaped off the porch and sprinted down the street.

Leaving her behind. She tried to scramble to her feet.

"Look at him go." A man's hard hand closed on her shoulder. "Ever heard the saying, '*if chased, I don't have to run fast, I just have to run faster than the other guy*'?"

After a second, she understood the joke. That shithead Sticks had made sure she was the slowest so he could get away. He'd left her to...

Ray looked up, and her heart sank.

A cop, uniform and all. He was huge, way tall, and had more muscles than Thor.

He tugged her handmade lockpicks from her hand and checked them out. "Nice crafting."

The tiny surge of warmth from the compliment faded fast because he was studying her like a hawk. "How old are you?"

Noooo. What to do? Be arrested as an adult or dragged back to foster care?

I don't wanna do either. He still had a grip on her shoulder. Running was out. He wouldn't be easy to fool. Hot tears pooled in her eyes, and her vision blurred. *I'm such a loser.*

The boys in foster care would beat her up. Again.

"How old," he repeated more softly.

I choose jail. She raised her chin to look older and made her voice all raspy. "Nineteen."

He snorted. "Try again, kid."

"Sixteen, but I won't go back; I *won't*. Put me in jail."

The sharp blue eyes narrowed. "Go back where? Home?"

Her breathing hitched when a sob caught in her throat. He'd dump her back there and—

"Hey, hey, easy there." The cop crouched beside her, ran a hand down her back comfortingly...and stopped. His finger traced sideways over the tight band she'd wrapped around her chest to flatten her breasts. "Oh, fuck me. You're no boy."

She stared at her dirt-streaked hands. Her knuckles were still raw from hitting the biggest of the foster kids. More scrapes were from defending her corner in the warehouse. Her skin itched from sweat and filth.

"You had me fooled, girl." With an exasperated grunt, the cop took a step back and after a second, took a seat on the steps. Casually leaning against the railing, he motioned to her. "Let's talk."

She eyed him. He wasn't yelling, didn't seem pissed off. Just waiting.

Slowly, she sat on the step, leaving space between them.

Although he still dwarfed her with his size, his deep voice was soft. "Tell me why you won't go back to wherever."

"Foster home," she whispered.

He swore under his breath. "Okay, you were in foster care. Tell me what happened to make you run."

She dared to look up at him. His jaw was firm—almost square—his face really hard. But he didn't seem mean. "Three older boys. They wanted sex stuff, like blow jobs." At the memory of being shoved to her knees, she felt her stomach twist. *Don't puke.* "The other girls—they give in to keep from getting hurt. I didn't."

"No adult would help?"

Her laugh came out bitter. "I told the foster mother, but one of them is her son. She called me a liar." Anger flared before tears burned her eyes. "The boys beat me up for talking, so I ran away."

His fingers closed on her chin and tilted her head toward the sunlight. His gaze was on her purple, swollen cheekbone. "That where you got this?"

"Nah. That was a fight at the ware—at where I'm staying. The foster home boys are real careful to hit where nothing shows." *Being as how they are total wankpuffins.*

His brows drew together, and his expression turned so pissed off she edged away from him. He huffed out a breath. "Which means you have sore ribs and gut?"

"Yeah." Everything hurt, really. "And back and legs and shoulders." She'd fought 'til she fell, then they kicked her and kicked her. She lifted her chin. "I gave one of 'em a black eye."

His grin was fast and wicked. "Good for you. What's your name, kiddo?"

"Ray." When he raised an eyebrow, she sighed and gave in. "Aralia Lanigan."

"Aur—say it again."

"*Ah-RAY-lee-ah.*"

"You prefer Ray?"

"I guess." And as always when she was nervous...or happy...or normal, the words spewed out in a river. "Before Pa d-died, he was a handyman, mainly a carpenter, and he wanted to call me after Ray Eames. She was, like, a furniture designer. Only Mom wanted me to have a girl's name. I think they had a fight about it."

"Parents, right?" He smiled slightly. "So your father called you Ray and your mom, Aralia. Where's your mother now?"

"Gone. Walked out when I was seven." She wrung her hands together. *Did Mom leave because of me? Maybe I talk too much, am too emotional and scatter-brained, am hard to tolerate...all the things Pa complained about. Only he said Mom was the same.*

Why didn't Mom want me? Take me with her? The question still squeezed at her heart like her ribs were too tight. "Pa got a notice last year that she died in a car crash."

"No other relatives?"

Ray shook her head.

"I see." He pulled out a notepad. "Tell me about the foster home. Who runs it?"

As she talked, he wrote down the names of everyone and how she'd ended up in the foster home and then more about Pa and about her lockpicks, so she told him about Pa's handyman business and how she helped. He even asked about her hobbies.

Her mouth was all dry when he finally shoved the pen in his pocket. "Time to be about solving this."

When he rose, her muscles tensed. She could leap off the steps and make a run for it. Might be able to get away...although he had really long legs, and she hurt enough it'd slow her down.

Maybe...maybe he might really help me? He seemed really nice.

When she stood up, his nod of approval showed he'd seen her thinking. And she'd made the right choice.

After stowing her in the back of his patrol car, which stank of cleaning stuff, he drove to a McDonald's and bought her lunch. Were cops allowed to do that?

She sat in the back eating while he leaned on the front of the car and made phone call after phone call. And she watched and listened.

When someone gave him trouble, his dark eyebrows would pull together, and his voice'd get really firm. Made her think of a movie star military dude who'd snap out orders. And it was all for her safety.

She wrapped her arms around herself. Maybe she didn't want a boyfriend or anything right now—not for ages and ages—but someday, maybe she'd find someone like him. Someone who just... liked her without wanting her to be different.

Hell, she even kinda enjoyed how he told her what to do, and wasn't that weird? When the principal of her old school spouted off his bullshit orders, she'd done her best to jerk his chain.

Eventually, he pocketed his cell and climbed into the car. "I won, princess. Doesn't always happen, but today things fell out right."

She shivered. "Am I going back there?"

"Back to Kitsap County, yes. To that foster home? Absolutely not. The foster mother will be investigated, and her license will probably be pulled. You're going to a friend of mine—the father of a buddy I served with. When I ended up here, George introduced me around. He's getting on in years, but he used to do short-term fosters and still has a current license."

A man. With a dick. Not good, *so* not good. But this cop—he *was* trying. "What's your name, anyway?"

He smiled at her in the rearview mirror. "Max or if we're being formal, Officer Drago."

The ferry across Puget Sound wasn't the same one she'd taken from Bremerton. When he drove off into a tiny town and onto a forest road, she frowned. "Where are we?"

"Bainbridge Island."

Whoa, really? Didn't only rich people live here?

The private drive he pulled into was almost invisible within the forest. A minute later, he parked in front of an incredible house. Two stories. Curving wooden decks all around and huge, fancy-ass windows in graceful arches.

It was like the wind and weather had rounded off all the hard corners and straight lines.

"I th-think you're in the wrong place." She tried to fade back into the seat.

He laughed. "No, this is where we're going. George calls the place 'WoodSong'." He opened the back door for her. "Jump on out now."

As the cop shut the car door, a man came around the side of the house. Past him, almost behind the house, a one-story building was barely visible. "Max. It's good to see you."

"And you, George."

As the men shook hands, Ray studied the man who owned this place that sure wasn't a foster home. He had a short beard and mustache, deep-set eyes, and olive skin. His straight black hair was going gray.

"George, this is Ray, the youngster I called about." Officer Drago smiled at her. "Ray, this is George Matsuda."

"Call me George. Before we even start, I should mention I

have an odd rule, one Max tries to ignore. I rarely allow visitors to WoodSong, which means you can't bring friends home."

He watched her as if expecting her to be upset, to back out. All she felt was relief. No strangers, no pressure. "Works for me."

One eyebrow rose, then his light brown eyes narrowed. "You're no boy."

So much for her disguise. Over a week on the streets and none of the homeless had caught on. It was kinda funny the cop hadn't told him.

In fact, Max was grinning.

"You're as bad as my sons." Shaking his head, George motioned toward the house. "Come on in, you two." He led them up the steps and paused in a blue-tiled area to remove his shoes. To her surprise, so did the cop.

Right, okay. She toed off her shoes and took a step up to the hardwood flooring and was handed a pair of slippers.

Uh, right. Following the two men into the house, she stopped to stare. She'd heard of open floor plans, but this was... *Wow, just wow.* Hardwood flooring, wood rafters, and trim with a grain so pretty she was in awe. A wall of windows overlooking the blue-gray waters of Puget Sound curved outward for the living area. There was a leather recliner, big comfy-looking couches, and overstuffed chairs, all in shades of white.

A fireplace on the back wall had a mantel of photographs. She sidled over to take a peek. You could tell a lot about a person by their pics.

At the left end were photos of George with two young boys and a pretty woman. Then the two boys as teens and only George. A batch of pics with different teens. Maybe the foster kids? Then him and...a man? Arms around each other. More than really close.

Was George gay? He wouldn't be *interested* in her? Yes!

Movement caught her attention. In a small alcove's window seat, two furry heads popped up from a pile of blankets.

He has kitties.

Pa never let her have pets, despite all her pleading.

She started to walk over, only... The shelves bracketing the fireplace were filled with the most interesting wood art. Lots of people doodled with a pencil to make cool pictures. This shelf had *wood* doodles. One was a spiraling twist. Candlesticks that almost swirled.

She managed to move away, but then the mahogany end tables beside the couch had legs so beautifully carved she bent to fondle them. Who knew something so basic could be art.

And the *coffee table*. The slab top had a swirling grain, and the edges weren't straight but somehow looked as if the wood had grown that way. Was still alive.

Unable to resist, she ran her fingers over the curves. "It's like it's breathing."

When George tilted his head, she realized she'd spoken out loud. He raised an expressive eyebrow. "We call the technique 'live edge' for a reason. Max says you love wood. Want to learn how?"

Yes, yes, yes. "More than any fucking thing in my whole fucking life." The words spilled out before she could stop. Too loud, too emotional. And she could almost hear Pa: "*Why can't you behave like other kids. Calm down, dammit, stop acting like your stupid mother.*"

She looked down to keep from crying. George would for sure turn her down now.

"You'll do, girl." The old man's laugh was deep and open as he turned to the cop. "All right, Max. She can stay. Tell the social worker to bring the paperwork."

"It's a plan." The cop grinned at her. "You going to be all right, little burglar?"

She couldn't even speak.

Words weren't needed in heaven, after all.

CHAPTER ONE

T*en years later*

"Turn left here." Ray pointed, and Theodore made the turn. Almost home. She bounced on the passenger seat, urging the car forward. It'd been so *long* since she'd seen George and WoodSong.

Ten amazing years ago, George had taken her in as a foster child, then a woodworking apprentice, then a partner. Truly, aside from one hellish incident, it'd been everything she'd ever wanted. These past months were the longest she'd been away.

Indiana winters lasted forever. To get her bachelor's degree finished up within the year, she hadn't even returned for holidays. But now... Back in Washington. Soon to see George. If she didn't vibrate right out of her skin first. "Turn into this drive. Almost there, almost there."

"Jesus, Ray, settle down." After making the turn, Theodore gave her a chiding glance. "You're hyper again. Nobody enjoys you going off."

The unspoken words—*especially me*—were plain as day.

Hunching her shoulders, she stared down at the floor mat and tried to control her emotions. Theodore hated when she was what he called over-the-top. Pa had felt the same way. "Sorry," she whispered.

"Hey, it's okay." He reached over to touch her tightly fisted left hand. "You're excited; I get it. But you're not a toddler. Act like an adult, yeah?"

Finally, the car came to a stop in front of the house, all curving lines and windows, somehow blending in with the forest around it. WoodSong, another name for home.

When she'd called, George made an exception to his no-visitors rule and said to bring Theodore. He was going to do a protective parental inspection. And wasn't that cool?

"He might be in the workshop and not hear us." Ray shoved the door open and jumped out. A long, happy breath brought air scented with fir trees and moss and the briny fragrance of Puget Sound.

The front door opened, and George stepped out.

She dashed up the steps to hug him...and stumbled to a stop. "What...?"

Gray tinted his olive skin. His cheeks sank inward, making the bones jut out. His clothing hung on him as if the shirt and jeans were two sizes too big, except the forest green work shirt was one she'd given him last year.

And it had fit perfectly then.

"No. Gods, no." He'd looked almost this bad before. Twice. Rather than grabbing him for a hug, she took his hands. "The cancer returned?" *No, please, no.*

His smile was wry. "I'm afraid so, Ray-chan." He looked past her. "Welcome. You must be Theodore."

"I am." Theodore reached around her to shake hands. "Good to meet you."

"And you." George put an arm around her shoulders. She could feel his bones, as if all the flesh had melted away. "Let's go inside."

He sounded different, too, as hoarse as if he'd strained his voice.

Pausing to remove her shoes in the genkan, she motioned for Theodore to do the same. He patted her shoulder and complied.

"Have a seat, Theodore." George motioned to one of the overstuffed chairs and then sat beside her on the couch.

Turning slightly, she saw how pain had etched lines around his deep-set, brown eyes. His short beard and hair were now almost all gray.

Her breathing was already hitching as dread lodged in her gut. "How bad, Faj?"

She saw Theodore's puzzled frown at the nickname. Come to think of it, she mostly used it when talking with George in person. A year after coming to WoodSong, she realized he didn't consider her a short-term foster. He was keeping her. How she'd cried. And soon after started calling him a foster-father kind of name, "Father G," which eventually compressed into Faj.

"Ray-chan." He took her hand. "It's my time."

"No." She rose so fast she staggered. "You beat it before. Twice. There are new treatments and..."

He was shaking his head. "Too many places, too advanced. The doctors say my time is short."

"No. No, no, no." She could hear her voice rise. "We can fix this—fix you again. I know we can."

Theodore sighed loudly. "Honestly, Ray. Shut it down. He doesn't need your drama now."

Flinching, she sat down quickly and put her hands between her knees. Tried to squeeze all her emotions into a cold, dark cave.

"Ray-chan." George's frown came and went so quickly she almost missed it.

"I'm sorry, George." Cold from hiding in her mental cave, she wrapped her arms around herself. "Why didn't you tell me? I would've come back right away."

He rested his hand on her hair. "That's why. I wanted you to complete your degree."

His love could warm the coldest room. She pulled in a shuddering breath. "There's nothing we can do?"

"No." His smile appeared. A genuine smile. "I already had the gift of extra time twice. And although living another couple of decades would be nice, I'm not averse to this. I have enough time to get matters in order before a quick exit. My father had Alzheimer's; I will escape his fate."

He was a very private person, and she'd always felt honored whenever he shared some of his past. Usually when they were together in the workshop. His soft voice would carry over the rhythmic sound of sanding. He'd told her of slowly losing his beloved father over several years. Of days when his father didn't recognize him or his mother.

But still...

Tears filled her eyes, and she let out a hiccupping sob. "I don't want you to die." She reached for him—

Theodore made a disgusted sound. "Ray, control."

"Sorry, sorry." She sat back, blinking hard.

Faj's mouth tightened, then he rose. "Theodore, I fear this is a poor time for a visit." He held out his hand. "Thank you for bringing Ray-chan home."

Caught in George's politeness trap, Theodore rose, shook hands, and headed for the door. "I guess you'll want to stay tonight, doll. I'll leave your suitcase on the porch."

She swallowed. "Yes. Thank you."

"I'll call you...uh, tomorrow so you can start moving into my place."

Move in? Sure, they'd talked about it, but she hadn't completely decided. He lived in Seattle, and she'd planned to continue working with George here on Bainbridge Island.

And now...

How could he think she'd leave Faj when he was...was...dying? She shook her head.

But Theodore had already left.

That evening, she carried mugs of hot chocolate into the great room.

Earlier, when she'd gone upstairs to her small bedroom, it was sparkling clean. A bouquet of pink peonies from the cottage garden sat on her dresser.

Although his sons were grown, Tomo in the military and Kaden with his own family, they each had a bedroom, and Faj had always welcomed them home with flowers in their bedrooms.

She'd never left for long before, but she still had a room here too. And his love, even if she was only a foster child.

Which was why she'd bawled her eyes out in the shower.

"Can we talk now?"

George was in his favorite recliner and accepted his drink with a soft, "Thank you, Ray-chan."

She managed to smile for him. Curling into a corner of the big overstuffed sectional, she automatically looked around for the cats.

Stupid me. No cats. The ache of loss intensified. Mikan had outlived Yuki by a couple of years but died this winter while Ray was away.

Gods, she'd loved both of the adorable furballs. When she moved in, sweet Mikan was immediately friendly. Eventually, aloof Yuki decided she was a nice *hooman* and added her to his acceptable lap-providers. But Mikan had been her favorite. The solemn ginger tomcat had placidly listened to her venting about whatever...as long as she kept petting him.

Their absence left a hole in the peaceful home.

What would she do when George was gone too? She swallowed hard. "Faj..."

"Mmmhmm?" He was considering her in that focused way he had. The one that made her feel like a mouse under a cat's paw... and the most important person in his life at the moment.

Even as warmth spread through her, she frowned. "*What?*"

A quirk of his lips said he recognized her mock defiance. "When did you and Theodore grow serious enough to plan to live together?"

She talked with George every week while in Indiana. Just to touch base. Although she should smack him for not telling her his cancer had come back. Then again, he never liked to share important matters over the phone. Their most meaningful conversations happened while working or cooking together.

As for his question... "I'm not sure we are serious. Or moving in together. A couple of weeks ago, I thought I was falling in love with him." She shook her head, feeling her face screw up in the wrinkled way Theodore made fun of.

Faj simply smiled. "That's your puzzled expression. Have you bumped into a boulder on the downhill slide into love?"

"Maybe?" She sucked down some hot chocolate, feeling the mini-marshmallows bob against her upper lip. The meeting between George and Theodore hadn't gone the way she thought it would. Faj hadn't been friendly at all. "You can read people so good. Almost like their personalities strip down and get naked for you. How come you're so much better at it than me?"

He never minded how her brain swerved off onto side excursions. Even as a teen, she'd known how rare his acceptance was.

"Having a cautious, analytical personality helps. You, girl, leap before you look. I'm also older, more experienced, and"—a corner of his mouth tipped up—"have some...training in observing people."

She did tend to jump into situations. "You didn't like Theodore." George hadn't given any warm smiles. His voice had been chilly, his posture stiff. She *could* kind of read people—her friends and family, at least—when she paid attention. "How come?"

"It would be more accurate to say I didn't enjoy how he talked to you or how you responded."

"I don't understand." Theodore hadn't talked to her. "Oh, you mean when he told me to calm down?"

"Yes, Ray-chan." The muscles in George's face had no padding to conceal the way they tightened. "Rather than offering support, he spoke to you as if you were misbehaving. Were too emotional even when learning someone you love is going to die."

It took her a moment to get past hearing *going to die*. She blinked hard and tried a light laugh. "Theodore thinks I'm a drama queen."

George rubbed his face with both hands, something he did when at a loss for the right words. "You said your father tried to fit you into a cold, emotionless shell. Is this not what your Theodore is doing?"

"What?" She turned her gaze away, toward the darkness outside the floor-to-ceiling windows. When she was younger, Faj worked with her to see how Pa's behavior had been verbally and emotionally abusive. She'd finally understood...intellectually.

But Theodore? She swallowed. In the beginning, he said he loved her energy, her open emotions. How alive she was.

Recently, his compliments turned to criticism. *"You're such a drama queen." "Stop acting out." "What are you, five?"*

"*Noooo.* Am I really dating someone who treats me the way Pa did?" Her belly hurt as her dreams of love twisted and cracked worse than a warped piece of wood. "I *am*." She threw her hands up in the air in pure disgust. "He doesn't like who I am. Not really."

George tilted his head slightly. Waiting for her to think it all out.

Had she misled Theodore in some way? "I haven't changed."

On her carved wooden ring, she rolled the tiny fidget beads back and forth. "We met after I won at darts in a bar, and hey, I went into a total screaming victory dance."

George laughed softly. He'd seen her various victory dances... for finishing a tricky carving, when a chocolate cake came out perfect, when she'd mastered intricate joinery. After she'd first arrived, she'd done one without thinking—and seen him, and her bones tried to shrink. Rather than making fun of her, he ruffled her hair and told her success should be celebrated.

Her father would've sent her to her room.

Months ago, at the bar, Theodore had *liked* her victory dance. "He seemed so wonderful, and we bonded over missing Washington's cool air and evergreens. He's the one who changed." She sighed. "I guess when we got serious. Now he wants me to be a quiet person. Soft-spoken. Placid."

"So it appeared to me."

Each time Theodore chided her, she felt stupider. Wrong. And now, when she got loud, she almost cringed, even if she was all by herself.

She was letting him smother her personality. "I can't believe I didn't notice."

Hell, it was because Pa had done the same thing. It didn't take a psychologist to figure it out. She'd fallen for someone like her father. "I don't want to be with a person who spends his time hushing me."

"No, Ray-chan, you don't. Expecting someone to change isn't a healthy way to love."

Theodore doesn't love me. Not the real me.

She pulled in a shaky breath. She'd get over this. She would. But... "Sometimes it feels as if no one likes me for who I am." Her eyes burned, and she blinked hard. "And I sound purely pitiful."

He opened his arms for a hug. "Ray-chan, in the years to come, many will love you exactly as you are. I'm proud to have been one of the first."

CHAPTER TWO

Breathing in the briny night air, Ray followed Marisol off the ferry and down the walkway. The last ferry from Seattle to Bainbridge Island on a Thursday night had been pretty quiet aside from a few noisy drunks.

"Thanks for inviting me to go with you and your friends tonight," Ray said. "*Les Misérables* was amazing. I'm glad you dragged me out of my cave. Although now, I'm going to be humming, 'Can You Hear The People Sing' for days."

Marisol snickered. "I know, right?" A nursing student at the University of Washington, Marisol was twenty years old, brown-eyed, brown-haired, and a total sweetheart. She and her mother lived next door to WoodSong, so Marisol and Ray ended up friends, despite the six year age gap. "I'm ready for the revolution. Burn the patriarchy."

"Hooyah, get out the pitchforks." Then Ray winced. "Ah, maybe not yet though. I need to buckle down and get some work done, or I'll be eating mac 'n' cheese for meals."

"That's way ick, woman."

As they entered the shadowy parking lot, Ray inhaled and stretched. She'd needed this night out to remind herself life was for the living. She'd mourned long enough. Two months where she'd done basically...nothing.

Maybe it'd helped being kinda prepared since, each time, the doctors had warned George the cancer would probably return.

It still hurt. And, to be honest, she'd mourn Faj for the rest of her life.

But she'd finally crawled out of the pit of grief and wasn't pouring out a fountain of tears every few minutes.

His sons had been pretty devastated, too, and they'd all cried together. A Marine, Tomo took leave and arrived the day after her, which was good since Faj only lived another week. Kaden had already been flying back and forth from the East Coast, dividing time between his wife who was recovering from a car accident and his father.

Tomo and Kaden had needed her, and gods, she was grateful to get to show Faj how much he meant to her. To be there for him the way he'd been her anchor for ten years.

"I was kinda surprised you were free to join us." Marisol bumped Ray's shoulder companionably. "George told Mamá you've been seeing someone."

Ray huffed a laugh. Marisol's mom did love to stay abreast of all the gossip. "Not since I got back, and I'm sure not looking to jump into another relationship."

In fact, Theodore had been pretty pissed off when she broke up with him. Then he proved Faj's point by demanding *why* but not believing her when she told him. "How about you?"

"*Nada.* I haven't found the kind of man I want. Still looking." Marisol walked alongside the line of trees toward where Ray had parked the car. "So what are you doing in the shop now? Anything as fun as your horror thingies?"

Ray snorted. "Always. One place in Pike Place Market will take anything I offer. I have a couple of Cthulhu statues complete with facial tentacles, a piece with a kraken crushing a ship in its tentacles."

"Mamá is still appalled at what you make. Way back when, you should've heard George telling her you were into Lovecraft and all things creepy. Mamá finally decided it was a teen thing and was grateful I was only into boy bands."

Too funny. Marisol's mother was such a sweet—read *proper*—person.

Marisol grinned. "I can't wait to see what she thinks of you adding the blue-green ends to your hair. I love it, by the way."

"Thanks." Laughing, Ray held up a strand of hair, still pleased with the way the red-brown turned into turquoise. She needed something…vivid…to remind herself she was alive. "Anyway, I do have normal woodturnings your mom would approve of. Candle holders, decorative boxes, and bowls to drop off at the galleries here and in Seattle." The small stuff provided a nice paycheck, especially during tourist season. "I need to get word out I'm back and available for custom work."

The desire to simply hibernate swept over her, and she shoved it down. "I'll make those calls. Plus, George had two contracts for projects he'd been working on."

"Oh." Marisol pursed her lips. "He was all about 'you finish what you start.' Did he ask you to complete them?"

"Actually no, he said the clients knew the jobs wouldn't get done." Reaching her red SUV, Ray leaned against the door. "And it's been a couple of month since he…"

She choked and set her mind on the projects. The beautiful work he'd already begun cried out to be completed. How could she leave it undone? It would make her feel…like she hadn't lost him completely. Her voice cracked as she said, "The wood is in the shop, and since he started the work, I'll see if they want me to finish. Our styles are similar, and I can change mine to be closer to his if needed."

Marisol patted her arm. "You know, George boasted about you all the time. Said you're already really well-known in the Northwest, and eventually, you'd be even more famous than him."

He'd been proud of her. Ray's eyes stung with sudden tears. *Gods, Faj, I miss you.* "Well. Let's get our butts home."

She pulled the door open and paused at the sound of a high-pitched, pained mew...followed by men's laughter. More than one man. "What's that?"

"Fuck, it scratched me." The man was slurring his words.

"You're more of a pussy than the pussy."

The laughter grew louder.

"C'mon, grab it. I wanna toss it in with your pitbull. See which one of them wins."

Ray stiffened. Surely the drunks weren't trying to catch a cat to kill it.

"My dog will rip it to pieces, no contest."

Those cum-sniffing dingleberries. Nope, not happening on my watch.

"Marisol." She kept her voice quiet. "Get in the driver's seat and follow me with the car.

"You're going to do something crazy, aren't you?" Cursing under her breath in Spanish, Marisol took the key fob, slid behind the wheel, and pulled the door closed. The window lowered. "Don't die."

"You got it."

Only...even though she still did the karate katas George had taught her, she'd be one female against several men. Faj would say to think twice.

Right. She opened the back door and grabbed one of the baseball bats from the back seat. Years ago, Tomo had gone all drill-sergeant bossy as he taught her self defense. *"Concealed weapons are illegal. But sports equipment is fine so long as you have all the shit needed to show you play the game."*

Swinging the bat to get a feel for it, she smiled grimly. *I've got all the shit, Tomo.* Even though she hadn't played baseball in years. "Turn the brights on when I yell." After a thought, she added, "Call the police if things go sour."

Peace-loving, quiet Marisol gave a soft whine of dismay.

THE LIVING EDGE

Ray headed toward the men's voices—and her heart began to pound. *This is so stupid. I'm outnumbered. But...it's a kitty.*

In the strip of trees next to the parking lot, several figures clustered together.

One big man held a small, dark brown cat by its scruff.

Anger swept through her. As she pulled up the hood of her oversized sweatshirt to hide her face, she heard the car tires on the pavement behind her. *Good girl, Marisol.*

With the baseball bat hidden behind her leg, she shouted in her deepest, raspiest voice, "Drop the cat and get the fuck out of here."

"Fuck." The second man, a lanky drunk, spun around.

The bearded man holding the cat looked Ray over and sneered. "Get lost, bitch."

He knew she was female. Her gut clenched with fear. She was going to get hurt.

The third man had a beer belly but was twice her size. He took a step forward. "Yeah, butt out."

The second one cupped his crotch. "Or stay. Another *pussy* to destroy would be good."

Her fingers tightened around the bat. *Yeah, Faj, maybe I should've thought more than twice.*

All three men took a step forward toward her.

"Now!" Ray yelled.

The car's brights came on and glared right into their eyes.

The men shouted. Blinded—and pissed off for sure.

Fast as she could, Ray slammed the baseball bat into the lanky one's knees. He landed on his back.

She stepped back, spun left, and continued the swing, upward into the side of BeerBelly's head.

The crack made her wince.

BeerBelly fell to his knees.

Beard-Face backpedaled—but didn't drop the cat.

Assbadger. His free hand drew back for a punch.

Lunging, she rammed the bat right into his crotch.

His scream hit an amazing high note. When his hands whipped down to his groin, the cat went flying.

Yes! She caught the kitty in midair with one hand and tucked it against her chest. Claws painfully pierced her clothes and into her skin as it hung on for dear life.

Spinning again, building up momentum, she swung the bat into Beard's legs. He hit the ground.

Tomo had a saying: *"Never leave the enemy in shape to chase you."*

She sprinted to the car. The passenger door swung open, and she jumped inside. "Let's go. Quick."

"*Madre de Dios*, you are cray-cray." Marisol backed the car up, changed gears, and stomped on the gas so hard the tires screeched before catching.

Ouch, ouch, ouch. How many claws does a cat have anyway? "Shh, shh, kitty, you're fine." Gently, she unhooked the sharp claws from her chest, settled the cat on her lap, and managed to fasten the seatbelt. Even as she tried to slow her breathing, she stroked the cat. Did a gentle cheek scritching.

Muscle by muscle, the tense little feline started to relax.

If only I could. Still quivering inside, Ray rested her head against the seat. What had she been thinking? The fight could have gone really bad. "You know, my goal for tonight was to get out and do something interesting. I thought a musical was just my speed."

"You mean beating up men with a baseball bat wasn't part of the plan?" For the next few minutes, Marisol kept busting into giggles.

Until the cat started to purr.

"Awww." Marisol smiled over. "Hey, do you have cat food and litter, or should we stop at a store?"

She hadn't thought past saving the cat. "Um." Her fingers traced over the cat's ribs and spine. This poor kitty hadn't been eating well at all. And it was a warm furry weight in her lap, purring like a miniature motorboat. "Oh, hell, I guess I got a new furbaby."

"Duh." Marisol smiled. "WoodSong has felt empty since Mikan crossed the Rainbow Bridge."

"Faj didn't want to adopt another cat until I got home from Indiana. We were going to visit the shelter together." The ache of loss remained, but it was getting easier to say his name. She stroked the soft fur. "No need for a store visit. There are still kitty supplies tucked away in storage."

"Okay then." Marisol turned the corner onto Sunrise Drive, then down the lane to her mother's house. "What are you going to call it?"

The cat rubbed its cheek against her fingers. Its instant acceptance reminded her of...

"Max. Boy or girl, its name is Max."

"Huh, okay." Marisol jumped out. "Thanks for an exciting evening."

"Anytime." Laughing, Ray kept the cat tucked against her as she walked around to the driver's seat.

A couple of minutes later, she parked in the garage and rubbed her chin on a furry head. "We're home, Max. You're gonna love it here." *Please love it here.*

Inside, she went upstairs to the master bedroom. *My bedroom.*

It'd been such a surprise. Before she'd returned from Indiana, George moved downstairs so he, Tomo, and Kaden could remodel the upstairs suite. For her.

Refinished the floors, the walls, the color scheme. All new furniture, draperies, linens. They'd locked the door and kept it all a surprise until...afterward.

Before he died, he said his sons encouraged him to leave her a "little something." He put the paid-off house and property in her name along with a trust for the hefty real estate taxes. Afterward, Tomo and Kaden showed off the new "mistress" suite, pointing out what parts they and Faj had designed or worked on. When she protested, they said they'd inherited a butt-load of money, and she damned well would keep the house and workshop to continue her career.

And they used the suite to show they and Faj really meant it. Gods how she'd cried.

Even now, at the memory of the love in their voices, she blinked teary eyes. She'd only been living with George for a couple of years when they started calling her "li'l sis."

Until she saw the redecorated suite, she hadn't realized they meant it for real.

I still have family.

In her arms, Max mewed as if to say a cat could be family too.

Her laugh came out a bit choked. "Yes, you will be." She pulled in a breath. "Which means, you'd need to get used to your new home. We'll start small and eventually give you the run of the house." Setting the feline down in the bathroom, she closed the door behind her.

A quick rummage in the downstairs storage room yielded cat bowls, cans of food, and all the necessary litter stuff.

"Look, Faj," she whispered. "The house has a kitty again." He'd be happy. He believed a house wasn't a home without a feline in residence.

Her mistress bathroom had a custom-designed, cat litter facility between the counter's double sinks. Ray lifted Max for a quick perusal of his underside. Male and neutered. She'd better notify animal services in case he was someone's lost pet.

But unless someone claimed him, Max was hers.

She set him on the floor and showed him the cat-sized doorway to the litter box. "Here's your special restroom, dude."

He entered, did a quick circle, and apparently found the sanitary arrangements adequate. The noise of litter being scratched sounded as she put his food and water on the other side of the room.

He strutted out, tail held high.

"Good job, buddy." She dropped a soft blanket in one corner —in case he wanted to hide out in here.

The bright bathroom lights let her see him clearly. Despite being way underweight and small, he had a stocky build. His short fur was chocolate brown and darker on the paws, ears, tail, and nose. Rather than slanted eyes, his were round and a gorgeous gold.

He came straight over to her, stepped onto her lap, and butted her stomach with his head.

"Wow, not a shy bone in your body. Max is the perfect name for you."

Looking up at her, he gave an enchantingly raspy meow.

"Oh, you want to know about your name? Max is the cop who saved me when I was sixteen. Brought me here to George. Even though he was a Seattle cop, he'd come over to the island every once in a while to see how I was doing." She grinned. "Faj hated visitors and grumped at him every time he showed up."

Carrying the cat into the bedroom, she pointed at a framed photo where two men, one white, one Black bracketed a pretty Black woman. "He moved in with his cousin in Florida, and they both fell for the same woman."

Max gave an approving meow.

"Huh, I guess tomcats don't mind polyamory." Shaking her head, she sat on the bed, smiling as he curled up in her lap. "Me, I prefer one man, one woman. But Max is a detective in Tampa now, and he sounds really happy."

Sinking onto the bed, she smiled at the picture. Over the years, the tough cop had turned into a friend. He really was a pretty special person.

She'd told him once that it was a shame he wasn't a few years younger. But maybe, someday, she'd find someone like him for her own. He'd been silent for a moment and then said he knew without a doubt she'd find someone. Because she was very lovable.

And then it'd been her who had to be all silent as she tried not to cry.

However... "*Without a doubt?*" For a cynical law officer, he was awfully optimistic.

Maybe in a few years, she'd try being optimistic and attempt dating again. Maybe. Or not. "After all, I do have my very own Max."

He opened his golden eyes and purred.

"Yes, you, furball. I don't need or want anyone else."

CHAPTER THREE

Ray's bright red Honda CRV splashed through the puddles left by an early rain.

To most Washingtonians' annoyance, summers had grown increasingly hot and dry. Shades of California, right? So this morning's cleansing rain and lingering moist air was lovely.

Unfortunately, the heart-lifting fragrance of green vegetation and sea brine couldn't drown out the underlying odor of city. Bainbridge sure smelled better than Seattle.

Her phone dinged with an incoming text, and she groaned. Undoubtedly, Theodore. Again. He seemed to think if he kept trying, she'd change her mind. He still couldn't grasp why she ended things, even though she'd explained. And explained.

Apparently, if *he* was happy in the relationship, she must have been as well.

Okay, it was true she'd been content at first. He'd been really nice. *At first*. He was intelligent, hard-working, well-spoken. They had many of the same interests. His mild bossiness was sexy without being aggressive enough to remind her of...the incident.

Until he'd decided her personality needed to be fixed.

Damn him. After his text late last night, she'd been awake too long. Her emotions had bickered like toddlers, until Hurt bashed Anger in the head with a toy truck and won. Yeah it really did hurt to realize he hadn't liked her the way she was. After stewing for too long, she went downstairs for a comforting hot chocolate, and the house felt so, so empty without George. But Faj was gone, and...

I need people to be with. Not a boyfriend, just friends.

Another goal to work on—along with getting back to crafting.

And caring for a kitty. Her heart lifted. Animal control had no reports of lost pets looking like Max. WoodSong had a resident cat again.

She glanced at the map on her phone in the dash holder. Almost, almost...

Google Maps' male narrator said in a boring tone, "You have arrived at your destination."

"Didn't I see a Facebook short with an oh-so-sexy GPS voice saying, '*Hello, gorgeous*'? I want *him*."

In the driveway, she shut the car off.

All right. Time to meet the client.

Her heart rate sped up, as usual. Despite years of custom wood crafting, the first meeting always sent her anxiety skyrocketing. She just knew they'd take a look at her and see she'd been a foster kid, had shoplifted, had tried to break into a house.

Now remember what George said: *"You were an abused child, Ray-chan, doing what you needed to do to survive. Would you blame a starving puppy for grabbing food from a table? No? You were a hungry puppy then, and now you're a very talented woodworker."*

Right. I am talented and skilled. Her lips quirked. Not a puppy any longer and haven't stolen anything since Faj took me in. *No one knows my past, only that I'm George Matsuda's protegee.*

Pep talk finished, she slid out of the car and retrieved her roll-around case.

Here I go.

She rang the bell.

A tall man with piercing blue eyes in a strong face opened the door. Short dark brown hair. Some gray at the temples. Twenty more years and he'd be a total silver fox.

A big black dog tried to push past him to get at her.

"Butler, mind your manners." The man's commanding voice sent a shiver up her spine, and she gritted her teeth.

Why, oh why, did she have to find authoritative men sexy? *Look out, everyone, the 1950s lost one of their housewives.*

"Ms. Lanigan, you're right on time. I'm Alex Fontaine." He held the door open wider. "Come in, please."

"Thank you." When the dog blocked her, she grinned. "Butler, is it? I love your name."

The dark eyes evaluated her as a possible threat, but his tail wagged ever so slightly at the sound of his name.

Taking a chance, she squatted down to his level and held out her hand. The worst he could do was rip off her arm and leave her with a bloody stump. *No problem, right?* "Hey, buddy."

He sniffed her fingers, probably smelling Max's feline scent.

As she'd hoped, having a pet meant she was good people, and his tail wagged in circles. When she stroked his head and ruffled the heavy fur on his neck, even his butt started waggling.

"Aren't you a sweetie-peach." Oh, heavens, now she sounded like her favorite gallery owner who was from Louisiana.

"She figured you out quick enough, boy," Fontaine told the dog. He offered her a hand and pulled her up easily. Damned strong for a rich guy.

"Thanks."

"Ray Lanigan?" The dark-eyed woman entering the foyer had a friendly smile and a mane of hair as beautiful as golden, wavy-grained ash wood. "Hi, I'm MacKensie. Welcome. Let me show you what we have in mind."

The family room had steel-blue walls with a pale, blue-veined marble fireplace, comfortable leather chairs, and mid-tone hardwood flooring. MacKensie waved at one bare wall and pulled out her phone. "I saw this picture of a tree trunk with book shelves coming off the branches."

"A tree sculpture. I was wondering why the shop has a six-foot, driftwood tree with a Department of Natural Resources permit." Ray checked the picture. "The tree is a close resemblance, and the silvery wood will look gorgeous against your blue wall."

Fontaine frowned slightly. "We were hoping for live edge shelves to match the tree."

"Of course. I can do that for you." Ray pulled her portfolio from her case and opened it on the coffee table. "Let me show you examples of live edge shelving I've done."

They were delighted.

Hey, they should be. I am an awesome woodcrafter.

As she started measuring and taking notes on her phone, she heard Fontaine murmur to his wife, "George did say his girl was as talented."

Her throat clogged with all the emotions, and it took a bit before she could speak. "All right. Here's a picture of the tree in the shop. For the actual shelves, you'll want wood that makes interesting edges and matches the color." She pulled wood samples from her roll-around case.

Sitting around the coffee table, they compared live edge examples, wood samples, and the tree photo, eventually reaching a consensus. Ray wrote up a new contract.

And couldn't stop smiling. This was one of her favorite things to do, a custom job that would honor the spirit of the wood, be artistic, and blend with the rest of the room. A challenge and a delight.

Lying by the doorway, Butler lifted his head and woofed, even as, from somewhere, a woman called, "Mac, I'm here."

"In the family room," MacKensie yelled, making Fontaine laugh, even as he stood up.

MacKensie grinned. "I know, your mother would be appalled."

A squeal came from the doorway. "I know you!" The woman's voice was deeper than years before but still recognizable.

"Hope?" In shock, Ray rose from the chair.

"Oh my God, it *is* you. Ray!" Dancing across the room, Hope grabbed her for a whirlwind hug.

"Look at you." Ray held her away to see her better. Still short and round. A fluffy pixie with a few freckles sprinkled over her nose and cheeks.

So many memories. Giggly lunches in the school cafeteria, sneaking looks at texts in the classrooms, gossiping about boys... She had to swallow hard.

"I take it you two know each other?" Fontaine asked in a dry voice.

"We were like sisters in high school." Hope's grip tightened. "She was always stepping in to save me from jerks who thought it was funny to pick on a short, pudgy girl. Even when she ended up with bruises and black eyes, she never stopped."

"Worth it," Ray muttered. She couldn't stand by when someone got bullied. And, although scrawny, she'd been pretty tough from working as Pa's handyman apprentice.

Stepping back, Hope set her hands on her hips. "You disappeared from school, and we heard your dad died, and you went to foster care somewhere, but you never called or anything."

So much for hoping no one would ever know I was in foster care. But it was impossible to get mad. Not at Hope.

All of four inches taller, Ray smiled down at her. "The evil foster mother didn't let us use the phone. And it didn't work out anyway." She suppressed a shiver at the memory of getting beaten, of curling into a ball, trying to breathe and sob at the same time.

MacKensie's expression held a wealth of understanding. "You ran?"

"Escaped on the ferry to Seattle. But no one hires teens, especially dirty, homeless ones."

Worry furrowed Hope's brow. "Seattle isn't exactly safe..."

"No city is safe for young girls." The bitterness in MacKensie's voice told Ray all she needed to know.

"It wasn't safe, but I got lucky. A cop caught me breaking into an empty house and arranged for George to foster me. And George taught me wood crafting." He'd opened the world to her. *Dammit, don't start crying.*

Sympathy filled MacKensie's gaze. "I'm sorry for your loss."

Fontaine's hard face softened. "George often boasted about you. He thought of you as a daughter, you know."

Warmth spread through her chest. Her voice came out choked. "It was mutual." Gods, she missed him. But even as she'd sat at his bedside, George had kept telling her, "Life goes on. So will you."

I will, Faj.

She managed to smile at Hope. "I did try to call you once I was with George."

"Oh, spit, we moved away a couple months or so after you disappeared. Dad got stationed down south."

Right, military family. "So...you live here in Seattle now?"

"I do. I'm married to a wonderful man, even if he is a lawyer" —she rolled her eyes—"and I teach fifth grade."

Once upon a time, they'd sat under a tree in the schoolyard, eating their bagged lunches, planning their futures. So long ago. "You always wanted to be a teacher."

Hope nodded, her gaze soft. "You were scared you'd end up stuck as a handyman forever."

Only too true. Pa had expected her to work for him until the end of time and endure the same fix-it jobs over and over. She'd never have gotten to create. To make something beautiful. "I guess dreams do sometimes come true."

Bad Ray, this is totally unprofessional behavior in front of a client.

She turned to Fontaine. "I believe I have everything I need now. Why don't—"

"This is yours?" Dropping down into a chair, Hope perused Ray's portfolio on the coffee table. "You do beautiful work."

"Thank you." Ray beamed. Compliments never got old.

Fontaine nodded at the portfolio. "You have a similar style to George's, although your work is, perhaps, lighter. More..."

As he searched for the right word, Ray smiled. "He said my crafting was more joyful."

"Yes." MacKensie was still sitting on the couch, looking over the portfolio with Hope. "That's it, exactly. Are we the only project of his you're planning to complete?"

"There was another contract, but I haven't managed to find the client. What kind of a business would call itself Chains? I thought a fence company at first, but they wouldn't want handcrafted items, right?"

All three of them broke into laughter.

Smiling slightly, Fontaine leaned his hip against the couch. "As it happens, Chains is a private club."

What am I missing? She turned to Hope who was the easiest to read. "What kind of a private club? A stuffy men's club or something?"

Hope flushed. "Um..."

"Close." Fontaine's expression held amusement. "Chains is a BDSM club here in Seattle."

Wait, what? George had a BDSM club for a client? For something called a tantric chair and a pentagram? She'd wondered if the client was a pagan church. "Wooden furniture for a place like that? Seriously?" she asked slowly. *I do not—do not—believe this.*

"Probably something to match the other live edge pieces he made," Hope said.

"Oh, you're thinking of the glorious spanking bench?" MacKensie noticed Ray's stare—and turned red.

A spanking bench? Surely not. George had always been... He

wouldn't... Ray crossed her arms over her chest. "Why would he take on work for a"—not going to say the BDSM word—"club?"

"The owner loves handcrafted furniture and talked him into making some pieces," Hope answered almost absently and turned another page. The last photo in the portfolio was of George, arm slung around Ray. The table they'd made together gleamed softly in front of them. "They're friends, and George was a member, after all."

Noting Fontaine's frown, Hope winced. "Sorry, guess it should've stayed private."

"George and a BDSM club? No way."

Smile growing, Hope pointed at her. "Miss Stubborn, you may have turquoise-tipped hair, but you haven't changed at all. I'll prove it to you, Ms. SwampDonkey AssClown."

From the dumbfounded expressions of the other two in the room, Hope didn't normally swear.

Bringing herself up to an offended stance, Ray shook her head. "Ms. TardyTwat Douche-Nozzle, I am shocked. Wherever did you learn such appalling language?"

"From my absolute best friend in high school who I've missed so, so much." Hope's smile wavered for a second. Then she glanced at Fontaine and MacKensie. "We used to vie with each other for the most creative vulgar invective. Truly shameful."

"Only shameful because you could never keep up." Ray sniffed. "Jealous much?"

"Totally." Hope grinned. "I've lost all my skill now, what with being around prudish principals and associates."

"Oddly enough, wood doesn't mind my language." Thank the gods for that, or she'd have to work with duct tape over her mouth. At least she didn't swear in public. Well not usually.

And...Hope was obviously a member of a BDSM club, as were Fontaine and MacKensie. Actually, she could see Hope being attracted to the lifestyle. As teens, they'd shared a preference for dominant men.

But Faj? Really? Ray sat down in the chair across from Hope. "Exactly how can you prove an association between George and this...club?"

"You'd recognize his work, right?" Hope asked.

"Of course." Every craftsman had their own finicky techniques.

"Oooh, I have the perfect plan. You can be my guest at the club and check out the stuff George made. You have to see the place anyway to finish the project he left."

"But..." Ray set her jaw. It'd been four years since...the *incident*. And it still felt way too soon to venture back into the world of BDSM.

Only she could see from Hope's expression she wouldn't let this drop. Talk about stubborn. Then again, her friend had a point. How could Ray finish the project without knowing what the piece was for and how it would fit into its surroundings?

And... This way she'd see Hope again. The thought of losing touch with her was intolerable. "Yes, okay. I'll come. Where is this place?"

"Wait. I want to come to the *show-Ray-the-club* night too." MacKensie bounced on the couch. "Please?"

"Sure." Hope laughed. "Ray might need both of us to hold her hands."

Ray squinted at her old friend, then huffed. "Yes, please." *How many panic attacks will I have?*

They had no idea what they were suggesting. Even as the three smiled at her in sympathy, Ray figured out her goals.

Get in.

Figure out what the project needed.

Reestablish her friendship with Hope—and maybe make a new friend—and...

Get the hell out. Fast.

Gods help me—a BDSM club.

Would anyone notice if she kept her eyes closed?

Getting out of his car, Drake paused to enjoy the cool night air and the view. The lights of the Seattle skyline and the iconic Space Needle never grew old.

A glance around revealed the parking lot for Chains, his BDSM club, was almost full. Very nice. The city had plenty of kinksters who appreciated a place to get together, to meet others, and for many, to learn or share their skills.

It was satisfying to know his club provided a safe community for them.

Unlike a normal business, the club's only entry was through the parking lot door. As with many BDSM clubs, it wasn't in a safe neighborhood. No one walked here. And this way, the very visible door guard could keep an eye on the parking lot. The members were safe whether inside and outside.

"Sir." The burly guard opened the door for him. "It's been a while since you were here. Good to see you back."

"*Merci,* Becker. How's your son doing?"

"He graduated top of his class. Going to the university next fall." Becker's chest expanded with pride.

"Congratulations to him—and to you as well. Raising an adolescent is a true test of courage." Drake grinned. "When you tell him the things not to do, do you share all the idiocies you did back then?"

"Oh, fuck no. Hell, I grew up in California. Got a fake ID so I could drink, then I'd go surfing while blasted out of my mind. Almost drowned more than once." Becker shook his head with a rueful smile. "I hope he's smarter."

"I'm sure he'll do well." Drake clapped him on the shoulder and stepped through the door.

In the entry, he smiled at the slender, brunette volunteer running the reception desk. "How are you today, Faylee?"

THE LIVING EDGE

Faylee rolled her eyes. "It's a madhouse tonight, Master Drake. Is this a full moon?"

Drake laughed. It was. "Did you have to call the police?"

"No—not yet. Three silver members tried to do a walk-in, but I explained *several times* Saturday nights are only for gold members, and they finally gave up."

"Some people can be quite stubborn." Friday nights were open to the public, although to satisfy the various zoning and business regulations, everyone had to be a so-called member. For a silver membership, a person simply filled out an application, disclaimer, and agreement to abide by the rules, paid the dues, and were admitted. On Fridays, the dungeon rules and equipment were tailored for newbies to the lifestyle.

Saturdays was for those serious about BDSM. The gold membership was more expensive and vetted.

Faylee wrinkled her nose. "Honestly, the memberships are explained everywhere. Including right there." She pointed at the wall poster. "Anyway, tonight we have three members who brought guests. The paperwork was signed, and they got the usual briefing."

"I do appreciate how efficient you are with paperwork."

"Thank you, Sir." She flushed pink with the compliment. The submissive had a rough past and had come a long way over the years. Making final reparations to Ghost, who lived in Florida, had been a big step in her healing—and opened the way for her to find love. She'd been with her Daddy Dom for several months now.

After giving her a smile, he walked through the door into the main room of the club.

Everything appeared to be going well. He'd known before opening the place years ago that BDSM clubs had a high failure rate. Thus he'd designated the nightclub-like ground floor for dancing and socializing. Putting the dungeon in the basement was not only nicely traditional but helped with noise.

Law enforcement disapproved of the sound of screams.

Having alcohol on the premises was disagreeable, but people, especially those there merely for the atmosphere, wanted it. After a few incidents in the dungeon, he'd added rules. The bartender marked anyone who was served alcohol, and no one with a mark on their hand could go downstairs.

Seemed fair to him. If a person wasn't safe driving while intoxicated, they sure weren't safe with a flogger in hand. Or safe to receive a flogging for that matter.

"Let's head downstairs. We'll do a scene." A man's loud voice drew Drake's attention. Ah, Riley, one of the newer members. Basketball player, tall and blond. The Dom was in his mid-twenties.

Drake suppressed a sigh. In college, he also felt he knew it all. It was a shame his gender took so long to gain a bit of humility.

Back then, he'd lost his cockiness quickly under Simon's mentoring. Simon had high standards for the Dominants he taught. Since he'd also been Drake's instructor in mixed martial arts, well... Pain swiftly cut an inflated ego into shreds.

As for now though...

Riley's companion appeared to be a couple of years younger and was shaking her head. "I don't want to do a scene. You said you'd show me around, nothing more."

"C'mon, Leanne. You're here; I'm here. It'll be fun." Riley rose.

Merde.

When Leanne stayed planted in the chair, her expression unyielding, Drake suppressed a smile because. *Good for you, young woman.* "Is there a problem here?"

"Listen, buddy, butt ou—" Recognizing Drake, Riley straightened. "Ah, sorry. We, uh, are just... Leanne doesn't..."

A teaching moment wasn't to be wasted. "Did you negotiate an agreement with your companion?" Drake asked gently.

"I... Well—"

"He said this would only be a tour." The young brunette slid her chair away from the table and farther away from Riley. "Now he wants to do a scene. He lied to me."

"Have you been together long?" Drake asked carefully.

"First date." Her lips pressed together. "Last date."

There would be no coming back from this mistake.

"Hey, I just wanted to—" Riley broke off when Drake crossed his arms over his chest and gave him The Look. "Right. C'mon, Leanne. I'll take you home."

"Yeah, I don't *think* so." She pulled out a phone. "I'm getting an Uber."

Drake looked around. As usual, security was observing. Drake raised his hand, and the stocky ginger hurried over. "Master Drake, can I help?"

"*Oui*. Please escort the young lady out and ensure she is safely in her ride."

"Sir, of course."

Leanne turned to Drake. "Thank you so much. I was getting really scared." Her eyes were moist.

Riley's expression turned surprised. Dismayed. "Scared?"

"You did very well at protecting your boundaries." Drake assisted her to her feet, and Shawn accompanied her out.

When Drake turned his attention to Riley, the aspiring Dom shook his head. "I-I thought she wanted to be pushed around. She said she was submissive."

"*Not. Necessarily.* Submissives enjoy giving control to"—Drake held up a finger—"someone they choose. Someone they *trust*."

At the emphasis on the word trust, Riley flinched.

"If you aren't that person, they are no more submissive than you are."

"She—she trusts me."

"Not any longer, Riley." Drake shook his head. "You brought her here, then broke your agreement and tried to verbally push her into something she didn't want."

"She... Fuck, she *did* say no." Riley slumped in the chair. "I can't believe I kept pushing her." Riley's remorse appeared sincere. His face had even gone pale. "She was *scared* of me."

Drake sat down at the table. "I was going to tear up your membership card."

Riley sank farther into the chair and didn't argue.

Oui, he could yet turn the attitude around. "So... If you repeat the beginning Dominant course as well as the consent workshop, I'll give you a second chance to prove you've learned from your mistake."

Relief filled Riley's expression. "I... Yeah, I'll take the classes again and get my act together." He held out his hand. "Thank you, Master Drake."

After shaking hands, Riley left for reception to sign up for classes.

Drake rose and headed for the bar.

"Oh, Master. It's good to see you here again." The high-pitched coo was like gravel abrading his skin.

He nodded to Justine. Dark-haired, dark-eyed, and lovely, but now he was as affected by her beauty as he was by a piece of perfectly sculpted ice. "Justine. Good evening." He tilted his head at the other two submissives at her table and moved away, allowing no opportunity for conversation.

When he broke off their relationship last winter, everything had been said.

He shook his head. Clear-sightedness about her own behavior, let alone anyone else's, wasn't in her nature. He was the one who'd been a fool.

And gotten burned.

Damned if he'd try again for a long, long time.

Three bottles of soda in hand, Ray slid between the clusters of people near the bar. MacKensie had stopped to talk with someone while Hope secured them a table.

Ray was concentrating on the drinks and keeping her feet moving. If she didn't focus, she'd end up in the center of the place, staring at everyone.

And freezing in place. Because if she thought about it hard, she'd be terrified there would be someone here from that night. One of those who'd assaulted her at the university.

Only, maybe not here. Hope had assured her the club had rules. Lots and lots of rules and people to enforce them. This sure wouldn't be the bastards' kind of place.

It's good; it's all good.

Now be cool. She pulled in a breath. *Right. I go to BDSM clubs every day. See naked people walking around all the time. Sure, I do.*

"Oops, sorry," a person muttered from her right and then there was the clang of something hitting the floor.

Ray glanced over and saw a skinny man with his head through a hole in an oversized serving tray carried on his shoulders. His wrists were cuffed to the tray. And some jerk had bumped him hard enough to knock a couple of bottles of water off.

With no way to pick up the drinks, the poor guy was battling tears.

"Hey, hey, hey, be cool, dude." Ray set her three bottles at her feet and picked up the waters and set them carefully on the tray. "Here's your waters. Did anything else fall?"

"N-no." He was snuffling, tears on his cheeks.

The poor baby. She grabbed a couple of napkins off a table and wiped his cheeks. "Is your Dom person really mean? Do I need to beat them up?"

Big brown eyes still swam with tears, but he was starting to smile. "No, he's really wonderful. I just w-wanted to do everything perfectly."

"It's hardly your fault when some dumbass runs into you. If

your Master person is so great, he'll understand. And you're all fixed anyway."

The guy's smile was truly there now. "Thank you. Really."

She patted his shoulder, picked up her drinks, and looked around for Hope. Ah, over there at a small round table with MacKensie.

"I made it." Ray set the drinks in front of the other two and took the seat between them.

"We saw," Hope said. "Did you get BetaBoi settled? He's a total sweetie. And he tries so hard."

"Still young," Ray said. "Give him a few years and he'll be more cynical than we are."

MacKensie snorted. "He's probably all of two years younger than you."

Opening the bottle and taking a good hefty gulp of the ice-cold Coke, Ray heaved a pleased sigh and started to look around.

And felt her eyes getting bigger. "You said the actual BDSM stuff is downstairs?" she asked in disbelief. The upstairs was plenty kinky enough.

When they first came in, she'd heard the music, seen the crowded dance floor, the people around the bar at the back, and it seemed like a normal nightclub. Along with relief, she'd almost been disappointed.

But then there'd been a couple of naked people.

Here, on the other side of the dance floor, there was a stage with an actual flogging going on. And people...

To her left, a woman in skintight black vinyl tugged on a leash to get her *dog* to follow her. However, the dog happened to be a robust man on all fours with a canine muzzle, ears, and a perky tail. Seeing how the tail was secured made her own asshole tighten up.

"We'll go downstairs soon," Hope said. "After you acclimate to the easy stuff." She and MacKensie exchanged grins.

Ray sniffed. "Patronizing brat." Yet she really was relieved to take things slowly. So she sat back and continued to look around.

Some of the fetwear was amazing. Some of the men were too.

Like the darkly handsome man who stood nearby, talking to a couple sitting at a table. He had flecks of gray in his black hair and goatee, so was probably in his late 30s, but *mmm*, that kind of leanly powerful musculature made her want to switch to sculpture.

When he crossed his arms over his chest and frowned, her mouth went dry. Talk about *intimidating*...and he wasn't even talking to her.

After a brief conversation, he lifted his hand, and a guy in a security vest hurried over to escort the woman out. The woman appeared almost tearfully grateful. Had Mr. Intimidation rescued her from her date?

The younger man might or might not be a Dominant, but the older one sure was. Authority radiated from him like solar flares as he focused on the younger man. Talked. The younger one's hostility changed soon enough to nodding in agreement to whatever Mr. Authority said. That was some seriously effective diplomacy.

Reluctantly, she dragged her gaze away and checked out the rest of the room.

On the low stage, the Top had switched to flashy two-handed flogging, what Hope called Florentine style. The bottom wore a leather jockstrap and was in la-la-land with a happy smile on his face. The rhythmic sound of the flogger punctuated with the dark electronic music of Alien Vampires.

Her view was blocked by a man walking by. He was dressed as a police officer, but the short-sleeved, uniform shirt was made of black latex—the better to display impressive biceps. His male companion wore a dark leather chest harness and nothing else.

"All this black clothing. Gods help us, we're surrounded by Goths," she murmured.

Hope giggled. "It's an easy way to differentiate Doms and Tops from submissives and bottoms. Bottoms and submissives go for more color—and less clothing."

"Lots less sometimes." MacKensie motioned to a man and woman in miniscule G-strings trailing a person dressed all in black.

"I thought I'd stick out like a sore thumb dressed in these clothes." Ray glanced down. She'd topped the silky black boxers she sometimes wore to lounge around the house with a green-and-black overbust bodice from her college Renaissance faire days. "Instead, I fit in pretty well. Thank you for the advice."

"You can never go wrong with cleavage and showing off legs." Hope tipped her soda up to get the last sip. "Done. Are you ready to go downstairs now?"

No. No, I'm really not. Goosebumps rose all over her body. "Maybe we could dance for a while?" And avoid the BDSM stuff...

MacKensie's eyes narrowed. "I recognize that expression. Have you had problems in the past with BDSM...or maybe with men?"

"Haven't we all?" Ray managed to say lightly. "Sometimes I wish my body preferred women, but being lesbian would only be a different set of problems."

"True enough." Hope bumped their shoulders together. "Less aggression and violence though."

"I wasn't raped, if that's what you were asking." *Probably* wasn't raped. Or fine, yes, she had been. Maybe she'd agreed to some of what he'd done in the beginning, only then there had been the others...

It was years ago, girl. Get over it.

"I know the dungeon is downstairs, but I don't want to...do anything. That'll be okay, right?"

"Absolutely." Mac gave her a reassuring smile. "Unless you're in a scene, no means no. And no one touches without permission."

"Okay then." Ray hauled in a breath. "Take me downstairs so I can see what George made. And everything else should be interesting too."

As long as she didn't have a panic attack, right? And really, it was time she worked through her worries about BDSM. *I'm not a fragile princess. Nope.*

"Right. Off we go then." Hope rose.

At the head of the stairs, security checked the back of their hands and let them proceed.

Downstairs was...

There were no words. Her only experience with BDSM was several years ago as a junior at the university. A kinky book led her to the campus BDSM club...and dating a man. After a taste of light bondage, she wanted more. He talked her into going to a private play party where her nightmare began.

She'd avoided even reading about BDSM ever since. Theodore was the closest she'd come—and he was bossy, not kinky.

Following Hope and MacKensie around the room, Ray couldn't keep from staring at everything. A bondage frame used for suspension occupied the very center with spanking benches and bondage tables around it. The middle of the massive space was open to the rafters so people upstairs could lean over the railings and watch.

Around the perimeter, more scene areas were cordoned off with black stanchions and rope. Between each area, doors opened into theme rooms with wide display windows.

Ray tried her hardest not to gawk like a tourist.

But...wow.

At the private play party, there'd been only one decrepit, portable St. Andrew's cross. Here were several of them—all being used.

Hope and MacKensie paused to watch a man tied to a bondage table. As his partner dripped wax on his chest, the poor man hissed with each drop.

Ow? Even as she shuddered, she couldn't look away. *No, no, I am* not *imagining how wax would feel dropping onto my breasts.*

A leather-clad woman wielded a whip in one roped-off area.

In the adjacent space, a man flogged a woman who yelped with every blow.

Ray's mouth had gone dry, and the whole room seemed too hot. Every couple of minutes, a sound or sight would remind her of...before...and make her shiver. Made her emotions whiplash so fast she couldn't tell if she was turned-on or terrified.

Clenching her fingers, she pulled in a slow breath. *I am strong; I can handle this.*

"What was George planning to make for Chains?" MacKensie asked.

Her words registered after a second.

Right. "Um, two pieces of equipment were ordered, but there weren't any specs." Ray wrinkled her nose as she thought. "It just said a pentagram and a tantric chair. Is there anything similar around here to give me ideas of what's needed?"

"Interesting." MacKensie glanced at Hope. "Maybe they're for Elfame?"

"I bet you're right." Hope explained to Ray, "It's like an enchanted room with new-agey décor. Wood-crafted furniture would fit better than metal or synthetic stuff."

"New age in a BDSM club? That's all kinds of wrong."

Hope sputtered a laugh and set off walking again. "For ideas... A St. Andrew's cross or maybe the spiderweb would show you the size a pentagram would have to be. George did the spiderweb."

"BDSM furniture has to accommodate a range of sizes," MacKensie added. "Someone tied to the pentagram might be anywhere from five feet tall to maybe six-three."

Tied to a pentagram. Oookay. Not wall art. A wooden five-pointed star big enough to what...restrain someone? The submissive could rest their head on the point at the top.

And restraints would probably be needed. Bind wrists to the

left and right points. Ankles would be pulled apart at the bottom points. Huh, might be really cool. Did a person have to be pagan or Wiccan to use it? She almost laughed.

But a range of sizes? Duh, the whippee might not always be a woman. "An example would be good."

After they checked out a couple of crosses in various shapes, Hope pointed to a six foot round wooden frame with a woman bound to intricate rope webbing.

"Yikes, it really *does* resemble a spiderweb." Ray shivered. "I'm glad it's not Halloween. Can you imagine if the Top dressed up like a massive spider? Talk about creepy."

"What a fun theme idea." Mac kept her voice low so as not to disturb the scene. "We could have a venomous creature night. Snakes and scorpions and spiders..."

Appalled, Ray took a step back. "You're more sadistic than I thought you were."

"Mac loves sci-fi and fantasy." Hope snickered. "Last spring, she helped decorate the science fiction theme room. Lynn and I have bets on when she'll talk the owner into an aliens-with-tentacles night."

Mac grinned. "Alex thinks it would be fun."

"Me too! Do submissives get to be Cthulhu?" Ray noticed the male Top was releasing the woman from the spiderweb. "Hey, when they're gone, I want to check it out closer. And...I saw you and Hope half-watching the whip session over there." She pointed to the corner. "Go watch it while I work."

"You're still really observant, aren't you." Hope grinned. "The whipmaster doesn't show up here very often, and I love to watch him work."

"You sure, Ray?" Mac frowned. "I don't like leaving you alone."

"I'm good."

"Well okay." MacKensie patted Ray's arm. "We'll be over at the corner. Come and get us if you need us."

"Sure."

So George made the spiderweb. In fact, she could see his craft in it, how the amber-colored rope webbing brought out the golden grain of the wood. It really was beautiful.

Finally, the Top and the woman were finished cleaning the equipment.

Ray pulled a tape measure and notepad from her boxers' pocket. Might as well get some figures. She could block everything out while she worked, focus on what Faj created...and *not* what he might have been doing while he was here.

CHAPTER FOUR

On his way to check in with the bartender, Drake felt the vibrations in his pocket and pulled out his phone. Ah, his executive assistant. "Tiago, what's the newest disaster?"

His EA laughed. "Only a minor one."

"There's a relief. Go on."

"It's about the BDSM convention next month. Your presenter for the flogging workshop called with apologies. His mother went on hospice, and he wants to stay close to home."

"*Merde.*" Drake sighed. "Of course he would. But this is inconvenient."

"Right? I thought maybe you'd ask someone from the club? Since you're there and can get anyone to say yes to anything."

He might have a talent for persuasion, but he wasn't *that* good. "Very logical. However, it's healthy to find presenters from elsewhere. Gives our community new ideas."

"Ah, got it."

"I'll have to call in favors to obtain someone on short notice."

"Good thing you know people from everywhere. But best of luck, boss."

"*Merci.*" Pocketing his phone, Drake sighed. As the owner of a

BDSM club, he considered education part of his responsibilities and was proud to be part of putting on one of the country's most popular BDSM conferences with excellent speakers and workshop presenters—ones who were more than merely well-known. Unfortunately, having a renowned reputation didn't guarantee the person was competent or ethical.

Drake tapped his fingers on the bar top. He did know someone who loved teaching flogging, and it'd been a while since he'd seen Simon and Rona. Could he lure them up here for a week or so?

"Master Drake." On the other side of the bar, the bartender lifted her eyebrows in a want-a-drink query.

"Thank you, nothing now. Everything quiet here?"

"Yes, everyone's playing by the rules." Nediva's husky voice had a pronounced New York accent. "As they had best be."

Drake grinned. No one messed with the tough Domme with a cap of steel-gray hair. Too many had discovered the extra-short crop worn on her belt was the perfect length to discipline anyone overstepping the bounds at the bar.

"Good evening, Master Drake." A brunette in her 40s, one of the newer members, slid onto a bar stool. "Have you already been downstairs and done a scene?"

"No, I haven't been here long." And hadn't planned to participate. No one had caught his interest since Justine, and he preferred something more meaningful than a quick pick-up scene. "How about you?"

"Not yet." The woman gave the bartender a meltingly hopeful smile. "I'd like to play later. Maybe when someone takes her break."

From the way Nediva's eyes heated, Drake thought the brunette's chances were good.

"Yo, Drake." Bob, a friend and one of the co-founders of Chains, joined him. Lynn, his submissive was tucked under his arm.

"*Mon ami*, it is good to see you and your Lynn."

The quiet submissive gave Drake a sweet smile.

"So anyone have plans for next weekend?" Bob asked. The conversation turned to sailing and picnics. Everyone wanted to take advantage of the predicted sunny August weather.

"If it isn't my favorite Frenchie."

At the familiar voice, Drake turned to greet Blaize. "It's been a while since we saw you here."

A few years older, in his late thirties, Blaize had maintained the beefy build of his college football days.

"Hey, Professor." Bob smiled. "How's the teaching business?"

"I swear the undergrads get dumber every year. And the tax laws get more convoluted and harder to teach."

Drake looked around, spotted Blaize's slave coming from the bar with a drink. She set it on a nearby table and settled on her knees beside the chair, eyes downcast.

"I see your slave is working hard at being correct," Drake said.

Bob and Lynn turned to look.

"Yes, slave-girl gets off on keeping me happy. Some women are suited to the role." Blaize grinned. Well respected in the community, he'd been in the lifestyle as long as Drake had. "And I enjoy being a Master. Didn't you try it once?"

"I fear the dynamic doesn't suit me." Drake shrugged off the memory of that time in his past. Although he hadn't been happy as a Master to a slave, Ramona was a lovely woman, and he'd missed her company afterward. "I was looking over the convention workshops. You're teaching a class on degradation in BDSM."

"My favorite subject." Blaize waggled his heavy eyebrows, one of which was bisected by a white scar. He glanced at his slave. "Eh, it's time to get some play in. See you later." He slapped Drake's back and headed off.

"Ew, degradation. I know he's very good at teaching, but I'm not into humiliation or degradation or objectification either."

Lynn rubbed her head on Bob's shoulder. "I'm so glad you're you. It's a shame others don't have a Master as wonderful as mine."

Bob laughed. "Sucking up, snookums? Are you wanting to negotiate something more intense for our session? Or...something sexy?"

As red rolled into Lynn's face, Drake grinned. "I fear I must head downstairs. One of the dungeon monitors is new."

"You go on. We have some talking to do." Bob pulled his submissive closer.

At the stairs, Drake stopped and held out his hands so the bouncer could see he had no mark confining him to upstairs.

"Very good, Master Drake." The bouncer grinned and waved him past.

The atmosphere in the dungeon was markedly different from upstairs. The chatter of conversation was missing. The music volume was lower. After all, it would be a shame to miss a huff of breath from the first stroke of an impact toy. A grunt of pain, panting. Or even better, a moan of arousal.

He didn't miss having a submissive. Although fun in the beginning, the relationship with Justine had deteriorated quickly. He did miss the delight of planning and carrying out a scene that would fill a submissive's needs—even ones she didn't know about. Bottoms had subspace, but for Tops, there was Domspace, a gratifying utter focus, and it was even better when the Top and bottom were on the same wavelength.

The crack of a whip came from the far corner. Closer was the buzz and crackle of a violet wand. Here and there were sounds of sobbing, the occasional scream, low-voice commands, groans.

Music to his ears.

Rather than the scent of perfumes and colognes upstairs, down here it was leather, sweat, and sex. Raw humanity.

Hands behind his back, Drake strolled past scene after scene. Smiling when greeted. Nodding approval when a new Dom displayed good techniques. Even Dominants liked positive feedback.

He always checked on the dungeon monitors, thankfully easy to spot in their orange vests. The new monitor still appeared slightly timid but was holding up well. Farther on, the most experienced DM was keeping an eye on a prior approved wax-play scene.

In the oversized corner space, a whip scene had gathered an audience, including Alex's and Peter's submissives. *Odd.* Were they here without their Doms?

Keeping an eye out for Alex and Peter, he noticed a young woman behind the spiderweb. Had she dropped something?

Who was she? Frowning, he detoured toward the scene area. He knew all the members.

Average figure on the slender side. Fair skin. Her shoulder-length, red-brown hair with scattered blue strands was so curly it sprang outward to dwarf her heart-shaped face.

Not a jaw-dropping beauty...but intriguing.

Was that a tape measure in her hands?

The dungeon was noisy enough he could barely hear her talking to herself. "Four foot, four inches. Remember it. Damn this stupid place's rules. I need my phone."

What in the world? Was she prepping for a scene? Drake moved closer.

She tried to bend to measure the lower restraint cuffs and couldn't. "Stupid bodice. Who invented this device of torment? Must've been a man. Imma find him, wrap the strings around his balls, and pull until everything squishes."

Interesting way to neuter someone. Was she a sadist? Her attire signaled submission.

Dropping to her knees, she used the tape measure between the bottom cuffs.

Why? Drake crossed his arms over his chest and cleared his throat.

Her head snapped up. Spotting him, she froze.

Zut, he'd frightened her. He didn't deliberately intimidate submissives, but sometimes he wondered if he gave off predatory monster vibes.

Ray couldn't draw in a breath. The man—holy cryptids—he was the Dom from upstairs. Not only gorgeous but *terrifying*. A good half a foot taller than her. Gray-flecked black hair, eyes as dark as the onyx studs in his ears. A thick, precisely shaped goatee formed a circle around his mouth and over his chin. A black shirt and black vest couldn't conceal streamlined muscles, and the way his arms were crossed made his biceps look like boulders.

"Um, hello?" Why had she let MacKensie and Hope leave? Shoving the tape measure, pencil, and notepad in her pockets, she tried to get to her feet but had crawled too far beneath the tilted metal frame. The boning in her bodice was less rigid than a corset —but still made bending...difficult. "I hate clothes," she muttered.

"*Permettez-moi.*" The deep voice was smoother than the bark of a young madrone and way too compelling.

Bending, he offered her his hand.

After crawling backward, she tried again to push up. Not happening. *Do people die of embarrassment? Oh, you betcha.* She could already feel a heart attack approaching.

When she set her hand in his much bigger one, he pulled her easily to her feet.

"Th-thank you." Flushing, she took a step back. Or...she tried. The stupid spiderweb was right behind her.

He didn't release her hand. Eyes as dark as a moonless night studied her. "Might I inquire as to what you were doing?" He pursed his lips.

Mmm, he had a great mouth, perfectly framed by the black mustache and beard, the bottom lip bigger than the top. How could lips look firm and soft at the same time?

Those lips tightened slightly.

Oh. *Oh*. He'd asked a question. "Measuring... I was measuring."

"I assumed as much considering your use of a measuring tape." His French-accented response was dry enough to dehydrate a swamp. "Does the scale of the spiderweb offend your senses? Or perhaps you feel you would not fit and wanted to ensure success?"

This conversational hole kept getting deeper. "Actually, I intend to create a similar piece of furniture and needed an idea of the distance between restraints."

"Interesting. Yet I doubt a measurement will give you what you need."

The words in her head jumbled together when his thumb caressed the back of her hand. The inescapable grip combined with the gentle stroking sent quivery sensations humming through her—and derailed her brain completely.

She blinked. "Ah, sorry, what?"

His lips twitched with his amusement. "Would you like to try out the spiderweb—and restraints—to see if you fit?"

"No." She tried again to take a step back, got nowhere, and panic rose inside her. "No, no."

"Easy, *ma petite*." Releasing her, he shifted back and smoothly gestured her away from the spiderweb.

She hurried around the web, tripped over the bottom rail. Catching her with powerful hands, he set her on her feet again. And let go immediately.

At the front, with plenty of space to escape, she could breathe again. She turned—and he was right there in front of her. Her eyes were at the level of his shoulder—and she couldn't help noticing the width of his chest. And the two top shirt buttons were undone, revealing the beginning of hard pectorals.

Get a grip, Ray. "Well it was nice meeting you. If you'll excuse me—"

"*Non, non.* To meet properly, we must exchange names." His black eyes held laughter. "You are...?"

"Ray. I'm Ray." Wait, was she supposed to use her real name in a kink club? Didn't people make up weird monikers like in online video games?

"Ray." His brows drew together. "This is Saturday, is it not? Gold members only. Why do I not recall a membership for anyone named Ray?"

He definitely had a French accent, although the dark hair, eyes, and olive skin suggested a Latino heritage, except he was at least six feet tall.

Aaand she'd lost track of the conversation again. How embarrassing. She totally didn't know how to socialize. It'd be best if someone simply locked her in the workshop.

"I'm not a member. I'm a guest," she said firmly.

"And yet, I see no escort."

His authoritative tone sent a shiver up her spine...and then she caught what he said. *Uh-oh,* was Hope supposed to stick close?

When he stayed silent, undoubtedly expecting her to respond with excuses or apologies, annoyance rose. "What are you, the Chains police?"

"*Oui,* you may think of me as such." His jaw muscles turned hard, the amusement gone from his gaze.

Ray's mouth went dry.

The finest of besties, Hope appeared and put an arm around Ray's waist. "Ray, I see you met Master Drake." She turned to the overwhelming man. "Did she tell you who she is?"

"We have gotten as far as her name and being a guest. Did you bring her?"

"Yes, Sir." Hope bounced on her toes like a Disney fairy godmother. "She needed ideas of how to do a pentagram and tantric chair."

"Pentagram and..." His expression changed. In fact, the man

had such a devastating smile, her own lips curved up. "*Ray*. You're George's protégé. Aralia, *oui?*"

"Yes. Usually it's just Ray though."

"I'm sorry for your loss. He is missed here in the club."

Here in the club. It really did sound as if Faj spent a lot of time here. At a BDSM club. "Right. Um. Thank you."

Joining them, MacKensie obviously heard. "Ray didn't know George was a member."

Drake's laugh was as compelling as his smile. "But of course not. He wouldn't share such information with a young foster-daughter."

"That's true," she said slowly. Faj was—had been—a private person. And apparently, she hadn't known him as well as she believed. How many times when she thought he was out with his buddies had he been here? Doing...things?

And making kinky furniture.

Her gaze traveled over the smooth circle of the spiderweb, now recognizing how George had turned furniture for a BDSM club into a work of art.

But there wouldn't be any new art for him to share with her. She put the grief aside and turned in a circle, hunting for other pretty craftwork. "Did he make other, ah, furniture or stuff?" Not spotting Faj's work, she glanced up at the man.

The amusement was back in Drake's dark eyes—and his voice. "He did. Would you like to see?"

Oh, she would, so much. "Yes. Please."

His smile widened. "I do enjoy polite submissives."

The obvious approval in his smooth-as-aged-whiskey voice heated her cheeks. How humiliating. *Don't blush, don't blush.*

Curse you, fair skin.

Then she realized exactly what he'd said. "What—wait. No. I'm not..."

He chuckled and turned to her friends. "MacKensie, Hope, I'll bring your guest back shortly."

"Okay. See you in a bit, Ray." Hope smiled at her and with Mac, took two steps toward the whipping scene.

Drake cleared his throat. "Ladies, did your Masters give you permission to be in the dungeon without them?"

They froze.

Whoa, he really was *the Chains cop.*

Mac whispered to Hope, "Busted."

Turning, Hope bowed her head slightly, "No, they didn't, Master Drake. They're not here tonight."

"I guess we'll wait for you upstairs, Ray." Mac wrinkled her nose, and the women headed for the staircase.

Leaving her alone in the dungeon.

"No, do not look so abandoned." Drake put an arm around her and steered her out of the path of a Domme and her bearded lipstick-wearing submissive in high heels and frilly lingerie.

"I don't. I'm fine." Ray tried to rearrange her expression as her feelings tangled worse than loose wire in a box.

He frowned, obviously aware she'd lied, but kept walking anyway. They passed a couple of scenes before he stopped at a roped-off area. He smiled at a burly Top with long tied-back brown hair who had his arm around a flushed, sweating naked man. "It appears you had a good scene."

"We did," the Top said with a pleased laugh, then motioned to the equipment. "All cleaned up if you want to play."

Play? Ray stiffened and tried to step back, but the arm around her tightened.

"Thank you, Bastian." Drake smiled down at Ray. "Relax, *ma douce.*" He motioned toward the device. "You wanted to see George's work. He made this spanking bench a few years ago."

"Ohhhhh." With a breath of relief, she stepped forward to look. It was a spanking bench design. She'd seen photos of cheap ones and even homemade ones from sawhorses. This one was as akin to a rough sawhorse as the *Mona Lisa* was to a child's artwork. Rich, dark walnut gleamed and demanded to be touched.

The dark red cushions incorporated in the design created a functional, comfortable—and beautiful—piece of furniture.

Realizing she'd gotten lost in examining and stroking the bench, she turned.

Drake was leaning against the wall, ankles crossed, totally at ease. "I saw George a few days before he passed on. Tomo said you were asleep, or we'd have met then."

Unable to speak, she nodded at Drake. When George had grown too weak to leave his bed, she'd volunteered to sleep during the days and sit with him at night. Faj had been awake off and on, and the quiet times with him had been a blessing.

"He let me know the two pieces he'd planned to make would not be completed." Drake lifted his eyebrows, his unspoken question obvious: *Why are you here?*

"I didn't want anything he started to remain unfinished." She pushed her hair back from her face. "I would've called, but his notes had no number or address for Chains."

The reason being Faj was a damn *member*. "If the club wants, I can complete the job he already started. Is there a person in charge of purchases I should speak with?"

"I would be that person." He studied her for a moment, then smiled. "It would be most helpful if you finish the work. Let me show you the room where they'll go." Drake motioned for her to walk beside him.

As they crossed the huge room, he seemed to know everyone. Other Dominants nodded. But the submissives...

No matter their gender, they greeted him with a breathy, "Master Drake." If the Chains cop had indicated any interest, every submissive appeared as if they'd bend and spread 'em. And not for a frisking.

Admittedly, he was shockingly good-looking. No, more than that. His personality was so confident and authoritative any submissive would melt in his presence.

Including me, dammit.

Halfway back across the huge dungeon, he stopped at a closed door. A sign read, "*Elfame. No impact or painful play, please.*" The door opened into a...very different ambiance.

Decorated in dark rich greens and browns, the room was softly lit as if with moonlight. It felt as if she'd wandered into Galadriel's high elf domain. Or a witches' forest nook. She turned in a circle. "This is different from the rest of the place." Ferns filled the corners. Ivy hung from wood-carved rafters.

"Not everyone wants pain or impact play or a dungeon atmosphere. This is a space for a more sensual experience."

It didn't even smell like the rest of the dungeon. She breathed in. The rich scent of sandalwood, green growing things, water. A hint of leather. Definitely sensual.

A flickering candle drew her attention to a woman restrained on a bondage table. The male Top was sliding an ice cube over her breasts.

Mmm. Simply watching it made her tits bunch up.

She turned her gaze elsewhere, to a wall covered with a tapestry of a boulder-strewn forest in the fog. The opposite area had a softly-splashing inlaid pool and fountain with candles tucked into hollows in the stones. The actual floor was aged red-brown tiles.

The room was so soundproofed she couldn't hear anything except a slow Celtic tune. And...uh...the woman's moans.

In a corner half-hidden behind ferns, a Domme teased her male submissive with a furry glove and a spiky wheel.

"The tantric chair will be positioned next to the pool." His mouth quirked. "You do realize what a tantric chair is used for? In this context?"

His eyes held hers, and she felt the blood rise to her face. "For sex in different positions."

"*Oui.* Both pieces, especially the chair, need a sensual appearance and feel to fit into the ambiance of this room. The tantric chair should be something a woodland elf queen might enjoy with her king on a moonlit night."

Drake motioned to a St. Andrew's cross. "The pentacle will be used for bondage and go against that wall instead of the cross."

"Right." The moans and sighs and music were getting to her. She felt way too hot, her skin far too sensitive.

As if he could tell, Drake inclined his head. "I believe you have the idea. Do you need further measurements?"

Focus, Ray. C'mon. She frowned at the cross on the wall. From the looks of it, the pentacle restraints would have to accommodate a wider stance than she'd imagined. "It would be helpful to get a range for arm and leg span."

"Easy to do." At the cross, he faced her, rested his arms over the horizontal bars, then spread his legs. "If you add a couple of inches to my measurements, you'll have the largest of our men covered."

She moved closer to get her measurements. And, oh, he smelled really good, his cologne so faint a person had to be within inches to catch the scent. There was a hint of lemon and spices and musk—incredibly clean and masculine.

No, no, mustn't put my face against his neck and sniff.

Pulling in a deep breath sure didn't help. With an effort, she concentrated on the task. Only...as she measured the distance between his hands, she noticed the solid bones of his wrist and how his forearms were thick with muscle.

Concentrate, woman. She jotted down the measurements.

When she knelt at his feet to get the measurement for how far his legs spread, the simmering heat in her body turned to a boil. Because it was far too provocative a position. Especially with her bodice pushing her breasts upward.

Seeing the smoldering interest in his dark eyes, she knew he'd noticed.

Yet he didn't say a word. Didn't leer. Didn't touch.

. . .

Drake hadn't had so much fun in a long time. This fascinating woman wasn't here for sex. Had no idea who he was. Was as wary as a mouse spotting the house cat.

Yet she, too, felt the chemistry between them.

Normally, in the heated setting of a BDSM club, attraction proceeded quickly to hooking up for a scene or sex. This much slower dance was far more unusual—and enjoyable.

Color rose in her cheeks when she touched him for the measurements. Her breathing sped up; her pupils widened. Kneeling between his legs, she refused to meet his gaze.

Truly adorable.

He waited as she wrote. After she rose, he said, "If you give me the tape measure, I will use you as the model." He studied her a moment. "You are perhaps three inches taller than our shortest member, so remember to reduce the ratios accordingly." He held his hand out.

"O-of course." Biting her lip, she gave him the tape measure, and they exchanged positions. She stretched her arms out to the side.

Tempting, but no. Men who pressed their attentions on the vulnerable were despicable.

Of course, he did enjoy the faint vanilla scent of her hair. And as he extended the tape measure from one wrist to the other, he noted the velvety skin of her wrist—and kept the contact brief.

After reporting the inches, he went down on one knee and tapped the inside of her knees. "Open as widely as possible, *ma douce*, because it is what would be expected."

As a Dom, he considered the faint tremor of her legs as she obeyed. Was it interest and arousal—or anxiety?

Under his hand, her muscles tightened. Looking up, he saw her entire body had tensed. Her mouth was tight, her eyes wide.

Fear then. He rose immediately. "Ray, look at me."

Merde, she was shaking.

. . .

"Look at me. *Now.*"

The authoritative words shattered Ray's nightmarish memories into ugly, painful fragments. Her chest lifted as if a boulder had rolled off, and she gasped in a breath of lifegiving air.

"Better, better." The man's eyes were so very dark. Warm with concern. A line between his brows disappeared. "There now, are you back with me?"

Oh. The Chains cop. Her throat was so dry, her voice creaked as she answered. "Yes. Sorry."

"Apologies are not necessary. Did we trip over a trigger for something in your past?"

His far-too-perceptive gaze dispersed the social courtesies she would have tried to use.

"Y-yes." Embarrassment and irritation and fear frothed inside her. "It's in the past."

"But it is not in the past if you get ambushed in the present, *mon petit chou.*" His deep voice was gentle. "Will you tell me what caused your fear?"

She shook her head, all the spit in her mouth gone.

"Ah, yes, I am still a stranger."

As he rested his hand on the cross, she realized she'd wrapped her arms around herself. And she couldn't relax them.

"Did you get help after whatever it was? Therapy, maybe?"

"I did. And it was years ago. I've worked past, um, most of the...stuff." Although she hadn't told George exactly what happened, he'd figured out enough to push her into therapy. The counselor *had* helped a lot. Truly she had. But she'd been older and motherly, and Ray couldn't bring herself to share or work through the kinky part of that night.

"Well then, you have choices. You have the measurements you need. I can take you back upstairs to Hope and MacKensie. Or if you'd prefer to eliminate this one trigger, we can repeat these actions over and over until you are no longer confronted."

She stared at him in dismay. "Do this again?"

A corner of his mouth tilted up, but he didn't speak. Simply waited for her to think it through.

She really wanted to thump him for coming up with such an unspeakable suggestion. Only... The ghastly night had occurred four years ago, and she was still avoiding mentions of bondage or anything to do with BDSM in books, movies, and conversations.

Drake didn't laugh at her, didn't back away. "Everything is up to you, *ma puce*. If you want to try, we can do a small amount or take it as far as you wish."

She tightened her back muscles, trying to find a smidgeon of spine. Damned if she'd let those jackholes ruin her life and continue making her afraid. She'd worked through the other triggers; she knew what to do.

She pulled in air through her nose. "Yes. I want you to do it again."

"Well"—his hard face softened with a smile—"then we shall proceed. However, this is not a scene, Ray. Simply say no, and I will stop."

She managed a jerky nod. Her fingers were cramping around the notepad. She stuffed it and the pencil into her pocket.

Once again, he measured between her wrists, the tape pressing against her breasts. Then he crouched and tapped her inner knees to get her to move.

Again, the memory dug deep into her brain.

Hard hands biting into her legs, forcing them apart. Her voice—crying out. Why was she so confused? The feeling of hands on her...wonderful... horrible. Who was touching her? How many of—

She shook her head hard. Forced her eyes open.

This is now.

She looked down and met Drake's dark eyes.

He wasn't moving, wasn't even touching her. Wasn't speaking.

She'd broken free of the memory on her own. *Yes.* She tried to smile and failed. *Deep breath, Ray.* "Again...please?"

"You have only to ask," he said softly and rose. He touched her cheek with light fingertips. "Another breath first, please."

The tightness around her chest eased further with the next inhalation. She gave him a firm nod.

Four more times he measured, knelt, touched her legs—and sent her into darkness.

But each panic attack was shorter. Easier to throw off.

With the last repetition, she managed to laugh as he regained his feet. "Are your legs getting tired? I hated doing squats in PE classes."

His chuckle was as low and dark as distant thunder in the night. "I can manage more if you wish. But I think you are past this trigger, are you not?" He tucked the tape measure into her boxer's pocket.

"Yes, thanks to you." She wrapped her arms around her waist again. "What a stupid thing to scare me. I mean...you didn't tie me down. Barely touched me."

His expression darkened.

Oh, damn, what had she revealed now? More than she'd intended, for sure.

Brows together, he was silent for a long moment. Obviously thinking. "*Zut*. Shall we continue to the next trigger point in this...scenario...from your past? Perhaps tying your wrists and adding more touch?"

"No!" Her heart rate doubled, tripled.

His gaze stayed on her, steady and patient.

She swallowed.

He moved his shoulders in a casual shrug. "If bondage will not be in your future, then you have, perhaps, achieved enough."

Bondage. She averted her face from his uncomfortably discerning eyes. Because stepping into the dungeon here had been terrifying. Also thrilling. Before the incident, it'd been incredibly exciting the one time she'd been tied up, helpless and dominated and—

Strong fingers curved along her jaw and forced her to meet his intent eyes. "You liked bondage in the past, *oui?*" His thumb stroked her cheek.

Her nod was tiny, but enough.

"Then shall we continue here and now, or have you had enough at this time?" It was obvious he felt she'd work through her fears sooner or later. His belief in her strength was heartening since she sure didn't feel very strong.

Only... Maybe the time was right. His concern for her was obvious, and he'd watched her carefully. Slowed when her breathing went funny. Did only what they'd agreed on. He'd taken no liberties.

"Now." She pulled in a breath. "With you. If...if you have time?"

"*Mon petit chou*, for you I will make the time." He tilted his head. "Is rope the right choice?"

It had been rope that night. She managed to nod.

But there was no rope here in the room.

His expressive lips curved upward as he eyed her bodice. "Your laces will do quite well."

With far-too-competent fingers, he untied her top, pulling the black shoelace-like cords loose. "As our law enforcement officers might say, assume the position." A glint of humor sparked in his eyes.

Her own laughter caught her by surprise and wafted away the fog of fear for a moment. "You're supposed take this seriously," she said sternly.

"Oh." His lips quirked as he tied her left wrist to the arm of the cross. "Forgive me, I had forgotten." Rather than a knot, he created a fat, easy-to-release bow.

Thank you for small mercies. If needed, she could twist her hand around to pull the string. Still... Her insides began to shake, then the rest of her. *Again.* "Does trembling burn calories, do you suppose?"

His surprised and approving laugh let her catch her next breath. She managed to keep her arm in place rather than yanking away as he secured her wrist.

The automatic way he ran a finger inside the bonds to check they weren't too tight was reassuring. So was the way he stepped back and narrowed his eyes to study her.

But when he remained still, just watching her, she couldn't keep from squirming.

"Very pretty." His smooth murmur caressed her ears. "Do you enjoy being bound?"

Her breathing started to speed up. Her heart was already racing. She was—

"Look at me, Aralia. Stay here with me." His hand was warm against the side of her face. His eyes trapped hers. "Do you like being bound by someone you trust? Someone you know won't hurt you?"

Oh.

His thumb pressed lightly on her lips, and she realized he was monitoring her breathing. Her panting slowed.

"You're safe." He stroked his thumb back and forth, and her body woke to the feel of the slight roughness against her lips. To the realization he was standing so close she could feel his body's heat.

Each breath brought her the clean, masculine scent of citrus and spices.

"*Très bien.* Now you remember why we indulge in such things." The hand against her face kept her trapped in his gaze. The other hand glided slowly down her bare right arm.

Every nerve in her body roused.

The fine lines at the corners of his eyes crinkled. For a long minute, he simply stroked her arm, before moving upward to caress her neck.

"*Oui*, this is how it should be." He cupped the back of her head, holding her as he kissed her, his lips as sensual as his hands, coaxing her to open. As if he had all the time in the world, he nibbled and sucked on her lips. His tongue teased hers as he toyed with her...and somehow, her anxiety disappeared.

The room disappeared.

She floated in space with only his hands and mouth anchoring her.

When he lifted his head and withdrew slightly, it took her a moment to focus.

He tilted his head, his smile wry. "You are full of surprises, are you not?" He rubbed a hand over his beard. "You are tolerating bondage quite well."

She really was.

"Do you wish to continue? To be touched while restrained? Or is this enough for now?"

Touched—when she couldn't get free? *No, oh, no.* When she pulled at the ropes, fear rose again. She couldn't get loose. A man stood in front of her. Her bodice hung loose, her breasts partially exposed. Her stomach quivered like a bowl of Jell-O.

He...didn't move. Simply waited with apparently inexhaustible patience.

She swallowed, half-terrified, half-aroused. And one hundred percent confused. And he recognized all of it. "I... Continue."

"Poor little submissive. Let us get your pulse down first." With a quiet chuckle, he stroked her hair much as she would an upset kitten. So very soothing.

Her frantic thoughts slowed.

After a minute, two, three, he nodded. "Now we will get you past this so you can return and indulge in something you obviously enjoyed in the past."

The words crystalized what she felt. What she wanted. Determination coalesced inside. "Yes."

"Then." His gaze met hers. "Pull on your ties."

She yanked—and nothing gave. Her wrists were securely bound.

He ran one finger down her neck, between her breasts where her bodice hung open.

Terror stabbed her. *Hands...touching, hurting.* Her breathing stopped.

"Aralia, eyes on me."

She shook her head.

"*Look. At. Me.*"

Heart hammering, mouth dry, she opened her eyes, shaking so hard the entire cross vibrated.

Black eyes met hers. "There now. Who am I?"

Who...? He was a stranger—*no, wait.* She swallowed. "The Chains police. Drake."

His slight smile held satisfaction. "*Bonne fille.* Breathe in. What do you smell?"

Sandalwood, leather, a faint hint of his cologne, "You, this place."

"Better." He waited as she looked around. As the world settled around her.

"Again." His stern chin rose. "Pull on your arms."

Oh freaking hell.

As she did, as fear swirled around her, he touched her intimately, his fingers brushing the insides of her breasts.

And then he brought her back from panicking.

Again.

And again.

By the fourth time, she was exhausted. Her knees finally trembled more from tiredness than fear, and when he ran his hand down her front, all she felt was warmth.

And then...she felt even more.

He leaned forward to kiss her lightly, as he cupped one breast. His thumb grazed her nipple.

Heat streaked through her body as if someone had opened a door to the sultry tropics.

Making a low sound of approval and enjoyment, he took the

kiss deeper. His tongue ravaged her mouth, sending shivers of arousal through her. His callused fingers teased her other breast. Kneading, plumping. When he tugged on her nipple, she rose on tiptoes at the shocking pleasure.

"*Très bien*," he whispered against her lips. And then he was using both hands, molding and kneading her breasts. Tugging on her sensitive nipples.

Her breasts swelled to an exquisite tightness.

"Aren't you sweet to touch," he murmured. After another quick kiss, he released her and stepped back. "But we must be done now. Your mind and emotions are not calm, and I will not take advantage."

She stared at him, shocked at his decision. And shocked in a whole other way. The man—the Dom—was honorable and kind. Simply, wonderfully *kind*.

With quick tugs, he undid the laces binding her wrists and wrapped an arm around her waist to steady her.

Moving her arms, she felt the ache in her shoulders at having been in one position so long.

"Poor *bébé*." Drawing her away from the cross, he massaged her shoulders firmly.

"Owwww."

As he dug his fingers into her tight muscles, the pain grew until they relaxed with a burst of warmth.

"Much better." With quick hands, he re-laced her bodice. "A pity to cover such magnificence."

At the rush of heat into her cheeks, she wanted to smack herself for feeling so...pleased...at his easy compliment. *Seriously, Ray, can you be more shallow?*

Even worse, this felt too much like before when she discovered she loved being submissive, being told what to do. Her obsession with the Dominant who wakened her interests had led her into disaster.

She pulled in a breath, straightened her obviously weak spine, and took a step back. "Well. Um...thank you."

He must have heard the change in her voice. He tilted his head, one eyebrow lifting.

She winced. Once again, she proved she was a social disaster. "Seriously, thank you. I know you must be very busy, and you've been wonderful to spend time with me and help me through...uh, this." Her words stumbled over themselves.

Elder gods, I'm such a mess.

He didn't look annoyed, although he moved another step back, leaving her missing his warmth like she'd been shoved into the snow. "You are very welcome. Before I leave you—"

"Master Drake." A tall, lanky man wearing a black chain harness hurried up. "There's an incident in the medieval torture room. Can you come?"

"But of course." Drake hesitated. "Please, escort Ray upstairs to her friends, Hope and MacKensie."

"MacKensie. Alex's submissive?"

"*Oui.*" When the Chains cop's attention returned to her, a totally unwanted thrill ran through her. He inclined his head slightly. "Be well, *mon petit chou.*"

"Um, you too." *No, Ray. Being attracted to him would be a totally bad idea.*

His smile appeared in his eyes. "When you want to actually... play, I'll be here."

Before she could respond, he was gone.

No, no, she didn't feel bereft. Not at all.

She smoothed her hands over her bodice, checked she was assembled correctly, and followed her escort. Her legs still trembled as she climbed the stairs to the second floor, but she didn't disgrace herself by needing assistance.

Despite the crowded room, the tall man easily located MacKensie and Hope who were seated at a table near the dance floor. He handed Ray over and disappeared.

"Did you get all the measurements you need?" Hope pushed a drink over.

"Yes." Ray dropped into a chair and chugged the Diet Coke down. "So good. Thank you. I *really* needed it."

MacKensie's eyebrows rose.

Bad Ray, too dramatic. "It's hot down there," she said hastily.

Hope laughed merrily. "And exciting, mmm?"

"Well, *yeah*. All that...stuff...going on?" Let alone participating. The urge to share rose, and she shut it down. Instead, she asked, "Weren't Alex and Peter supposed to be here by now?"

"Oh, they got dragged down to some altercation in the dungeon." MacKensie waved toward the stairs. "Apparently, a Top gagged his bottom and didn't give him a squeaky toy to use to safeword. That's breaking the rules. The people watching thought the bottom was in distress and was being ignored."

Ignoring the safeword. Ignoring consent. The unbearable memories radiated through her, and her surroundings blurred.

No, no, I'm here. With friends. Drinking a nice soda. Another swallow of the icy liquid helped ground her in the present. "A squeaky toy?"

"Oh, right, you're new. You know what a safeword is?" Hope asked.

When Ray nodded, she continued, "If you're gagged, the Top and bottom work out other ways to signal for a stop. Gestures or hoots."

"Or squeaky toys." MacKensie grinned. "In Chains, it's required to provide the bottom with a squeaky toy if gags are used. The dungeon monitor needs to know if there's a problem."

Hope nodded. "It's like the club safeword here is red. No matter what anyone uses privately, if someone yells red, DMs show up."

"But this bottom didn't get a squeaky toy," Ray said slowly. "So other people called for a dungeon monitor?"

"Exactly. When in doubt, call for a DM." Hope wrinkled her

nose. "But when Kenyon tried to intervene, the Top threw a fit and got aggressive. So a bunch of the longtime members went to deal with it. Drake usually handles really bad stuff though."

"I don't think anyone knew he was showing me the Elfame room." Or maybe they saw he was...involved...with her and didn't want to interrupt. How embarrassing.

Her breasts tingled with the lingering sensation of being squeezed by callused hands. Feeling her face heat, Ray said hastily, "What will happen to the Top?"

"If it's the first transgression, and they fix the problem," MacKensie said, "they'll probably just get a lecture."

"In this case, he got belligerent with the DM. I bet his membership gets canceled." Hope nodded. "Consent is big here."

Consent is big here. Ray's tension seeped away. A submissive had needed help and wasn't ignored. Help had come. The others listened and acted.

If she wanted to explore BDSM—more than the taste she'd gotten years before—Chains might be a safe place.

Maybe.

But not tonight. "Sooo, although the evening was great, it's time to head out. I have a kitty to get home to." Wasn't that wonderful? "And I don't want to miss the last ferry to Bainbridge." The stupid ferry didn't run all night.

"Then we should wrap this up. Did you have any questions?" MacKensie asked with a smile.

"No...oh, actually, yes. About something else." Ray pursed her lips. "Exactly what does *mon petit chou* mean anyway?"

"Oh, she's definitely been around Drake." Hope snickered. "Literally? It means my little cabbage."

You have got to be kidding. Ray wrinkled her nose. "I was kind of hoping for something...else. Like my exotic beauty or heartstoppingly intriguing."

As the two busted up, Ray sighed. *He thinks I'm a cabbage.*

Later, in his downtown condo, Drake showered and changed into loose pants. Beer in hand, he strolled into the living room and paused. From this high, the floor-to-ceiling windows gave a magnificent view of the glowing lights of the waterfront.

Seattle was a special city, a bastion of high-tech industry as well as a hub of outdoor activities. The mountains were close, the water closer. People loved hiking, camping, kayaking, and skiing. And prided themselves on never carrying umbrellas in the constant winter drizzle.

Finest city in the world, and he'd seen quite a few of them.

Taking a seat on the couch, he rested his bare feet on the coffee table and leaned his head back to watch the night. Past the wharf, the waters of Elliott Bay were black. During the day, he could see the ferries from Bainbridge and Bremerton making their way to the city terminal.

Ray Lanigan would have returned to Bainbridge on the ferry. George's protégé. Drake sighed. His friend would not be pleased his foster daughter showed up at Chains. And certainly wouldn't have approved of Drake restraining her.

Touching her.

He smiled and shook his head. He *had* tried to stay in a mentor frame of mind. She wanted his help—and the scene had been difficult. There was no guaranteed method of dealing with sexual trauma. What might help was different for each person.

Apparently, counseling had helped her work past much of the trauma. And she'd done very well this evening.

Merde, she'd been brave.

He took a sip of his beer, remembering how she'd looked. Brave and vibrant and so damn appealing. "I'd like to see you again, Ray Lanigan."

George would have fits. "Sorry, *mon ami*, but she's all grown up now." He half-smiled. "And not the innocent you thought she was."

She hadn't known her gay foster-father had been a switch at the club. Not that George had been open about it. In turn, George hadn't known his cherished girl had done some experimenting.

Drake's smile faded. Her experimenting had gone wrong somewhere along the line.

Now she had two projects to make for the club. She'd seemed to appreciate the tranquility of the Elfame room, and he was looking forward to seeing what she created.

Would she have the courage to return to the club? Or would George's last two projects get delivered without a spirited young woman accompanying them?

Thoughtfully, Drake stroked his fingers over his goatee. Did the club he'd founded feel welcoming enough—safe enough—that she'd want to visit again?

CHAPTER FIVE

Over a week later, Ray still couldn't get the memory of Drake out of her head. And honestly, her head was busy enough that nothing should stick like this.

Ah well, it doesn't matter anyway. She wouldn't see him again, at least, not for anything except business.

Because she'd gone to Chains last night. Fridays were for Silver Members, basically a token membership for walk-ins. Before paying to get in, she'd asked the receptionist to let her peek inside on account of it sounding a whole lot louder than last weekend with Mac and Hope.

The atmosphere was totally different, far more sexual, and the younger crowd wore garish and provocative fetwear. Two men her age headed straight toward her, resembling a video she'd seen of wolves taking down a deer.

Despite the receptionist's obvious concern, Ray said, "Sorry, changed my mind," and fled back to her car. Her heart rate and breathing hadn't returned to normal until the ferry was halfway across Puget Sound.

Yeah, total fail.

"Hey. Earth to Ray."

Ray blinked and shook her head as the cheerful sounds of the coffee shop around her registered.

Across the marble-topped round table, Marisol laughed. "Where'd your head go?"

"I was riding on a ferry." Ray buried her grumbling with a sip of her coffee. Good coffee. She needed to stay here, in the moment with her friend. Besides, the coffee house was the best of places. Floor to ceiling, it boasted so many different kinds of wood it made her think of home.

After a fight with her mother, Marisol had dragged Ray out of the workshop. They'd ridden their bikes into Winslow—the downtown area of Bainbridge Island—for coffee and pastries. The center of the ivy-covered brick coffee house was the perfect place to people-watch on a weekend.

"Did you have a good weekend?"

"Eh, I picked up a few hours on the evening shift at Harborview trauma unit. Weekends always get busy." Marisol narrowed her eyes. "Nice try at diverting me. You're stewing about something, I can tell."

At Ray's scowl, Marisol snickered. "See? That look is sus as fuck. Wassup?"

"Pushy brat." Ray sighed and went for the more amusing story. "It's nothing serious. Just...a totally hot man I met at a club called me *mon petit chou*, which apparently is affectionate, but means *my little cabbage* in French. Ugh."

Marisol burst out laughing. "At least he didn't call you *gusanito* —a little worm—like Mamá does with me. And my first boyfriend called me a marshmallow—*bombón*."

"He thought you were pale and squishy? Ew." Ray rolled her eyes. "It's annoying how men think women are food items— cupcake, sweetie-pie, sugar. Gotta say, cabbage is a personal low."

Marisol giggled so hard she started snorting. "I'm sure he meant it nicely. Oh, wait—does this mean you have a guy? Where's the club? Sure isn't on Bainbridge."

"It isn't. But, girl, you don't want to go to Chains." Ray wiggled her eyebrows. "I was there for the wood crafting project I'm finishing up for George—and would you believe it's a BDSM club?"

"O. M. G." Marisol leaned so far forward she almost fell off her chair. "I've wanted to try that stuff for-evah. There's a group on campus I'm planning to check out."

"At the university? No!" Her heart crammed into her throat. "They're..." She swallowed hard. *Don't over-react.* But, dammit, why did her past keep slapping her in the face?

"Ray?"

After she'd called and reported the incident to the club president, the abusers must have been kicked out if nothing else. Surely, they wouldn't be there four years later.

Nonetheless, a warning wouldn't hurt. "Listen. I've, uh, heard, bad things about that UW group. And really, you might want to play...um, vanilla, until you have more experience or something."

Seeing Marisol's expression close down, Ray winced. Maybe she was only a few years older, but sometimes it felt more like a generation. And apparently, she sounded like it.

"I'm almost twenty-one, not fifteen," Marisol said in a cool tone, "and probably have more experience than you, Ms. Live-in-her-workshop."

"Ouch, good point." Especially since after that night, she'd avoided dating for a long time. "Sorry."

"S'okay. Hey, did I tell you Mamá is going on vacation the middle of August? She and my aunts are doing a women-only trip to San Francisco for a week. "

"Oooh, fun. Wish I had sisters."

"I know, right?" Marisol grinned. "The Latinas take over Chinatown."

Marisol's mom was a force of nature. Three of them together? Ray was giggling when three noisy men entered the coffee shop.

A short ginger-headed man was saying to the others, "I want a place right on the water like Drake's. Can you believe the view he's got?"

Ray stiffened. Drake. Surely he hadn't said Drake. Her imagination had gone bonkers.

The bearded blond snorted. "Since when can you afford to live on Bainbridge?"

"Yeah, okay, it'll be a while," the ginger grumbled.

"If ever." The bearded blond's eyes fell on Ray, and his eyebrows went up. He took a step toward her. "Hey, aren't you Drake's plaything from last week? You disappeared and—"

A hard thump on his shoulder interrupted him. The third man, maybe a decade older than Ray, said in a low voice, "You know better. What happens in..."

Old gods, they were from Chains.

Blondie's tanned skin turned a dusky red before he nodded to her. "Sorry."

The older man who'd reprimanded him was good-looking with the hefty build of an ex-football player. His clothing, although casual, was expensive. Then again, Bainbridge Island had a lot of over-the-top rich people.

He inclined his head at Ray. "Sorry for disturbing you."

Before she could respond, Marisol piped up, "Are you a member of the...the *club* too?"

"Why yes, I am." His smile was thoroughly charming. "I'm Blaize. And you are...?"

"Marisol, but I'm not a member." Her gaze edged toward Ray. "Not yet. I have other things to do first."

"Ah, your studies, of course. Good for you. The world is in dire need of more nurses." His expression turned wicked. "And everyone in the lifestyle loves nurses." He nudged Blondie toward the counter and added, "Have a nice day, ladies."

The ginger followed.

Talk about awkward. Another reason to avoid Chains in the future.

Marisol's brown eyes were alight. "How interesting."

"More like way indiscreet." Ray frowned. "How did Blaize know you're a nursing student?"

"You're so blind." Marisol motioned toward her T-shirt. The graphic had a half-filled syringe with NURSE IN PROGRESS; PLEASE WAIT, underscored by University of Washington.

"Too funny. I didn't even notice." Angling her chair to put her back to the annoying man, Ray lifted her drink. Time to change the subject. "So what unit are you on for your clinical now?"

"I rotated to pediatrics, and sometimes it's so fun and then"—Marisol's eyes welled with tears—"not. Children shouldn't get so sick. Or die."

Ray put her hand over Marisol's. "No, they shouldn't. But they're lucky to have nurses like you. Want to tell me about it?"

Marisol did, and all too soon, they were both sniffling. Losing George had been heartbreaking, but at least, he'd had a full life. Children—just no.

Eventually, Ray turned the conversation to something happier. "So what's your cohort been up to?"

"Oh, wait'll you hear this!" Marisol bounced on her chair. "Bezzler totally hates one of the idiot medical interns; he's such a patronizing twat. Anyway, she smeared melted chocolate all over an incontinence pad. I took it over to the desk an' said the patient complained of abdominal pain and pooped all over. Bezzler takes the pad, sniffs it, and then swipes a finger through the so-called BM. Then she sticks it in her mouth and says, 'Seems fine to me.'"

Ray's jaw dropped.

"Right? The intern gags and runs for the staff bathroom." Marisol was giggling. "Honestly, I almost puked, and I even knew it was only chocolate. Best prank ever."

Ray was still laughing as they got up and bused the table. A glance around showed the Chains members had already left.

Squinting in the bright sunlight, she followed Marisol onto the sidewalk. Across the water, Mount Rainier was out in its full glory.

Marisol's cell phone buzzed. She answered and listened a moment. "Yes, Mamá, on my way." Tucking her phone into her purse, she grinned. "Mamá's over being mad. She did my laundry, and my payback is making supper."

"Sounds fair."

The sigh was huge. "Some of my friends go home, and their moms do it all for them."

"Bet she took lessons from George. When I was in the dorms, he let me bring laundry home, but I had to wash his at the same time." Ray's eyes teared with the bittersweet memory. "He was a firm believer in *TANSTAAFL*—There Ain't No Such Thing As A Free Lunch."

He'd been such a mentor, happy to teach her everything he knew. But he was enough of a traditionalist that, as the student, she got stuck with the most tedious jobs in the shop. At least doing housework had netted her an allowance. "When I wanted cake or cookies, he bought the ingredients, but I had to do the baking. From scratch."

"Oh. yeah, he got real salty about people being lazy."

"Truth. On the upside, I ended up being a pretty good cook, especially with sweets.

"You really are." Marisol scowled. "Now I have a craving for cookies."

Grinning, Ray unlocked her bike and led the way back.

A few minutes later, Marisol turned into her drive while yelling over her shoulder, "Next time you make cookies, call me."

Ray laughed, continuing farther down the road before turning into her own drive.

Once the bike was in the garage, she headed into the house. Dammit, now she wanted sugar too.

She'd been a bottomless pit all through her teens and into the twenties, and it hadn't changed much. Thankfully, wood crafting required a fair amount of activity, or her belly'd be bigger than her butt.

A thud sounded and a beige-brown furball scampered over, greeting her with throaty complaints about being abandoned for days and left to die.

"Oh, so pitiful." She picked him up and got purrs. "Lots of food, a warm house, kitty beds and a catio and wall-trails. You have a rough life."

Max voiced his complaint again. *But you weren't heeeere.*

She looked around to share with George how funny this cat was and... The house was empty. "I know how you feel, baby. How it feels to miss someone."

Faj isn't here.

She rubbed her chin against the furry head. "I'm so glad you found me, kitty. It'd be awfully lonely without you."

It was the honest truth.

Ray'd been almost done with high school when she came here and didn't attend long enough to make real friends. The island didn't have a high percentage of single people her age, and they usually commuted to work in Seattle and partied there. Marisol shared an apartment near the university campus and only came to Bainbridge now and then.

Feeling grumpy, she gave Max some scritches.

Trying to join Chains sure hadn't worked out. Rather than making friends, she'd slid right into a panic attack. Sure, MacKensie and Hope said the club was safe, but unless they were there, it wasn't really true, was it?

Or maybe it's me. She didn't feel comfortable without people she knew. After all, look at what happened at the play party she'd attended.

Yeah, no BDSM clubs in my future.

Even if that smooth-talking, French-accented Chains cop had called her a cabbage.

Speaking of which, she needed to finish the projects for the club. *That's the only reason I'll go back there.*

An hour later, she was making serious progress on the tantric chair. The cherry wood was a satisfyingly rich reddish-brown, and she'd picked a piece with an elegant wavy pattern to the grain.

So beautiful.

Of course, Pa would've insisted she paint the wood. He'd wanted everything orderly and matching...and for people to be predictable rather than interesting. He'd wanted her to be flat and smooth, but she was like this wood grain, full of waves.

Before she could spiral back down into grumpiness, a ringing came from the workshop entry. The small enclosure was where she changed into scrubs and tied up her hair to prevent hair or dirt from ruining a glossy wet finish.

Didn't it figure she'd left her damn phone there?

And now, she had to answer—it was on her business line, after all.

In the entry, she pulled it out of her jeans pocket. "Creations by Ray. How can I help you?"

"Hey, Ray, it's Hope. MacKensie gave me your work phone, since I stupidly forgot to ask for your number. Peter and I are having a Sunday afternoon barbecue tomorrow with some friends. You should come."

When Ray didn't answer, Hope's voice turned coaxing. "C'mon, Ray. MacKensie and Alex will be here."

"Um." Unfamiliar people and territory weren't a problem. What strangers thought of her wasn't high on her worry list. But if *Hope* or *MacKensie* decided she was too emotional, too wired, too...

In her head, all the disapproving remarks from Pa and old boyfriends swept past and required effort to ignore.

Then again, her high energy had never bothered Hope. In fact, most of her friends, at least the female ones, hadn't minded Ray's quirks.

Faj used to quote Emerson when she got frozen by worry: *"He who is not conquering some fear has not learned the secret of life."*

She pulled in a breath. "I'd love to come."

As Hope burbled about the party, Ray could only smile. It'd be fun, right? And a summer barbecue was way far away from Chains and any BDSM stuff.

CHAPTER SIX

Holy kraken, there's a lot of vehicles here. Finding an empty space, Ray parked her SUV and walked up the curving private drive. Trying to ignore her stomach quivers, she followed the big party signs pointing to the side gate of the three-story brick house.

The backyard held a large paved area and a wide green lawn... and too many people.

On the patio, guests were standing around with drinks, getting food from a long buffet, or sitting at tables to eat. A couple of people were cooking on a massive built-in grill. The tantalizing aroma of meat reminded her she hadn't eaten lunch.

Okay, here goes. She headed down a charming stone path toward her doom.

"Ray, you made it!" Hope hurried over and caught her up in a hug. "I'm so glad. I want you to meet everyone."

"How fun." *It'll be fine. I wanted to meet people.* "I don't see any children. Is this an adult-only party?"

"It is." Hope linked their arms and tugged Ray toward the patio. "Parents host the alcohol-free, children-inclusive parties since their houses are already kid-proofed. Us childless ones hold the parties with drinks...and occasionally kink."

"Kink?" Ray stopped short. *I should have asked more questions.*

"Relax, woman. I'd have warned you if it was that kind of party." Hope bumped her shoulder. "This is a nice, normal, vanilla barbecue. Probably a third of our guests have never heard of Chains."

"Whew. Okay." Ray nudged her friend. "Stop smirking. For one really bad moment, I had visions of a rubber mat covered in baby oil and a lot of naked people."

Her scowl sent Hope into gales of laughter, drawing grins from everyone within hearing.

Ray rolled her eyes. "Oh yeah, here's Ms. Cork-poppin' Champagne—bubbly to the max." She'd used the term back in high school—and not always as a compliment.

"*Maaaybe.*" Hope's blue eyes danced. "Are you still a fireworks display, brilliantly explosive?"

The question brought back so many memories—of the friendly teasing from her small group of high school friends. "Not quite as hyperactive, though, I'm no couch potato. Not like you, always napping up in the sun like a cat."

"Now that's just mean." After delivering a quick elbow jab, Hope stopped in front of the grill. "Peter, see? I told you I could talk her into coming. Ray, this is my husband, Peter. Peter, Ray Lanigan, George's girl."

Tall and lean, the man turned. When he smiled affectionately at Hope, Ray felt an ache of envy, but it was followed by happiness. Because Hope deserved all the love in the world.

"Welcome, Ray. I'm glad you made it. And I'm sorry I missed meeting you last weekend."

He meant at Chains. Really, she was seriously happy he and Alex hadn't arrived before she left.

"Hope said you're single." Peter glanced at the other guests. "If you see someone interesting you'd like to meet, let me know."

Ray's mouth dropped open. Was the fancy lawyer trying to matchmake?

"Oh, good idea." Hope beamed. "I was thinking she should meet the other submi—um, friends like Lynn and Tess. I didn't even think of romantic stuff."

Ray froze. "No. No, no. Don't you dare introduce me to men."

"That sounds quite vehement." Peter eyed her. "Are you ace—or do you prefer women?"

"Het, but you can consider me asexual for now."

"Ah. Got it." He nodded. "As you wish."

Hope's brows drew together. "That sounds like a relationship went sour or something." When Ray winced, she added, "I'm sorry, whatever it was that happened."

"Thanks." Being Hope, *she'd eventually get the story*. Ray waved at the buffet table. "So how about a drink? And is MacKensie here?"

As Drake parked his black SUV in Peter and Hope's circular drive, his cell rang. Pulling it out, he swiped to answer. "Simon, how are you?"

"Very good, actually. And you?"

"Good, good. Except for a problem with our local BDSM convention. Chains is one of the hosts, and two of our speakers have canceled. The weekend is August 23rd through the 25th. Might you be interested in teaching a couple of the workshops? We would, of course, pay for travel and lodging for you and Rona. And before or after, stay with me at the Seattle condo or on Bainbridge."

"Interesting idea. Rona has vacation time coming up and does enjoy conventions. What workshops did you have in mind?"

A few minutes later, Drake headed to the party with a smile. One speaker position was filled—and he was looking forward to seeing his martial arts and BDSM mentor again.

The convention attendees would have a treat. Simon was a superb instructor.

Back when Drake had been in college in San Francisco and learning about mixed martial arts, Simon had taken him as a student, then introduced him to BDSM and the ethics of domination.

Simon had strong opinions about how a good man should behave.

Drake shook his head. In all reality, his mentor's beliefs were a reversal of Drake's father's. In Marseille, Papa had worked his way up through the organized crime ranks and expected Drake to follow in his footsteps as an enforcer. Expected obedience and blind loyalty.

Drake had been trying to find a way out when his parents and father's side of the family were murdered in gang warfare. All of them. He'd have died too if he hadn't been elsewhere, recovering from a beating his father had given him.

Would have died if the mob learned he was alive. But his mother's family had taken action, and his US-based uncle brought him to America and adopted him.

In college, Drake had still been trying to figure out where he fit into the world when he met Simon...who became the big brother he never had.

"*Merci*, Simon," he said under his breath.

There would be time to catch up with his mentor during the convention. And he had a feeling Simon would adore Ray.

In the backyard, the party was still going full swing although he was running rather late. Not that it mattered today.

Peter, being a lawyer, loathed formal dinner parties. He and Hope usually had much more casual gatherings where people could simply graze the buffet table when hungry.

Drake strolled through the crowd, stopping to chat occasionally, and eventually ran into a group of friends. Alex, Peter, Blaize, and a stranger.

"I wondered if you were going to make it." With a smile, Alex made room in the circle for Drake. "We've been talking about Chains."

Peter noticed him and grinned, then continued speaking to the man Drake didn't recognize. "Why don't you come as my guest next week? It sounds as if you're ready to learn more about the lifestyle, and since you're single again, this is a good time."

The man's face tightened. "I'm not pleased about being single, thanks."

"But it happens—and you were only together a few months." Peter thumped his arm. "Visiting the club will get you out and about."

Drake almost grinned, having been treated to the same annoying cheerfulness after his two relationships went sour. Peter had no tolerance for moping.

"Drake, good you could join us." Peter motioned to the stranger. "Let me introduce Theodore Prescott who's been in my firm for a few years now. We wanted a specialist in international law and sent him off to get his LL.M. in Indiana. He just got back in May."

Drake nodded politely, acknowledging the introduction used when guests were work associates. Occupations and business affiliations were given rather than actual interests.

Prescott was a couple inches short of six feet and appeared fit, so possibly indulged in a sport more active than the usual golf. But his brown hair was side-parted and cut conservatively, his button-down shirt a muted blue. He looked like a lawyer.

Peter continued. "Theodore, this is Jean-Pierre Dragomir, who owns Dragomir Real Estate & Development. His company put together some of Seattle's most innovative big projects, including the high-rise you admired that overlooks the wharf."

Drake smiled and shook hands politely. "A pleasure to meet you."

"Likewise."

Alex raised an eyebrow. "Why Indiana?"

"I grew up there and still have siblings near Indianapolis." Prescott grinned. "I'd forgotten how annoying the snowy winters are. It's great to be back in Seattle."

"We're pleased to have him back," Peter said. "There's a need for lawyers familiar with international law."

Blaize as a professor of tax law nodded agreement. "Global markets are growing."

Prescott looked at Drake. "I can hear a French accent. Does your company have developments overseas?"

"*Non, non.* I have some family there, but my business interests are in the US"—he smiled slightly—"to avoid the convoluted area of foreign investment and—"

Noticing a woman with eye-catching, curly red-brown hair, he paused mid-sentence.

Ray Lanigan. He hadn't expected to see her here. How delightful—and wasn't she a pretty sight?

Her white jeans were casual but more upscale than shorts. The blue-green color of her tank matched her eyes and the turquoise strands in her hair. Even better, it fit nicely enough to showcase fine breasts and toned arms as well as the tree tattoos on her deltoids. He hadn't been able to see the ink well in the dungeon.

Intriguing designs. One tattoo was of a blooming tree, showing the form of a woman in the curving trunk. The other was a gnarled old trunk, not only enduring everything but in full autumn foliage. The fall-colored leaves matched the freckles on her face and arms.

He did love freckles.

"See someone you like?" Blaize followed Drake's gaze. "Ah, the new one from the club. Not as stunning as some of your women, but she looks interesting. Like fun."

Ray had been fun. And interesting. And had tugged at his heart as well. Quite a mix for one woman. As for stunning? "I find her more than stunning, actually."

Drake ignored Blaize's blink of surprise.

Ray was with Hope, Tess, and Mac near the drink table. The women were talking animatedly, hands waving, laughing, not noticing the glances from unattached men. They obviously didn't need a man's company to have a fun time.

Blaize glanced at Peter. "Is she a Chains member?"

"No, but her foster father was," Peter said. "I don't know if you knew George...he was a switch. My wife ran into Ray unexpectedly and turns out they knew each other in high school. Hope was thrilled to reconnect."

"Ray?" Prescott glanced over his shoulder and froze. "That's *my* Ray." Turning, he headed straight for the women.

His Ray? Irritation drove a spike between Drake's ribs. Was it because Ray hadn't mentioned a boyfriend—or because he wished her to be free of commitments?

"Hmm." Peter's brows drew together. "I hope she's not the girlfriend who broke up with him."

Drake stiffened. Would Prescott be the cause of her trauma? Probably not. It hadn't seemed as if whatever happened was recent. But still... "I'm in need of a beer. Anyone else?"

When no one took him up on the offer, Drake headed for the drink table...conveniently close to the women and Prescott.

Surprisingly, Ray was enjoying herself. The day was lovely, and the guests at the party were interesting and just plain nice.

A light buzz fizzed in her veins since she'd had a couple of the dark and malty Holy Mountain beers. Seattleites totally embraced local breweries. And coffee shops. And ethnic foods. *Cold, damp weather turns us all into foodies.*

Speaking of food, she'd sure eaten her share. Shrimp and veggie kabobs. Grilled salmon. Green salad, sourdough bread, corn on the cob.

It was a wonder she had enough room to laugh—but laughing she was. Hope was her usual irrepressible self. MacKensie had a wicked sense of humor.

Tess, a redhead in her forties, was married to a sheep rancher and seemed really sweet.

Right up until she told a very graphic story about their new high school interns who'd been helping with castrating lambs and docking tails. Too funny.

Although I'd probably throw up all over my shoes too.

Giggling, Ray noticed someone approaching from her left and turned slightly. "Theodore." She stared at him. "How are you here?"

He gave her a look as if the screws holding her brain in her skull had fallen out. "I live in Seattle, remember?" After a second, he added, "Peter is an attorney at my law firm. He invited me."

"Oh, well." She couldn't say it was nice to see him; it wasn't. And he stood too close—like a lover, not a friend. Unable to step back with her friends behind her, she edged sideways. "You're, um, looking well."

"I don't know how. I've been miserable. I miss you, doll." He reached for her.

She took another step away, but her retreat was separating her from the women, which would result in her talking to him rather than with her friends. She planted her feet. "Theodore, we had this discussion. Several times. And this sure isn't the place for arguing. This is a party."

"I agree—this isn't the place." His expression turned stubborn. The man clung to his beliefs like a rusty, pitted bolt that would break rather than loosening. "We can get together and talk more privately."

Her hands closed into fists. In counseling, she'd learned how girls who'd been programmed to be "nice" were easy to manipulate by male predators. Theodore thought she wouldn't want to cause a scene, and he'd get his way.

Wrong, dude.

She spoke louder. "Did you know naked mole rats are practically deaf? You are totally a mole rat. Since you obviously can't hear, read my lips. *No.* No private discussions. No discussions at all. *We. Are. Done.*"

"Jesus, Ray, shut it down," he hissed. "You're loud and hyper again. You're embarrassing yourself."

Her shoulders hunched as her confidence splintered like poorly dried wood.

No. No, he would not make her ashamed of who she was. "Right there, those words, are why we are finished." She drew herself up, regretting she wasn't another foot taller. *I want to be the giant in* The Princess Bride. "Keep harassing me, and I'll use your bones to craft toys for toddlers. Now go. *Away.*"

Turning her back on him, she rejoined her friends. When Hope put an arm around her, and Mac closed in from the other side, tears burned Ray's eyes.

"As I was saying"—Tess's alto was louder than before—"being ranchers, we castrate baby rams. Now my husband prefers to use a burdizzo to get rid of those pesky balls, but me—I'm old-fashioned. I use a knife." Her brown eyes held a wicked glint as she cupped one hand around an imaginary testicle and cut it open with an equally imaginary knife.

Ray's mouth dropped open. "You are not the person I thought you were."

"I had to find a threat to match your toys for toddlers."

The others burst out laughing.

"Love the toddler threat." Mac high-fived Ray and then Tess. "And Ms. Knife, every man within hearing squeezed their legs together...including the bastard who gave Ray grief."

Ray grinned at the women. "Can I switch sexual preferences and marry the three of you?"

"Mmm, tempting," Mac murmured before looking over at Alex who stood nearby with Peter and a couple other guys.

Alex was apparently close enough to hear her. His gaze didn't waver from Mac's as his lips formed the word, "*No.*"

There was so much heat in his gaze Ray wanted to fan herself.

Hope snickered. "You're really asking to get yourself spanked, woman."

"Duh." MacKensie blew Alex a kiss and waggled her butt. "He has the *best* hands."

Alex grinned—and the Dom had a devastating smile. Yes, the temperature had definitely gone up.

A few minutes later, Theodore left the party. *Yes!* She'd simply wait a while to make sure he was really gone.

"Hey, Ray." Lynn was a slim brunette—and also a Chains member. "Have you hit the ice cream sundae bar yet?"

"Uh, no?"

Lynn grabbed her hand and pulled her over to the long table. "My dear, this is a party. Sugar is mandatory." With happy chortles, she filled a bowl with vanilla ice cream, added berry topping and fresh-cut strawberries, sprinkled on chopped nuts, and smothered it all in whipped cream. "Besides, it has fruit so it's healthy."

"Sure it is." Ray eyed the towering concoction. "Aren't there laws against something so hedonistic?" The Chains police would surely arrest her.

Gods, it'd probably be totally fun. And hot.

"Nope. Although I might go straight to hell for the sin of gluttony."

"Well I can't let you be tormented down there all by yourself. Let's see how decadent I can be." Ray topped her vanilla ice cream with hot fudge—so yummy—nuts, and a token cherry. "Oh, yeah. Add whipped cream, and I'm for sure heading for everlasting punishment."

"Indulging, Aralia?" The deep masculine voice was smoother than the ice cream she'd just scooped.

Turning, she stared into brown eyes so dark as to seem almost black. Whoa, did thinking about someone summon them? "Mr. Cop."

"*Oui*." His smile was wicked. "It appears I'm in time to deliver some necessary discipline."

As if she'd been zapped by lightning, her skin turned supersensitive. Waiting for a touch. His touch. Instead of backing away as she'd done with Theodore, she barely caught herself from moving closer.

On Ray's other side, Lynn let out a snort of laughter. "I'll be at a table when you're...free, woman."

Ray could feel a blush stealing up her face, drowning her freckles in red. "I'll be right there."

"Perhaps you should add some substance to your dessert. Did you see the brownies?" Drake asked.

If stomachs had ears, hers would have perked up. "I love brownies."

"I love feeding women who enjoy their food," he murmured and held up a piece of a brownie. "Open, *ma douce*."

When she obediently opened her mouth, he popped the bite in, making a satisfied sound deep in his throat.

And the bones in her body started to melt.

Then he dropped a full-sized portion of brownie into her bowl of ice cream and fudge. "Enjoy, and I'll talk to you later."

He ran his thumb over her lower lip to swipe off the brownie crumbles, smiled into her eyes, and strolled away...leaving her hot enough to melt the entire ice cream bar all by herself.

A while later, Ray had finished her dessert and was chatting with Lynn and her Dom, Bob, as well as Hope and Peter. The conversation had turned to Chains, and she glanced around to see if any vanilla people were within hearing.

Huh. The few remaining guests were members of the BDSM

club. *My bad.* She'd gotten so caught up in the discussion she hadn't noticed people leaving.

At a break in the conversation, she took a step back. "I didn't realize it was so late. I should be going. But it was wonderful meeting you, Bob and Lynn and Peter. And seeing you again, Hope."

Hope caught her arm before she could escape. "Uh-uh. I can tell what you're thinking. You realized most of the crowd was gone, and now you feel guilty."

Ray's brain stuttered. Was she really so obvious?

"You did the same thing in high school." Snickering, Hope told Lynn, "She's so fun. It's even better when she pushes boundaries and then is terrified she hurt someone's feelings."

"But—" Ray shook her head. "The people still here are your good friends. I shouldn't—"

"You're my oldest friend, silly." Hope tucked an arm around her. "And you've been to Chains, so it's all good."

"I was only there to finish George's projects—not to, um, *play*."

Peter studied her. "The question is: Would you like to...play?"

Oh my terrifying elder gods.

"Impressive, my Lord and Master." Hope was laughing so hard her words came out almost garbled. "You silenced her completely."

Some friend. Ray leaned in to mutter at her, "I'm going to shave you bald and tattoo *mean girl* on your shiny, hairless head,"

The threat wasn't quiet enough. Everyone in the group started to laugh.

Peter cleared his throat. Waiting for her answer.

Yikes, he really was a Dom.

Do I want to participate in BDSM play? "Um. Maybe?" How could a person be so torn? She did want to...only what if she panicked? Again?

Last week, only Drake's patience and understanding—and

knowing Hope and MacKensie were there as backups—kept her from fleeing.

But she'd gone yesterday and the "open" night was terrifying. Because she had no safety net. *I'm not going to admit I totally ran when someone leered at me.* "I'm not exactly comfortable..."

Maybe if she paid the hefty dues to be a real member? Then she might make friends and might have people around to watch out for her.

But... Getting to know people wasn't quick or easy. "It's...it's too scary to be there when I'm new. I only know you and—"

"You should volunteer," Lynn interrupted. "You'll get a discount on the dues *and* meet lots of the members."

Ray pursed her lips. "That might work."

"I had the same problem when I joined." Lynn gave her a sympathetic smile. "None of my vanilla friends wanted to visit a BDSM club. And since I'm quiet, going alone was awful. So I tried the volunteer route. When you work with others, you don't have to come up with small talk, and making friends is easier."

"I can vouch for volunteering as a method." Bob had brown hair and a full beard, and was built so stocky and muscular, he resembled a bear. "It's how Lynn and I met."

Interesting. Ray smiled. "I...yes, okay. Volunteering sounds like something I should try."

Lynn's smile was smug as she turned to Bob. "There, I got you a new recruit."

"Good job, snookums." Bob nodded at Ray. "As it happens, I manage the volunteers for Chains. I always need new recruits."

She frowned at Lynn, then couldn't help but laugh. "You totally set me up."

"She really did," Hope agreed. "But it's still good advice."

Volunteering might work. If she had friends at the club, she could play without being afraid. The anticipation of being... touched, bound, dominated simmered inside her.

"Ray is joining Chains?" Drake set a hand on her lower back for a second as he joined the group. "And volunteering?"

Did he sound pleased—or annoyed?

"It appears Bob has a new minion." Peter snorted, then grinned at Ray. "George would be appalled you even set foot in Chains."

"True. However, as an adult, it is your decision." Drake smiled ruefully. "Although now I want to apologize to him for encouraging you."

Bob and Peter had equally sheepish expressions.

Ray snickered. Faj really would be appalled. He'd never talked about anything sexual. When she left for college, he handed her a box of condoms, asked her if she wanted to see a doctor to get on the pill, and added if she had questions, he'd find a woman friend to answer them. His olive coloring had actually flushed all the way to a dark red.

Tomo was the one who told her his parents divorced when George finally admitted he was gay. During the time Ray lived with him, Faj never brought a lover home.

He sure never talked to her about BDSM.

"Women should be protected from anything having to do with sex." Leaning toward the women, Lynn whispered, "Men and their double-standards, amiright?"

Hope and Ray grinned.

Bob cleared his throat loudly, then pulled out a business card, wrote something on the back, and handed it over. "Here's the URL for volunteer positions at Chains and my cell number. Give it a look, call me, and we'll talk about what you might enjoy doing."

She glanced at it and then the other side. Apparently, he was a human resource manager at a Seattle hospital.

"Ah, excellent idea." Drake pulled out his own card and also wrote something on the back. "My personal number. We need to set up a delivery for your woodworking projects. And I need your invoice, of course."

Delivery and invoice? Her eyes narrowed. If he was handling those, he wasn't some random person who'd helped plan the Elfame room's décor.

A glance at the card in her hand showed: *Dragomir Real Estate & Development. Jean-Pierre Dragomir CEO.* "I guess you're more than just the Chains police?"

From the laughter around her, she'd missed something. With her evil sense of humor, Hope might not spill, but Lynn seemed sweet. Ray turned to the brunette. "Lynn, help?"

"*Non, non*, no need," Drake said before Lynn could speak. "I thought Hope would have told you, although I did enjoy being just the Chains police."

"Tell me what?"

He gave a very Gallic shrug. "I'm one of the co-owners of Chains."

The club *owner* had caught her measuring the equipment...and she'd taunted him about being the police. Why couldn't the ground swallow her up?

"Actually, he owns over half, although several of us invested," Peter said, sounding like the lawyer he was. "He also runs the place."

Drake inclined his head at Peter. "With assistance and advice."

"Uh-huh." Bob snorted. "When we don't agree with him, it's more like"—his voice deepened—"*Vous êtes des connards stupides.*"

She caught the words for stupid—and assholes—and smothered a giggle.

"He does hate me telling him he can't simply beat up any Top who oversteps the bounds." Peter gave a litigator's long-suffering sigh.

"If a Top ignores a submissive's limits, Drake *should* be allowed to flatten them," Hope said.

"Agreed." Mac crossed her arms over her chest.

"Same," Ray said under her breath, her shoulders hunching as shame slid through her.

When she glanced up, she realized Drake's eyes had narrowed. His gaze was on her face, her shoulders, her hands.

She flinched. Over and over, the counselor had said the assault wasn't Ray's fault. It wasn't a crime to mistakenly trust an abuser. It still felt as if she'd done something wrong. A good person wouldn't have been taken advantage of the way she had.

Drake set a warm hand on her shoulder and squeezed lightly, even as he said to the others, "Next time I want to chastise a misbehaving Dom, I'll use the upstairs stage and call it a S&M event. Chains could use the publicity from a blood-drenched beatdown."

Peter threw his hands up with an exasperated huff. "You're hopeless. And don't even think about doing something like that at the convention."

"A convention?" Ray asked. "Like a…a kink convention?"

"It's a BDSM convention." Hope beamed at her. "Every year, the local clubs host one at a big hotel. We'll turn the ballroom into a giant dungeon."

Lynn added, "There are classes about the lifestyle and workshops on different skills."

Ray snorted. "Like Whipping 101?"

"Exactly," Lynn agreed, not realizing Ray was being sarcastic.

"You're serious—workshops on how to whip someone?" When everyone nodded, she asked, "What…else?"

"Oh, the usual impact stuff. Flogging, caning." Mac grinned. "Spanking."

"Other kinks too. The interrogation one last year was terrifying," Hope said with a shiver. "I had nightmares."

"Relationship dynamics. Bootblacking," Bob told Ray. "Pony play as well. All the different kinds of bondage."

A tremor ran through her, and when Drake's hand tightened on her shoulder, she realized he was still touching her.

Funny how just a simple touch—from him—grounded her. Gave her courage.

She looked up. At the concern in his eyes, she managed a smile. Hey, she'd had her wrists tied and managed all right...eventually. This was something she wanted. She really did.

"Sounds like fun. I'm in."

CHAPTER SEVEN

Coffee cup in hand, Drake walked out onto his back deck to watch the sunrise over the Cascades. It still amused him that his condo in Seattle looked out over the Sound toward Bainbridge Island, and the view from here at his Bainbridge home was toward the city.

Tossing a blanket over the slightly damp chair, he settled at the table. To the south was the ferry terminal and downtown Winslow. Directly east, the Cascade Mountains served as a backdrop for the Seattle skyline. Slowly, the sunlight turned the gray water of the Sound to a molten gold.

Did Ray get up to enjoy sunrises? Admittedly, five-thirty was rather early.

George's WoodSong house in the forest had a fair view of the Sound—although not as fine as this one. George had preferred forest to beach. He'd been all about the wood.

Did his lovely protégé feel the same?

Such an intriguing woman. Energetic, emotional, expressive. When she was excited, her words ran together, and her hands waved in the air. She reminded him of the way sunlight danced on rippling water.

He took a sip of his coffee, thinking of yesterday. The interaction between her and Theodore Prescott had been...ugly. Apparently, Prescott wanted the relationship to resume, despite his disparaging comments about Ray's behavior.

The bastard should be grateful Ray had rallied and sent him packing. Drake had been only seconds from rudely interrupting to handle things *his* way. But she had done quite well.

However, it was doubtful Prescott was the Dom who'd caused Ray's PTSD. He'd struck at her self-confidence, but she'd shown nothing like her fear when they'd spoken of Tops ignoring limits. Or about bondage.

It would be good to find out exactly what happened to her. To do what he could to help her past those fears.

Leaning back, he sipped his espresso. It was a good blend. Rich, flavorful, with a touch of creamy sweetness to smooth the slight bitterness.

Below, the ferry made its stately, slow progress over the Sound to Seattle, escorted by a few hopeful gulls.

No harm in being hopeful. He had his own hopes, after all. Like to get a chance to explore the chemistry between him and Aralia. To talk with her, to make her laugh. She had a hearty laugh —and sometimes, the most infectious giggles.

Damned if she didn't have him reconsidering his no-relationship stance. She was nothing like...well, anyone he'd been with before.

However, if she wasn't interested, he'd step away. Consent mattered.

Since she'd signed up as a volunteer at Chains, there would be time to talk with her at the club. It'd be good to show her there were honorable Doms in the world, ones who didn't ignore a submissive's boundaries.

And he'd do his best to be worthy of her trust.

CHAPTER EIGHT

Mouth more spitless than a pile of sawdust, Ray followed Bob into the BDSM club. Sure, maybe her heart was tap dancing against her ribs, but she was doing far better than last week when she hadn't ventured two steps into the room.

Tonight, she had an escort.

Over the past week, she'd jumped through all the hoops. Her application and preferences list. A background check to rule out being a sexual offender. She'd even done the optional STI testing.

Since she had to show up for the orientation, she'd hitched up her work trailer and dropped off the first project for the Elfame room—the pentagram.

It'd been disappointing Master Drake hadn't been the one to take the delivery.

Oh well.

Now here she was, ready to be a volunteer and make friends. Bob had assured her she didn't have to participate in any scene stuff. She'd watch and get comfortable, and after another three or four visits, she could try playing.

If she liked it here.

Her membership was a heavily discounted trial one, so no real risk. Although she did need to "invest" in some new clothes.

She glanced down at the outfit she'd pulled together for tonight. The white, button-down shirt came from Tomo's closet. Now wasn't she glad she'd insisted George's sons keep their rooms for when they visited? Leather straps to look like a waist and chest harness had been easy to craft since some of her woodworking projects had leather surfaces. Sexy fishnet stockings with an elastic thigh top. She matched the red bra and thong with red ballet flats. It all worked—and hadn't cut into her budget.

Shaving down below had been disconcerting. Because, this time, she kept thinking of Master Drake's hands.

No, Ray. He was the owner of Chains, after all.

Bob led her across the room, past the busy dance floor. On the stage on the other side, a Top was demonstrating electro-play.

Now there was something truly scary. Yet *sooo* intriguing.

"We'll start you off serving drinks at the bar," Bob said over his shoulder.

She frowned. "I didn't think BDSM clubs allowed alcohol."

"Most don't. Consent, safe play, and drinking don't mix." He sighed. "However, many people like a glass of wine or beer when socializing. On Fridays, which is basically a walk-in membership, no alcohol is served, only soft drinks. Saturdays are exclusive for the gold members, who really are members and have passed the orientation. Saturdays, it's BYOB—and any alcohol has to be fetched from the bar in person so the bartender can stamp their hand to keep them out of the dungeon. And security will toss out anyone caught sharing drinks. Drake is inflexible about no intoxicants before playing."

Bob waved her behind the bar and rather than abandoning her to strangers—face it, that's what it would have felt like—he joined her and continued his instructions.

"Sodas in this fridge. Juice packs and bottled water in this one.

Ice and glasses are over there." Bob pointed to the different refrigerators under the counter on the back wall.

"Got it." Ray ran a hand over the lovely bar top. The black walnut was a beautiful deep chocolate color with intricate grain patterns. Just lovely.

And oops, Bob was still talking.

"If they want alcohol, send them to the other end of the bar. Claudia's handling that side. She knows who owns which bottles—and will mix a drink when needed and mark their hands."

Ray glanced over at the older woman. Petite and curvy, she was chatting with someone while filling a glass. "Seems straightforward enough. I can handle dispensing soft drinks."

"I think you'll enjoy it, and I'll stay with you for a while. Your shift lasts until eleven when the next pair of volunteers takes over."

"A couple of hours doesn't seem too tough."

In a long jean skirt and fringed denim crop-top, Tess slid onto a barstool. Her mid-back length hair was strawberry-blonde, several shades lighter than Ray's auburn color. "The hours are short since Bob wants his volunteers to have time to play."

Bob laughed. "Playing is the point, right? Where's your Master, and how're the woolies?"

"The sheep are good. My man will be over shortly." She waved at the alcohol refrigerator. "Can my Sir and I have a couple of beers, please? We've already had our fun."

Ray looked her over.

Hair damp at the temples, lips slightly swollen and red. And she'd taken a seat on the stool gingerly, as if her butt was sore. Fun, huh?

"Coming up now." Bob headed for the spirits fridge.

"Love your outfit, Ray. And how are you doing?" Tess' brown eyes were warm.

They weren't friends yet, not really, but the concern was real—

and heartening. "Pretty well, actually. It helps knowing some of you are around."

"Good. Yell if you ever need help or backup." Tess reached over and patted her hand. "There are dungeon monitors downstairs. Up here, we have a couple of bouncer types—one on the stairs and another free-floating." She pointed them out.

Bouncers and monitors. "That's more policing than I'd anticipated."

"Drake has a thing about submissives—anyone actually—feeling safe. He'll step right in if he sees someone getting pressured."

How...satisfying. Reassuring. "Good to know. Thanks, Tess. Actually, I did see him in action when I was sitting with Hope and Mac." He'd summoned an escort for a woman and scolded a younger Dom—or so it appeared.

Bob interrupted their conversation when he set a beer and a mug in front of Tess. "Hand, please." When she put her hand on the bar, palm down, he swiped a purple magic marker across the back.

Ray noticed he hadn't given Tess the second beer. He'd obviously been serious about people having to get marked up if they were drinking.

"Purple? Seriously?" Tess scowled at her hand. "I hate purple."

"Me too," Ray muttered. "Although lavender is worse."

Tess shuddered then grinned. "Redheads have to stick together, yep. I do love the turquoise tips on your hair though."

A couple of young women stepped up to the bar.

"Time to get to work. Excuse me, Tess."

"Have fun."

Ray served the women, chatting with them as they checked out the various singles on the dance floor.

Next to arrive was a group of four gay males. One broke away to get a drink from Claudia while Ray served juices to the other three. They also gave her a hearty welcome.

The club must be small enough everyone knew each other, at least by sight. It felt very friendly—and so much nicer than her Silver membership night visit.

When a burly, gray-haired man showed up, Tess waved Ray closer. "Ray, this is my Sir, Zachary, but our girls have been calling him Papa Bear for so long that even our friends now call him Bear."

Ray laughed. "Bear it is then."

"Nice to meet you, Ray." Bear collected his beer from Bob along with a long purple mark on the back of his hand.

"All right then." Bob smiled at Ray. "I think you're good to handle the bar. I'll be nearby." With a wave, he walked out from behind the bar and joined Tess and Bear at a table.

For the next couple of hours, Ray met people, handed out drinks, chatted when there was time. And actually had fun.

The bar stayed nicely busy, enough she'd made a dent in the drink glasses shelved on the back wall in place of expensive bottles.

In the center of the wall was a vivid, hand-painted sign with the words: SAFE, SANE, and CONSENSUAL, denoting the club's slogan. She loved it.

"Hey, it's the pretty redhead from the coffee shop." Wearing a black sleeveless top, black jeans, and a thick belt with a flogger attached, a blond man approached the bar.

Oh, great—it was the over-muscled jerk who'd outed her at the coffee shop when she was there with Marisol. She barely kept from wrinkling her nose.

His gaze went immediately to her half-open shirt that gave glimpses of her red bra.

Ray gave him a polite but cold smile. He'd called her Drake's plaything. Definitely a jerk. "Good evening. What can I get you?"

"Ooooh, I can think of lots of things." His leer made her want to retch.

Note to self: don't leave openings for idiots. "Let me rephrase—would you like a soft drink?"

"Spoilsport." He turned toward a group of men. "Blaize, look who's here."

The older man who'd spoken to her and Marisol was in a finely tailored black suit. And there was the red-headed one in a casual black T-shirt and jeans. Another man was dressed more like a biker.

"If you're behind the bar, you must be a member now." Blaize's smile was as charming as at the coffee shop. He did seem really nice. "Welcome."

"Thank you." All of the men were in black. "I guess you're all Doms or Tops or something?"

"That's right." The ginger leaned on the bar with an elbow, his blue eyes keen. "And you?"

"Not a Dom, no." She smiled politely. "What can I get you to drink?"

They all wanted coffee, which Bob hadn't mentioned. Turning, she spotted the pot and cups. A small tray held creamers and sugars. Good enough.

She served them, one by one.

Taking his coffee, Blaize lifted his eyebrows. "You didn't answer Jago. Are you submissive or a Top or Domme? Single or attached to someone?"

Irritation scratched at her nerves—which was silly. She wanted to make friends and maybe, eventually, actually play. It made sense people wanted to know what side of the—how had the orientation instructor called it?—what side of the slash she played on.

Aside from the big blond who suffered from foot-in-mouth disease, the men seemed nice enough. Blaize had a smooth manner, even if he was pressing for answers.

Woman up, Ray. "I'm single...but only on a recon mission tonight."

"Can't discover what you like if you don't put a foot in the water," the blond said. "I'm Kiefer. Want to do a light scene?"

Her mouth dried, and she had to force herself not to step back.

"Ray, when are you done there?" Drake's smooth voice came from her right. A few feet from the other Doms, he was studying her, a line between his brows. "I'd like your opinion on the wall attachment for the pentagram."

Relief flooded her, leaving her almost dizzy. Swallowing, she glanced at the small clock on the back wall. "As soon as my replacement arrives, I'm free."

"Ah, but are you easy?" Kiefer asked and wiggled his eyebrows.

Why did men have to be such jerks? *Grow up, dumbass.* "No. I'm not," Ray snapped.

His eyes hardened. "You—"

"Are you Ray? You must be Ray." A tall woman joined her behind the bar. Her voice was a low alto. "I'm Calliope, and you're relieved from duty. Oh, and welcome to Chains!"

The sheer exuberance made her smile. "Thank you, Calliope. It's wonderful to meet you."

"She didn't say that to us," Kiefer muttered to the biker Dom. "You think she's lesbian?"

As she headed for the end of the bar, she heard Drake saying, "Kiefer, I don't want to hear you making sexually suggestive comments to women. I want to think you're better than this."

"Hey, this is a BDSM club—sex is on the table."

Drake paused for a moment, then said mildly. "At Thanksgiving, turkey is on the table. But you'd be unhappy if your father rammed a drumstick into your face. To a woman, your behavior comes across like you're shoving your testicles in her face. Like you're desperate for sex, no less. Your reprehensible behavior makes women uncomfortable and is not acceptable here. Do better."

Oh, burn. Ray barely managed to keep from hugging the

Chains cop. How often did men call out other men for their sexually aggressive behavior? Like never.

Drake turned to Blaize and said something in a low voice.

Blaize nodded, setting a hand on Kiefer's shoulder. "With me. We need to work on your lack of social skills before they get you tossed out of the club."

Yes, yes, yes. Of course, she shouldn't be pleased Kiefer had been taken down a notch, but...damn, it'd been awesome. She beamed at Drake. "Okay, Chains police. I'm all yours."

"All mine?"

She flushed—and realized she was standing much closer than she usually did with men.

Amusement glinted in his eyes as he stroked the back of his fingers down her cheek. "*Ma chérie,* if you say this to a police officer Dominant, you might well be tucked into a jail cell and... used. With your consent, of course."

"O-of course." He'd have his hands on her again, restrain her, maybe take her... The bottom of her stomach slid right down into a pool of lava.

His mouth curved. "This appeals to you, I see. Perhaps we should discuss your interests."

Oh, oh, what was she doing? "Uh." She shook her head. "This...tonight I planned on only meeting people. Making friends. Not doing anything."

"I see." A corner of his mouth tilted up. "I would hate to disrupt your planning. Or give young Kiefer a bad example."

She frowned. He was right. "Why is it different?" Old gods, but this was confusing.

He chuckled. "First...we are not strangers. I've kissed you. Touched you."

Oh, he so had.

His lips quirked. "But what happened in the past isn't a guarantee you'd still be interested. And if you'd been reserved, I would have given you your space, and I will at any point if you ask for it.

But when you approached, your distance from me suggests you might enjoy something else."

She realized she was still standing too close. Intimately close. "Oh."

Before she could decide if she should retreat, he smiled. "Come, let's go look at your pentagram." He put a hand on her lower back, moving her toward the stairs.

Her bare arm brushed against the soft fabric of his shirt, against the solidness of all those muscles underneath. And somehow, she was far too aware of his warmth.

Down, body. Behave.

The security at the top of the stairs checked their hands—even Drake's—for purple slashes and waved them past.

At the foot of the stairs, she stopped to look around.

In the center of the room, a naked woman stood with her arms restrained over her head. Not one, but *two* male Tops took turns using a cane on her. She was crying and wiggling to get out of the strike zone—and yet her nipples were erect and arousal was obvious on her wet inner thighs.

People upstairs were looking over the railing and watching.

Ray swallowed, feeling the sweep of excitement. What would it be like to be the woman, in the center of the room? It was close enough to her nightmare to raise a ball of anxiety inside her, yet... Being restrained, touched by someone special while being watched by strangers was one of her fantasies.

One that'd turned so very wrong. She shook her head hard and met Drake's eyes.

His gaze on her was like the sun, warm and heightening everything she was feeling. He made a sound deep in his throat.

"What?" She frowned at him.

"You are so very conflicted." He lifted her hand, kissing her fingertips, then lacing their fingers together. "Come, we have a pentagram to check."

Holding hands. Something she'd never done with a guy. How could it feel so intimate and grounding at the same time?

They wandered past so many interesting scenes. Floggings. Then something...a crop, yes, that was what the stick with leather patch on the end was called. The next scene showed tiny cups lined up on a man's back like grotesque nipples. And farther down, a woman was caning another woman.

The door closed behind her in the Elfame room, shutting away the noise from the dungeon. Here, there was peaceful music and the trickle of water from the fountain.

Holy kraken, look at this! She smiled so hard it probably took up her whole face. *My pentagram is in use.*

Holding an ice cube like a crayon, a woman drew patterns on a naked submissive bound to the pentagram. On a nearby table lay fur mittens, a feather, and a sharp-toothed pinwheel thing. The woman's breasts had thin red lines and were wet from the ice cubes. Her eyes were half-closed, dazed almost.

Even better, she looked comfortable with the pentagram tilted enough to support some of her weight and let her rest her head.

"It works," Ray said under her breath. Satisfaction blossomed at the fulfilment of her vision.

"*Oui.* It's perfect." Drake put his arm around her shoulders, gave her a squeeze, and guided her back out the door into the regular dungeon.

Her sigh was happy. "I should have the chair done in a few more days. It still needs more coats of polyurethane." She wanted a sexy-satin finish on it.

"Very good." Drake looked down at her. "Do you have time for another project? It has a short turn-around."

"Maybe?" Consumed with finishing up George's projects, she still hadn't informed her previous associates and contractors of her return.

"You know about our upcoming convention, *oui?*"

"Yes."

"On the last day, we give out useful awards—bondage items, sex toys, impact toys. Handcrafted wooden paddles are always popular. Can you make some for the convention?"

"Paddles...like for spanking?"

His lips quirked. "Exactly for spanking." He guided her toward a scene off to the left. "Hands get sore and bruised. Belts require skill to avoid welts. Paddles are useful."

He motioned to where a brunette in a siren-red catsuit walloped a man bent over a padded bench. She was using what looked like a cheap Ping pong paddle.

"Something more...artistic...is needed for our convention," Drake murmured.

It actually sounded like a fun project. Only... "I don't know anything about, um, spanking paddles."

"Easily fixed." The wicked expression in his face sent a jolt of alarm—and heat—through her.

"Uh...how about you give me one to use as a sample?"

"I can. However, isn't it important to know how it feels to the user—and to the recipient?" His expression was all innocence except for one raised eyebrow.

Dammit, he had a point. Sure, she could make something like the ping-pong paddle, but she had too much pride in her work to create something half-assed. "Yes, it's important."

"Then let's give you the opportunity to try a variety—from each side of the slash."

Each side of the slash? *Wait, wait, wait.* "You mean spanking and *being* spanked?"

"But of course." He moved toward two people farther down the room.

The tall, mixed-race woman had a feminine warrior body in a sleeveless vinyl dress, a black brace on her arm, and platform boots.

Ray suppressed a sigh of envy. Preteen, she'd longed for a Wonder Woman body and to be a total boss. Had thought she'd be the type to stand over a guy with a stilettoed foot on his chest. Instead, she was short. Lean rather than muscular. And sure, she could hold her own in everyday life, but in bed? Totally submissive.

Life sucked lemons sometimes.

"Evening, Drake. And who is this?" the woman's voice a firm contralto.

"Jasira, this is Ray, George's protégé. She will be crafting wood paddles for our convention awards. Ray, this is Jasira and her slave, Casper."

Casper's name—totally on target. His skin was a milky-white, his hair blond. He didn't speak but, eyes downcast, bobbed his head slightly.

"It's good to meet you, Ray." Jasira had a warm smile. She was probably around fifty, her slave maybe in his thirties. "We all loved George here." Before Ray could speak past the sudden ache in her throat, the Domme turned to Drake. "Bastian mentioned you might be adding new awards."

"We want to encourage more community service and mentoring." Drake nodded toward the other side of the dungeon. "Like Blaize has been doing with the newer Doms."

Ray followed his gaze and saw the charming Dom who'd been with the fuckwit Kiefer at the bar. Mr. Mentor really needed to be more proactive rather than needing Drake to tell him to deal with jerks. Eh, with luck, Kiefer would have learned his lesson.

"Bribes can be useful in motivating behavior." Jasira winked at her slave, then asked Drake, "Do you need my help with something?"

"*Oui.*" Drake looked around, then led them to a quiet corner scene area. It had an odd, padded bench in the shape of a half-barrel on its side. Two tall, padded blocks of wood were positioned in front of it. "Ray is new to the scene. I want her to experience how different paddles feel when she's using them—and then how they feel on her ass. Could we borrow your slave for some fun?"

Ray stared at him in shock. He expected her to hit a strange man?

"Obviously, you heard I sprained my wrist." Jasira touched the brace on her arm. "Hey, minion, want to get your masochism beat out of you today?"

"Yes, please, Mistress." Casper turned to Ray, his tone eager. Needy. "Please."

Ray blinked. Now she'd feel guilty if she *didn't* beat the man.

"I'd say we're good to go." Jasira waved Casper to the stand. "Do you have paddles, Drake, or should I send someone for mine?"

"I've already gathered a sampling for Ray." He fetched a large leather bag from a nearby bench.

Down to only a G-string, Casper knelt with a knee on each of the padded blocks and bent forward over the spanking barrel. His butt was at the highest part of the curve with his upper torso angled downward on the other side. To her relief, his closed thighs kept his package all in front. She wouldn't have to worry about accidentally hitting his balls. *Whew.*

As Jasira pulled a strap over her slave's waist to secure him in place, Drake laid out a line of paddles on a table.

"I had no idea they came in so many shapes." Ray ran a finger down a long, rectangular one with a narrower handle. Maybe a foot and a half long, two inches wide. Carved from one piece of maple, sanded smooth, and polyurethaned.

He chuckled. "These are only the wooden paddles. There are other materials like silicone—or the classic leather." Drake turned to Jasira. "Would you instruct Ray where to hit, how hard, and any specifics for your slave."

"Of course."

Drake smiled at Ray. "As you work, I want your impressions on how the paddle feels in your hand, how it hits, and whether you like it. Later you will share how it feels from the other side."

As it hits my ass, he means. She tried for a sour expression yet couldn't suppress a shiver of excitement.

The two Dominants exchanged smiles.

Damn them.

"Girl," Jasira said. "Never be shamed by or afraid to express your needs. We all have them. To find someone who wants to receive what we want to give—it's a blessing."

At the sound of agreement from her slave, the Mistress smiled and ran her hand up and down his naked back. "You, my sweet slave, are my blessing, and I never forget that."

Awww. At the sting in her eyes, Ray blinked hard.

Somehow, when she considered submission and kink, she hadn't thought love was included. But the love between this Mistress and slave was plain for anyone to see.

"In Chains, red is the universal safeword. If he uses it, you stop the scene completely." Drake pursed his lips thoughtfully. "However, he *is* a pain slut. I believe your arm will give out before he does."

Head still down, Casper snickered.

Biting her lip, Ray went over to the table. One of Faj's favorite proverbs was *"The sooner begun, the sooner done."* She picked up a well-carved paddle of prettily-shined, lightweight pine. She slapped it against her hand to test how it felt.

Ow. It had a bite.

"Unless the goal is punishment, it's best to warm up the play zone...which is the meaty part of the buttocks from here to here." Jasira indicated a line from Casper's upper buttocks to the lower cheeks. She started rubbing and lightly spanking the designated area with her uninjured hand. "Stay below the tailbone and inside the hip bones. The upper thighs are valid targets, but stick to his ass for now. When the area is a pretty pink, you know you've got a nice blood supply going."

Stepping back, she motioned for Ray to begin.

Ray felt her breathing speed up. *Am I really going to hit this man?* She couldn't seem to move.

"Aralia." Drake put an arm around her. "Being injured, Jasira hasn't been able to give Casper this kind of pain—something he enjoys—and needs. You'll be doing them both a favor."

Right. She pulled in a hard breath and nodded.

"Stand to one side so you can swing easily," Drake said, "and take light swats to check your positioning."

"Got it." Ray edged to the left of Casper's butt, swung, landed an easy blow—and quickly checked his face. Had she hurt him?

Head turned so his Mistress couldn't see, he rolled his eyes and mouthed: *harder. Much harder.*

Drake *could* see, and his cut-off laugh wasn't nearly silent enough.

She shot him a dirty look, lined up, and gave Casper a firm swat. The sound was appalling, but his pleased sigh made up for it.

Okay then. Honestly, if she had to go to a two-handed swing, she was calling it all off.

"Very nice." Drake pulled out a notebook and pad. "How does the paddle feel in your hand? How is the weight? Does it make you happy?"

By all the old gods in all the oceans. She hadn't thought about anything except trying to strike Casper.

She glared at the Chains cop.

"Such a face, and no, you can't gag me." Drake's dark eyes held laughter. "Answers, *bébé*."

Ray growled under her breath. Hefting the paddle, she checked the balance and the feel. Her next swat hit Casper's other cheek.

And he made a happy sound.

I don't want to be the one hitting someone. Being the...the Top. Not comfortable! But Casper wants it so I'll focus on making him happy. And checking out the paddles. Oh, right... "Um, the balance isn't great. Minus two points. The curve of the blade is pleasing, but the weight feels too light, and..."

When she was finished with her evaluation, she picked up the next paddle in the line. It was black walnut—a lovely wood—and startlingly heavy.

Mouth firm, she settled down to deal out the swats and dictate her evaluations.

This is not what I thought I'd be doing this evening.

A while later, Drake helped Jasira unbuckle her slave. Casper's ass was a nice red. And the way the masochist glowed with satisfaction was a delight to a Dom's heart.

"Thank you both for helping with Ray's lesson," Drake said, with Ray murmuring her thanks as well.

"You're quite welcome." Jasira gripped Casper's hair. "Come along, minion." From her heightened color, she'd undoubtedly drag him to a quiet room and satisfy them both.

Since Drake had cleaned the paddles as used, they were ready to go again. However...

He considered the worry furrowing Ray's brow. "You did a fine job with Casper. Tell me, did you enjoy giving out pain?"

She scowled. "No, not at all. Only...he loved it, and I liked seeing him smile. I'm so confused. Does this mean I'm a sadist?"

"You're not a sadist, no." At her relieved sigh, Drake grinned. Setting two fingers under her sweetly pointed chin, he kissed her lightly. "To give someone what they want, but not take pleasure in the pain, indicates you're more of a service submissive. Making someone happy makes you happy."

"Oh." Her thoughtful expression was delightful. Smart submissives—hell, smart people—made his day.

"Now it's your turn to be on the receiving end." He ran a

finger over his goatee, trying to decide how to phrase the next question. "So. Since for you to evaluate the feel of different paddles, I can simply duplicate what you did with Casper. However..."

"However what?"

"You aren't a masochist, Ray Lanigan." He slapped a paddle against his hand. "If I hit you with this, it will hurt, and I doubt you'll enjoy it."

"Oh." Turning right and left, she studied the scenes around them—many with impact play. "Are all of those bottoms masochists?"

"No, bébé. At one end, some people hate pain—no matter what kind. At the opposite end, some *need* pain." He motioned toward the scenes. "And many of those are in the middle.

"The middle."

"*Oui*. Within a sexual context, pain and pleasure can be indistinguishable—and pain can heighten pleasure to a remarkable degree." He studied her face. "I get the impression your previous experience with BDSM was limited?"

"It was." She folded her arms around herself in a self-comforting motion.

It was a shame she didn't trust him enough to let him wrap her in reassurance. Too soon. He could be patient.

After a moment, she added, "I tried bondage and D/s. Not pain."

Whereupon her bondage experience had apparently turned into a nonconsensual assault of some kind. Suppressing rage at the thought, he kept his voice soft. "When it comes to spanking—especially with wooden paddles—most spankees who aren't masochists either want a disciplinary type of scene for an emotional outlet or an erotic scene which may or may not end in physical release."

Her cheeks turned a pretty pink. "Oh. Um, huh."

"Ray, it's your choice which we will do." He held up a finger for each option. "1: an uninvolved evaluation of each paddle. 2: a roleplay discipline scene. Or 3: an erotic paddling which would include being touched and aroused."

"Touched, like last time?" She bit her lip. "That'd be extra work for you."

So sweet. He moved closer and smiled into eyes the color found in high mountain lakes at the foot of a glacier. Wide eyes, right now. "Work is not the word I'd use. Touching you is a pleasure. One I'd like to enjoy again."

Color rose in her cheeks, and she swayed toward him slightly. "Oh."

"Ray. It's your decision." He paused before adding, "Until the scene begins. Then—within what we have negotiated—the decisions are mine. My preference is erotic. I would like to touch you...everywhere...with my hands. To put my fingers inside you. To arouse you."

Her pupils dilated. Her lips parted. Then she took a step away and turned slightly so he couldn't see her face.

He waited. It truly was her choice, and he'd do his best to give her what she wanted. He wasn't her Dom so giving her what she *needed* instead wasn't within his purview.

"Own it, Ray," she said under her breath, the words not for him. A deep inhalation lifted her chest as she turned to him. "I—I'd like the erotic version."

Self-awareness and honesty in a partner were traits he'd learned to cherish. And were some of the reasons he was so drawn to Ray.

"Very good." He ran his knuckles over her cheek. "I'll try to keep the pain around a five—and we'll test where that is for you." Now for the more difficult decision for her.

"I'd prefer to restrain your arms. If it hurts, you'd most likely use your hands to cover your ass, and a wooden paddle can break fingers."

She took a step away from him, her color fading.

"Ray." He made his tone stern, and her gaze shot to his face. He spoke slowly enough the words would get through her fears. "The dungeon monitors will intervene if you use the club safeword, which is *red*. And you will be able to easily escape any binding I use. *Oui?*"

"Oh." Her hands unclenched. "Yes. Right. Okay."

More forward progress. Excellent. "Then, we begin. Disrobe, please."

Her appalled expression almost...almost made him laugh. He took a step back, crossed his arms over his chest. And waited.

Simon, the Master who'd started him off on the road to being a Dom, said silence and patience were excellent tools. His words had proven to be right.

Ray looked at him. Looked down. She wanted to obey; he could see it. And more. It took a significant amount of trust for her to bare her body and hand over control to him.

Earning such trust was a precious gift.

She chewed on her lip, looked at him, and dropped her gaze again. Her muscles relaxed.

There we go.

Slowly, she bent to remove her red shoes, which gave him a sweet glimpse of her round ass. The man's white shirt really was an inspired clothing choice.

She rolled down the fishnet stockings. Wiggled off the thong. And finally shrugged out of the shirt and red bra.

He'd have enjoyed stripping her himself even more, but acquiescing to his order, removing her clothing, baring her body, would shift her into the proper headspace—the one where she acknowledged that for the next span of time, her body was under his command.

Ray felt his gaze on her body as she dropped her bra to the floor, and she was oh-so-naked. Why was it so difficult to keep from covering her breasts and pussy?

It wasn't body shame—not entirely. She had an okay body. Some cellulite on her thighs, sure. A roundness to her tummy. All in all, it was a pretty good body.

It just wasn't supposed to be *naked*. Not out where anyone near the thankfully-almost-secluded corner area could see her.

So could Drake.

Firming her jaw, she straightened, lowered her arms, and stared across the room. Waiting. There was a flutter in her chest. If he said something insulting, it would really hurt.

Silence.

Unable to bear it, she looked at him.

He had a faint smile as he met her eyes. *"Tu es si belle."*

Belle. Even she knew that *belle* meant pretty or beautiful or something good. A smile pulled at her lips.

"And you have given me permission to touch."

Her whole lower half clenched. Whyever had she said she wanted an erotic scene?

But how could she not? She'd dreamed of how he'd touched her previously. Dreamed of him taking it further. Dreamed of his voice. This was what she wanted. *Own it, Ray.*

He curled his fingers around her nape and kissed her. His lips were firm, coaxing her to respond. When she did, he nibbled on her jaw, then ran both hands down her arms. He cupped her breasts, weighing them, his thumbs stroking lightly. "I do love your breasts."

The feeling of his callused palms on her bare skin gave her goosebumps.

He turned her to face the spanking stand and with his shoe, separated the heavy wooden blocks, pushing them a couple of feet apart. "Kneel, please."

Carefully, she set a knee on each tall padded block—and felt air touching her widely spread private parts. Instinctively, she tried to pull her legs together...and the blocks wobbled under her weight.

And Drake chuckled. "If you don't want to fall, *chérie*, you must stay still."

The blocks would tip over if she wasn't careful. Was that the point? Another kind of torture. "This is plain mean."

"This spanking barrel with the knee blocks was designed with discipline in mind. It's one of my favorites."

Wait, what? "D-discipline?"

"It is what happens to submissives when they've been bad. Or teaching control. I enjoy teaching...and even disciplining if needed."

When a shiver of anticipation and longing ran through her, he made a satisfied sound low in his throat.

"For now, you will be a good girl." With a firm hand in the middle of her back, he bent her forward over the curved bench. The padding was cold against her skin as her upper torso tipped downward leaving her ass high in the air.

Only, unlike Casper's position, her legs were spread wide apart. Unfair—why had she gotten stuck with a man-spread?

"Easy now." Drake ran his hand over her butt, massaging her cheeks, teasing the crack. When he began lightly slapping each inch of her buttocks, she jumped.

Right, right, Jasira said to warm up the skin. That was what he was doing.

Only each flurry of swats was followed by his hand stroking downward, over the backs of her thighs. And inward. When his knuckles brushed her clean-shaven pussy lips, she squeaked, jerked, and the knee blocks rocked precariously.

His next swat held a slight sting. His voice was softer, deeper. "Stay still, Aralia."

Don't move, don't move.

He repeated the same actions, touching her pussy, stroking

over her, so, so intimately. And she could tell from increasingly slick slide of his fingers she was growing wet.

"Very nice. We'll have some fun, won't we?" The French-accented voice held such warm approval, her embarrassment melted away.

After stroking her back, he put Velcro cuffs on her wrists and clipped the right one to an anchor near the floor. She could feel all the muscles in her body tense.

He added a chain between the left cuff and the anchor. "There now. If you need to, you can use your teeth to undo this cuff."

She pulled her hand up toward her mouth. Yes, he'd left enough chain. Once she ripped the Velcro open with her teeth, she could unfasten her right cuff. Her breathing slowed. *Okay. Okay then.*

"Panicking and trying to get free will be forgiven...for now." His jaw was stern...his eyes laughing. "Trying to escape for fun, such behavior will earn extra swats."

It sounded too much like a dare. Unable to resist, she pulled on the restraints. Tugged harder.

"Yes, *ma douce*, you are bound and quite nicely open for my attentions." He touched her again, grazing over her clit, and the shocking pleasure made her gasp. "We will start with paddle number one."

He withdrew to get a paddle, and her mind grew frantic. The sounds of the dungeon somehow grew louder...as did her thoughts. Would she be able to sit down for crafting tomorrow?

What is Master Drake thinking about me?

Is my butt as far up in the air as I think it is?

She glared at the floor. Someone must spend a lot of time cleaning it. Why is Master Drake taking so long? Does he have—

"And this adorable ass is right where I want it." A second later, there was the sound: *Slap*. The impact and right afterward, the sting.

She was speechless. He'd...he'd *spanked* her. No one had ever mentioned the rush of humiliation.

"Ray, give me a pain number. One is almost nothing, ten is unbearable."

It felt as if her whole body was flushed red—but the pain hadn't been bad. "Um, a three, maybe?"

"What else? Stinging, burning, thudding. Pleasurable. Irritating?" Even as he spoke, he was touching her, rubbing the sting away. His fingers slid between her legs but didn't touch where she wanted to be touched.

Dammit.

Her clit felt swollen. Demanding to be rubbed.

He cleared his throat.

Oh, yes, she was supposed to be evaluating the paddle. "It stings a bit. I'm...not sure."

"All right. We'll keep going, and if you can't decide which ones you like, we'll repeat the cycle as many times as we need to."

Her eyes went wide. *Oh, no. No, no, no.*

But the sting wasn't bad, and somehow her whole body was just waiting for him to touch her. Her skin felt as sensitive as if it'd been sanded down, ready for the primer.

He hit her with paddle two, hard enough there was a decided sting followed by a low ache.

I like this. No, no, I don't.

As she gave her evaluation, he played with her. He even lifted her torso off the barrel so he could tease her breasts. Now they throbbed too.

Paddle three was skinny and heavy, and her eyes filled with tears after two swats.

"Talk to me, *chérie*. Do you need to stop?" His hand stroked down her back and over her stinging bottom. Comforting and yet...arousing.

I can't stop yet; I want to see what this is about. Like...there's something I'm not quite reaching. "No, I...I'm good."

"Then breathe through it. Take deep slow breaths through your nose, exhale through your mouth."

As she did, the pain...changed, and somehow sent all the blood to her groin. To where Drake was sliding a light finger over her clit, circling the sides until she wiggled to get him to touch the very top. Only she'd moved enough to make the blocks under her knees tip.

"Eeks!" She froze.

The bastard laughed—and slid a finger up inside her.

The rush of pleasure swamped her. "Ooooh!"

Paddle number four was wide and round. One cheek and then the other. The stinging turned to a sweet burn.

Gods, she was being tenderized like a hammered steak heading for the grill. *Do steaks get all excited about the hammer?*

Or maybe the one beating on them?

"Now number five." This paddle was small, like an artistic version of a wooden spoon. The curved portion made a bulls-eye circle of burn. And the sadist swatted her again and again. Her whole backside felt seared.

She pulled on the restraints, needing to cover her butt from the abuse.

Hot tears rolled down her cheeks as he massaged the pain in, and then destroyed her by playing with her clit.

The pain transformed into a heavy liquid heat low in her pelvis. In her pussy. Everything down there throbbed. Her mind had emptied out, leaving only the pain, only the need to come. She panted, her knees trembling.

"Ah, you are quite fun." He knelt beside her, lightly kissed her.

I pleased him. The knowledge of his approval warmed her through and through.

His gaze ran over her body, and awareness of her arousal showed in his pitch-black eyes. Tenderly, he wiped the tears from her cheeks, kissed her, and rose. "Number six."

It was the one with holes. The firm swat landed, and she let out a half-yelp, half-scream. The sting was bitey, like she'd sat on a pile of yellow jackets. "Ow, ow!"

"You are doing very well, but do you need a break, *bébé*?" His voice and his hand stroking her spine pulled her back. The panic receded.

He was concerned about her. Would stop if she needed it. Knowing made *all* the difference. "N-no. Keep going."

"Breathe, Ray." Still, she was sucking air like a bellows, and then his hand was between her legs. His finger slid around and around her clit and up inside her.

"Ooooh." In and out, and as everything transformed again, a wave of pleasure shook her. The pain...wasn't pain.

She couldn't think.

It went on. Pain and pleasure and pain. Only those, no thoughts, no worries.

His dark, resonant voice pulled her upward, asked her questions, even as pleasure swirled around her like a warm fog.

"All right, you've been a very, very good girl. You deserve a reward." He knelt beside her, one hand in front, sliding his fingers over her clit.

Reaching around from behind, his other hand impaled her on his fingers. More than one finger. Penetrated. Filled. In and out, deeper, driving her upward even as his other hand teased her clit.

This time he...didn't stop.

Every muscle in her body tightened. Tightened more. And like the inevitable ocean tides, the waves of an orgasm crashed over her. Tossed her head over heels as her entire body filled with pleasure, and she bucked against his hands with the mercilessly heart-stopping sensations.

Sucking air, the blood pounding in her head, she lay limp on the barrel, as flat as if an eighteen-wheeler had driven over her.

An eighteen-wheeler named Drake.

Eyes closed, she felt him remove the cuffs from her wrists. He gently massaged the ache in her shoulders.

"Up you come now." With firm hands, he lifted her to her feet, holding her until the swirling in her head eased, and she found her balance.

Kind of. Her feet felt awfully far away.

He kept an iron-hard arm around her waist as his free hand tilted her chin up. "I didn't expect you to slide away so easily. Are you back with me now?"

Was he talking about subspace? She'd heard of it. But her? She swallowed, unable to look away from the dark concerned eyes. "Yes, Sir."

The involuntary respect slipped out, and she saw the sunlines crinkle with his smile. "Very nice."

Whoa, what am I saying. "No. I mean, I'm not..." She tried to push away.

His eyes darkened. "You will accept assistance until your mind and body are functioning again. I want you to sit quietly, right here, until we go upstairs to the aftercare room."

Every tiny bit of resistance fled under the steel in his voice. The safety it promised.

A minute later, wrapped in a soft blanket, she sat on her burning, throbbing butt. And somehow, kind of drifted.

By the time her thoughts were in a semblance of order, he'd cleaned everything and packed away the paddles.

"Up you go." With the duffel bag over his shoulder, he lifted her to her feet and guided her to the end of the long room.

The elevator opened onto the ground floor, and he escorted her through a door into a quiet room decorated in calming blues and greens. It was filled with comfortable furniture, the music was soft, the air faintly scented with orange and lavender

To the right, a man sobbed against his Domme's shoulder. Farther to the left, a brunette lay curled up on a couch, her head on her partner's lap, as he stroked her hair.

Drake guided Ray to a soft, overstuffed couch near the wide windows overlooking the dance floor. No one in the public space tried to see into the aftercare room. Actually, when she'd been in the main room, this area had looked like a mirror. Was this one-way glass?

He helped her sit—*ouch, ouch, ouch!*—then fetched a couple of Gatorades from a fridge. Sitting down next to her, he opened the bottles, handed one to her, and pulled her against his side. Settling in.

Dammit, why was it so comforting to be tucked under his arm, nestled against his hard, lean body. She wanted to burrow against him like a puppy against its mother. "I'm okay. You don't have to—"

He chuckled. "Ray, you are here for fifteen minutes or so, then I will decide if you're ready to leave."

"But you have things to do."

"None that are more important than you right now."

That... That made warmth blossom in her heart.

He put his feet up on a convenient ottoman and drank some Gatorade before setting the bottle on an end table.

She rested her head on his shoulder, plastered like stucco against his side. *So fucking happy to be right here, right now.*

"Everyone has different needs for aftercare. Some submissives don't want to be touched at all. A few want to be alone or with only their friends." He gave her a squeeze. "You like being cuddled and cared for, *non?*"

She opened her mouth and closed it. He was right.

"You only worry you might be a bother. I assure you—you aren't."

Nothing like being read like an open book. And she'd never been so content. Felt so safe and happy.

No, no, no. She couldn't possibly be falling for this man she barely knew. This person who owned a BDSM club. A terrifying Dominant.

Talk about being an idiot. *Didn't you learn anything from last time?* She'd been so obsessed with Crypto, the Dom on campus, and he knew it. Had done everything he could to pull her in.

How'd that work out for me last time? Drugged, bound, assaulted.

Even if Drake wasn't a Dom—and face it, he was one to his bones—there was probably no future with him. She'd dated enough to know guys disappeared around the third date.

At first, men were attracted by her "high spirits." That was what one date had called her hyperactivity. A few dates in, they tired of her energy, of what they named incessant chattering, her distractibility, her need to work until she reached the right stopping point even if she missed meals.

Drake probably wasn't that interested in her anyway. He was simply being kind. Although it sure felt as if there was some chemistry between them. "Um, Sir. Thank you for this evening. I appreciate the time you've taken with me."

He stiffened slightly. She could almost feel the heat of his gaze as he looked down at the top of her head. "I sense a 'but' coming."

"But…it can't go further than this. Although I really enjoyed" —enjoyed was far too tame of a word—"tonight, I'm not interested in anything more than…fun."

He rubbed his chin on the top of her head. "Fun, hmm?"

"Um, yes?" Had she hurt his feelings? Surely not. He had women falling all over themselves to talk to him. She'd seen it.

Would more explanation help? "I don't do well in relationships." Oh, now that made her sound pitiful. "I mean, I'm not interested in relationships. With anyone."

"I see. Thank you for letting me know." After a moment of silence, he asked, "Do you wish to stay a member of the club?"

The thought of never returning here was distressing. "Yes. Please." All the same, when she thought of having a scene with anyone else besides Drake, it felt wrong. Jagged. Like a project where she was sawing concrete rather than wood.

But the connection to him was probably just the aftereffects of a fantastic orgasm. *I'll get over this attraction soon enough.*

I will.

Drake studied Ray. It seemed the little submissive's emotions and mind were stable again if she was fretting about the future.

But wasn't she delightful, worrying about taking up too much of his time?

He helped her dress, and as he buttoned her shirt, she looked up, so trusting, so wide-eyed at being cared for.

He treated himself to another kiss...because Aralia Lanigan put all her singular attention into kissing. He could happily continue this for the rest of the night.

Nonetheless, she'd made her boundaries clear, so he pulled back. "What would you like to do now?"

"Oh, it's time for me to leave. Really." Her voice was beautifully husky.

"As you wish." As he escorted her into the main clubroom, a quick glance told him everything was running as it should. About half the tables were filled.

On the stage, a married couple demonstrated how to tag-team a caning, working over an attractive woman in a pillory.

The dance floor had a newly transitioned transman teaching the crowd a suggestive line dance.

"Hey, *Ray*." At a table with Mac and Alex, Hope rose to her feet and waved.

When Ray immediately veered toward her friend, Drake smiled and followed. He was beginning to see that, no matter how shaken emotionally, this woman would never deny the people she loved.

"Did you have fun?" Hope asked as they approached. "We saw you, but you didn't see us at all."

MacKensie laughed and echoed, "At *all*."

Flushing, Ray glanced at Drake...and turned even redder.

He pressed his lips together to keep from laughing—and saw Alex doing the same.

"Just so you know, I'm ignoring you all." With a huff, Ray dropped onto a chair, squeaked adorably, and rose even faster.

That did it. He laughed—as did the rest.

Ray gave him a squint-eyed frown before sitting...very carefully. "All of you"—she made a circling gesture—"I will get revenge."

"Sure you will, Ms. Sweetie Woodcrafter," Hope said with a giggle.

"I," Ray stated firmly, "will replace your hardwood floors with bright orange shag carpet."

Alex choked on his drink.

"Sweetie, my ass," Mac sputtered. "You've got a real mean streak."

Drake grinned and kissed Ray's cheek, murmuring, "Excellent threat."

The dimple beside her mouth appeared.

"Drake." Clad in his usual battered leathers, Steel strode over. "I'll teach the class at the convention."

"*Très bien.*" Keeping one hand on Ray's shoulder, Drake shook hands with the big trucker who looked as if he'd lost more than a few bar fights.

Steel nodded to Alex and smiled at MacKensie. "Girl, good to see you."

"Which class?" Alex asked.

"The consent-nonconsent one."

Drake tilted his head at Steel. "What made you change your mind?"

"Ran into a fucking noob who thought CNC meant rape, pure 'n' simple. Made me want to pound on him, but he was just clueless, not a total asshole."

Under Drake's hand, Ray's muscles had tightened. Drake bent

to murmur in her ear. "He is a hardass, *oui*, but he has a solid core of kindness."

Gaze still on Steel, she gave a single nod.

Alex was smiling slightly. "Did the way you and MacKensie met have anything to do with it?"

"That I almost whipped an innocent because I hadn't taken enough precautions? Yeah, it did." Steel's gaze was hard, but then he burst out with a big, booming laugh. "Gotta say, I was working out the legalities and ended up with a sideline business."

MacKensie leaned forward, frowning suspiciously. "What kind of business?"

Drake grinned. He'd helped Steel set up the guidelines.

"Kidnappers for hire."

MacKensie choked.

And Ray was gripping Drake's hand—something he found surprisingly nice.

"No, no, don't give me those big eyes, girl. I learned from the mistake with you, we only kidnap the person who hires us, and that's after they provide a shitload of ID and sign even more paperwork." Looking satisfied, Steel scratched his chest. "It's risky business, and we charge accordingly."

Hope shook her head. "Kidnapping or raping women doesn't sound exactly..."

"Not politically correct? Except it's not only women." Steel shrugged. "Started off with one or more guys getting hired by a woman. The business got a good rep, and then I'm getting requests for gays to grab gays, and then hiring dominant women. Did ya know submissive men fantasize about being kidnapped and beat up by a woman or a gang of women?"

Ray released Drake's hand and leaned forward. "Really?"

"Yep." Steel laughed. "Now, a woman denting my balls with her stiletto heels doesn't rev my engine, but everyone to their own, right?"

Alex narrowed his eyes. "I'd be worried either law enforcement or your client would say they were pushed into signing the papers and all that."

"Nah, we record everything and do it outside their place of business—not their home—making it real clear there's no coercion. And if a woman is hiring us, I send a woman employee to do the interview." He jerked his chin toward Drake. "He and Peter gave me advice."

"Now that I believe." MacKensie smiled at Steel. "You're looking really...oh, happy these days. Contented."

Steel shot a look at Alex. "You have a good one here." Then he told MacKensie, "I'm in a...eh, like a leather family, looser than poly. A *chosen* family. Makes me a contented man. Some are planning to help me out with the CNC class. We all want to make sure whoever attends understands the first letter in CNC stands for *consent*. Period."

And this was why Drake wanted Steel to teach the class.

After thumping Drake's shoulder, Steel headed toward a table full of people. His family.

"You're not sitting?" Alex asked Drake. "No time to join us?"

"I regret not." Managing the club included checking on cleanliness, supervising the dungeon monitors, instructing newer Tops, confirming rules about consent were followed, and ensuring the club was welcoming and happy. "Will you escort Ray to her car when she's ready to leave?"

"Of course. It will be my pleasure." Alex smiled at Ray.

Drake lifted her chin for a quick kiss, enjoying the way her mouth softened under his. She had reservations about starting something new, of course she did. But he wasn't in a rush. They'd get to know each other and would go as slowly as she needed. As long as she melted at his touch, he would listen to both her body and her words. "I will call you."

"But..." She frowned. "I told you—"

"For fun, I do remember. I will call you for *fun*." Before she could respond, he kissed her again and left.

. . .

Ray watched him walk away. *Men.* Or should that be *Doms*. Either way, the Chains cop was a rascal. A reprobate. *Huh.* How come historical romances had lots of publicly acceptable terms for a scoundrel while the current century was lacking? *Dickhead* and *asshole* didn't convey the same mischievously decadent description.

"So, did you get a ticket for the convention?" MacKensie asked.

"I...no. But I plan to get one tomorrow." Although that CNC class wouldn't be one she'd take.

"Remember, when you order, members of the sponsoring clubs get a big discount." Hope looked over Ray's shoulder. "Oh, there's Peter. Finally." She waved.

Mac wrinkled her nose and said in a low voice, "This might be awkward. Want to go over to the bar?"

"I don't understand. What's awkward?" Then Ray saw Peter with *Theodore* beside him. "Oh, freak my life."

Before she could tell Mac yes, the men sat down at the table.

"Ray." Theodore stared at her in shock. "What are... You shouldn't be here. This is no place for a respectable person."

"And yet, here you are. Or did you mean respectable women?" From his blink, it was exactly what he'd meant. "Double standards much?"

When his expression soured, she shook her head. What a great way to end the night. "Yes, let's go," she said to Mac and rose.

"Wait, no, don't leave, doll." Theodore grabbed her wrist. "Is this why you broke up with me? You wanted me to—be more commanding? To be your Master?"

It was true, his bossiness had attracted her. But she'd cut him loose because he didn't like who she was. "No, Theodore. If you'd listened, I told you why I called it quits."

She tried to pull away—and his grip tightened.

"Stop." Alex set a hand on Theodore's forearm, and his voice went dark. "You don't touch—*anyone*—without permission. If you continue, I'll throw you out of the club myself."

Theodore jerked his hand back, releasing her.

On the other side of the table, Peter was frowning.

Blaming her for hurting a man's ego, she bet. She clamped her mouth shut to keep from being rude. And walked away.

Before she got two steps, Mac joined her. "I'm in the mood for a gin and tonic—if you like gin, I'll share." She put an arm around Ray's waist. "Let's go talk about volunteering."

Ray pulled in a breath and released her irritation with stupid men. "You're on."

A second later, Hope was on Ray's other side. "I heard that. We should sign up to do the convention reception table at the same time."

Friends could brighten a person's life like stars in a dark night.

CHAPTER NINE

The next evening while undressing in her brightly lit bathroom, Ray looked over her shoulder at the mirror to check her bare bottom. Her slightly swollen, still reddened, beginning-to-bruise butt.

"Holy kraken, no wonder it hurts to sit down. Those paddles were awfully effective." And Drake had a very...firm...swing.

Just firm enough though. From paddling Casper, she knew Drake could have hit her much, much harder. But if he'd gone softer, she wouldn't have been able to evaluate the true sensation each paddle gave.

The hardwoods ones had been too painful for her, but were perfect for spankees like Casper. She could use the beautiful rosewood or the beautifully grained zebrawood. Cocobolo would be stunning but...no, it could cause allergic reactions. Talk about adding insult to injury.

Two shapes. Yes. Some long and narrow paddles. The others shaped like ping-pong paddles to spread out and lighten the sting.

Cuz there had definitely been a sting. She eyed her butt again. "Ouch?"

So why was she grinning? *WTF?* "What is *wrong* with you, woman? Happy about bruises?"

Maybe. A bit, yes. The marks were souvenirs of a very interesting evening. Of being someone's center of attention.

And that someone was Drake. Her whole body shivered.

He was definitely the whole package. Not only gorgeous, but that resonant, French-accented voice... She'd be happy listening to him reading *War and Peace*, the most boring book in the world.

His voice as he touched her... She had to swallow hard.

And his hands—his far-too-skillful, way-too-creative hands. He'd played her like a master conductor directing an orchestra through a symphony. Speeding up, slowing down, circling, stroking. Sliding his fingers inside her.

Aaand now she was all aroused. *Way to go, idiot.* But he really was something.

She froze at the thought.

Falling straight into obsession again, Ray? Haven't we done this before?

No, this was different. Drake was a good person. Admittedly, her own judgment sucked, but Hope and Mac both liked him. They would know, right?

Last winter, she hadn't been in college long enough to make good friends, which was a shame. Friends would probably have disapproved of Theodore like Faj had.

She shook her head. And four years ago at UW, she had friends but didn't tell them about trying out BDSM. Total mistake.

But Hope and Mac approved of Drake.

With a huff, she kicked off her jeans. Cloth and a tender ass? All day, she'd regretted the combination.

Being naked was a relief as she walked into the bedroom.

He was interested in her. Kind of. How much of it was a casual interest though? As the owner of the club, as an experienced Dominant, he had to be in demand. Oh yeah, she'd noticed other submissives drooling over Master Drake. He could have all the women he wanted.

No, Ray, he's not someone you should even try to get involved with. None of her relationships with men lasted. Like with Theodore, who'd gone from saying she was fascinating to telling her to stop acting like a child. When it came down to it, maybe she was happier without men in her life at all. Friends were awesome. Men not so much.

But...she could do an occasional scene at the club once she got to know more people and confine her interactions with men to Chains. Maybe even occasionally enjoy some...coital bliss.

For now, she had her BOBs. Many, many battery-operated boyfriends. *Hey, a girl needs variety. Especially me.*

Opening the nightstand drawer, she considered her choices. *Not AquaBob. No. What about Bilbo, the dildo, or BuzzyBoy, the vibrator? No. Oh, hey, how about a rabbit? Not Bugs*—*he didn't quite do it for her, but Thumper?*

"C'mere, Thumper. It's you and me, buddy. Let's have us a good time and forget all about the Chains cop."

You know, as a Chains cop, he probably owned handcuffs...

Holy kraken, stop thinking about him!

CHAPTER TEN

Having worked long hours all week, Drake took Friday off. After sleeping in, he wandered out to his back deck, breathing in the cool briny air. Across Puget Sound, the Seattle skyline stood out against the blue sky. With hopeful squawks, some gulls circled the slow ferry as it neared the Bainbridge terminal.

"George." Sitting at the table, Drake lifted his cup of coffee in a toast to the departed woodcrafter. "You were right. I do love the island."

Last fall, when Drake complained of the stress of double jobs —owner and CEO of his real estate development company as well as running Chains—George talked him into buying this house. He insisted the ferry commute wasn't much longer than driving into Seattle from the east side and would be far more peaceful.

"Thank you, *mon ami*." Drake pulled in a slow breath. "You are missed, you know."

There were more than a few club members mourning the loss of the quiet switch. George hadn't wanted any serious relationships, but he'd been part of the BDSM community for years. He'd been content with his work and his family. His two sons adored him as did Ray.

Drake winced. George wouldn't be pleased his girl was a member of Chains...or of what Drake had done with her, let alone what he'd like to do. "Sorry, old man, but she is incredibly appealing."

More than physically, in fact. Certainly she had a tempting body with her sweetly rounded ass and plump breasts. And those freckles on her face, her arms and shoulders, and the tops of her breasts were captivating. He'd definitely noted how well her light skin held the marks of the paddle.

But Chains was full of lovely submissive women.

Women realized earlier than most men that they wanted more from a partner than good looks. Eventually many men learned personality was more important than appearance. Here was a woman who followed a code of honor, who had a sense of humor and intelligence, kindness, confidence. Then there was the chemistry and compatibility between them. How could he resist?

He sighed. Even vanillas had trouble finding partners. Add in balancing D/s dynamics, and it was a wonder anyone in the lifestyle managed a serious relationship. He sure hadn't.

His friends had better luck. Alex and MacKensie, Peter and Hope, Bob and Lynn. Down in Florida, Z had his Jessica and now two little girls. Max and his cousin had found a woman to share.

Simon had Rona. It would be good to see the two of them—even if he'd have to hide his envy.

He tapped his finger against the table, thinking back to last Saturday in Chains. When an intelligent, beautiful submissive had drawn the lines. *Fun only*.

The scene had roiled up her emotions, no doubt about it. A thorough spanking often offered an emotional release, but could also bring insecurities to the surface.

And she'd backed away.

Normally, he wouldn't try again after a woman said no. His ego was healthy enough to take the hit if and when a woman wasn't interested. But she was attracted to him, and she hadn't actually rejected him as much as she'd rejected a relationship.

After seeing her ex, Drake could understand why she was wary. Especially since she'd also experienced something traumatic further back in her past.

However, she trusts me. Or she wouldn't have sought security in his arms after the scene.

He took a sip of coffee and watched the gulls skim the water.

A submissive wasn't the only one to have concerns about moving forward. Dominants could, as well. When Ray had said fun only, he hadn't protested. Because...face it, his track record wasn't one to boast about. Two relationships, two fails.

At one time, he hadn't planned to try again.

Yet now...

He picked up his phone. A woodcrafter might enjoy a walk in the forest.

"Um. Okay. Yes." Ray pocketed her cell phone. *I said yes. Why did I say yes?*

"Now there's a puzzled expression." MacKensie turned away from the newly finished shelves on her wall.

Puzzled was an understatement. "I... Hmm..."

Frowning, MacKensie walked over to set a hand on Ray's shoulder. "Is anything wrong? Can I help?"

Ray had to smile. "You are a really nice person." The unexpected burn in her eyes made her step back and blink hard. "Sorry, sorry."

"Oh *frak*, I'm sorry." MacKensie's expression held panic as she hugged Ray. "I didn't mean to make you cry..."

Ray choked on a laugh. "You didn't do anything wrong. Just made me realize how much I've missed having friends."

"Oh." MacKensie blew out a breath. "Okay, I get how feelings can sneak up on you. But"—she frowned—"you're good with people. Why..."

"Why don't I have friends?" Ray dropped into a chair, and the big black mongrel came to rest his big head in her lap as if to say *I'll be your buddy*.

"Butler, you're such a sweetie," she whispered.

His tail thumped against the floor.

Okay, explanations for the human. "I lost my college friends when I dropped out, then I buried myself in my career. Last winter, I got into a relationship with Theodore who I thought—briefly— was my *destiny*." The sarcastic emphasis on the word said it all.

"Gotta watch out for those so-called fated mates." MacKensie grinned.

"Big letdown there, yes." Ray picked up her iced tea for a sip. "Anyway, it's been wonderful to reconnect with Hope and also to make new friends, especially ones who...um..."

"Oh, I hear you." MacKensie snickered. "There are a fair number of smart, kind women. But not so many go to Chains and can give advice on how to rile up a Dominant."

Ray choked on her iced tea. "Rile up a Dom... You mean Alex? Are you *delulu*?"

"Maybe a smidge? But it mostly only happens when I'm mad at him. Or bored. Or sometimes, for the pure fun of it." Grinning, the crazy person motioned to Ray. "C'mon, the housekeeper left apple fritters in the kitchen."

"Oh yum." Ray kissed the top of Butler's furry head and rose.

"Now, since we're friends and all, who was on the phone?"

Ray huffed. "You're one of those are you—never forget a dropped conversation even if everyone else has moved on?" Pretty much her opposite.

"That would be me." MacKensie pulled the top off a storage container. "Were you talking to your ex?"

"Hardly." Ray took a fritter, glossy with glaze, and bit into it. Cinnamon and apple bits and sugary icing. "Mmm."

Maybe MacKensie would have advice. "It was Drake on the phone."

MacKensie's hand froze halfway to her mouth, then lowered. "Drake like in Chains?"

"Ha, there's a visual." Shiny metal chains over tanned skin. Over those supple muscles. "That Dom would never let himself get put in chains." Restraining him would be like trying to handcuff a tiger.

Mac snorted. "The mind boggles. And...?"

"Yes, it was Drake on the phone. He invited me to go for a hike at Bloedel this afternoon."

"Bloedel—the nature preserve over on Bainbridge?"

At Ray's nod, Mac's lips curved. "Nice. But why did you look so confused? Did you think he wouldn't call you even though he said he would? Or did you not enjoy the sexy-time paddling?"

The heat in Ray's cheeks was from embarrassment, right? Surely not from the way-too-arousing memory of his hands, his voice, the sheer intimacy of how he'd touched her. She took a bigger bite of the apple fritter and concentrated on chewing. And avoiding MacKensie's knowing gaze.

"After I...after the *scene*, I told him I didn't want anything more than fun—no relationships or anything. And he agreed. Didn't even hesitate."

"Consider what he said—he'd call you. For fun." MacKensie scooped her snow-white cat named Chef off the floor and cradled it to her chest. A loud purr showed feline approval.

"Uh-huh. On the phone, he said hiking was fun. And would be the first step." Ray shook her head. "A first step to *what*? There is no second step. I'm not going down that road again."

MacKensie's lips twitched as if she was trying not to laugh. "Mmm. '*You may test that assumption at your convenience.*' "

Was that a quote? Ray narrowed her eyes. "Captain Picard's way of saying fuck around and find out, right?"

Mac beamed. "Another Trekker. I knew I liked you."

Smiling back, Ray sighed. Because Master Drake was fully as commanding as Captain Picard...and she knew exactly what'd happen if she fucked around with him.

She would be...assimilated.

In Bloedel Park, Ray slid out of her SUV and smiled up at the clear blue sky. When she was young, there'd been far more rainy days in the summer. But California's dry weather had crept north. Rather than moist mosses, the air smelled of flowers.

Leaving the parking lot, she approached the gatehouse.

And there he was, leaning against the building, arms casually crossed over his chest. Just a totally gorgeous, dark-haired, dark-eyed man. The carefully shaped goatee framed his mouth, making her remember kissing him. How his lips had moved over hers. Had made her respond.

No, you stupid brain, don't go there. This is a friendly hike. They were simply friends. Maybe not even that.

"Hi." She kept her voice casual. "Have you been waiting long?"

"*Non*, not at all." He smiled, took her hand, and kissed her fingers. "Although you are worth a wait."

The feeling of his warm lips on her skin, the slight French accent, the way his dark gaze held hers... Had she relocated from the Pacific Northwest into a scorching Saudi desert?

"You..." She cleared her throat—and her mind. "Mas—um, Drake. This is a friendly hike. Just friends."

"But of course." With a wicked smile, he laced his fingers with hers so they were holding hands. "We can be friends."

A year ago, George had introduced Drake to the wonders of Bloedel, a 140-acre nature preserve with carefully laid-out winding trails. Timed tickets ensured the peacefulness was maintained.

Today, Drake and Ray started off on the trails through the forests and down to the famous moss garden. As they walked, the sound of trickling streams accompanied the faint rustling of wind in the higher branches.

He hadn't thought of hiking as a kind of friendship test, but maybe it was. Ray turned out to be a most enjoyable companion. Quieter than usual as she took in the beauty but offering occasional remarks. With her artistic eyes, she spotted details he missed, like where orchids had been planted in a decaying log. How vines were trained to grow up and over twenty-foot-high tree stumps.

Away from the intense, rarified atmosphere of Chains, he had a chance to see another side of her. She liked color, preferring vibrant blooms to the foliage like varieties of ferns and mosses.

A couple of times, she'd stopped to touch the older trees, just...breathing...with them, as if sharing their life stories. She said she loved how they'd been left to grow unrestrained.

Interesting. Had she felt restrained in her childhood?

"Did you enjoy your visit with MacKensie this morning?" He stopped to admire how someone had woven thin branches into a calf-high wattle fence.

"I did." Ray walked for a few steps, then glanced at him. "She's incredibly nice. And a veterinarian. I wish she lived on Bainbridge so I could take my cat to her."

"Last winter, George mentioned missing his cats—and you. Did you bring your cat back from college?"

Although her eyes reddened slightly, she smiled, the dimple appearing for a moment. "No, I've only had Max for three weeks or so. But he's made himself at home on the cat wall playground and catio."

"A...catio?"

"A screened-in, cat patio. When I first moved in with George, he had two cats, Mikan and Yuki. The vet said they needed more exercise, and I saw the catio in one of Faj's woodworking magazines. It was one of my first projects." Her sigh was almost inaudible. "I think he wanted me to feel it was my home too."

"By having you put your stamp on it." Drake nodded. Before Ray, George had raised two sons as well as being an experienced Dominant. Of *course* he'd recognized the child felt lost.

Blinking hard, Ray kept her gaze on the trail, grief pouring off her.

"*Bébé.*" Putting an arm over her shoulders, he pulled her close. "We are all richer for having known him. He won't be forgotten."

When she leaned into him, accepting his comfort, it filled his heart. Kissing the top of her head, he released her.

Each turn of the trail brought something new to see. Cedars and firs. Hydrangeas in full bloom. White wapato flowers with a glimpse of one of the ponds. "Aside from expounding your wonders as a woodworker, George didn't share much about you, although Tomo said his father disliked a new manfriend of yours. Was the man Theodore?"

"Yes." Her lips pressed together in a telling way.

Ah now, how could a Dom resist? Especially since he'd learned over the years that however skilled he might be, he wasn't omnipotent when it came to reading body language. It was not only wise to ask for clarification, but a submissive's choice of answers could be quite revealing. "Your expression says..." Running a thumb and finger over his beard, he studied her. "Actually, I'm not sure whether you're pissed off or unhappy."

When she didn't offer the answer, he waited, and as with most well-socialized people, she couldn't take the silence.

"Both." The look she shot him showed she knew she'd been nicely played.

He grinned—and waited.

"You're worse than a counselor," she muttered.

Yes, she said she'd had counseling. In his opinion, the therapist had left some work undone. "Is this where I should ask what happened and how you feel about it?"

Her exasperated snort turned into a real laugh, and he grinned. There was nothing as delightful as someone who shared his sense of humor.

"I guess there's no secret. I fell for Theodore. We planned to live together when we got back here. I loved him." She scowled. "Or maybe I fell for someone who didn't really exist. I don't think I changed, but in the beginning, he was full of love and compliments, and in the end, my personality and behavior got only insults."

The breath she pulled in was shaky enough that he reached out and took her hand to remind her she wasn't alone.

Ray felt Drake's big, warm hand close around hers. How could such a simple gesture be so comforting? Everything he did made her feel cared for.

Huh, she'd never felt like this with Theodore, but she had when she'd come to live with George. The feeling of being safe and protected and...and even precious.

With Drake, there was more though. With him, her body hummed at being near a supremely sexy man. One who was an experienced, powerful Dom.

"So you broke up after you got home—here. Do you have regrets?"

"No." She bit her lip before adding, "Breaking up wasn't as painful as it should have been. As shallow as it makes me feel, I think I was more in love with the idea of being in love than with Theodore himself. I haven't missed him."

Okay, not quite true. She missed having someone to snuggle with, to talk with over meals and share jokes in movies. The sex—

well, had been okay, but her various BOBs and a good imagination actually gave her a better time.

And wasn't that pitiful?

"Ah now, what was that thought?" The smooth voice yanked her back, and her face heated.

"N-nothing."

He had a smoky, low laugh as he gripped her shoulders to make her face him. His hand cupped her chin, forcing her to meet his eyes. "Tell me, *oui?*"

What a stubborn Dom. Let's see if he's ready to be embarrassed. "I was thinking my BOBs give me bigger orgasms than he ever did."

"Bobs?" Drake's dark brows pulled together. "Ah, I remember now. Battery-operated-boyfriends." His teeth gleamed white in his tanned face, and then his laugh rang out, full and hearty. "Such an insult for your poor ex."

So much for trying to embarrass Drake.

She tried to pull away, but he still had one hand on her shoulder. After planting a light kiss on her lips, he let her go, but took her hand again as they resumed walking.

The man sure liked to stay in physical contact.

"Um." She looked down at their laced fingers. "As you can imagine, I'm not interested in another relationship."

"Not ready yet?" He didn't release her hand.

"Not ready ever. I'm done."

He stopped to look at the Residence, the Bloedel family's neoclassical villa, and then the view out over the calm waters of the Sound. The brisk, cool wind ruffled her hair.

"*Mon pauvre bébé.* I know how that feels."

She shook her head. "Sure you do, Mr. Sex-on-a-stick, Ultra-Dom owner of Chains."

"*Non, non, non*, this is not worthy of you, Ray Lanigan." He made that deep-throated, super-French tsking sound. "Appearance, financial status, power—none of those things guarantee a happy relationship. I think you know this."

Ouch. His polite reprimand made her wince. She'd been guilty of reverse snobbism. And worse, acting as if her hurts were the only ones to have ever happened. "You're right." She pulled in a breath.

He watched her, his expression unreadable. His face was masculine angles with firm, sensuous lips that made her want to kiss him again.

"So, Master Drake, I told you my sad story. What's yours? Why aren't you with a mesmerizing submissive?"

With a huffed laugh, he lifted her hand and kissed her fingers. "But I am."

She had one moment of thinking she was holding hands with a man already involved with someone. And realized his gaze was steady on her.

He means me.

Oh.

Her delight at the unexpected compliment was confounding.

"Ah, there's that smile." He squeezed her fingers and stopped to look at a beautiful pond.

The pond was lovely. But he wasn't going to escape answering her. "You made me talk about my relationship fail. It's your turn."

"Eh, this is fair." He shrugged. "I have had two serious, long-term relationships, and both were derailed due to mismatches in what we wanted in a power exchange."

A power exchange? After a second, she got it. The Dominant/submissive stuff.

"The first, Ramona, loved everything about being a slave. Wanted to leave all decisions to me, from her clothing choices, her food, even to when she used the bathroom. Everything."

When he grinned, she realized she'd wrinkled her nose. "Sorry."

"*Non, non.* You are honest in your feelings." He stroked his goatee, thumb on one side, fingers on the other. "I was—mmm, mid-twenties—in the scene for maybe five years. I thought of myself as a Master."

He used past tense. Wasn't he a Master any longer? People in the club used the title for him. Or maybe there was a difference in an honorific and a lifestyle? "It sounds like a rather intense life."

"It was. I was uncomfortable with her need to be micromanaged. M/s and 24/7 D/s relationships don't have to be so all-encompassing. But since she needed to be comprehensively controlled to be content, I helped her find a more suitable Master."

Ray blinked.

His expression was slightly rueful, but without anger. He really *had* helped his girlfriend find a new man.

"So you don't like the Dominant/submissive stuff at home?" There was an odd stab of regret in her chest.

"Actually"—he smiled down at her—"I very much like the D/s stuff at home."

Huh. "Okay, I'll bite. What happened to your second serious relationship? I'm guessing it wasn't a Master/slave sitch?"

"No, my ex wanted the kind of D/s where the power exchange is limited to the bedroom or the club only. You have heard of such a dynamic, *oui?*"

She nodded. She and MacKensie had talked about it. "Bedroom only wasn't what you wanted?"

"As it turned out, I don't like quite such a restrictive rule on where and when. Exclusively in the bedroom makes BDSM all about sex, but I enjoy the D/s dynamic for itself, not solely for sex." He moved his shoulders as if still feeling fettered. "If you think of D/s as a range where a total power exchange is at one end, and bedroom-only at the other, well..."

"You want something in the middle."

"Exactly." He guided her to one side of the trail to let a party of four go past. "After my last relationship fell apart in an ugly fashion, I wasn't interested in trying again."

The lingering hurt in the smooth, low voice made her heart ache. "I'm sorry you went through that twice."

"Eh." Like the sun coming up over the horizon, humor lit his face. "A friend with children said my attempts at finding the right D/s relationship reminded him of *Goldilocks and the Three Bears*."

What in the world? Ray frowned, then sputtered a laugh. "The first, the power divide was too big, the next one was too small?"

He grinned. "He insists I must try at least one more time."

"Relationship advice disguised in a fairy tale." She couldn't keep from snickering.

Drake veered off onto a small trail. The path through the trees ended at a small pond. A long wooden bench perfect for viewing sat on the grassy bank. "Let's sit for a bit." He drew her down beside him.

In all reality, her feet were happy to have a rest. Stretching her legs out, she breathed in the moist air. The dark pond was calm with odd, tiny islands dotting the middle.

Drake followed her gaze. "Floating islands for the ducks to keep them safe from four-legged predators."

"Sweet." It must work. Across the pond, a pair of ducks had fluffy babies paddling between them.

So peaceful. She pulled in a long happy breath. "Thank you. I haven't visited this spot before."

His strong face held a puzzled expression. "It's a beautiful view."

"It is but too secluded for my comfort. Bloedel has a lot of security measures, but still..." She shrugged, trying not to feel as if she was over-reacting and paranoid.

His gaze darkened. "I'm sorry so many of my gender are more predatory than protective."

She tried a light laugh. "George used to say it was because modern life is too easy, that if men had to risk their lives bringing home supper, their testosterone aggression might be less."

"Do you remember Bear, the rancher? He says civilization

circumvents natural selection, resulting in too many males. To add to it, in nature, rogues are killed or driven out." Drake grinned. "Which our society won't do. But preying on our future—women and children—is a danger to civilization, so he thinks we should geld men who savage females or children. Take them right out of the gene pool."

"Seems awfully extreme." Bear was Tess' husband—and a sheep rancher. Of course he'd think in terms of herd dynamics. And improving the flock.

And yet... What would it be like to walk alone at night or in a secluded forest without fear? She wrapped her arms around herself. "I might agree with him."

The muscles in Drake's jaw tightened before he, so very gently, ran a finger over her cheekbone. "I'm sorry you were hurt in the past. Someday, I hope you'll trust me enough to tell me more about what happened."

She stiffened—and lightly answered, "Who knows...maybe." Right about the time the planet fell into the sun.

Obviously reading her expression, he huffed a breath and kissed the top of her head. Turning, he leaned back and returned to watching the pond.

Letting her breathe again.

Eventually, Ray stretched. "We should—"

Voices sounded on the hidden trail and were growing closer.

"Ah, finally." Drake turned toward her. "We now have witnesses, so you can feel safe."

Before she could parse what he meant, he tilted her chin up and kissed her. Soft and gentle, teasing and retreating.

Excitement swept through her. Her whole body had been waiting for this—for him to kiss her. To touch her.

When she wrapped her arms around his shoulders, he pulled her closer with one arm behind her back. Unbuttoning her shirt, he slid his hand beneath her bra to fondle her breast. His fingers were warm and callused. Skillful.

She gasped as every nerve wakened.

"Mmm, yes." He kneaded one breast, then his thumb swept around her rigid nipple. His next kiss deepened to a full possession.

Everything in her melted.

Voices came from nearby.

"Oh, whoa."

"Nice."

When Ray stiffened, Drake gave a throaty laugh and continued kissing her and fondling her breasts.

Didn't he realize people were watching? Her heart thudded against the inside of her ribcage. She could almost feel their eyes.

Each breath she took seemed sultrier. His hands seemed hotter. Her nerves were tingling with excitement. Her arms tightened around Drake's neck as she kissed him harder.

"Lucky man," someone said. And then there was the sound of people moving away.

After more kissing, Drake lifted his head. His thumb rubbed over her aching nipple. "So, my little submissive, it seems you like being watched."

"What? I do not."

"Mmm, but you do." His dark eyes examined her as he smiled slowly. "Perhaps our next scene in the club should be in the center of the dungeon. So everyone can watch what I do to you."

The thrill of excitement shooting through her was appalling.

Not waiting for her response, he rose, pulling her to her feet. "We should leave before I get us in trouble by stripping you down and letting everyone here enjoy our fun."

The rush of heat was way, *way* concerning.

His lips quirked.

Damn Dom.

An hour later, smothering laughter, Drake settled Ray on the couch in her living room. When he'd hoped she would eventually invite him to her home, *this* certainly hadn't been in his plans.

"Seriously, Drake. I'm fine." Her face scrunched up into an endearing scowl.

"No, you are not. Must I remind you, we have a deal." He'd given her the choice of accepting his help or a trip to urgent care.

Her lower lip poked out.

"That pout." *Adorable.* Bending down, he kissed her, slow and thorough.

When he straightened, her mouth was soft, her eyes unfocused, not a pout in sight. *Much better.* "Your leg needs to be elevated, and the pants have to go so I can monitor the swelling."

If ice didn't improve things, he'd haul her to a doctor, deal or not.

She stiffened, fear filling her eyes.

Of not being fully dressed? *Merde.* She didn't appear to have friends on the island and her neighbor was gone on vacation this week. Hope and Mac were in Seattle—and she'd insisted she needed to be home for her cat. "Can you can trust me to not attack you, *ma douce?*"

At the blunt question, the tension slid out of her body. "I...yes."

"Good. And we will do this, to ensure you don't feel without backup." He typed in a text to Mac and Hope: *Ray injured her knee, so I am assisting her for a day until she can walk without hurting. She'll call you tonight and tomorrow before noon to let you know I am behaving myself. If she doesn't check in, here's her address.*

Showing Ray, he chuckled at her befuddled expression. After adding in her home address, he sent off the message.

"I can't believe you wrote that. They'll think I'm...I'm..."

"Being practical and careful." He went down on his haunches beside her and took her hand. "Arranging a safe call is standard practice when a submissive first gets together with a Dom." He read her expression and squeezed her hand. "A public club doesn't count. It never hurts to have a check-in when first alone together."

"Standard practice?"

"*Oui.*" His phone chimed, and he showed her Hope's answer: *I have the evening call. If I don't hear her voice before 8 pm, you'll have a cop in the driveway. Give her a hug from me.*

A second later, from Mac. *I'm on the morning call. After 8 am, please. If I don't hear from her before 10 am, I'm sending a big beefy police officer to take you out, Drake. Tell her she can come and stay with me and Alex anytime she wants.*

Tears welled in Ray's eyes.

Leaning in, he kissed her cheek. Friends could unravel the hardest heart—and Ray had a very soft one.

"Now, let's get your jeans off."

She sighed. "Yes, Sir."

"That does sound nice."

Scowling at him, she unzipped her jeans and struggled to push them down.

"Allow me." Sliding his hand under the back of her jeans to support her ass, he helped her slide her jeans down. And had to suppress a smile. Her high-rise briefs were a leopard print with black edging.

It suited her. From what he'd seen in the park, her bra matched.

Focus, Jean-Pierre.

"I can't believe we walked for three miles—and then I trip over a branch in the *parking lot.*" Her hands waved in a pattern of frustration. "That's just *wrong.*"

"It does seem unfair." She'd probably hit him if he openly showed how much he enjoyed her energy and passion.

He laid a blanket over her waist and lower legs—truly a shame to hide those panties—and uncovered her right knee. Only slightly swollen with no obvious dislocation of the knee cap. No purpling bruises.

"Do you have sports ice packs and a compression wrap?"

"Yes—Faj had a bad ankle. There's a first aid kit under the master bathroom sink, and I have leftover pain pills in the medicine cabinet from when I sprained an ankle." She rolled her eyes. "Although that makes me sound accident-prone, doesn't it?"

"It does. Are you?" Drake asked. But he knew better. George had mentioned she'd picked up karate like a champ.

"No!" Her glower was as cute as her pout.

Having visited before George's death, Drake knew the house layout. "I'll be back in a minute."

Supplies gathered, he wrapped her knee and positioned an ice pack.

After taking a pain pill, she leaned back with a sigh. "Thank you, Drake."

"My pleasure." He told only the truth. Caring for her filled a need inside him.

A movement caught his eye. The far wall of the great room had a vertical maze of hand carved wood shelving for books, DVDs, and plants as well as customized cat hammocks and perches.

At the highest level, two round, golden eyes peeked over the edge.

"Now, who do we have up there?"

Ray followed his gaze and smiled. "That's my Max. I was wondering when he'd poke his nose out."

A nose was now visible.

"Max, c'mon down and meet Drake." She clicked her tongue a few times.

The feline bounded from shelf to shelf, over the tops of bookcases, and across the paw-size, hanging bridge.

"Quite the obstacle course." A very impressive one. A

climbing tree would take a cat right to the top. Two sisal rope-wrapped scratching posts probably saved the furniture.

"That was the idea," she agreed. "I need to get Max a friend. Mikan and Yuki used to chase each other up and down the wall until they were exhausted."

"I'm pleased he's an inside cat. The foxes and coyotes consider cats to be snacks."

"Birds too. Marisol next door lost her kitty to a bald eagle. It was horrible." She wrinkled her nose, so cute, he bent for another kiss.

With a low meow, Max padded across the hardwood floor. He had plush-looking, brown fur, darker around the muzzle and tail. Sturdy bones, rather skinny body.

Drake knelt and politely offered a finger.

After a careful sniff, Max rubbed his cheek against Drake's hand.

"You have a friendly cat."

"I know, right? The vet said he looks Burmese, which means he's totally friendly and trusting—and what everything else in the world calls prey." Her expression went flat. "It's how I met him."

Drake scooped the cat up—*oui*, very accepting—and settled in the adjacent chair where he could watch her face. "This sounds like a good story. Tell me."

With Theodore, Ray knew better than to tell an exciting story. If she got into the telling, he'd end up calling her a drama queen.

But Drake was waiting patiently. And when she saw sweet Max snuggle down on the Dom's lap—her kitty had never met a stranger—anger fired in her blood. How could those men have been so cruel?

She launched into the tale, how she and Marisol were in the ferry terminal parking lot, what she'd heard. As Drake stroked her sweet-hearted kitty, her anger rose higher.

"One of them said, '*C'mon, grab it. I wanna toss it in with the pitbull. See which one of them wins.*' She sat up straighter, muscles tensing as she remembered. "I grabbed a baseball bat from my back seat and headed for them."

"You...what?"

"Marisol followed with the SUV. I confronted them, and they saw I was female and wouldn't put the cat down. When Marisol turned on the brights to blind them, I used my bat." She made a swinging motion with her hands. "End of story—and I ended up with a cat."

Drake was on his feet, cat cradled against his chest. His eyes had turned darker than dark—or maybe it was the effect of his black eyebrows pulled together. "I do *not* believe you."

The words were a knife to her chest, slicing through her heart with a icy pain. "I...It's *true*." But...so many skeptical voices lived in her memory.

Pa never believed her when she'd excitedly told him of her adventures. Theodore always thought she was lying. "*Stop exaggerating.*"

Hands dropping into her lap, she swallowed down the hurt and tried to even her voice. "I wouldn't lie to... I never lie."

As if he'd believe her

"*Merde*," he said under his breath and put Max on the floor. Taking a seat on the heavy oak coffee table, he captured her hands. "Aralia Lanigan, that's not what I meant. I never thought you were lying. But you...you are a small woman, and you took on three men. In the dark. With a baseball bat."

When she stared at him, he drew an audible breath in through his nose. Leaned forward right into her space, and growled, "Are. You. *Insane?*"

The hurt dissolved, and she half-choked on a laugh. He sounded like Faj when she'd scared him—only even more upset.

More protective.

He believes me. Her eyes filled with tears. Her voice came out raw. "I didn't want to...but I couldn't let them hurt a cat."

"No, *chérie*, I suppose you couldn't." He cupped her cheek, and she could actually see him set his anger aside. His thumb stroked over her skin. "However, if you do something so dangerous again, we will learn how many paddle strokes are needed for you to eat standing up. For a week."

Wait...what?

"Awake, *bébé*?"

Still on the couch, Ray yawned and looked at the sunlight slanting through the western windows. It was evening? "How long was I asleep? What time is it?"

"A couple of hours and around seven. Speaking of which, before you forget, it's time to call Hope."

"Oh, oops. Wouldn't want you to be hauled away in handcuffs."

"No, let's not have that happen. I prefer to be the one doing the cuffing."

When she shivered at the thought of him putting her in cuffs, the faintest smile appeared on his lips. Damn Dom saw everything.

"Time to eat, *oui*?"

Her stomach growled in agreement...and wasn't the only bodily function complaining. "I...uh...need to get up."

"Ah, of course." To her relief, he didn't make fun of her but simply scooped her up and carried her into the downstairs bathroom. He left her there, saying he'd be in the kitchen and to open the door when she was done. Handing her the cell, he reminded her to call Hope.

He really is a nice person. Because, face it, how could she pee if he was outside the door listening? Which, if she was being logical, was kind of stupid. Seriously, what idiot in the beginning of civilization thought it was clever to make normal bodily functions something to be hidden and embarrassed about? Animals didn't have any problems with pooping in public. In fact, Yuki would use the litterbox and then yowl to inform everyone she had a successful bowel movement.

But Americans—oh, the shame if anyone hears the toilet being used. *So stupid.*

Ack, how'd I get sidetracked onto this rant? Okay, brain, get off the hamster wheel. With a huff of exasperation, she finished and washed her hands.

So, knee, how's it going? She limped in a couple of trial circles around the bathroom before opening the door.

Obviously having been watching for her, Drake strolled over from the kitchen. He studied her. "Since you undoubtedly tried putting weight on your bad leg, how does it feel?"

"Considering we just met recently, you seem to know me awfully well."

His lips quirked up. "Some people are like obsidian, impossible to see through. You, *bébé*, are a diamond, transparent to read but with so many facets."

That...was a compliment. She had to smile. But still... "So much for being a woman of mystery."

Laughing, he swept her into a bridal carry and took her breath away.

She should've felt like annoying baggage being hauled around. Instead, he made her feel like a princess.

Every woman should get to feel like a princess.

And what kind of thought was that?

Disney has a lot to answer for.

"I'm sorry I'm so much trouble," she said as he carried her across the great room.

"I enjoy having you in my arms"—he grinned—"and at my mercy." Bending his head, he kissed the top of her nose teasingly.

The brush of his beard against her skin made her shiver. Why did it feel as if she'd been waiting for him to touch her all day.

What rule said she had to wait?

She pulled his head back down and kissed him. Totally kissed him.

Under her mouth, she felt his lips curve up.

And then he sat down on the couch, settling her with her butt on thighs, her legs stretched out on the cushions, and leaning back into the curve of his right arm. With his left hand, he laced his fingers into her hair, gripped, and pulled her head back.

And then *he* kissed *her*.

In a slow, determined exploration, he learned her taste and gave her his, invading seductively, slowly, before turning wet and ravenous. She couldn't move, and a thrill ran through her. For a moment, he sucked on her bottom lip, then took her lips again until her senses spun.

When he lifted his head, her skin felt sensitive, hot all over her body.

He made a sound like *pffft* and gave her a rueful smile. "We will go no further, *mon petit chou*. Not with you on pain medications, no matter how mild."

"But..." She was willing to go much, much further.

"*Non*."

She scowled at him. "I'm not a cabbage, by the way."

"You aren't a what?" His brows drew together, then he laughed. Gods, she loved his laugh. "I'll remember. Perhaps." He moved her to a corner of the couch and stood up. "Supper is prepared. You should eat."

"You cooked while I was asleep?" Oh, she could smell something wonderful. "Seriously?"

"I did. Do you have TV trays?"

"Faj hated those flimsy things so he made something better." Scooting to the corner of the couch, she motioned to the three-shelfed cherry wood end table. "The surface of this is actually two layers of wood with both on rollers. Pull the table forward, then the top part rotates around to the front of the couch."

"Interesting." He scooted the top of the end table around to make an L-shape. "Clever—and sturdy."

"It's mostly because I was kinda clumsy and tipped over a TV tray." She sighed and confessed. "Twice. It's one of the reasons he taught me karate."

"I would have said his plan worked—you don't seem clumsy at all, except"—he tugged on her hair teasingly—"you did trip over a twig in the parking lot."

"It was a *branch*, you, you *douchenoggin*." She kicked at him with her good leg. *Oh, hell, I insulted and tried to kick a Dom.*

Not even close to upset, he was laughing as he stepped out of reach. "That cannot be a compliment."

"Sorry?"

"No, you're not." He adjusted the end table on the other side of the couch. "I made chicken—what pieces do you like? Drumstick, breast..."

"My favorite is the thigh." She pursed her lips, remembering his touch in the club. In the park. "Don't tell me... You're a breast man."

His instant grin delighted her. "In every way, *oui*."

He brought her a plate with succulent chicken, broccoli with cheese sauce, wild rice, and biscuits.

Discovering she was starving, she abandoned conversation and inhaled it all.

Smiling, he did the same.

"Oh, that was awesome." As she picked up her fork with the last bite, Max jumped up on the couch beside her, tiny nose lifted.

"Cat, you know better." And yet, who could resist? She offered him a tiny shred of the chicken. "Faj would have my head."

Max gave her a look as if to say only sadistic dogs wouldn't feed a hungry feline.

"He's as expressive as you are." Smiling, Drake took their

empty plates to the kitchen and returned the end tables to their original position. "How does your knee feel? Your pain meds should have worn off. Do you need more? Or...I saw a bottle of Grand Marnier."

"Actually, my knee only hurts when I move it now. I'm totally up for a glass of liqueur, please."

After removing Max from her lap, Drake positioned her legs on a pillow on the coffee table. An ice pack went on her knee, then a warm quilt.

She shook her head. "Were you a medic in your last life?"

He laughed, warm and dark. "*Non*. I learned to fight when I was young and, later, took up mixed martial arts in college." His smile was rueful. "Injuries from sparring happen often enough."

After another trip to the kitchen, he brought back cognac glasses with a nice pouring of bronze liqueur. "Here you go, *ma chérie*."

"Thank you." After her hand's heat on the glass warmed the Grand Marnier, she took a sip. He'd picked Faj's favorite—the Centenaire. Lovely and sweet with smoky hints of orange at first, then a touch of fruit and also vanilla-y. Was that a word? "Perfect. But I can't have more than this glass. Tomorrow I'm helping fill swag bags for the convention."

"Ah." He smiled. "The convention couldn't happen without volunteers. Your help is appreciated." Leaning back, Drake put an arm around her shoulders and picked up his own glass. He took a sip, obviously enjoying the taste.

Max jumped back onto the couch and settled on her lap. She ran her hand down the soft fur. "He's such a carefree guy. He made himself at home within a day of being here."

Putting his glass on the end table, Drake reached over to stroke the cat, getting a happy purr in response. "His name suits him well. It is short for Maximillian or Maxwell or...?"

"Huh, I'm not sure. I named him for the police officer who found me breaking into a house in Seattle, and I was terrified he'd hand me over to children's services who probably wouldn't believe me, and I'd end up back in the foster home I ran away from. Instead, he brought me here to George."

Whoa, what was she *saying*? She scowled at the glass of Grand Marnier. Okay, the stuff was strong, but she'd only had a few sips. Not nearly enough to explain why she'd blurt out stuff about her past.

Surely it wasn't because Master Drake made her feel...cared for. Because there was a warm arm around her shoulders and fingers playing with her hair. Because all her barriers were down.

Unsettled, she looked up at him.

He was studying her again, hard face softened. "A bad situation for a child. Might I ask why you ran away?"

She sighed. In for a dime, in for a dollar—wasn't that how the saying went? "The foster mother's son with two of the other foster boys were..." Slowly, under his quiet gaze, she explained what had happened.

His mouth tightened, anger growing in his eyes. "What happened with the boys?"

"Uh, Chains cop, this happened years ago. You can't go beat them up."

"I can check on them and ensure they didn't continue this behavior." A corner of his mouth tipped up. "If they have, *then* I can beat them up."

The euphoric rush deep in her belly was surely from the liqueur, not his words.

Drake was enjoying running his fingers through Ray's curly hair and watching each silken lock spring back when released. Such beautiful colors, ranging from rich reddish-brown to golden red where bleached by the sun...along with the blue-green strands.

Now that he knew her better, the added colorful strands not

only matched her eyes but also her vibrant personality. Her beauty was far more than skin deep.

"*Anyway*"—she waved her glass—"Max is named for the patrol officer who put so much work into saving me. He talked Faj into taking me in and talked my social worker into the ton of paperwork to allow the change. Afterward, he kept coming back to check on me. I still get an occasional card from him even though he moved all the way to Florida."

Drake raised his eyebrows. "Impressive." The officer really had gone above and beyond. "I hope he's doing well."

"So well." Her sigh held happiness. "Lots of sun and sand…and he's in a poly relationship with his cousin and a woman."

Poly relationship. Cousin. Cop. And a friendship with George… "He doesn't, perchance, live in Tampa, does he?"

Ray stared at him. "How could you possibly know that?"

"Max Drago—*oui*?" At her nod, he laughed. "We were teased about our names—Drago and Dragomir."

"He…he wasn't a member of Chains, was he?" Her eyes got wider. "Oh, oh, I bet he was!"

Drake didn't out his members, so he changed the subject. "Max is short for Maximillian, if your cat would like to use the longer form at times."

Her nod showed she wouldn't push. "Longer names are useful when scolding." She smiled at the feline she'd woken with her excitement. "Don't you agree, Maximillian Felinus Lanigan?"

The cat gave a throaty mew in response.

Drake laughed, then kissed Ray's temple. "Let us get you upstairs, washed up, and comfortable for bed."

"It's early yet."

"You look tired, *ma douce*. Being in pain is tiring—and I fear you will be hurting by the time you finish preparing for bed."

Her eyes narrowed. "You are definitely a Dom."

Non, he was merely being reasonable. "This is what my ex had a problem with."

"What, you wanting to take care of her?"

"If it didn't involve sex, she didn't want any hint of dominance."

She pressed her hands over her mouth, but the snorting laugh came through clearly.

"And what do you find so funny?"

"She tried to put boundaries around your dominance. It'd be like someone telling George he could only craft wood in the morning hours. She was an idiot."

Her understanding was like light breaking into a dark forest.

"Hmm." Her eyes lit with laughter. "What would happen if I said no, I won't go to bed?"

She really did enjoy poking the bear, didn't she. "You mean, would I beat you until you agreed?"

"Uh-huh." She waggled her eyebrows at him, not a trace of fear showing. Delightful.

"Most tempting, but I can do nothing without consent. Of course, being quite intelligent, you will see my...suggestions...are always correct."

She had the cutest giggle. "More like I can see that what you don't win through domination, you win through charm."

"But of course." Setting her glass to one side, he put Max on the floor, tossed the quilt and ice bag to one side, and picked her up.

"We'll take the lazy way up." Drake carried her to the small elevator near the stairs.

Reaching out, Ray pushed the button. "When I moved in, I thought Faj was crazy to have installed an elevator. Talk about a luxury. But he said he built the place planning to stay even when he was old and decrepit." Her eyes filled with tears.

Drake rubbed his cheek against her hair. "He had a good life, even if shorter than he might have hoped. But he was happy with how his days came to an end—with a quiet death in his own home with his family around him."

She rested her head against his shoulder and nodded.

Upstairs, Drake walked into the light-filled master bath and took the time to look around. A white freestanding tub by a large window looked out over the shadowy evening. The beautifully grained, light wood in the cabinets and vaulted ceiling along with swirly, blue-green marble in the glass-enclosed shower made the room feel part of the forest outside.

"Almost minimalist, but cozy." Whoever had designed it had chosen marble the same shade as Ray's eyes. "Now, shower or bath?"

"Shower. There's a cane leaning against the wall in the closet. With it, I should be able to get around. My knee does feel better. Really."

"All right." There was a chair beside the marble-topped counter. He helped her into it and found the cane. Much as he'd like to help more, he wouldn't. In many ways, he was still a stranger.

In one cabinet, he found clean towels and arranged them on a hook beside the shower. "What do you want to wear to bed?"

"Um."

Her startled expression was a dead giveaway. She normally wore nothing.

And now, he was getting hard. *Merde.* "A robe instead?"

"Right, right. On a hook in the closet."

"Very good." He brought it in, checked she had everything close, including her phone, and gave her a stern look. "I will be answering my emails in the bedroom. Take your time—but you *will* call me if you need help. If it sounds as if you fell, I will come in. I dislike breaking down doors, so please don't lock it."

"Yes, Sir." Her expression was that of a contented submissive. Unlike Justine, she liked being directed.

So very satisfying.

Settling into a chair in the bedroom, he pulled out his phone and grimaced at the long list of emails. Didn't anyone observe weekends anymore? Then again, he usually put in a few weekend hours himself.

Today had been rare—and very enjoyable.

In the bathroom, the shower came on. Singing accompanied the sound of the water, and Drake smiled at the "We're Not Gonna Take It" by Twisted Sister.

Someone liked singing to metal? Nice. Then he blinked as she not only switched genres but went off the track entirely as she sang, word perfect, the "You'll Be Back," from the musical *Hamilton*, belting out *Da-da-da-dat* with enthusiasm.

Intriguing. Sometimes she was quite subdued—maybe a lingering effect from her last relationship—and sometimes so filled with energy she sparkled.

Her bedroom didn't say shy and retiring—and was nothing like George, who had preferred quiet and subtle in shades of gray and white.

This room had a dark hardwood floor, vaulted ceiling, and unique trim—and vivid colors. The draperies and bedspread were a dark teal. Oriental carpets added complexity. The color scheme went well with the dark wood trim and the graceful furniture and was brightened by numerous foliage plants and floor to ceiling windows.

He smiled slightly at the very romantic king-size, canopy bed. And noted it would provide quite effective anchor points.

Now...how could a Dom resist?

Not tonight, Jean-Pierre.

There was time.

CHAPTER ELEVEN

Ray woke the next morning with a heavy weight on her chest—and she froze. She opened her eyes slightly, but the pressure on her breasts wasn't a man's arm but a very smug cat.

Am I happy or sad it's not Drake?

Last night, wide awake after her shower, she'd invited Drake to watch a movie with her, thinking they'd go back downstairs. Instead, he saw the screen on the wall, tucked her into bed, piled up pillows against the cushy tufted leather headboard, and joined her.

As they were scrolling and discussing the available shows, she spotted a movie George had talked about—*Jaws*. She loved horror, especially fantasy and sci-fi kinds. *Jaws* wasn't fantasy, but the movie was so old—how could it even be scary?

Mistake.

Gods, she might never go swimming again.

But when she was scared, Drake had pulled her close, and she'd curled up against him. He'd rubbed her shoulder comfortingly, and then when the movie was over, he'd given her a squeeze and switched over to cartoons.

And she'd fallen asleep.

Turning her head, she saw the pillows were still piled up on the other side of the bed, the covers undisturbed. He hadn't taken advantage of being here.

She rubbed the funny ache in her chest.

In college, she'd learned the hard way that when a man said he only needed a place to crash and wouldn't try anything, they lied. How many times had she woken up to being groped or having a dick nudging her ass as if the fact that a man had a hard-on obligated a woman to do something about it.

There were times she hated the male gender.

But Drake...hadn't tried anything. Oh, they'd shared a few kisses here and there. She'd been willing for more. Being a Dom, he could probably tell.

Instead, he'd been what George would consider *honorable*.

Thinking of which, she picked up her phone from the nightstand and texted Mac to say she was alive and well—and Drake was a gentleman.

Getting back a happy face and a thumbs up, she laughed.

She stroked a hand down Max's plush fur. "You, Sir Feline, are no gentleman cat. Look how you simply assumed I'd be okay with your paws on my breasts."

He purred.

"Yes, I know they're nice and squishy. But you're not the one I wanted doing pushy-paws on my breasts."

A smoky-sounding laugh came from the hallway. "I might remember how to—how is it said—make biscuits?"

"Drake." She felt her face turning hot.

Max jumped off the bed to collect a quick stroking, then Drake sat down on the bed. His hip was against hers as he smiled down at her. "You look much better today."

She swallowed, trying to think of something to say, all too aware of how close he was. Of the thinness of the aged T-shirt he'd pulled out of her drawers, to wear as a token nightgown. Of his clean, fresh scent, and the whiteness of his teeth against dark facial hair.

His gaze held hers as he reached out, pausing over her chest, giving her time to protest, then slowly ran his knuckles over one breast. Over the jutting nipple. The lightest of touches and it sent an electric pleasure blossoming outward.

The sunlines at the corner of his eyes deepened. "Yes, we will have to play. Soon." He lifted her arms over her head, securing her wrists with one hand. And his other hand firmly cupped one breast, lifting it, kneading, the pure exquisite sensation of being fondled making her toes curl.

She managed to haul her brain back long enough to ask. "Soon. Not now?"

"Ah, non, désolée. I let you sleep late." He tugged on one nipple, then the other, making her gasp. "You're scheduled to assemble swag bags for the convention. We must get moving now since you wanted to get your car from Bloedel on the way to the ferry. You can leave it at the terminal, and I'll drive in Seattle."

He was talking about her car, and she didn't care what he was saying.

Under his firm touch, her back arched up in an unspoken demand for more.

She wanted to beg.

Dammit. Duty sucks.

With Drake beside her, Ray walked down the hallway in the hotel, pleased at the lack of pain in her knee. The clamor in the hotel conference room was loud as Ray walked through the doorway.

Drake squeezed her fingers—and wasn't it fun he liked to walk holding hands?—and tugged her to the left to clear the doorway for others.

Leaning back against the wall, she took a slow survey of the room. A room full of people could be overwhelming, but getting an overall picture helped.

Cthulhu's tentacles, but this time, she'd need every trick in her toolbox. The frantic energy in here was like an overturned anthill.

Doubled-up conference tables ran from one side of the room to the other. Each seat at the table was marked with a number and had an opened box or bin. Some had additional boxes stacked behind the chair. People milled around, greeting old friends, and looking for their places.

Beside her, Drake waited, letting her take everything in.

When she looked up at him, he smiled. "All right?"

"I guess. It's actually not as bad as I thought." Near the door, volunteers were quickly checked in and assigned to specific chairs. One by one, people were sitting down, checking their boxes, and cheerfully conversing with the others around them. "It's well organized."

"This is the convention's sixth year. Each year, we get more efficient and eliminate more glitches. Like in our first year, we weren't prepared for how popular the dungeon would be—not enough space, not enough staff." Drake's cheek creased with his smile. "Of course, there are always new problems cropping up."

"Huh. I wonder what you'll run into this year." Maybe she'd get to help with fixing things. It was something she did enjoy doing and—

"Ray." Resting a hand on the wall over her head, he leaned in close enough she could feel his body's warmth. Could breathe in his light citrusy scent that made her want to nibble on—

"Aralia."

Yikes, focus, Ray. "Uh-huh?"

His voice deepened as he asked, "Are you going to invite me over for tonight?"

Did he want to see her again or...was this him being responsible? "Um, my knee is fine now."

"I'm aware." His lips quirked. "I am asking if you want company in that big bed of yours."

Oh. Oh yes.

No, Ray. You're one-hundred percent asking for heartbreak.

Yes, Ray. Pain is part of living.

She looked up into patient black eyes. He hadn't moved, was waiting for her to work things out in her head. And his self-control was as compelling as his invitation to have sex.

Okay then. She wasn't going to hide in a box to stay safe. *Life is for living.* "Hey, Chains cop, want to come and commit some crimes in my big bed?"

His laughter wasn't loud, but was full-bodied and...oh, so contagious. "Yes, *ma chérie*, I'd be delighted. Although I should handcuff you and teach you what happens to little criminals."

Her mouth dropped open—and flames roared up, so hot and passionate she could actually feel herself flush.

His gaze heated, and he lowered his head. An inch from her lips, he murmured, "Text me when you're finished here, and I will pick you up." Cupping her face, he kissed her with a demanding, thorough possessiveness.

Lifting his head, he rubbed the wetness from her lips with his callused thumb. "Soon, *mon petit chou*."

And he straightened and strolled out of the room, lifting his hand in greeting to the people at the door.

Ray took a minute to get her breathing back under control.

Wow.

And the bastard Dom had called her a cabbage again. Deliberately when she didn't have any brain cells left to respond.

She pulled in another breath. *Okay. Time to work.* Trying not to notice the people staring at her, she joined the line in front of the sign-in desk.

"That looked like a pleasant kiss." Rather than gushing, the lean, brunette woman behind Ray sounded as if she was simply offering a conversational opening.

Nice. With a smile, Ray admitted, "My legs are still shaking."

The older, short woman in front of Ray turned. "Getting kissed by Master Drake? I am not surprised in the least. Hi, Ray, remember me? Claudia from behind the bar."

"It's so nice to know someone." She beamed at Claudia, then turned back to smile at the tall brunette. "I'm new."

"Hi, Ray. I'm Faylee and tend to be terrified of new places and strangers. You're brave." The brunette crinkled her nose in a teasing way. "And taking on Drake? *Very* brave."

Ray laughed. Had Drake offered much of a choice? No, not true. He'd given her the chance to say no every step of the way.

She had only herself to blame.

After getting signed in and given a chair number, she went in search of her seat. And was delighted to realize Claudia and Faylee were stationed on each side of her.

Yay! Two people who'd be fun to talk with.

As the assembly tables filled with people, the person in charge gave instructions. Each person was to put a promotional item from the box in front of them into a swag bag, then pass the bag on.

Ray's box held pens with a BDSM equipment store brand. Claudia had hand flyers promoting a Master/slave organization. Faylee's tub contained tiny hand sanitizer bottles from an online sex-toy store.

"There are so many cool things." Looking down the table, she saw flyers, lanyards, temp tatts, pins, snacks, sunglasses, and shot glasses as well as kinky-themed condoms, tissues, and disinfectant wipes.

Across the table from her, a clean-shaven man was looking through the lube packets in his box.

"Lube is so appropriate for a BDSM con." Ray tilted her head. "Are you doing quality control?"

He laughed. "Checking out the different varieties. Like"—he held up a green-colored packet—"this one has peppermint in it. Perfect for a masochistic bottom."

Peppermint on the tender bits? "Ouch. Oh, I'm Ray."

"Shawn from Chains. What club are you with?"

"Oh, right. I forgot they got volunteers from all the sponsoring organizations. I'm from Chains too."

He looked startled. "Yeah? I know Claudia and Faylee"—he smiled at the women on each side of her and got smiles back—"but I must have missed you."

"She's new, Shawn. But a good one. She worked the bar with me last weekend," Claudia said.

"And Drake likes her." Faylee waggled her eyebrows.

Shawn's mouth dropped open. "Wait, you mean *likes* her, likes her?"

"Oh yeah." Claudia made kissing sounds.

Ray's face turned hot. "Behave. What are you—in middle school?"

Thank the elder gods, the assembly line started up, diverting their attention.

Bag after bag came down the table. Faylee would toss in a hand sanitizer, hand the bag to Ray who'd put in a pen and give the bag to Claudia. At the far end, the line turned the corner and bags flowed down the other side of the tables.

As people mastered the art of filling and passing on, conversation started back up. To Ray's delight, the others started discussing the various kinds of BDSM they'd gone through over the years.

Faylee had tried Master/slave and D/s, and found her niche being a "little girl" with her own Dear Daddy.

Shawn was a switch—something Ray had trouble wrapping her head around.

In contrast, Claudia wasn't submissive *or* dominant. She called herself a pain slut and was in tight poly relationship with two people as well as being extended kin in a leather family.

So confusing. *Where would I fit?*

The thought of taking charge was a big ugh. *I'm definitely submissive.* And, huh, coloring books sounded cool, but being treated like a child? *Noper, not for me.*

Pain slut—no, but... The spanking. Mmm, it'd been all kinds of erotic.

Sheesh, how many kinks were there?

The line paused as Faylee switched her empty box for a new one.

With a relieved sigh, Ray stood up and stretched—odd how bag-filling used muscles wood carving didn't—and looked around.

A woman farther down the table saw her stand up. Ray smiled at the woman who was quite striking with smooth dark hair and eyes. Rather than smiling back, the woman compressed her full lips and turned away, saying something to the woman beside her. Who then frowned at Ray.

All right then. Guess not everyone here is friendly. Feeling totally awkward, Ray turned her back, pulled another box out from under the table, and emptied the last pens from the old one.

Sitting back down, she checked the two women out of the corner of her eye. They were laughing and kept glancing at Ray.

Great, nothing like being laughed at.

Why don't humans come with shells like a turtle? It'd be nice to be able to tuck my head and arms inside something unbreakable.

Perhaps she should develop thicker skin. After all, anyone Master Drake kissed probably ended up as gossip fodder.

With a sigh, she tossed a pen in a swag bag...and kept going.

Faylee started another round of telling stories about the club with Claudia chiming in with tidbits. Some of the stories were hilarious. Or terrifying.

After a couple of hours, no more bags came through. Ray blinked at her empty hands. What happened?

The person who'd checked them in climbed up onto a chair. "We are done! Way ahead of schedule as it happens. You've been wonderfully efficient. There are other volunteers to pack away the boxes, so your work is finished. Since we'd planned to have a break about now with snacks"—she pointed to the back of the room—"go ahead and grab a cookie and water to go. And thank you!"

The man beside her with military-short hair yelled, "Dismissed."

Laughing, people began to move away from the assembly line.

"I'm for some water and a cookie or two," Claudia said.

"Me too," Faylee answered. "You, Ray?"

"Bathroom break." She needed to move. Between the overload of too many people and having to stay in one place, she felt as if her skin had ants on it. "Afterward, a cookie will be good."

Outside the room, Ray eyed the line at the bathroom door and turned away. Instead, she stretched her legs on a long walk down the carpeted hallway. The edginess eased up and finally disappeared with a third trip down the hall. And her knee didn't complain at all.

After a bathroom break, she returned to the room, detouring between clusters of people to the snack area.

Cookie, cookie, cookie.

The water was cool and refreshing; the oatmeal cookie had exactly the right chewiness. *Yum.*

Near the table, people were still chatting in small clusters.

Maybe I can make more friends? Unfortunately, Claudia and Faylee had left.

From serving soft drinks at Chains, she recognized a few of the club members in one group. She met a woman's gaze, and they looked away with a curled-up lip. Two of the others gave her cold stares before turning so as to not have her in their sight.

What in the world?

Oh, hell. Had she been too annoying today? Laughed too

loudly at Faylee's stories. Or talked too fast or too much and disturbed others in the area.

She didn't think she had. *Am I being hypersensitive? Overreacting?*

Maybe. Then again, why else would they be acting like she smelled worse than a rotting pile of aged manure?

With a thick lump in her throat, Ray left, dropping her cookie and water into the trash on the way out.

So much for her goal of making new friends.

Her stomach hurt as she walked out of the hotel. And all she wanted was to go back home and hide out—turtle style.

She was supposed to text Drake.

No. The thought of seeing him again... She bit her lip. After this, she'd be thinking of how she sounded, not wanting to talk, to laugh.

I know I'm being too sensitive to...to rejection, but...

In his office, Drake pulled out his phone and read the incoming text from Ray.

The assembly line finished up early. I didn't want to mess with your schedule and am boarding the ferry back to Bainbridge now. Since I'm way behind on everything, I'm going to spend today in the shop. Thanks for looking after me when I got hurt. It's appreciated.

Drake read the message again and considered the tone. Formal. Distancing. Very different from when he'd dropped her off.

Hmm. He could understand her having second thoughts if their time had been acrimonious or even uncomfortable. But she'd been all in with open enthusiasm. *"Want to come and commit some crimes in my big bed?"*

What had happened in the last couple of hours?

His jaw tightened. Ray was as friendly and open as a golden retriever. But not everyone else was. BDSM communities tended to be welcoming...but people were people.

Perhaps she'd heard gossip about him and had second thoughts? Doubtful, since he wasn't a sadist or into any of the more unusual kinks. Wasn't an abuser.

His brows drew together. She had at least one ugly incident in her past, maybe more. No telling what might bother her.

If she truly wanted him to go away, he would do so. First, it'd be good to know she hadn't tripped over a trigger and simply panicked.

Now how to find out what had sent her to hide in her cave.

Three loud thumps on the workshop door startled Ray so badly she dropped the sandpaper block. "What the heck?"

More thumping. Ooooh, someone was knocking.

As she straightened, every vertebrae in her spine cracked. *Ouchers. How long was I in here sanding?* No sunlight came through the windows.

A shiver of anxiety ran through her. She was alone. And it was dark.

"Ray, it's Drake."

Her tension disappeared. He wouldn't hurt her. Not Drake. Then her brain came online. *No, oh, no, no, no.* He was *here*. Hadn't her text given the right message? Okay, so she hadn't spelled out *—don't call me again—*but he wasn't stupid. In fact, she'd never met anyone more capable of reading between the lines.

He opened the door and halted in the entry. George must have educated him since he didn't open the inner door. He leaned against the wall, arms crossed over his chest. His level, patient gaze met hers. The black beard didn't conceal the sternness of his jaw.

He didn't appear angry, but...

"Come out, Aralia Lanigan. Let's talk." His baritone was calm. Controlled. He'd used her formal name in the same way George would when he wanted her complete attention.

Why couldn't she summon up any defiance?

Because her heart was already breaking? *Why can't I be normal?*

She stepped out, skin covered in sawdust, hair yanked up in a messy top bun, in stained, gritty scrubs. "I don't think there's anything to talk about. This"—she motioned between him and herself—"it won't work. You should just go."

"Ah." He paused for a moment. "No is always no, but it would make me feel better if I could know your thoughts on why things won't work. Can we talk for a bit?"

When she didn't manage to come up with a reason immediately, he put an arm behind her back and ushered her out of the workshop, down the tiny path, and up the front steps of the house.

He took a seat on the porch swing, the one Faj had made for her, despite teasing her it belonged in the deep south.

When he pulled her down beside him, she tried to edge away. "I'm filthy and sweaty and—"

"And I have never seen a sweaty woman before?" His deep chuckle silenced her, reminding her he was a Dom...and exactly how sweaty and tear-stained she'd been after being paddled.

How he'd held her afterward.

"Tell me, *chérie*. Why do we not work?" He touched her chin lightly, only enough to bring her head around so his gaze could meet hers.

Tears prickled a warning at the backs of her eyes. "I know you're attracted to me now, but... that'll change. Like with Theodore. You'll get to know me and won't want me anymore."

He made an uncomprehending sound. "What didn't Theodore like?"

Honestly, did she have to spell it out? She threw her hands in the air—the way Theodore had hated. "I'm too loud, too scattered, talk too fast. Too emotional, too dramatic."

He eyed her hands, and amusement lit his eyes. "Ah. Go on."

That...was not the response she'd expected.

"Theodore says I act like a toddler, complete with tantrums." Even saying the words made her mouth taste bitter.

The displeased sound Drake made came from the back of his throat. "He's a lawyer. Lawyers cover their emotions like a cat covers its scat in the litterbox, and they think everyone else should do the same." He tilted his head. "Your emotions are unguarded, unrehearsed. I like that. And I enjoy the drama."

Oh, guess she hadn't exactly tried to hide her personality, had she?

"What else? Give me the awful whole." He moved close enough she could feel his hard thigh against hers. His arm along the back cushion touched her shoulders.

"I... I jump from activity to activity, lose track of time. Miss meals and dates. And get bored easily."

His lips twitched. "Now, in all reality, as a Dom, I'd probably look for ways to ensure you didn't miss important times—like dates with me or meals." His fingers cupped her chin, forcing her to face him, and she had no defenses left to push him away.

His voice dropped to a smooth—intimate—murmur. "Keeping you from becoming bored will be a pleasing challenge."

Her heart sped up. The owner of a BDSM club, an experienced Dom, he probably had way too many ideas.

"Um." What would he do? She could feel herself getting damp. "No, we were talking about, um, personality clashes and—"

"I see no clash. But I am remiss." His lips curved...and she remembered how his mouth felt against hers. "Is there something you don't like about me?"

Her mind went blank.

No way would she let him think he was perfect, true or not. *Come up with something, anything.* "Um. You're pushy?"

"*Zut*, is that a question? *Oui*, I am pushy, and you appear to like it, *non*?" His gaze intensified.

Oh, hadn't he said his being a Dom too often was what upset his ex. *Stupid, Ray, what an objection to throw out there.* Even worse, he'd caught her. "Yes. I do like when you go all Dom...even if I feel as if I'm betraying the sisterhood."

"And sometimes male Doms feel as if we're reinforcing a toxic patriarchy. What redeems us are the other genders who are submissives and female Dominants. Power exchanges aren't about gender." He ran a finger down her throat. "You gift me with your trust and submission...just as I work to take some of the decisions from you and let you exist in the moment without worrying."

Oh. Yes. The gift went both ways.

"Nonetheless, it will take some discussion to learn how much and when D/s is wanted." He leaned in, rubbing his cheek against hers. "I like you very much, Ray, and you like me. Why don't we see where this attraction will take us."

Every muscle in her body simply sagged.

A stronger person would fight longer.

"I brought pizza," he murmured. "Say yes, *ma chérie*."

"You... I see what you're doing—taking this decision away too?"

His dark eyes lit. "But, of course."

She laughed, knowing full well she could say no, and he'd respect it. And then she summoned up all her courage. "Yes. Let's see what happens."

Please, let it all work out.

Drake took the pizza from the oven and tilted his head. The faint sound of the shower upstairs had stopped a while ago, but...no Ray. Was her knee giving her trouble?

Doubtful. She'd said it no longer hurt, and the swelling was gone.

Was she having second and third thoughts? Maybe he should check.

Upstairs, Ray was standing in front of the dresser in the master bedroom. A towel was wrapped around her hair. A second towel wrapped around her torso, plumping up her breasts and revealing appealingly long legs, toned arms and shoulders. Her skin was pink from the hot shower. She carried the delightful fragrance of raspberry-scented soap.

Merde, taking her to bed now would be wrong. She needed to know he liked who she was, that he wasn't here for sex.

He'd take it slow—even if he had to throttle his testosterone faucet. Intimacy might or might not happen later on. He cleared his throat. "Is there a problem?"

She jumped and spotted him. "No." Her gaze returned to the dresser, and her scowl deepened. "Yes."

He managed to smother a laugh. Shy and yet straightforward. Delightful. "Tell me what is wrong, *chérie*."

She sighed. "Normally, I'd lounge around in an old T-shirt of Tomo's, only it feels as if I should wear something nice for you." She pulled the towel off her hair and tossed it into the laundry hamper. "But that's not who I really am and—"

"Ah, I understand." *Tell her to discard the towel and wear nothing? Bad Jean-Pierre.* "Since I am hoping for a relaxed, quiet evening, it would please me if you chose the T-shirt option."

He could see her tight shoulder muscles relax with her sigh, and the look she gave him was filled with gratitude. "Sounds good to me. Thanks."

"You are very welcome." De-stressing a submissive pleased the Dom in him. "Pizza is out of the oven. Come down and eat."

"I'll be there in two minutes."

She was exactly as fast as she'd said. Surprised, he set the bottle of a good Barbera red wine and glasses on the coffee table, then took a moment to study her.

No makeup. Hair still damp, beginning to curl around her face. Her oversized T-shirt wasn't a military one of Tomo's. No, he'd bet she bought this one. It was a pale green that brought out the color of her eyes—and the graphic was a stack of books and the words: *Imagine being scared of drag queens and books.*

Yes, he did like this woman. As she padded over in in fluffy green socks, he put an arm around her. "You do look comfortable."

Max jumped up onto an arm of the couch, nose pointed toward the pizza.

"Is anything left to prepare?" Ray asked.

"Not unless you require a salad or vegetables."

"You got George's favorite." She grinned. "And a supreme pizza has plenty of vegetables." She took a seat next to Max.

The scant scattering of peppers, onions, and tomatoes on the pizza was...*plenty*? And she'd mentioned missing meals when she was working.

Hmm. Would he be coaxing her into eating healthier? He poured the wine before sitting beside her. "What do *you* prefer on your pizzas?"

"Mmm, it varies, depending on what I feel like at the time." She pulled off a slice, swiping a finger through the string of cheese.

He took his own slice and handed her the shaker of parmesan cheese he'd found in the fridge. "In that case, what don't you like?"

"I know it's a controversial topic, but"—she pointed at him sternly—"fruit does not belong on a pizza."

Fruit? Ah. "No Hawaiian style. Understood. How about white sauce?"

"Mmm, once in a while. There's a spot near the driveway where I pick chanterelle mushrooms—and they're awesome on white pizza." She grinned. "What about you?"

There were so many dishes he could make with fresh chanterelles. "I'll have to cook for you during mushroom season." He took a bite of pizza, savoring the tang of tomato sauce and the smoothness of the mozzarella. "Be warned. I do enjoy an occasional Hawaiian pizza."

She hissed. "Sacrilege. You truly are evil."

"Mmm, it appears we will be role-playing in the future." At her confused expression, he added, "The devil visits a convent and finds a virtuous, virginal nun."

She sputtered delightfully as her face turned pink. "That is so wrong."

And she was enchanting. He took a sip of the deep red Barbera. Medium bodied and dry with a touch of fruit. Very nice and went well with the complexity of the supreme pizza. "So what movie would you like to watch?"

When she didn't answer immediately, he wandered over to the bookcases along one wall, filled with books and DVDs. One section for nonfiction, especially wood crafting books. In the fiction and movies were a variety of genres: mysteries, science-fiction and fantasy, historical romance, comedies, and... "Horror?"

"I love it—well, some. Not the psychopath slasher bloodbaths. But monster—uh, creature horror is awesome. *Godzilla*, *Alien*, *King Kong*. Oh, and *Tremors*—so good."

He had to laugh at her enthusiasm. And that their interests overlapped rather nicely. "Well then, have you tried foreign monster flicks?"

"No. I don't think I've seen hardly any."

"Then, do you want to try a South Korean one called *The Host*?"

Two hours later, they were lying stretched out on the oversized sectional with her tucked in front of him. Curvy woman in a soft cotton T-shirt. Smooth, warm skin. He'd lost track of the movie a time or two.

After the explosions and flames, new beginnings, and the scrolling credits, he moved her hair away from her neck and nibbled beneath her ear.

When she shivered, he smiled and cupped her breast. The nipple bunched to a peak against his palm. "*Ma chérie*, take me to your bed."

True to her open nature, she didn't even try to protest. "Yes."

CHAPTER TWELVE

At the foot of the stairs, Ray hesitated. She wanted the bathroom. And to brush her teeth and... "I need a few, um, minutes."

"Of course." Drake tugged her hair with a smile. "Go. I'll get my bag from the car, clean up in the guest bath, and lock up the house."

Theodore would've been annoyed she had spoiled the mood. She bit her lip and eyed Drake. Was he displeased or—

"How is your leg?"

"Fine, it's fine."

"In that case, when I get upstairs, I will expect you on the bed. On your knees. With the shirt gone and your hands behind your back so I can enjoy the sight of your breasts." With a hand on her back, he nudged her forward. "Off you go."

Just as well he didn't expect a response from her; her mind had gone blank.

As she climbed the stairs, she felt his gaze. By the time she reached the top, her whole body simmered. Ready to boil over the minute he touched her.

After visiting the bathroom, she entered the bedroom and

frowned. *Way too much light.* She turned the dimmer switch to set the chandelier lights to a faint glow.

Way too quiet too. Must have music. But what if he wanted to pick it? Doms did, right? Only, what if he didn't? *I like music, covering up...sounds.*

Biting her lip, she set the sound system to play a dark, sensual playlist she'd copped from a friend last winter...and never played it for Theodore. He made fun of her when she tried to add romantic touches to their bedroom times.

Would Drake also think she was stupid?

She clenched her jaw. If he did, it'd be a red flag—like the ones she should have caught with Theodore.

Shaking off the memories, she looked around the room. Now what?

Obey the Dom's directions. Merely the memory of his confident orders erased every worry from her head.

Kneeling in the center of the bed, she pulled off the T-shirt. As cool air flowed over her bare breasts, she swallowed hard and laced her fingers together behind herself. The position arched her back and lifted her breasts.

Holy kraken. Tingles of anticipation ran over her skin...and then she heard a sound.

Her head jerked up.

He was already here, leaning against the doorframe, arms crossed in a deceptively lazy posture. A five o'clock beard shadow softened the lines of his goatee and hard jaw. His unbuttoned shirt exposed the solidly packed muscle of his chest. As he looked at her, black eyes filled with masculine appreciation. "Very nice, *bébé.*"

Turning, he said, "You'll have to wait. Sorry, Max," and closed the door. In stocking feet, he silently crossed the room and set a leather bag at the foot of the bed. After putting his phone and a condom on the nightstand, he sat facing her on the bed. When she started to move, he said, so very softly, "Stay still for me."

A shiver ran through her.

He tilted his head, obviously listening to the music. "Quite suitable for tonight."

She released the breath she'd been holding.

He smiled and, with no urgency whatsoever, leaned forward and kissed her. His lips coaxed hers to open, sweetly seductive rather than demanding.

The temperature in the room grew warmer.

Straightening, he smiled into her eyes and ran a finger over her lower lip, her chin, down her throat and between her breasts. "I do like you naked."

Her breathing stuttered to a halt as her nipples tightened to urgent peaks.

As if hearing her wish, he cupped one breast, weighing it in his palm. "We will take a moment to talk first. We both want sex, *oui?*"

She nodded.

"Out loud, please."

"Yes." No, she wasn't a child to whisper—even if her mouth was dry. She spoke louder. "Yes. Absolutely."

The laugh lines beside his eyes crinkled. "Firm and enthusiastic. Perfect. Next—I expect to be dominant in the bedroom." His smile reached his lips. "And often at other times."

He was telling her what he wanted—and carefully, so she didn't feel railroaded. In fact, her anxiety settled, leaving only excitement behind. "I'm in."

"Perfect. Tonight, you will have some choices and can say yes or no. Later, other nights, those choices will go away...except for a safeword."

No choices. Quivers of anticipation ran through her.

His hand moved to her other breast, squeezed gently. "Tonight, no physical bondage. You aren't ready for it." He studied her, lips slightly pursed in thought. "Perhaps a touch of anal play—although I will not take you there. Yet."

Oh yikes. Heat and worry fizzled in her blood.

"Light pain—nothing like your paddling. Some toys and—" When she glanced at her nightstand, his grin flashed.

When he leaned forward and opened the drawer, embarrassment scalded her face.

"I have some in my bag, but for now, we'll use yours, and I will learn what pleases you." His eyes were purely wicked as he added, "Later, we can explore others."

Pushing a pillow out of the way, he pulled out her toys and lined them up. His eyebrows rose—because she had a *lot*

"I, uh, like variety." Her voice sounded as if it would crack any moment.

His deep laugh made her skin tingle. "*Ma petite Ray*, no matter how tempting to use all of these tonight, you wouldn't be able to walk tomorrow." Planting a quick kiss on her lips, he caressed her breasts.

When he studied the way-oversized dildo, she shook her head quickly. "No, not Beast. The online description lied to me; he's too big. I prefer Phil."

"Beast? Phil?" His lips quirked. "Which one is Phil?"

Twisting around to face the head of the bed, she pointed to the dark purple dildo. "Phil."

"Old boyfriend?"

"Short for Fill-Me-Up."

Gods, she loved his laugh.

"Do they all have labels?" He pointed to each in the line, and she dutifully named them.

The dildos—Bilbo, Pinky, Bruiser. Thumper and Bugs, the rabbits. Donald was a vibrating duck. Warlock, a wand.

By the end, he was laughing hard—and she knew she was bright red.

"*Non, non, chérie.*" He cupped her cheek and kissed her. "Your imagination is a treat. Sex—with and without toys—is normal, no matter what idiocy prudish people spout."

Of course, she agreed... Only having someone studying her very intimate belongings was as mortifying as having him look at her intimate parts.

How would it feel if he actually used her toys on her. *Ooooh.* Everything inside her trembled.

"All charged, ready for use?" A corner of his mouth tilted up. "Say *yes, Sir*—or *no, Sir* like an obedient submissive. For the rest of the night, disrespect will result in punishment, which I'll enjoy. You...might not."

The open pleasure in his caressing voice made her voice come out hoarse. "Yes. Sir."

"*Très bien.*" He rose and unzipped the leather bag. The dim light shadowed his face—and made it impossible to tell what was in the bag. "I do have some things to...use...on you."

She leaned forward, trying to see what was in the bag.

His brows drew together. "*Zut*, you are more curious than your cat. Easy enough to remedy." He set a black blindfold over her eyes and adjusted the Velcro fastening to fit it securely.

Everything went dark. Her hands rose instinctively—and were caught in an unbreakable grip.

"*Ma chérie*, you will use the usual safeword tonight. Red for stop, yellow to pause and talk, green to continue. Have we reached red?"

She swallowed, feeling her hands quaking in his. "No, not red." She pulled in a breath for honesty. "Green, please, Sir."

"So brave." He held her face between his hands and kissed her, long and slow.

"I want you to kneel up and hold onto the top of the headboard." Since she couldn't see, he helped her turn and guided her hand up past the tufted leather to the wood frame. It was fairly high, leaving her up on her knees close to one side of the bed.

"Now don't let go, *bébé*."

Oh, oh, why did that sound ominous?

She strained to hear what he was doing. The zip of something

—his jeans? Or the toybag? Then his warm hands closed over her breasts, massaging, tugging on the nipples, sending streams of pleasure through her. With her vision gone, everything seemed more sensitive—especially, her body.

"Pretty little breasts—and so fun to touch," he murmured. And then something bit into her right nipple, like cold, tiny teeth, and she yelped in shock.

He chuckled, dark and low, and a second later, her left nipple was attacked, no...*clamped*. Nipple clamps.

Ow, ow, ow. She had to force herself not to grab the damn things and—

His hands landed on hers, preventing her from releasing the headboard. "Breathe slow and deep until the pain decreases."

But, but, but. She sucked in several breaths, hard and fast—and got a stinging slap on her bottom.

"Try again, Aralia," he chided, voice quiet. Not at all upset. "Slow and deep."

She hated—*hated*—to admit she'd deserved the swat. Carefully, she pulled in a breath, held it, took her time releasing. Another. Another.

"There now. Is the pain bearable?" He stroked a slow hand down her back, much as she did when Max got nervous.

The pain *was* better, although the tingling ache sure wouldn't let her forget something was pinching her nipples. "Yes," she whispered.

He tugged on one clamp and made her hiss, and then he patted her bottom. "Keep breathing."

Why did it make her stomach quiver to know he was willing to hurt her, to know he'd comfort her even as he made her obey.

He was still stroking her back, the calluses on his warm palm slightly abrasive.

Tingles followed the movement as his hand continued, down over her stinging bottom. Down the backs of her thighs. Back to her ass to massage the cheeks as if demonstrating he could and would touch every part of her body.

"Spread your legs farther apart." One hand pushed on the inside of her thigh, and she edged her knees outward.

Which let his whole hand cup her wet pussy. Let him tease her clit—right where she was aching for his touch. He pressed a finger, then two inside her, and her hips wiggled involuntarily at the shocking zing of pleasure.

He pressed one cheek outward, and his finger rimmed her. *Whoa, there, really?* Only, he'd said something about anal.

But she didn't have any of *those* toys. Maybe he'd just—

"You may call this one *backdoor bob* and keep it for your own."

Cold, slick gel dripped onto her back hole. He circled the rim, wakening *sooo* many nerves, and then something was pushed firmly inside. *Not huge, thank you, Elder Gods*, but it felt so, so weird. Wrong and embarrassing—yet those nerves jangled fiercely.

When she whined, he patted her butt. "Now, let go of the headboard and lie down on your back, *ma chérie*."

She scooted to the center of the mattress and onto her back. The quilt was cool against her overheated skin. Her breasts felt alien with clamps clinging obstinately to her nipples. She bumped one with her still half-closed hand.

Drake made a tsking sound low in his throat, took her hands, and massaged them. "You held onto the headboard rather tightly, *bébé*."

Her hands ached, her stiff fingers twitched when she tried to straighten them.

"So, so, I will give you something else to cling to." And the amusement in his tone was a warning. Not being able to see his face was really a handicap.

He pulled her knees up so her feet were wide apart and flat on the mattress, then used her hands to push her thighs apart. "Don't move your hands from where I've put them."

He wanted her to...to hold *herself* open?

Ah, Drake thought, he did love forcing a submissive to participate in her own submission.

Her fingers trembled under his as he held her hands in place. Anticipation or fear?

Sitting beside her, he placed one hand between her breasts, enjoying the accelerated thudding of her heart.

Hmm. Was she too worried?

He paused to caress her face...and she rubbed her cheek against his palm.

All right then. The clamps looked lovely, darkening her pink nipples. He fondled her prettily plump breasts to make them swell, to make the clamps tighter.

Such charming squeaking sounds she made.

Now what would work well with the anal plug? Ah, how could he resist using Bilbo the dildo? It was fairly slim. He'd use it first and upsize to his thicker dick.

After setting the dildo beside her hip, he stretched out on the bed, his shoulders between her knees. Propping himself up on one elbow, he used his free hand to tease her smooth pussy.

She was nicely slick, and her clit was already poking out from beneath the hood. Leaning against her left thigh, he slowly drew his finger around the ball of nerves, making a mental note of what pressures and locations made her muscles tighten, her breathing falter.

Soon, she was making adorable whining sounds...that abruptly stopped.

He halted and studied her face.

Her lips were pressed together, the muscles in her jaws locked tight. Not letting any sounds escape.

This little one came with some interesting baggage, didn't she? He moved her hands, letting her legs down, and lay down beside her. Propping his head up on a hand, he pulled off her blindfold so he could see her eyes. His fingers curled around her left breast gave him a way to track her breathing and feel her heart thumping. "Now *bébé*, tell me why you don't wish to make any noise."

Her chest stopped moving. Her gaze didn't meet his. "I...just... It doesn't seem right to make sounds."

Perhaps a slice of the truth, not the entire pie. Odd, she was most straightforward normally. Was this related to her bad experience? If so, it would be best to deal with it before the problem grew. "Aralia..." How could he say this? "Do the sounds you make bring back bad memories?"

Under his hand, her body tensed. Then she sighed. "Yes. Sometimes it sounds too much like whimpering...and a bad time. And I guess I worry about annoying you if I make noise."

His jaw clenched against the need to swear. If those *bâtards* who abused her were within his reach, he would introduce them to *real* pain.

"I understand." He took a moment to cool his rage, then ran his hand down her skin in long comforting strokes over her stomach—and felt the tension easing from her body.

It was a delight when she found the courage to meet his gaze again.

Smiling, he traced a finger over her lips. "So. Hmm. Silence isn't a problem although your jaw might get sore. I also like to hear moaning, whimpering, whining, cursing, screaming, begging, or even yelling."

Under his finger, her mouth tilted up. "You're saying anything works?"

"*Oui*. Unless I hear you giving orders, in which case, I'll find a way to get different sounds from you."

The threat sped up her heartrate, flushed her cheeks, and dilated her pupils.

So very submissive.

"However, tonight, I'll take this worry about noise away. The only sound you are allowed to make—aside from your safeword—is 'yes.' It can be as soft or loud as you wish, but I must hear the word. Or else. Now what sound will you make?"

She swallowed. "Yes."

"Good." He ran his finger around her lips again. "Since you interrupted my play, you pay the penalty." He rose. "Let's see how well you can use that mouth."

Oh gods. Ray felt her breathing hitch. Why did the thought of giving him a blowjob make her totally aroused? Then again, this was hitting all her hot points.

Across the room, Drake pushed the ottoman to one side, took a seat, and sprawled in the lounge chair like an indolent king. When he unzipped and opened his jeans, his cock rose hard and proud from a nest of trimmed black hair. "Kneel between my legs, *ma chérie.*"

She slid out of the bed. Once in front of him, she went to her knees—and his hard thighs closed on her shoulders, trapping her.

And everything inside her melted.

Her hand closed around his shaft...and she froze. *What if I do stuff he doesn't like? Or he's bored?*

"So many worries." Making a dark sound in his throat, he gripped her hair with one hand. Not hurting her, but oh, so firmly. "Lick up and down. Like an ice cream cone where the very top is the best and the part under the glans is pure chocolate."

She snorted at the thought—and relaxed. *I can do this.* Her tongue circled the underside of the head, flicking around it. And the slit at the top had a drop of salty precum for a reward almost as nice as his low *mmmm* of approval.

"Cup my balls in one hand—gently. Treat them like...mmm, oversensitive breasts before your monthly."

Oh, the Dom sure understood women. But—now she knew

exactly how to touch him. She fondled one heavy testicle, then the other, pausing to lick his erection in between.

"*C'est parfait.* Now wrap one hand around the base, take me in your mouth as far down as you can. Then up. Close your lips around me tightly."

He was so big. But having her hand there let her feel a bit in control—but only a bit. She bobbed her head, swirling her tongue around the spongy head on the upswing. Rubbing her tongue over the thick, bulging veins. Each breath brought her his musky, masculine scent.

She looked up at him. He was watching her, his dark eyes half-lidded in open enjoyment.

"Now suck as you go up and down." His grip in her hair tightened, pulling her down. His other hand closed over hers, moving her fingers in rhythm on his shaft. "*Très bien.* Harder now."

She got into the rhythm—and it was wonderful to not worry if she was doing it right. He had no problem telling her what to do. So nice.

"Now hum as you lift your head."

What? She stopped completely until he cleared his throat, setting her back on task.

Right, right. Lift and hum.

Oh, hey, she could feel the vibration she was giving him. And she almost laughed. *I'm a Ray-vibe.*

His low-throated growl of pleasure sent happiness straight through her.

And heat too. She was so wet. Pressing her thighs together, she squirmed a little.

He laughed. "*Oui,* you have paid your penalty, and I want my own taste." He tugged her hair, lifting her head. Once free of her mouth, he rose and closed his jeans. Lifting her to her feet, he laid her onto the bed with her butt close to the side of the mattress instead of in the center.

She lifted her ass up slightly—because...*plug.*

"Do you remember where your hands go?"

Feet flat, toes curling over the edge, thighs held open with her hands.

"Very good." To her shock, he pulled the ottoman over and sat on it. Right where he could see—and touch—her pussy. "Ah, you did enjoy your penalty, didn't you?"

He just *had* to notice she was soaked.

"That makes this easy." He picked up one of the toys—Bilbo—and without a pause, opened her folds, and firmly slid it in.

"Aaaah."

"Wrong sound. What is the only sound you are permitted tonight?" He made a tsking sound and slapped her puffy mound lightly.

Her pussy stung from his hand—and *eeeks*, she'd almost come right then. Her pulse was roaring in her ears, and what had he said? *Oh. Right.* "Yes."

"*Oui*." His teeth flashed white, set off by the dark beard and tanned skin. "Next mistake, I will hit harder...and lower."

Her eyes widened. Like...right over her clit? *No, no, no.*

He was still smiling as he pushed her hands outward, forcing her to open her thighs more widely. Then he bent, and his mouth was right *there*. His tongue traced circles around her clit and over the top, sending pleasure bursting through her.

Teasing, circling, flicking. Until all of her focus was on his mouth.

And then he started moving Bilbo—in and out, slow and steady in a contrast to the erratic hard and soft, fast and slow rhythm of his tongue..

She came, all in a rush, pushed right off the cliff with incomparable skill. Waves of pleasure shook her—and the dildo firmly moving in and out, made it last and last.

When her panting and her speeding heart slowed, she moved her hands, reaching down for him. "You didn't come before. Your turn."

The corners of his eyes crinkled. His smile was wicked. "*Ma chérie*, you do not give me directions in bed." He slapped her pussy—harder this time.

"Eeek!" The bright pain was shocking, even as her insides convulsed with another spasm of pleasure.

Bending his head, he tongued right over her stinging clit.

"You—" *Don't talk*. Her gaze met his black eyes. "Um, yes."

How could he laugh even while he was using his tongue in such a way?

When he started pulling on both the anal plug and the dildo, she came again, even harder.

Drake watched the little submissive go limp after her second orgasm. Perfectly delightful. "Over you go now, *bébé*."

After removing Bilbo, he rolled her over, onto hands and knees, then positioned her so her knees were near the side of the bed. Yes, this was a perfectly usable height.

Her creamy-white ass cheeks almost glowed in the dim light of the room, and he took a moment to massage them.

Her whimper broke off into a whispered, "Yes, yes." Trying so hard to obey.

She tugged on his heart in a way he hadn't felt before. Bending, he pressed light kisses from her neck down her spine.

And reached around to fondle her breasts. Time for the clamps to go. Gently, he removed one, then the other, and the evil side of his dominance savored her squeaks as circulation was restored to the abused nipples.

She was trying to lean on her shoulder to free her hands—but his hands were there first. He ruthlessly massaged her tender breasts.

More squeaks sounded before she remembered and hissed a "Yessss." He could almost hear the added, "You bastard," she had enough control to keep from saying.

"You are being a very good girl." She couldn't see his grin, but from the tiny growl she gave, she probably heard it in his voice.

He hadn't had so much fun in years.

And it was time to provoke some more squeaks and growls. Opening his jeans, he released his rigid, increasingly demanding cock and rolled on a condom.

On his phone, he tapped the anal plug remote app and set it to a pattern of building and declining intensity.

As the buzzing started and ramped up, she barely managed to change her yelp to a yes. Her hips wiggled as if giving him a target, or so his cock apparently thought.

He picked up the small wand from the toy lineup at the head of the bed and set it beside her right knee.

After sliding his shaft along her pussy, he set himself at the threshold and entered her without stopping, slow enough she could accommodate his size.

She was hot, her cunt giving tiny convulsions around him as she inhaled sharply, her head tipping up.

With the anal plug in her, she was very tight—and the vibrations through the thin membrane added to his pleasure.

Sheathed completely, he kneaded her ass cheeks. "Still green, Aralia?"

He could see her shoulders rise and fall with her fast breathing. After a moment, she nodded, then laughed. "Yes."

He grinned at her quirky sense of humor, pulled almost out, and filled her again. Out, in, adding a circular motion now and then for fun. She'd come twice already. One more.

As he moved into deep driving thrusts, he picked up the wand, flicked it on. Reaching around her, he set the big head a few inches above her clit.

She let out a keening cry, her muscles going rigid. And within a few more thrusts, she was coming. He let her recover for a moment, slowing his thrusts also.

And then speeded up and applied the wand on one side, then

the other, of her clit. She came again, wailing loudly. Well, he wouldn't punish her this time.

There was nothing like the feeling of a woman's cunt convulsing around a rigid dick.

One last time with the wand directly on top.

Oh, oh, oh. Every nerve in Ray's body seemed to be focused in one place. And she was coming again, pleasure raging through her—again! It didn't stop, and it was too much. She could hear the pleas coming from her. Could hear the satisfaction in his voice. "Take a little more, for me." And her back arched as another wave ran through her, a feeling like she'd never felt before,

"There, you should sleep well tonight, *bébé*," he murmured. The torturous, horrible, wonderful wand was gone, and she was slumping.

His hands gripped her hips hard, still thick and hot inside her. As he set up a driving rhythm, her insides kept spasming in tiny explosions of pleasure around him.

His hands tightened as he sheathed himself even deeper inside her and held there with a low growling, "mmmph," of satisfaction.

Everything inside her echoed that satisfaction.

She'd given herself into his care, and he pushed her past what she thought she could take, pushed her into pure sensual torture, forced pleasure on her. Forced her to come.

There was nothing she could say to express the pure contentment and the happiness welling inside her.

Smiling, he gripped her hips firmly. His dick was swollen and hard, pulsing with brutal need as he released his control.

And then, the pleasure was exploding inside him, sizzling from his spine, through his balls, and out his shaft.

As he jerked with the last few tremors inside her, he heard the happiness in her whisper. "Yes, yes, yes."

The next morning, Drake felt alive and...happy. Yes, that was the word. Happier than he'd felt in a long time. He knew why, of course.

The reason was the adorable woman who was now trudging into the kitchen in a fluffy bathrobe. Despite a shower that left her hair wet, she still didn't appear fully awake.

Her lips were still swollen from his kisses and... The memory of the magnificent blowjob caused his dick to thicken, despite all its work last night. It was a wonder he wasn't raw.

He wasn't the only one, considering how gingerly Ray was moving.

A fine night indeed.

"Good morning, *ma chérie*." He pulled her against him, all soft woman enclosed in fluffy fabric. No slinky silk for this one, and he liked her all the better for it. Washington was cool in the mornings, and she obviously preferred comfort over looking sexy.

"Morning."

Smiling, he bent to kiss her. "I made coffee."

"You're my hero...although waking a person up in the middle of the night might mean you're really a villain." Her voice was husky, partly from sleep, possibly a bit strained from the screaming she'd done when he'd gotten her off during round two. Admittedly, she hadn't been fully awake when he began.

"Now, now, *bébé*. You seemed to be enjoying yourself. Especially when you climbed on top."

"You mean when you pulled me on top." Her lips twitched as if she was trying not to smile. "And held my hips to make me move the way you wanted."

"*Zut*, I'm no villain." He bent his head and nibbled on the sweet curve between her neck and shoulder and felt her soften in his arms. "Just a Dominant."

"*Just*, my ass," she said under her breath, making him laugh.

He handed her a cup, waiting to release it until he knew her grip was secure. "I have a meeting in Seattle and must leave soon."

"But it's Sunday."

"It is. I often work on weekends." Perhaps it was time for a better balance in his life. "Are you working in your shop today?"

"Sure." She doctored her coffee and took a sip. "Mmmm." He could almost see her brain cells coming online. "I'm ready to gloss the tantric chair and have a couple of other commissions to work on. And I need new artsy projects for the stores and galleries who carry my work."

"All on Bainbridge?"

"Only the downtown gallery here. I also have a contract with places in Pioneer Square, Fremont, and Pike Place." She grinned. "The gallery sales let me create without worrying about what a client wants. And provide an additional income stream."

Such an intriguing woman. She might call herself flighty, but he admired how she used her exceptional self-knowledge in financially inspired ways. In her case, "flighty" went hand-in-hand with brilliant.

"When you stay over with me in Seattle, I'd like to see your Pike Place outlet. My condo is only a block or so away." He ran his hand through her damp hair to untangle the locks. Each strand would pop back into a curl. Quite mesmerizing.

"I thought you lived here on Bainbridge."

He guided her over to the kitchen table where he'd left his coffee. "George talked me into buying a house here last year. I kept the city condo for late nights when the ferry isn't running or when I need to be closer to work. I'd like you to stay with me there this weekend during the convention."

"You have a condo in Seattle." She looked to one side, a line furrowing between her brows. "It shouldn't be a surprise to realize I don't really know you."

"We understand much about each other as a result of the scenes and sex. But our backgrounds and all the noise in our current lives—those things we don't know." He kissed away the worry line on her forehead. "There is time."

He held a chair for her to sit and joined her at the table.

There was a thud, and Max padded into the room, tail high. Nose up, apparently checking for breakfast nibbles. Drake grinned. The former stray was one pampered cat.

Leaning back in his chair, he sipped the full-bodied coffee. Nice. Ray's kitchen had three varieties of coffee as well as an espresso maker. All hers since George had preferred tea.

"You have good taste in coffee." He held his cup up in a toast. "Obviously we were meant to be together."

She actually giggled. "We're fated mates...because of our coffee preferences?" Picking her cat up, she whispered in the furry ear, "I think Master Drake has gone off his meds."

Drake tsked. "I compliment you, and you imply I'm insane? Appalling manners, *mon petit chou*."

He did enjoy hearing her laugh.

Still smiling, she tilted her head. "I've been wondering. If you started Chains years ago, then you've been in the States a long time, but you still have an accent and..."

"Ah. You are observant." He rubbed a finger over his goatee. "When my parents were killed in Marseille..." He still remembered his cousin's face, the way her voice broke when she said *they're all dead*. "...I was a teen, and my mother's brother brought me here and adopted me. Gave me his name—Dragomir."

The name had meant safety to Drake. A way of cutting ties with the half of his family in the mob.

"I'm sorry." Her gaze was soft, and her hand covered his. "I didn't mean to bring back bad memories."

He knew his voice had been even, unemotional. That she could read him so well was...interesting. "It was long ago. I tried to lose my accent, become all American. When my new high school friends decided Dragomir was another way of saying dragon—it isn't—and male dragons are drakes, I ended up with a new name. And I welcomed it."

He shook his head. "But... Eventually, my uncle took me back to France to see my mother's family." They said his mother had been appalled when she learned Papa was in the mob—but she loved him and cut ties with her family to keep them safe. "Hearing my language again, seeing family, I realized I didn't want to become wholly American. So I visit once or twice a year and resurrect my accent; if words slip in, I enjoy them. And my uncle has been happy to speak his birth language as well."

Setting the cat on her chair, she rose and gave Drake a gentle hug. "Dragomir is a great name. But...is it French?"

"*Non*, Romanian. Papa was Corsican. My mother was Romanian, Latino, and probably a few other things."

"Aha, that's why the dark hair and eyes." She grinned. "When I first saw you, I thought you looked like a pirate out of South America. Only then, you started talking and made one of those French expressions"—she pursed her lips in a way that made him laugh—"and so much for you being Latino."

A pirate, hmm? They might have to explore roleplay.

"I bet your accent is really popular with your amorous interests." She blinked, obviously realizing what she'd said, and pink colored her cheeks.

Would he ever be able to anticipate the way her mind worked? He barely smothered a laugh. "That may be true. Would you be among those amorous interests who enjoy a French accent?"

The pink deepened. "*Maaaybe*."

"In that case, *Chaque matin est plus beau avec toi*." Smiling at her frown, he translated, "Every morning is more beautiful with you."

He took her hand in his. "*Je me sens vivante à tes côtés.* I feel alive beside you." He kissed her palm. "*Je suis fou de toi.* I'm crazy about you."

"You...you shouldn't be allowed to say things like that." She pulled her hand from his, her eyes wide, pupils dilated. So adorable in her confused response. Picking Max up, she sat down in the chair, holding the cat on her lap as if he'd provide a defense. "Bad Dom."

Perhaps the cat did provide an adequate defense, given that he had an overwhelming urge to pull her into his arms. No, to take her right back to bed.

Bad Dom indeed.

"So. What with my meetings today and early Monday, I won't be back on Bainbridge until tomorrow night." Perhaps this was better. He wouldn't keep his hands off her, and she was obviously tender. "I'd like to see you tomorrow evening. Unless you are becoming bored."

Although she snorted, her gaze was on Max as she stroked the cat into happy purrs. "It worries me how very unboring you are. How interesting you are. It doesn't happen often, but I can get, almost obsessed, in a way." She bit her lip.

So sweet. He moved, going down on his haunches beside her legs. "Aralia, look at me."

Her blue-green eyes were beautiful. And worried.

"New lovers are often obsessed with each other—and you might be more susceptible because you focus intensely. A bit of obsession isn't unhealthy as long as you evaluate your lover to ensure they are a wise choice. Just as you'd check a lake for rocks before diving in. *Oui?*"

Her brows drew together. "You...obsess too?"

"You have been much on my mind. And at the moment, I would like nothing more than to spend the day with you, preferably with several of those hours in bed and several hours to simply talk and get to know you."

She must have heard the sincerity in his words. Her frown eased, then reappeared. "You're right. In the past, I didn't take time to...evaluate...before jumping."

"And you did with me?"

The way a corner of her mouth tipped up told him the answer before she spoke. "I asked Mac and Hope about you." She snickered. "You get excellent reviews, Master Drake."

"As I should." Rising, he kissed her lightly and ran a hand over Max's soft fur. "I must leave, or I'll miss the ferry. Tomorrow night?"

"Yes. Yes, I'd like to see you."

"Then you shall." He picked up her phone from the table where it was charging, held it out for her thumb to unlock, then went into the clock app. "I should arrive around seven, so I'll set your alarm for six to give you time to finish in your shop and clean up." He raised his eyebrows, chuckled at her stunned expression, then hit SAVE.

Did she think he wouldn't remember what she'd told him? How she needed to set alarms because she got lost in her work? But she often forgot to set an alarm. As fast as her brain worked, as creative as she was, of course trivial matters got missed.

As it happened, he was excellent with details.

He kissed her again. "As a Dominant, it makes me happy to help set your day in order. You may tell me—tomorrow—if it bothers you."

"Hmm." She bit her lip. "I'll think about it."

It was all he asked. Although he tried to respect boundaries, he also had to be himself—and he enjoyed making order out of chaos and fixing things.

Her personality didn't need to be fixed, not at all. But he could help to ensure minor details didn't trip her up.

With luck, she'd see the difference.

With even more luck, she'd share her thoughts on the subject.

He'd never met anyone so fun to talk with. Especially when she was passionate about a subject.

The doorbell rang as Drake retrieved his bag from the great room.

A woman's voice came from the entry. "Hey, I got your email. What's up? I only have a few minutes before I need to be in line for the ferry." There was a disgusted sound. "Then I have to study all the way over for the labor and delivery exam."

"Poor baby." Ray laughed. "Oh, I made you a present. You should take it with you."

"Oh Ray, this is totally fire."

Curious, Drake walked into the entry.

A short, brunette woman was clasping something made of wood, colored dark blue with a mirror in the center. Hooks ran along the bottom. Ah, an entryway organizer.

"Oh, fuck, I'm dead; it's so perfect. But I can't take it—"

"Marisol, you can and will. You and your mom used to pet-sit for George, and now I have Max, so more kitty sitting will happen. This is just a thank you. And you need a place to hang your stethoscope and car keys, right?"

"Yes!" The young women grinned. "I love it. And—" Her eyes went wide when she spotted him. Her voice went high. "*Sheeeeeesh*. Um—hi?"

Drake chuckled and moved forward. "Good morning." He turned. "*Mon cœur*, I must run, or I will miss the ferry." Ignoring the young woman's presence, he molded Ray against him and took a kiss that would last him a couple of days. "Monday. Obey your alarm."

The way she'd sagged against him was delightful. "Right, Sir." Recovering slightly, she stepped back, narrowed her eyes. "We'll talk."

"*Oui*." He lifted her chin, kissed her again, and headed out.

Behind him, he heard Marisol squeal. "That's a Dom. Yo, baby, he is the GOAT! Way more...*more*...than that Blaize guy. I want one. I went to the campus group and—"

As he got into his car, he was grinning, imagining the look on Ray's face.

And already looking forward to seeing her tomorrow night.

CHAPTER THIRTEEN

Who are you and what have you done with Ray Lanigan? Ray gazed at herself in the window of the hotel. *A BDSM convention. Seriously, woman?*

Pulling her wheeled carry-on, she walked into the hotel. Signs for FetishFest pointed the way to the convention registration. The large room had small tables scattered in the center with registration tables against the back wall.

Ray selected the one labeled: *Last names starting with J-K-L* and lined up behind two others.

What a week. Somehow, her life had been completely overturned. *Is this what wood feels like when I carve it into something different? From a wood slab to a curvy coffee table?*

She'd gone from ending a relationship with Theodore, being so very lonely—and now, she had new and old friends...and Drake.

Especially Drake.

Since her leg injury at Bloedel Gardens last weekend, they'd been together almost every night. And texting off and on during the day.

Thank gods for texting, or she'd never have finished the presentation paddles. Master Drake could completely derail her thoughts with his dark voice and his too-sexy-for-words French accent. Let alone his body... So finely sculpted with rippling muscles *everywhere*. Wide, strong shoulders tapering to a ridged abdomen. The man was simply drool-worthy.

Ray noticed the line had moved forward and shuffled ahead a few steps.

So...I'm dating and sleeping with a Dom. Yeah, mama, he was definitely dominant. And he noticed every single time she lost focus on what was going on. Like last night when they were cooking and she got mesmerized by the bubbling sauce. Usually it would mean stuff got burned. But instead, his saying her name pulled her back into the real world—and to what she was supposed to be doing. His white teeth had flashed in a grin, and he'd swatted her on the ass, just hard enough to sting. "*Stay on task,* ma petite *Ray.*" He'd probably been able to see the effect of the swat. His voice had dropped to a smoky murmur. "*I will reward you suitably if you keep your mind on cooking.*"

She sighed. He'd worried she might not like him being a Dom outside the bedroom. But she sure couldn't find anything to complain about. The "rewards" were amazing.

Like when he'd said, "*You were such a good girl making supper. You deserve to come again.*"

And now, every time she thought of him and his hands, his mouth, his...ahem, endowments...she had such a *craving*. Truly the Dom should come with a label—*WARNING: Dominant. Risk of overdose and addiction.*

"Hello." A woman's voice broke into her thoughts.

Ray blinked. Her turn at the reception desk. *Oops.* "Sorry. Daydreaming."

"Understandable. Waiting in lines is boring." The middle-aged brunette volunteer smiled. "Welcome to FetishFest. Can I have your name and an ID, please?"

"Aralia Lanigan." Ray dug her driver's license out of her mini backpack.

The woman held the card down for her teammate at the laptop to enter, then handed it back.

Red-haired, freckled, with numerous piercings, the teammate grinned. "Got it. All checked-in."

Meanwhile the brunette woman searched a box on the table and pulled out an envelope with Ray's name. She handed it over along with a swag bag.

When Ray snorted, the two volunteers looked startled.

"Sorry. It just seemed funny—I helped fill these." Ray held up the bag. "And I'll be back here in"—she glanced at her phone—"yikes, all too soon. To work the next registration shift."

"Oooh, another volunteering idiot like us." The redhead laughed. "Go get oriented before we chain you to a desk."

"Good plan."

Ray settled at a round table to get organized. The envelope held the conference program, an extra information booklet, a pamphlet with a map of the hotel, and her name badge lanyard showing RAY with her preferred pronouns, she/her.

A shame she didn't have a cool scene name.

She put on the lanyard. The swag bag went into her carry-on and the booklet into her mini backpack.

Drake had booked a hotel suite here for them and his two San Francisco friends. They'd all stay at his condo at night, but he wanted a room onsite to unwind, clean up, and change clothes during the day and for the dungeon.

Even better, she could leave her carry-on there. Swinging by the hotel registration desk, she gave her name and got a key.

No one was in the suite. After cleaning up, she headed back downstairs. Darn it, she'd hoped for enough time to walk around but *nooo*. Stupid ferry times.

"Ray!" At a round table, Hope jumped up and pulled Ray in for a bouncy hug.

Like Ray, Hope had dressed in the recommended volunteer attire of jeans and a light-colored polo shirt.

Weren't button-down shirts the service industry choice in the past. When had polo shirts become the standard? She started to get out her phone for googling, but Hope's squeal interrupted the beginning of squirrel brain.

"This is going to be so much fun!"

Ray had to laugh at all the enthusiasm. "What part—the reception table or the weekend?"

"All of it. Especially the dungeon."

The dungeon, right. Ray shifted her weight, then shoved her hands in her pockets. "Um, is it like Chains? The activities and everything?"

"Activities?" Hope's eyebrows lifted, then she smiled. "Ooooh, you mean like sex?"

Ray scowled. "Go ahead and shout the word for everyone to hear. But yes, it's what I mean."

"I guess you know not all clubs or conventions permit sex— aka penetration. Depends on the various state, county, city rules, and what the club wants to deal with. But!" Hope grinned. "You're going to have so much fun. Like Chains, sex is allowed in the con dungeon."

Oh...boy. Her heart started skipping inside her chest. Because Master Drake said she'd enjoy the scene he was planning, and she couldn't tell if she was terrified or thrilled. Even worse, he'd said it when they were having anal sex.

He wouldn't, would he? The thought sent a zing of heat through her.

"You'll have to go to some workshops—and then tell Drake what you're interested in trying." Hope pulled her lanyard ID out of her jeans pocket and put it on.

"Right. Sure. I'll do just that."

After a look at Ray's undoubtedly flushed face, Hope was laughing her ass off as she dragged her to the volunteer table.

Thank goodness for work.

Two hours passed quickly. They were assigned the letters: S-T-U at one of the reception tables. Thankfully, Hope had chosen to man the laptop...because *boring*. Ray had the more interesting job of collecting names, IDs, and handing out stuff.

Finished registering, an older Dominant nodded to her and strolled away.

Standing behind the box of swag, Ray watched him—and blinked at the vision entering the room. Whoa, the person looked almost like Prince in skintight blue pants, a yellow tank, and a vivid red-and-blue striped short jacket.

Ray glanced at her friend. "I've never felt quite so bland before."

"I know." Hope wrinkled her nose at her clothes. "We'll dress up tonight. Promise."

As a woman stopped at their table, Ray launched into her spiel. "Welcome to FetishFest. Might I have your name and an ID, please?"

"Justine Tepper." The woman was tall, tan, and nicely built with overly plump lips that didn't look quite natural. Why did she look familiar?

Justine handed over the ID.

Ray held the ID in Hope's view in case she needed to see the spelling...and noticed Hope had tensed slightly.

"Thanks, Ray, got it."

Justine turned. "Hope, how nice to see you here. How are you?"

Hope finished typing and looked up. "I'm good, thank you. Uh, have you met Ray? She's a new member at Chains. Ray, Justine is also a member."

Ray handed back the ID. "It's nice to meet you."

"Charmed, I'm sure." Smile gone, Justine gave Ray a chilly nod and returned her attention to Hope. "This looks to be a great convention, don't you think?" Her Boston accent reminded Ray of the Kennedys.

"It should be a lot of fun." Still looking uncomfortable, Hope tilted her head. "I think at least half the club will be here. And the workshops and classes look great."

When Hope stopped speaking, Ray set Justine's registration envelope and a swag bag on the table. "Here's everything you need. Have a great weekend."

Taking her stuff, the woman walked away.

"Brrr." Ray pretended to shiver. "I don't think she liked my looks or something."

"Or something is definitely the case." Hope stood and stretched her arms over her head, then frowned. "You didn't recognize her name?"

"What, is she famous or something?"

"Not outside the club." Hope turned and gave Ray a serious look. "She and Drake were dating for a while."

Oh, Justine was his ex? The one who wanted him to smother his dominance. She was certainly beautiful, but that didn't really matter when it came to ending things. And he'd said the breakup was ugly. Poor Master Drake.

Hope pursed her lips. "I bet she's heard Drake's interested in you."

"She sure did get cold fast. But I thought they broke up ages ago." No one was in line so Ray sat down and stretched out her legs. Her feet were throbbing.

"Mmmhmm, the breakup was last winter, but she's trying to win him back."

A sharp pang stabbed Ray under her ribs. Her voice came out hard. "She can't have him."

He's mine.

Only he wasn't really. They'd only known each other a month. Been seriously sleeping together for a week. They hadn't even talked about other people and monogamy—or what the community called fluid-bonding.

Does Drake consider me his girlfriend?

Ray rubbed her chest where an odd ache had taken hold. After this weekend, if nothing changed, they needed to talk about expectations. He'd probably call them boundaries.

"Hey, I'm pretty sure Drake wouldn't take her back—even if he wasn't involved with you." Hope patted Ray's arm.

"That's reassuring." Ray watched Justine move across the room, confidently greeting other people. She really was beautiful with her long dark hair and brown eyes. Like a quiet version of the actress Marisa Abela. No wonder Drake had dated her.

"You know, she always reminds me of Ms. Wendell." Hope put her short nose up in the air in a snooty manner. "Our English teacher in high school?"

Oh the memories. Ray laughed. "Like *I'm cool and know everything, and you're a moron?*"

"Exactly. Remember how you blasted her for making Chaz cry." Still standing, Hope put her hands on her hips and imitated Ray's voice. '*Miz Wendell. Seriously? Is crushing someone's spirit really an appropriate method of instruction? I don't think so. If you keep it up, our class will be calling and mailing complaints to the school board about your abuse of a student.*' Girl, the words are engraved in my head—and still rev me up."

"Huh, I barely remember what I said. I was just so...so *angry*. What I do remember is how I froze afterward, cuz I'd spoken for the whole class." Ray blew out a breath, feeling the sickness that'd risen in her gut back then. "But when I looked around, every single student was nodding. And the guys were saying stuff like *damn right.*"

"It was epic."

Ray had to force a smile. When Pa heard about it, he'd used other words—ones starting with *stupid* and ending with *damn fool drama*. "It could have ended badly. I swear, my brain turns right off when I see someone getting bullied. I have to jump in."

Hope slung an arm around Ray's shoulders. "Speaking as one of the victims, we all appreciated it. I was incredibly grateful for you back then."

"It went both ways." Her few friends had added the happiest moments to the hell known as teen years.

Especially since she'd lacked a mother at home after her mother had walked out. Only... Pa kept saying Ray was just like her mother, too emotional and all that. If Pa had been as critical of Mom as of Ray, maybe her mother had fled in hopes of salvaging whatever self-esteem she had left.

You could have taken me... Only Pa was always saying Mom had no skills, that she couldn't survive without him. Of course she'd left Ray where she had a home and food.

A ding-ding-ding rang in Ray's head, as if she'd scored a prize. Or figured something out. *Mom didn't leave because of me. She left because Pa was ripping her to pieces.*

"Volunteers, your time is up," a voice called.

A pretty, petite blonde and a redhead were holding hands as they approached.

"We're the next shift," the blonde said.

The redhead gave them a charming military salute. "Y'all are relieved from duty."

"Free at last," Hope crowed. "Ray, I have to hit our hotel room and prep handouts. Peter and I are part of a panel on informed consent. Want to come up to the room with me?"

Slinging on her mini-backpack, Ray shook her head. "I want to take a quick walk-about and check out the workshops and classes."

"Save the vendor room for later. I want to visit it with you—it'll be a blast."

"You got it."

As Hope headed toward the lobby and elevators, Ray went the

other way. Tall screens restricted the convention section entrance and blocked people from seeing anything down the hallway.

Two burly guys in jeans and polo shirts blocked the way. "Badge?"

What? Oh, oops. She pulled her lanyard out from under the backpack strap and held it up.

And got smiles. "Welcome," one said.

The other added, "If you're dressing up later on, remember only streetwear is allowed outside of this area. So either change once you're here or wear something to cover up. Same with toys. Bring them in a bag. We don't want to freak out the vanilla hotel guests."

Ray grinned, anticipation rising. "And inside?"

The man with the bushy beard laughed. "Anything goes."

"Fun." Ray almost danced through the narrow opening, then stopped in a lounge-type area. People milled here and there. Others relaxed in seating arrangements of couches and chairs or tables and chairs. Along the left wall, vendors at tables were selling water, sodas, and snacks.

The right wall had two doors, widely separated. The signs said: DUNGEON, 9 pm until 2 am.

She swallowed. Drake planned for them to visit—to play—in the dungeon, possibly tonight or tomorrow. And that was all he'd say.

The thought made her squirm.

On the far side of the lounge were the two hallways to the classrooms and workshops. "Follow the yellow-brick road," she muttered.

Sitting at a nearby table, a woman in a black latex suit gave her a once over and smiled slowly. "Have fun, Dorothy. Come and see me when you're ready for the wicked witch."

Ray couldn't help but grin back.

As she walked the hallway, many of the classroom doors were closed so she checked the signs for what was going on inside: Negotiation and consent. Fisting. Power Exchange. Shibari.

One big room with an open door was labeled *Want a Taste?*

Oh, Hope had told her about this room where stations demonstrated various BDSM skills. Like violet wands or flogging or bondage. It would be going on for the entire convention.

I'll be back, she promised herself.

She passed more classrooms, then paused at a large room where people sat at low tables with coloring books and crayons. Most wore short skirts or shorts with bright socks. Some had their hair in pigtails and braids. Giggling, throwing crayons at each other.

I found the littles room.

Farther in, pillows and vibrant plush rugs covered the hotel's low-pile carpet. In the far corner, people wearing kitten and puppy ears and tails gamboled about with balls and happy barking.

The sheer energy and happiness in the room had her smiling.

A pitiful whine came from the littles table. "I wish we had cookies." A couple of others at the table joined the whining.

Huh. Ray glanced around. Two obvious "grown-ups" were doing one-on-ones with their littles.

Across the room, a table had plates filled with cookies—and a pitcher with glasses.

Looking back at the littles group, she frowned.

One with her short brown hair in stubby pigtails noticed. And recognized her.

Faylee squealed, "Ray-Ray, hi. Hi!"

After giving her a wave and a laugh, Ray gestured toward the cookies and drink.

Faylee's smile blazed. "Yes, pleeeze, Auntie Ray!"

Okay then, I'm the helpful auntie today. She fetched the cookies, setting them on the table with an admonishing, "Good children get one cookie. Just one."

The high-pitched giggles, even from the two dressed as boys, made her grin. She poured them drinks—laughing under her breath as she poured one for herself. Cherry Kool-Aid. How long had it been?

As the group ate and drank, bouncing and coloring, Ray headed out, grinning at the chorus of thank yous and bye-bye, Auntie. They were all having so much fun.

I might have to get a coloring book.

She continued on past more classrooms.

At the far end of the U-shaped hallway, the vendor's room was huge, filled with tables and booths. Looked as if they sold everything from books to BDSM equipment to sex toys to fetish wear. There were racks of corsets. *Hmm.*

Yes, visiting with Hope would be great.

She continued down the other side of hallway. More classrooms.

A rhythmic smacking sound made her stop at an open door labeled ADVANCED FLOGGING, FLORENTINE STYLE. People sat at tables in the center. Roped-off areas were on the sides and front with what were probably demonstration equipment. A big pillow attached to a tall stool was in one area. Another, a clothes rack with a heavy coat. A mannequin with sandbags holding down the base. Her favorite was the giant teddy bear restrained across a tall stool.

At the front, a man was wielding not one, but two floggers on a woman's bare back and buttocks. The way each set of strands spun and hit, perfectly placed, was mesmerizing.

As Ray leaned against the back wall to watch, the instructor stepped back and lay the floggers on a table. He talked about safety, using the woman's body to show where to avoid the kidneys and spine. What areas were best to target.

Finished, he handed the woman a long wrap-around dress. With her back still to the class, she put it on, tying it closed. Reaching up, she released a cascade of dark-blonde hair from the bun on top of her head before turning around. She was a mature woman, and the dress showcased her curvy body.

The instructor smiled at the class and motioned to the roped-off areas. "Take turns practicing on the demonstration models. I'll be wandering between sections to give advice. Use only light flogging on our inanimate victims, please." His voice deepened. "If you rip a pillow, *you'll* pick up the feathers until the room is clean."

Holy kraken, the Dom looked as if he could easily enforce his threat. He was, maybe, in his forties, about six feet tall, and solidly built. No beer gut on this man. With silver-flecked black hair and eyes as dark as Drake's, he looked as if he should be modeling.

Pulling floggers from bags, the learners lined up at the various areas.

As the floggings started, Ray put a hand over her mouth to smother her snickers. *Bad Ray.* But damn. The two-handed style wasn't easy. Some picked it up right away; others could manage one flogger but had trouble getting into the flow of two. Or couldn't aim at all with their non-dominant arm. She winced when the mannequin got strands whipping around her sides to lash her breasts.

Thank goodness they weren't using real people.

Over at the poor teddy bear, a scruffy-bearded Top couldn't get the two floggers going in sync at all. Even worse, he missed the target areas. A lot.

One watcher raised his voice. "Yer recipient's gonna be pissing blood, dude. You gotta avoid the kidney area."

"Stuff it, asshole." Scruffy-Beard turned far enough for everyone to see his food-stained black t-shirt, pudgy muscles, and pale complexion.

Not an enticing sight. A while back, Marisol termed a man with a similar appearance a neckbeard—and had to explain. Poor social skills, poor hygiene. Looked like he lived in his mother's basement, playing video games.

Around the room, the teacher was making the rounds and giving advice. The students would practice on the test dummies and then make way for the next person. Some went to the end of their lines for a second shot.

Reaching the teddy-bear area, the instructor watched the neckbeard for a few swings and shook his head. "I'm sorry, but this isn't the right class for you. Before trying the Florentine weave, you need to master basic flogging. There is a Flogging 101 class being offered later today."

"Yeah, well, that's bullshit. I'm here now, and I got a place to practice. Good enough for me." The bearded idiot turned his back and kept swinging away.

The instructor stiffened, apparently searching for patience—and coming up empty. As his jaw tightened, Ray tensed. The teacher looked as if he was going rain down holy hell on the rude asscrack.

Not good, so not good. Master Drake would be really upset if there was a classroom brawl.

As Ray straightened up, her belt snagged on her pale blue-green shirt. And she started to grin. She was still wearing the stereotypical volunteer uniform of polo shirt and black jeans. She dug the volunteer badge out of her hip pocket and clipped it onto the lanyard. *There—all official.*

Donning a pompous attitude like an overcoat, she marched across the room and stepped right between the instructor and the neckbeard. Facing the dumbass. "*Excuse* me, please. The convention has rules—and does *not* tolerate disrespect to instructors."

Neckbeard scowled. "I paid to attend these workshops."

Not an argument she wanted to have. "Security has been called. When they arrive, you'll either be thrown out or"—she paused to heighten the moment—"they'll color your badge yellow as a first warning."

She could see the fool relax as if a warning wasn't so bad.

"A yellow badge shows everyone that you are a problem. No

one will want to have anything to do with you. You sure won't have anyone wanting to play with you in the dungeon."

His mouth dropped open. Because a hot babe in a dungeon was what every young wanna-be Dom would dream about. "Uh... Yeah, okay." He looked over her shoulder at the instructor. "Sorry, guess I'll go to the other class."

A second later, he was gone.

Ray blew out a breath. That could have gone a lot worse. Now to pacify the instructor. "Sir, I'm sorry—" When her gaze lifted to meet his, her voice died.

Like Drake, this Dom was utterly self-confident and radiating power. Rather than angry, he was...amused. "Very nicely done. Can you flog as well as you intervene?"

"Oh hell no. I was just watching. I'm not—"

"Not a Top." His eyes narrowed. "No, you're a very brave submissive." He glanced at the blonde who'd joined him. "She's much like you, lass."

The woman had a warm, throaty voice. "Thank you for stepping in. The young man was close to getting a fist in the face." She directed a reproving stare at the Dom. "And you already have enough damage to your hands. *Bad* Master."

As he laughed, Ray backed away, waving the next student forward. "Go on, let's keep the line moving."

Her retreat continued right out the door. Obviously, the madness of Cthulhu had taken her over. Talk about jumping in before thinking.

And...she'd told more than one little fib.

Security hadn't been called.

And coloring a badge yellow? She'd totally made it up.

Hopefully, no one would ever tell Drake.

She popped into another classroom, watching an intricate demonstration of shibari. It was like artwork—although it took forever. She'd probably be bouncing in the ropes before the poor Top could finish.

As the class finished, people flowed out of the room, discussing what they'd learned. Heading off to other classes or to the open area for drinks and snacks.

And Ray...sighed as loneliness hit. Drake was doing convention administration stuff. Honestly, the man's super-power must be diplomacy. Everyone liked him and came to him when there were problems.

Mac and Hope were both busy. Faylee was still in the littles room.

I need more friends, obviously.

She wandered down the hallway, eyeing the classes. There was a panel discussion on funishment versus punishment. Interesting topic.

"Dammit, I hate lazy—"

Ray recognized the irate woman standing inside the door of a classroom. "Hey, Claudia, problem?"

"So many problems. Both volunteers who were to distribute papers and handle the mic for attendee questions didn't show. I have to handle intros and facilitate the Q&A, so—"

"So you're stuck in the front. Let me help."

"Seriously? I mean..."

"Sure, I'm even wearing a volunteer uniform. Where are the papers and the mic?"

It was a great hour. The panel discussion had been lively, the ideas inventive—and a bit eye-opening at times.

The speakers and attendees ended up knowing her name since Claudia used it so often. *"Ray, can you hand out these papers?"* And she'd trot to the front, accept another panelist's stack and hand them out. Or take a mic to someone in the audience with a question.

"Thanks for the help, Ray," one Mistress said, echoed by the switch beside her.

"Claudia kept you moving." The male Dominant panelist smiled at her. "And from your smile, you enjoyed it. Service submissive?"

"Um, sometimes?" Her smile was rueful. "I think it depends on who needs help. Some people—no way."

"And for a special one or two, all the way?"

"Um." She thought of Master Drake and laughed ruefully. "Yes, I guess so."

Claudia hugged and thanked her. Spotting the other two members of her throuple in the back, she introduced Ray. One woman gave off Dominant vibes and had attended a predicament workshop. The other woman was all enthused over the class about switches.

Then they started talking about visiting the vendor area. "Want to come with us, Ray?" Claudia asked.

"Oh no, I promised Hope I'd wait for her. I'm sure I'll run into you all again this weekend." She headed off, checking the doors again. She could simply sit down with the schedule and pick out an interesting class...but right now, her body totally wanted to move.

Hadn't there'd been a class about submission to start now? Like farther down this hall? Either this classroom or... The door was shut so she slowed to read the sign.

"You disgusting cunt. Piece of fuckmeat. Not worthy of—" The man's voice blasting out, audible even through the door, was straight out of her nightmares.

Out of her memory of...that night.

The blood drained from her head. Her knees went weak.

No, no, don't pass out. Get out of here!

Holding onto the wall for support, she staggered away, down the hallway, back to the pre-function lounge area. To the wide open area with lots and lots of people. *Yes.*

At an empty table, she almost fell into a chair. Planting her forehead against her knees, she panted...and shook.

Breathe slower, stupid. This is a public place. I'm not tied up and helpless. Not in a house.

One inhalation. Purse lips. Breathe out. Wiggle toes, wiggle fingers.

That man's voice... It'd sounded like one of her assailants, but was it really? Her memory was...unreliable. Full of holes and crazy emotions from whatever drugs had been in her drink. It was why she hadn't gone to the police. How could she when even *she* didn't remember exactly what had happened?

Maybe it wasn't the same voice. Only...the words were the same. Such ugly words.

Ray swallowed against the nausea. Pulled in a breath. Breathed out slowly. Swallowed again.

"You okay, girl?" The woman's voice was...welcome. Another woman felt like safety.

Ray straightened. Tried to smile—and blinked at the tall, muscular, dark-haired Domme. The one who'd taught her how to paddle Casper. Her name was... "Mistress Jasira?"

"Very good." The Domme sat in a chair next to Ray and glanced at Casper. "Minion, go fetch her a bottle of water."

"Yes, Mistress." The blond slave gave Ray a worried look and hurried to the beverage station.

Bending again, Ray used the bottom of her shirt to wipe the fear sweat from her face. *Guess my panic attack is over if I can be embarrassed.*

"Please tell me someone didn't use you for a demo and leave you in this condition." Jasira's eyes narrowed as she glanced toward the hallway as if she'd beat up whoever it was.

A half-hysterical laugh burst from Ray. *I want to be like Jasira when I grow up.* "It wasn't"—she sucked in another breath—"a demo. I had kind of a panic attack." Talking was easier now her heart wasn't clogging her throat. "It wasn't something anyone did."

The Domme studied her with serious brown eyes before leaning back. "All right. Heaven knows there are triggers to trip over in some of these classes."

Ray wasn't about to tell her she'd triggered on a voice rather than some BDSM activity. "I'm good now." She huffed a laugh. "I just needed to shake for a while."

Casper appeared, went down on his knees next to Jasira, and offered up a bottled water like a gift. "Mistress."

"Thank you, my sweet," Jasira murmured.

As Casper glowed, Jasira opened the water and handed it to Ray. "Drink up. Get yourself back in your body. Can I call someone for you?"

Ray started to feel forlorn, like there was no one, only...there actually was. Hope. MacKensie. Claudia and Faylee would undoubtedly come if she needed help. *Wow, friends.*

And...Drake. She didn't doubt he'd show up. Not even a doubt. Huh. "I—Actually, I'm good."

"And you're smiling."

Ray's smile grew. "I realized there are people I could call if I needed them."

"Ah. Always a good realization." Jasira eyed her again in consideration, then nodded. "You look back to normal. The minion and I need to go get set up for a M/s roundtable."

"Thank you both so much."

As the two headed down the hall, Ray concentrated on drinking her water. Untensing her muscles. Staying in the present.

Later she'd think some more about that voice. Although everyone had worn masks that night. She wouldn't recognize anyone who'd been there, except for Crypto, the college student who'd taken her to the play party. But she wasn't even sure he'd stayed for the...rest. He might well have abandoned her.

A while later, after finishing the water and using the restroom, Ray felt her phone vibrate.

The text was from Drake. *"Want to eat a late lunch with me?"*

Her heart leaped. Here was what she needed to forget the last hour. And face it, he made her feel so very secure, simply by being himself.

"Sure, where r u?"

"Meet u in the con lounge."

How easy was this? She was already in the lounge. She sent back a thumbs-up icon.

A couple of minutes later, she spotted Drake entering and felt the buzz of anticipation and pleasure she got every time she saw him. His black hair was swept back. His eyes were dark under equally dark brows.

Everyone seemed to know him, calling greetings.

And then he frowned and stepped right in front of a person. Folded his arms over his chest.

Uh-oh, someone was in trouble.

The person he'd stopped had a precision-cut stubble beard, glitter eyeshadow, and dangling earrings. They wore a pencil skirt and a bright fuchsia corset low enough to show chest hair. And freckles.

Ray smiled. Colors and courage—whoever this was, she liked them already.

But why was Drake giving them a rough time? Her smile faded. He'd never seemed narrow-minded. Could she have been mistaken?

When Drake finished talking, someone called him over to a table—and Ray made a beeline for the colorful person. She checked the name tag. "Are you all right, Neon? Drake looked irritated with you."

"And you were worried? Bless your heart, my dear." She got a warm smile.

How could Drake possibly have picked on this sweet person?

"No need to worry." Neon shook their head. "Master Drake noticed I'd signed up to be a demo model for two whipping sessions. Back-to-back so to speak." Eyebrows waggling, Neon gave a booming laugh. "He said I needed a break between sessions and to trade with another masochist."

"Oh." The Chains cop was guarding...everyone. Her heart simply melted. More than melted.

No, no, no. I am not falling in love with the owner of a BDSM club. No, absolutely not.

Oh Gods, she *was*.

Neon looked over her shoulder with a fond smile. "You're way too protective of us all, Master Drake."

"Occupational hazard."

The sound of his smoky, dark voice sent sparkles fizzing through her bloodstream.

Drake wrapped an arm around Ray, drawing her in until her side was against his solid frame. Looking down, he studied her for a moment. "Are you all right, *ma chérie?*"

Yikes, could he see she'd had a panic attack earlier? "Fine. Ready for food."

"We'll be off then." He smiled at Neon. "I take it you've met Ray?"

"It's rare to find someone as sweet as she looks." Neon waved their hand in a showy benediction. "I approve."

A corner of Drake's mouth rose. "But, of course. I knew you would."

"She has other attributes too." Neon eyed her. "Like me, your skin must show handprints quite nicely."

Ray's eyes went wide. "What?" She sputtered, looking for a suitable retort.

"Yes, it's most satisfying." Drake laced their fingers together and started toward the exit. Laughing.

The sadistic jerk.

No, she didn't love him at *all*.

"MacKensie, how about this one?" Ray held up a set of pajamas with teddy bears, knowing the veterinarian loved clothing with animal prints.

"Teddy bears, fun!" Mac's eyes narrowed as she moved closer. "Wait... Teddy bears in bondage? *Frak*, that's just wrong."

Furry paws cuffed together. One teddy bear wore a blindfold. Another held a paddle.

"Seriously?" Hope laughed maniacally and pointed. "This one is holding up a paddle."

"Bad bear. Me, I prefer a barehanded spanking," Mac said. "But to each bear his own."

"Barehanded spanking?" Unexpected carnal curiosity heated Ray's blood. "Um. It does kinda sound more intimate than paddles."

"Oh look," Hope's voice rose. "This one has a ball gag."

"Interesting." The man's voice came from behind them. "Someone doesn't want Teddy using a safeword."

Mac spun around. "*Alex*." She hugged him. "How'd your panel on domination go?"

He hugged her back and kissed the top of her head. "Quite nicely. Drake picked a diverse group of people to be on the panel with me, which made for good discussions."

"Hope. Ray." But when he nodded at Ray, his expression held amusement. Like... Gods, he hadn't heard her talking about spanking, had he?

Turning away, he eyed the pajamas and told the vendor, "We'll take a women's size ten."

Mac laughed. "Butler will be appalled. He's so straightlaced."

Ray blinked. Wasn't Butler the dog?

"You know, some people wear pajamas to go shopping. Or to work." Hope's eyes danced with merriment. "You could—"

"Bears in bondage at the vet clinic? Absolutely not." Mac

shook her head. "I can't believe I thought you were a nice person when we met."

Hope snorted and murmured to Ray, "Considering I met her at one of Alex's private play parties, I really doubt that."

Ray could only laugh. Hope, with her big blue eyes and pixie hair, *did* look sweet. Cute, even.

After paying, Alex took the sack. "After that panel, I feel the need to release some dominance." He took Mac's hand. "Come with me, my little submissive."

And he led MacKensie straight out of the vendors' room.

"Huh." Ray glanced at Hope. "She sure didn't fight back."

"Not even a little." Hope sighed. "I'm the same way when Peter pulls out the Dom card."

"Mmm, I get it." Drake never lost his seamless air of authority, but when his voice got a little slower, softer, deeper—and the look in his eyes changed, she felt it right down to her toes. As if her stomach got on an elevator going down, down, down.

What would it be like to *live* with someone who had such power over her? In the past week, she'd had a bit of a taste. "Is Mac happy with Alex being a Dom?"

"Definitely." Hope dragged Ray to the next vendor and a rack of colorful corsets. "She wouldn't be comfortable being submissive to just anyone though. But Alex is a really good person. Trustworthy, you know?"

"Trust takes time..." Ray said slowly.

"And enough occasions where trust might be broken—and isn't." Hope's serious blue eyes met Ray's gaze. "A lot of us have suffered when a Dominant ignored our boundaries or broke our trust. Afterward, it's tough to let someone in again."

"Isn't that the truth," Ray said under her breath and absently started looking through the rack of corsets. How rare was a trustworthy person—let alone a man.

But...she was discovering she could trust Drake. Even if it was really annoying how he managed to tell she'd had a meltdown and got her to talk about it during lunch.

While he'd held her hand and simply listened. His ability to focus completely on a person—on her—was devastating.

Wonderful.

She shook her head, realized she was flipping through the rack of corsets without seeing them—and then stopped. "Hey, this blue is a match for your eyes."

The corset was a beautiful, royal blue in a floral, overbust style. Hope held it up against herself. "Mmm, it'd hold the girls up. Pull my waist in. I like it."

"Of course you do—I have great taste."

"Peter loves me in corsets." Hope's lips tilted up in a smug Cheshire smile. "He considers them almost like bondage. Like how you can't really bend except at the hips, and when you get bent over—"

"No, no, stop." Ray stuck her fingers in her ears and tried to drown out the images. "La, la, la."

Her laughter died when she spotted Drake's beautiful ex, Justine, whose plump upper lip was raised in a contemptuous sneer.

Ray turned her back...and felt her happiness dying. Damn the woman. *She's totally an assassin of good moods. Or no, maybe something uglier like an exterminator. I should find her a gray coverall and—*

"What should I wear with this?" Hope held the corset out at arm's length to study it.

"Maybe a short, frilly—" Ray's eyes widened as she spotted Theodore approaching. In her head, she could almost hear the warning cry of: *"Flee for your lives. Incoming..."*

Her mood spiraled downward. "Theodore, what a surprise."

Moving too close, he ran his gaze over her, head to toes. "I heard you'd be here. But I was hoping to find you in fetwear, doll."

If she rolled her eyes as hard as she wanted to, she'd sprain something in her head. "Fetwear is for dungeons, not classrooms."

"Speaking of dungeons, I've been practicing. I'll pick you up at your room and we can—"

Freaking hell. "No. Don't you listen? We're done."

"But—I can be your Master. Give you what you want."

Under the frustration, her heart ached slightly. He probably thought he was trying, but he still didn't have a clue.

Because he wouldn't listen.

"Theodore, I already told you no when you asked if you being a Dom would make a difference." She shook her head. "And I can tell you from experience, a good Dom listens—and hears—what a submissive says."

"I knew it." He tried to stand straighter. "I knew you were submissive. You're made for me."

"No." She could feel her face flushing. Her voice rose. "No, I am not *made* for you."

"Dammit, if I hit him, Peter will get mad," Hope muttered from behind her. "But I'm up for it if you want."

A fistfight between Theodore and Hope. Ray burst into laughter, half-snorting. But no. "Go *away*, you idiot."

"*Shhh.*" Palms down, Theodore made lower-it motions. "Don't go all drama queen and loud here. Shut it down, doll."

"*You* shut it down." When she poked a hard finger into his chest, he stepped back. "I have had it with you. Stay away from me."

"Christ, you act like a toddler having tantrums. What is wrong with you?" Realizing people were watching, Theodore stomped away.

Ray shook her head as anger warred with frustration.

And shame and didn't that piss her off. She'd been taught a good woman would never cause a loud altercation. Even as she told herself, to hell with patriarchal brainwashing, she couldn't quite lose the guilt.

She heaved a sigh and... *Oh great.* Everyone was watching, including the snooty Justine and her friends who were staring at Ray as if she was the clown of the hour.

Talk about embarrassing.

"Needy men can be such dicks." Shoving her bangs out of her eyes, Hope held up the blue corset. "So you think I should get this?"

Ray stared. When had they moved from an altercation to shopping?

Unless hyper-focused, her thoughts were a jigsaw puzzle where all the pieces would fit—except they were scattered everywhere.

Hope's brain was linear. Like a train, only she could switch tracks at the drop of a hat.

Clothes. We're now talking about clothes. "Ah, right. You should absolutely get the corset. It's made for you."

"It is!" Hope grinned.

Hmm. "You know, I budgeted money for clothes. A corset might be fun."

"Yes!" Hope bounced on her tiptoes. "Let's see. Maybe something turquoise to match your eyes? Or red-brown to bring out your freckles?"

"Hope," Ray growled.

"Oh, right, I mean, to match your hair. Sorry." Hope's smile was unrepentant.

"I should have drowned you in high school." Ray noticed a rack of leather corsets. *Interesting.* She pulled one—a black one. No, it stopped beneath a person's breasts—and she'd rather be a bit more covered. The next one though went higher...

Zipper up the front, lacing in the back. Shoulder straps. Long though. The corset would go down to the crease of her hips, probably because it had O-rings with garters to hold up thigh-high stockings.

"I like these cups." Rather than under or over the bust, it had semi-cups.

"Ooooh, nice. They'll push your girls way up high." Hope tapped the O-rings on each side of the waist. "I bet Drake could find something to do with those."

Like...bondage? Ooooh, yes. Her insides went into the melting sensation she got every time she thought of sex with him. Or when he restrained her—no matter how he did it. With his hands or ropes or...

Begone, lusty thoughts. She shook her head hard, then glanced at the price tag. Way higher than she wanted but... The garment was well made. She could wear it again and again.

She put it on over her clothes and zipped up the front. "Can you tighten the laces, Hope?"

"Sure."

Tugging and more tugging until it was nice and snug.

Ray looked down at herself. "Sweet. Okay, this'll be my indulgence for this month and give me something special to wear tomorrow night."

Grinning, Hope led the way to the register—and handed Ray a pair of fishnet stockings on the way there.

Drake exited the elevator and strolled down the hotel hallway, enjoying the cooler air and quiet. *Nice.*

It'd been a long day, but the convention was off to a rousing start.

It was a shame he hadn't gotten more time with Ray, but the convention's sponsoring clubs took turns with troubleshooting problems, and today had been Chains' turn. Another club had the hot seat tonight, and he was off duty.

Earlier, Simon had texted to say they'd arrived but were booked for two workshops and would see him tonight. He and his submissive were staying in the other bedroom in the suite Drake had booked.

At the hotel suite, he used the key card to unlock the door.

"Drake, finally!" Rona rose from the sofa and caught him in a warm hug.

"Rona, it's good to see you."

A moment later, Simon took her place for a hug and a hard thumping on his back. Stepping back, he gripped Drake's shoulders for a quick once-over. "You look in excellent health. A bit tired, but...happy."

Interesting. "*Oui*, I am. Both."

"So sit and put your feet up. Let's talk."

Before Simon could continue, Rona called from the kitchenette area, "Want something to drink?"

"Some juice would be good, *merci*." He dropped down onto the other sofa as Simon resumed his seat.

She handed him a glass of apple juice, then joined Simon, curling against him in a way that made Drake smile. Simon had been alone a long time, and it was good to see him with a submissive who complemented the powerful Master so very well.

"How did your day go?" Drake asked. "Were your workshops well attended?"

Rona rolled her eyes. "Both classes were packed full."

"Of course. You are well known, and dual-handed flogging is flashy enough many Tops want to learn how."

"Not to mention it's simply fun. Fun to teach as well"—Simon sighed—"except for pups who never held a flogger before."

Drake frowned. "The write-up for your class clearly states it's only for those experienced in one-handed flogging. The title includes advanced."

"The prerequisite should include *ability to read*." Rona laughed. "Or the willingness to read, I should say. I have doctors who can write a page of orders but can't be bothered to read directions."

Rona had been a surgical and ICU nurse before going into

hospital administration. Along with an incredibly caring disposition came a delightful helping of cynical.

"I assume you kicked anyone unqualified out or, maybe, used them as a demonstration dummy?"

"It was tempting," Simon murmured. "I came close to thumping one fool who hogged the practice mannequin and refused to leave."

Merde. A past champion of the MMA circuit, Simon could inflict an unimaginable amount of damage within seconds. "I appreciate your restraint."

"It wasn't restraint." Rona elbowed her Master. "One of your volunteers intervened and told the idiot the security guard would color his badge yellow as a first warning—and no submissive would play with a tagged troublemaker. You would not believe how fast the wanna-be Dom left the room."

"A colored badge appears to be an effective constraint. One I hadn't heard of." Simon raised his drink to Drake in a toast.

A yellow-tinted badge? Drake frowned. "As it happens, I've never heard of this deterrent."

Simon started to grin. "The volunteer made it up on the spot?"

"So it seems. Did you notice the name of the volunteer? I'd like to speak with him."

"Her," Rona corrected. "Her name was—"

The door to the suite clicked open, and Ray walked in. She smiled at him, warm and—he could swear—lovingly, then noticed Simon and Rona. Her eyes widened.

"How convenient," Simon said smoothly. "Meet the volunteer who came to our assistance."

Oh, no, no, no. Ray couldn't believe her eyes. The instructor and model from the Florentine flogging workshop were *here*. From the way Drake was eyeing her, the two had told him what she'd done.

Freak my life. She took a step back in retreat.

Laughing, Drake rose and captured her hand. "*Non, non*, you will be explaining this to me, *mon petit chou*." He pulled her down beside him on the sofa and secured her with an arm around her shoulders.

"I-I'm sorry." Twisting her wood-and-copper rings, she stared at her hands. "I lied to the neckbeard. I knew you'd be upset if an instructor and student had a fight and..."

"Ray." Drake's voice was deep and smooth as he lifted her chin, forcing her to look at him. "I *would* be upset at fighting in a workshop. Thank you for keeping Simon from taking the miscreant apart. Bloodshed doesn't belong in a classroom."

She'd been thinking the conflict would be a push and shove or maybe a punch. "Bloodshed?" She eyed the instructor.

Drake made a French-sound of amusement. "Simon likes to grease his fists with blood."

Ray saw the instructor had scars all over his hands.

The woman choked on her drink. "What a phrase. Isn't there a law against allowing barbarians out in public?"

"Now, lass," the instructor reproved, then smiled at Ray. "It's a pleasure to meet you in a more relaxed environment. I'm Simon Demakis and this is Rona McGregor. Thank you for your help earlier."

"Um, Ray Lanigan. Nice to meet you." Ray wanted to slide behind Drake and hide. Simon and Rona were so very assured, at home in their own skins. Would she ever feel as comfortable with herself? With others?

Drake put his hand over hers, and it was warm and real, pulling her back to the moment. "Tell me about this yellow marking on the badge."

"It...seemed logical. Young man, kind of insecure, poor hygiene and verbal skills. At a BDSM con. Of course, a wanna-be Top would daydream about playing in the dungeon. All I had to do was show him his behavior would shatter his dream."

"Ingenious." Drake ran his hand over her arm in a comforting stroke. "We should incorporate your warning system into the convention protocols."

"I like it," Simon agreed. "You have a good head on your shoulders for dealing with turmoil."

Rona nodded. "I look for that talent in my charge nurses."

"I might be good during a crisis." Ray moved her shoulders and had to confess. "And then minor problems have sent me into left field."

"I'd only be upset with you if you put yourself in harm's way, but you didn't." Drake tightened his arm around her shoulders in a comforting squeeze. "So... If you manage the occasional disasters, I'll handle minor problems—and you."

The word was out before she even had a chance to think. "Deal."

CHAPTER FOURTEEN

After showering that night, Ray left the ensuite bathroom with only a towel around her.

Drake was lounging in the easy chair by the window, and his gaze was warm enough to flush her skin. "Very pretty."

She was probably turning red from her toes up to her face—and almost all of it would be visible. "Um, you said you would choose what I wore tonight?" Why wasn't there any clothing laid out on the bed?

His lips curved. "Such a worried expression. I won't insist you be naked or only in a G-string."

Whew, okay then. But still... What was she going to wear? "The convention packet suggested roleplay costumes for the first dungeon night. To break the ice or something."

"Exactly so, and since Chains is a sponsor, you'll be one of the examples." He pointed at a sack on the dresser. "While you get ready, I have some calls to answer." Sauntering out of the bedroom, he closed the door behind him.

She stared at the sack. So very small. Whatever clothing was in there would be...skimpy.

The first thing she pulled out was very sheer…a black dress? It had white lace on the top and bottom. *Ooookay*. Then there was a white square with white ribbon ties. Perhaps an apron?

The small, white headpiece nailed it. "Oh, you did *not*!" Her French master got her a French maid outfit.

Laughter started in her belly and erupted. If she'd thought of it, she'd have bought one herself.

She pulled it on and checked the mirror. *Oh niiiiice!*

The stretchy, off-the-shoulder top meant she couldn't wear a bra. Midriff stitching drew in the bodice to showcase her breasts. Despite being black, the fabric was so sheer her darker nipples showed against her pale skin.

Even worse, the hemline barely covered her crotch in front, and in the rear, it completely opened in a V to display all of her ass. The bright white ruffle on the barely-there black panty would ensure no one missed her butt being exposed.

Well. No jewelry needed for a maid. Her shoulder-length, curly hair might as well stay down.

She took her makeup bag into the bathroom and kicked the door shut. For tonight, she went for dark and sultry eyes. Then a soft-pink lip stain topped with cherry-flavored gloss. *Just cuz*.

And that was it. She never wore foundation or blush; it felt too weird if her freckles disappeared. Stupid Irish ancestors.

Huh. She started grinning, imagining getting arrested by the *Gardaí*. "*For shame, Miss. Being as you're Irish, wearing a French maid outfit is against the law. To gaol with you.*"

Ack. Stop! She shook the scampering squirrels out of her head and left the bathroom. And stopped.

Drake stood in the center of the bedroom in black dress pants and an unbuttoned, white silk shirt.

Oh mama, he is so fine. Unable to resist, she ran her fingers over the hard ridges of his abdomen. *Yum*. "For a businessman, you're sure fit."

"I work out, *ma chérie*, or I'd possess a fine beer belly." He turned her to face the mirror and moved behind her. His gaze in the mirror held open heat. "You are lovely...and I am tempted to take you, here and now."

Reaching around her, he cupped her breasts in his strong hands, thumbing her nipples and sending zings of pleasure straight to her pussy. His thick erection pressed against her barely clad ass. "But I will wait. For a while."

She swallowed hard. Wanting him to just take her. To heck with the dungeon.

"But first, some warming up, *oui*?" Without moving away, he reached around her to pick something up from the desk. He slid it inside the front of her frilly panty. A black magnet on the outside secured it in place. Right over her clit.

A vibrator—it had to be a vibrator. "Drake..."

One hand pressed it against her mound, the other fondled her breast, and his shaft was still against her ass. The whole room grew warmer.

He kissed her neck and pocketed the remote. "The toy is simply to ensure you have an enjoyable evening." In the mirror, his black eyes danced with laughter, the jerk.

Enjoyable? Yet the thought of him turning on the device when they were in public, of him being in control of what she felt, sent a thrill through her.

She swallowed hard. What was she letting herself in for? "Are —are Simon and Rona going with us?"

"*Non*, they're going out with friends tonight but will join us in the dungeon tomorrow night." He put his arm around her waist, his other hand caressing her breasts. "Yesterday, you told me what you wanted to try this weekend. That, aside from your restrictions on the list—no water sports, no blood play, etc., you wanted to hand over control of your body to me. I can touch or take you at any time, restrain you, punish you. Is this what you want?"

The melting sensation grew inside her. She nodded, and when he didn't continue, managed to force out the words, "Yes, it's what I want."

"Then so it will be. Since you are dressed as a powerless maid, I will treat you as one. Bear in mind"— his lips quirked—"I already know you don't mind being watched."

She could feel herself stiffen. At the party, it had started with them watching and then—

"*Bébé*, I am the only one who will touch you. No one else. Others may watch. Watch only."

Her muscles relaxed, then she frowned, remembering his ex was here. "No one else will touch me. But...um, does it go both ways? You won't, um, *be* with other women?"

He pursed his lips in that way he had, taking her seriously. And made her fall even harder in love with him. "Agreed. As it happens, I prefer only one sexual partner—and prefer my partner agrees to the same."

She let out a breath. "Yes!"—and winced, modulating the volume. "Sorry, but yes." Only he wasn't angry or upset with her vehemence. Was actually amused.

"Very good. Now, some power exchanges remove the ability to use safewords. I am not comfortable with that. Your safeword can always be used and will be honored."

She relaxed back into him. "Yes. Yes, I trust you."

"I am honored"—he kissed her neck—"and will do my best to deserve it."

Drake nodded to the two volunteer security personnel who were checking badges carefully as well as warning others about phone and camera restrictions. "Good job, Shawn," he told the one from Chains. The other guard was from another club.

"Thank you, Master Drake. Enjoy your evening." Shawn smiled even as he gave Ray an appreciative look.

As he should.

In her red, calf-length, wrap-around dress, she looked lovely. It was a shame to cover up the French maid costume, but street attire was mandatory outside of the screened convention area.

He smiled and ran a finger down her soft cheek, appreciating skin free of sticky face makeup. She had however, lined and shadowed her eyes. And those glossy lips would look perfect around his cock.

Once past the screens, he stopped. "We're now on convention ground. No need for covering up in here." He undid the fabric belt and slipped the dress off her shoulders. It rolled up easily and went into his toybag.

The air was cooler than in the hotel room, and beneath the very sheer black top, her nipples were visibly pointed.

He grinned, enjoying the sight. "You make a most adorable maid."

"Thank you." Then she followed his gaze, looking down at herself.

Ah, so delightful. He would never tire of watching how blushes rolled upward from her breasts to her face. "Now, while behind the screen tonight—and actually, anytime we are in a dungeon, I expect medium protocol toward me and other Dominants. Be very respectful, don't speak unless spoken to, use honorifics, eyes down. We've talked about this before."

Her tongue wet her lips. "Yes, Sir. I understand."

"I know you'll make me proud." He caressed her cheek, and she leaned into his palm. Giving him her unspoken submission.

A power exchange sounded so neutral, so cold for the trust and affection in a D/s relationship like they were coming to have.

After picking up the toybag, he smoothed his suit coat. He'd dressed as an aristocrat to set off her maid costume. Since he wasn't planning anything strenuous, his classic black dinner suit and vest, white dress shirt, silk tie, and pocket square would do.

Tonight he wanted only to give her a psychological taste of power dynamics.

"Perhaps a quick look inside the dungeon, then we'll come back out here."

"Yes, Sir."

As he guided her into the hotel's biggest ballroom, her eyes widened. Twenty thousand square feet of dungeon was impressive, and he stepped to one side of the doorway to let her take it in.

"*Hooooly* cryptids."

He couldn't help grinning at the phrase. "Someone watches too much Lovecraftian horror."

She was right though. The volunteers for the setup had done a magnificent job. St. Andrew's crosses stood high among suspension stations, cages, spanking benches, and slings. One of the clubs had sent a GYN table so one corner was set up as a medical room. The far wall was roped off for whipping and flogging scenes.

He bent to murmur in Ray's ear. "Tomorrow, we'll be in here. I'll even let you choose which equipment we'll start on."

The tiny tremor he could feel with his arm around her waist was pleasing. All tomorrow, she'd be thinking about what was to come. Anticipation was good for a submissive.

For tonight though...

The pre-function areas surrounding the ballroom were for socializing and dungeon foreplay, so to speak. Signs pointed to other rooms for aftercare where experienced volunteers were available to help in case of post-scene meltdowns.

"Drake." Alex was seated near the center of the area. "Join us." He and Bob had their submissives kneeling at their feet. Not surprising. Bob enjoyed ratcheting up the D/s dynamic during play periods.

This was perfect for tonight.

Drake settled into a comfortable leather chair and squeezed Ray's hand. "Please join the submissives in kneeling, *ma chérie*." He pointed to a place on the floor between his legs.

Her instant obedience was as pleasing as her gracefulness. Woodcrafters probably were up and down from the floor all day.

"Very nice." Leaning forward, he rested his hands on her shoulders in a possessive gesture. *This body is mine.*

Bob's eyebrows went up for a second before he smiled in open approval.

After ending it with Justine, Drake had stuck to short-term hookups, much to the disapproval of his friends. But now...

He looked down. At Ray's autumn-colored, curly hair with the intriguing bluish strands. Freckles over her cheeks and shoulders. Her blue-green eyes were bright as she smiled up at him.

Not only submissive, but intelligent, generous, creative, and simply fun.

Warmth filled his chest. What was growing between them was deeper and more satisfying than anything he'd known before. She was a friend as much as a lover—although admittedly, he certainly looked forward to enjoying all the sexual aspects later tonight.

Before that...well, she'd given him her body to enjoy.

He ran his finger along the lacy edge of her top that exposed just the tops of her shoulders. "Alex, have you seen Ray's tattoos?"

"No, I haven't." Alex's mouth quirked. The Dom undoubtedly knew where Drake was headed.

"The one on her right arm is my favorite." He pushed the sleeve down to expose the tattoo on her deltoid...which dragged the bodice down almost to her right nipple.

She stiffened, gripped the cleavage area, and started to pull it up. "M-Master Drake," she whispered.

"Hands on your thighs, *bébé*," Drake said, his voice softer than before.

"I..." The way she bit her lip was charming.

It pleased the hell out of him when she obediently set her hands on her thighs, palms-up, imitating the posture of the other two submissives.

"Much better." Drake ran his fingers over the tree tattoo and asked Alex, "See the woman's form in the trunk?"

"It's beautifully done," Alex said.

Bob, with a half-smile, lifted his eyebrows. "Is there one on the other arm?"

"As it happens, there is. Let me show you." He pushed her left sleeve down. Now the lace of her top barely covered her plump breasts.

"Ah, I like the ink. The colors blend well with her freckles and her hair." Bob nodded approval, his hand on Lynn's shoulder.

Lynn stole a quick look before her gaze returned to the floor. Drake had to smile. The introverted brunette was an excellent complement to Bob's sociable personality.

Drake looked down at Ray. Her cheeks were flushed from being almost exposed in public. Her lips were reddened, her nipples erect with arousal.

Even so, all her muscles were tense. Perhaps with uncertainty? This was new to her. He must not let himself forget that.

When he set his hand on her nape beneath her hair, she startled. "*Mon cœur*, you put yourself into my keeping for tonight. I will touch as I want, show you off as I want. No embarrassment is needed because this isn't your body tonight; it's mine. There is nothing for you to think about. Your job is to keep your eyes lowered. You do not talk or move unless so directed. If you need to move, you may sit—as long as you're still between my legs. Clear?"

He could feel the tension flow out of her. Barely hear her relieved exhalation as she murmured, "Yes, Sir."

For many submissives, turning over the reins was a respite from their need to please, to be perfect, even to serve society's impossible expectations.

· · ·

When Master Drake lowered her sleeves, Ray had felt as if an entire anthill set up residence in her chest. Prickling and biting, making her breathing shallow.

What should I do? Cover myself? Look away? How was she supposed to act?

But he'd laid out just what she had to do now and... Gods, the *relief*. Simply kneel here. Not think, not talk. Not even decide if she should be embarrassed or not.

Those decisions were...his.

It might be different if he told her what to do all the time, but his time in charge had boundaries. And this was Drake. *I can trust him.*

She breathed out. The low carpet was soft beneath her knees. His hard thighs bracketed her upper arms. His warm hands rested on her shoulders. She was enclosed in warmth and safety.

Her squirrel thoughts slowed, as if happy to wait for orders.

The music of Sierra's "Unbroken" with the distinctive heavy bassline spilled out of the dungeon as if to accompany the hum of conversations. The sounds—footsteps, people talking, glasses clinking—swirled around her without landing. She was tucked in a bubble of peace.

The Doms were talking about something. Now and then, she listened. Or not.

Time passed. After a while, she realized the voices around her had changed.

Drake leaned down, rubbing his cheek against hers. "You've been such a good girl. How do you feel now?"

"Comfortable," she whispered, paused. "Happy."

He made a pleased sound. "Good. Although, comfort isn't in my plans for your entire night."

Wait...what does he mean?

Hands around her waist, he drew her closer between his legs

and pushed the stretchy top of her maid's uniform to her ribcage. Exposing her to...everyone. "She has the most beautiful breasts I've ever seen."

Voices came from around her.

A rumbling baritone. "Yes, lovely."

"I prefer bigger, but there's something to be said for perky." A man's tenor.

A woman's voice. "Pretty nipples too."

Ray's head jerked up. Nediva, the Mistress who'd bartended at Chains sat in one of the chairs.

Drake's callused hands were under her breasts as if offering them up—and he squeezed lightly with a low admonishment, "Eyes down, pet."

She squeaked and lowered her head, forcing her gaze to stay on the floor. But shades of the elder gods, he was touching her, cupping her breasts, his thumbs circling her nipples.

Her whole body jolted completely awake. Tingles flowed from his touch, spreading across her skin until every inch was waiting for more.

"Nediva, have you found someone to play with tonight?" Drake was asking.

"No, I'm looking forward to some pick-up play sessions. Lots of people here from out of the area and new equipment to play on. Did you see the bondage table that looked like someone mated it to a pillory *and* stocks. So cool."

One of the male Doms laughed. "I saw it. We should get one for Chains, Drake."

"I'll take a look at it. Inventive equipment is always welcome. I also need to get a replacement for the back bar painting." Master Drake sounded annoyed.

Did he mean the lovely SAFE, SANE, & CONSENSUAL artwork? What happened? She almost blurted out the words.

Someone else asked the question for her.

"An altercation at the bar and one culprit thought it was a

good idea to throw his glass of red wine at his boyfriend—who ducked. The wine hit the painting."

"Damn," Nediva groaned. "There's no coming back from red wine."

Ray bit her lip, feeling almost as if she'd lost a friend. The artwork had been a symbol of what Chains stood for—and had made her feel safe there.

"We'll find something to replace it eventually." As if seeing her unhappiness, Master Drake squeezed her shoulder.

The conversation moved on for a minute before he bent forward and said softly, "*Ma chérie*, I'd like you to bring me a Perrier and whatever you wish for yourself from the drinks table." He raised his voice. "Anyone else? Ray would be pleased to serve."

The words hit her with a shock of truth. Because there was nothing she wanted more.

A voice came from her left, a male Dom. "A Mountain Dew would be great, thanks."

She glanced up quickly to ensure she knew who to deliver the drink to.

No other takers.

"Off you go then." Drake handed her money, closed his hard hands around her waist, and lifted her to her feet.

She took a step and unthinkingly started to pull her bodice up.

Drake made a sound low in his throat. A glance showed his lips tilted slightly, his eyes filled with amusement.

Oh, damn. *He owns my body tonight*. And was in a mood to show off her breasts.

Damn Dom.

Okay then. Easy for him to tell her not to be embarrassed. Her whole-body blush was probably giving off heat waves as she crossed the room.

"Oh nice." A man in black leathers stepped directly in her path. "You with someone, pretty woman?"

Drake had said, "*You do not talk*," so now what? After a

confused second, she turned and pointed to her Dom...who was watching.

Drake shifted his dark gaze to the black-leathered guy and shook his head—*no*.

"Fuck me, you're with Drake. Shit. Sorry. Tell him *sorry*."

And her path to the drinks table was clear.

Well, cool. How reassuring he'd kept an eye on her in case she needed help. She glanced over her shoulder, and he was lounging in his chair. Still watching.

She smiled at him and got a wink in answer.

A few minutes later, she returned, gave Drake his change, and handed out the drinks. And... *Yikes, I'm the only submissive in the group now.*

Lynn and Mac were probably with their Doms in the dungeon. Good for them, only... The appreciative looks from the Dominants in the sitting area made her nervous.

It was such a relief to take her place at Master Drake's feet. Even better when he pulled her backward between his legs again. Bracketed by hard thighs.

Safe.

Keeping her gaze lowered, she drank the small apple juice she'd gotten for herself.

He took the empty glass from her and set it on the end table. Then he curled his hand over her bare shoulder and...

Right over her clit, vibrations started up. She startled—and his grip tightened, keeping her from jumping up.

But... *Holy kraken, here?*

The soft pulsing vibrations didn't stop even when she squirmed, trying to get the vibe away from the acutely sensitive spot. This was just...just wrong.

Master Drake's legs on each side of her closed in, subduing her wiggles. He leaned down and whispered, "Stay very still and very quiet, Aralia. It's your only job right now." He chuckled under his breath and added, "You *do* have permission to come. This time."

Permission. *Permission*. Ooooh, that was taking dominance way too far. She'd come when and—

The grip on her shoulder tightened. The deep whisper was silky smooth. "My body, you said, which makes those orgasms mine to deny, *ma petite*. Punishment for disobedience is also my right this evening, mmm?"

Heat shuddered through her, at his words, at the threat—with the memory of his hands on her body, paddling her and arousing her at the same time.

The slow, soft vibrations on her clit changed, escalating from low to high, pausing, and starting over again at low.

Maybe this was good? She never got off from the oddly patterned speeds some vibrators had. One of hers had over a dozen rhythms. Who needed that?

With this vibe's pattern, she wouldn't have an orgasm in front of everyone.

She gave a whuff of relief, tried to move and got nowhere. His legs kept her pinned in place...and the floor felt as if it'd dropped a foot.

Drake's hands closed on her breasts. "Tonight, you will take everything I give you. Unless you safeword out. Otherwise"—he tugged on her nipples, rolling them gently, sending shocks of pleasure coursing through her—"you will have an orgasm." His voice held only complete certainty.

She started to turn, to look at him.

"Mmm-um, eyes down."

And then he was talking to the other Doms. Greeting someone else. She couldn't even see who was present. Could only...feel.

Gods, she needed to come. *Only, I don't want to. Do I?*

His hands were so strong, so warm, so...expert. Her breasts swelled, the skin tight. Sensitive. Sometimes his touch was gentle, dancing lightly over her nipples until she wanted to strain forward for more. Except she was trapped in place.

Sometimes, his touch grew rough, pinching her nipples until she tried to draw back—and again—couldn't.

The sense of his controlled, ruthless power made the molten pool in her pelvis grow deeper.

And the vibrator didn't stop. When it increased in speed, it sent her to the precipice, but then it'd pause and slow. Damn Master Drake, this was driving her crazy. Her thighs clamped together, and she barely managed to suppress a frustrated whine.

The bastard was talking with the other Doms. Laughing.

More cycles. Sweat beaded on her skin. And she really wanted to turn and...and hit him.

The hands on her breasts tightened. His voice murmured in her ear, "Do not move, make no noise—and come for me."

The vibrations changed, hard and fast. No pattern, no pauses.

From teetering on the peak, she was tossed right over the cliff in a flood of sensation. *Don't move, don't move.* She barely kept her hips from bucking as overwhelming waves of pleasure swept through her, over and over. Her vision went white.

She gritted her teeth—and the effort of not making a sound made the orgasm last. *Forever.*

Her heart pounded so hard it roared in her ears and was all she could hear. Her breaths were still fast and shallow when the vibrator stopped.

The air moving around her made her realize she was covered in a fine sweat. Her muscles were seriously overcooked noodles. Closing in on mush.

Spine, stay straight.

And, oh man, her panties were soaked. Had anyone seen her getting off? Hopefully not. She'd been quiet, right?

"Thank you, Aralia. You are beautiful when you come," he said.

Freaking buggering spit, Master Drake hadn't lowered his voice at all.

"Excellent control. The quivering was adorable," a woman said.

Oh no, no, no, the others did see me.

"The little squeak, yeah, great sound," came from a man.

More chimed in, and the blush scalded her face.

"Thank you for sharing with us, Drake."

"My pleasure." Drake leaned forward and whispered in her ear, "Your specialty in crafting is wood art with a living edge. Mine is... edging the living."

No, he did *not* go there. She sputtered a giggle, tried to choke it down, and totally failed.

Probably only she heard him chuckle before he straightened and started talking to the other Dominants again. "So what did you think of our new workshops? The one on primal play and Blaize's panel on degradation."

She managed to regain control, although her stomach still quivered with the need to laugh. *Edging, my ass.*

A few minutes later, she realized she needed to pee. Rather urgently, actually.

Before she'd squirmed more than a couple of times, he bent. "You seem uncomfortable, *bébé*."

She turned to whisper in his ear, "Restroom, please?"

"But of course." He rose and lifted her to her feet. "It's been good to see you all here. If you would excuse us, please."

With an arm around her waist, he guided her across the room —responding to greetings with smiles and short comments. But not stopping. *Thank you, Master.*

At the door, he curled his fingers around her nape and kissed her lightly. "I'll be nearby, reading my messages." He motioned to a table. "Take the time you need."

She looked up at him, startled at his...kindness. "Thank you, Sir."

His fingers trailed down her cheek, then he stepped back. "Off you go."

Once inside, she gave a sigh of relief as the door closed out all the noise and activity. After peeing, she used a few paper towels to clean up as best she could.

Why, oh why, do guys get the fun, stand-up-to-pee appendage and gals the drippy-messy-innie and hard-to-locate-fun bits? It wasn't fair at all.

Leaving the stall, she tossed the towels and washed her hands. As she took a moment to finger-comb her hair, she checked out what fetwear the other women were wearing. And recognized some of the women.

Uh-oh, one was Justine, Drake's ex.

Her stomach dropped as Justine looked back at her. And scowled. "Oh, look what the cat dragged in. Didn't you look smug sitting at my Master's feet. As if you belonged there, in your slut clothes."

Damn, I used to love a hearty Boston accent, and she's ruining it for me.

One of the other submissives turned. "Justine, it's roleplay night. What she's wearing is perfect. I've seen three other maid outfits."

Justine ignored her, keeping her gaze on Ray. "Skank. He'll get bored and dump you. Or he'll get tired of all your drama, how loud you are. I hear you can't even remember your head unless someone screws it on for you."

Ray's shoulders hunched to weather the too-accurate attack. *How can she know all my faults?*

Had Drake complained about her?

She shivered. Too often, she'd heard Pa grumbling about her to his friends. Her boyfriends had too. Theodore even criticized her in front of others.

If Drake had...then she was wrong about him.

Stomach knotting painfully, she walked out.

"Look at her run, the cowardly bitch." Justine's voice scraped like a blade. "Worthless."

A coward. Am I? Uh...maybe?

Drake's eyes and smile warmed at the sight of her. "Shall we walk around in the dungeon, and you can tell me what intrigues you."

Everything inside her wanted to take his hand and ignore what Justine had said. Only she couldn't.

Trust...it was important.

"*Ma chérie*, what is wrong?" He moved closer and ran his hands up and down her arms, as if he could tell how chilled she was.

And she could feel the urge to run again. *No, I won't run. I'll ask him what I need to know.* She stiffened her spine. "In the restroom, some women were saying you'd get tired of my drama, how loud I am, how forgetful, and I thought maybe you'd been complaining about me and, and I need to know if..."

"Ray." He took her hands, as if wanting the physical connection to her. "When I have talked about you—and I have, *oui*—it's to tell my friends how pleased I am to have met you. How you're everything George said—more, in fact, considering your mentor didn't see you as an intriguing woman or a fascinating submissive."

Seriously? She stared at him in shock.

And his lips quirked. "You don't believe me." He pulled her slightly closer and kissed her forehead. "You've been hurt by criticism from those who should love you. Such behavior between lovers isn't honorable. Is...*mmm*, toxic, is the word. *Non*, I do not behave in such a way."

"Oh."

His expression was open, his gaze steady, his hands warm around hers. "I assume, eventually, we will find things to complain about, but Aralia"—he released one hand to cup her chin, lifting her head, holding her gaze—"I haven't found anything yet. You are...eh, dramatic because you feel intensely, not because you seek attention. You can be forgetful when involved in work." His shrug said he didn't care. "You are never boring, which I very much appreciate."

Warmth was growing inside her, so much warmth. Tears burned at the backs of her eyes.

No, no, I can't cry here.

He pulled her into his arms and laid his cheek on top of her head. "*Mon petit chou.* Perhaps there are times your thoughts are as erratic as a spring wind, but...your emotions, your loyalty is as solid as the mountains."

That did it. She felt the first tear slide down her cheek. *Gods, I love this person, this Dom.* She opened her mouth to say it—and nothing came out. Nothing.

He chuckled. "There will come a time when you won't choke on whatever you want to say to me."

Smiling, he kissed her forehead, laced their fingers together, and led her across the room.

It was a good convention this year. Sitting in the pre-function area, he sipped his drink and enjoyed the buzz of conversation around him. Nodded at the greetings from various people.

And scoped out possible choices for play in the dungeon later tonight.

A young woman with auburn hair caught his attention. Ah, yes, the redhead named Ray. She was heading for the dungeon with Drake. The know-it-all bastard did have good taste. The French maid outfit set off all the cunt's best attributes.

Earlier he'd enjoyed watching her climax—although spending the time and energy to get a woman off was time wasted. If he wanted to display his control over a submissive, he'd demand she give him a blowjob.

Drake pampered the submissives. In fact, it was galling how contented the bitch looked.

Yes, it had been several years, but he remembered her. She'd recovered far too well. He took pride in his ability to break a woman and to leave her so confused in her head she'd know she was violated but still feel as if she asked for it. Might even remember begging.

He smiled slowly.

The redhead might not be broken now, but...

Wouldn't it be interesting to do it all over again? Only go much further the second time.

Oh yes.

CHAPTER FIFTEEN

In his condo tower's fitness area, Drake finished his early morning workout and was stretching out. The equipment in the room was state of the art with a variety of cardio machines and strength-training equipment. There was good natural lighting and ample floor space.

This early on a Saturday, there were only three others working out.

And at the far end of the room, Simon was shadow boxing, displaying his usual fine footwork.

It was difficult to believe he was a decade or so older.

Of course, staying fit was high on his priority list. Simon owned an international security company and often sparred with his ex-military and ex-mercenary employees.

"Old man," Drake called, even though the insult would garner bruises. "I designed this gym so the end can be roped off for sparring. Care to indulge?"

"Yes, I want to see how out of shape you are. Along with the usual caveats, today the head is also off limits."

Drake laughed. "You don't want to lecture with a black eye and fat lip?"

Simon only grinned.

Drake set up the sparring ring ropes to keep idiots from blundering into a fist. "Let's glove up—I have an extra pair."

Ready to go, they squared off, moving in a slow rotation, each searching for an opening. Smiling slightly, Simon led with a fast punch, got blocked, and his other fist hit Drake's ribs. Not full force, but hard enough.

His mentor definitely hadn't slowed down.

"Is your Rona enjoying the convention?" Drake threw a flurry of punches.

Simon knocked him sideways with a knee to the flank followed by a side punch. "She is. She says the classes for the submissives are the best she's attended."

"Good to hear." Drake feinted a roundhouse and twisted to throw a body shot. Got it in although Simon turned enough to lessen the blow. "All too often, conventions focus on skills for topping. We're trying for a better balance—and trying to ensure those new to BDSM feel welcome."

Drake blocked Simon's crisp jab and returned a right hook.

"What does your young woman think of the classes?" Simon asked.

Even while thinking, Drake avoided a foot sweep. Considering how reticent Ray had been about her panic attack, she probably didn't want others to know. "She's enjoying herself, which probably means we haven't let the newbies down."

"And the dungeon? Did she enjoy it?"

"We haven't been yet. Last night, I gave her a taste of power exchange dynamics in the pre-function area."

"Interesting." Simon raised his eyebrows—and grunted in annoyance when Drake didn't fall for a rear low-kick feint. "Newbies usually want to play in the dungeon."

"We will tonight." It was something to look forward to. "She can get overwhelmed by too much activity and noise, and the convention dungeon is pure chaos." Starting out in BDSM was unsettling enough without adding in a frenetic dungeon filled with kinksters from everywhere, all wanting to try out new equipment.

Private clubs were different, Most developed their own flow and culture over time, and Chains was less hectic than many others.

Simon moved in. The give and take of blows and kicks was as invigorating as a hearty tennis exchange.

Stepping back to recover, they circled again.

"I like her," Simon said after a minute. "I'm pleased by the way you are together."

Drake's concentration faltered, and he took a step back. "You met Justine. And Ramona when she was my slave. I don't recall you giving *any* opinion on them."

"I wasn't impressed by either, but maligning a person's lover is short-sighted—and tactless." He punctuated that opinion with a side kick that almost took Drake out.

"*Bâtard*." Drake's forearm burned from deflecting the kick. He countered with a quick reverse punch.

"You never looked at either woman the way you look at Ray." Blocking, Simon stepped off the line of attack and punched toward Drake's ribs.

"As it happens, I love this one." *And she loves me.* How could he concentrate on fighting when he simply wanted to smile? With a step back, he broke off for a moment.

Unusually for his mentor, Simon let him, a smile on his hard face. "I look forward to getting to know her better."

"Oh. My. Gods." Ray stood inside the fitness center and stared at Simon and Drake. A fist hit a muscular abdomen with a meaty slap. "Are they trying to kill each other?"

Rona laughed. "Seems to be a pretty relaxed sparring session. They're having fun."

Simon punched Drake's ribs hard enough to make him grunt. Grabbing Simon, Drake tossed him over a hip onto the floor.

"Ow," Rona said in sympathy. "They're going to have some bruises."

"But they're having fun?" Ray blew out a breath. She'd thought sparring with Tomo was rough; apparently, the Marine had gone easy on her. A quiver of worry ran up her spine. "Drake said Simon likes to grease his fists with blood?"

Rona laughed. "He's not blood-thirsty. Really. But he was one of the top fighters on the MMA circuit. Before my time, thank goodness."

Whoa. She'd seen clips from MMA fights. There had been blood. "He-he shouldn't be fighting Drake." *My* Drake. She took a step forward, intending...what? To yank Master Drake out of the ring?

Only Drake landed a solid fist in Simon's gut—and blocked a roundhouse kick, saying something that made Simon laugh.

Ray frowned. "He's not getting stomped into the ground."

"Hardly," Rona said. "Simon taught him everything he knew in exchange for the dirty fighting techniques Drake grew up using in France."

Wait, what? "Dirty fighting?"

"Mmmhmm." Rona's gaze was on the fight. "Under all that French polish, there's a sad history and a steel backbone."

"Huh. I know his parents died when he was a teen, and he came to the US to be with his uncle." Ray frowned. "Getting the rest of the story might be difficult."

"Definitely. Although that can be nice." Rona rolled her eyes. "Some people will spill their entire life story over a beer."

"Or in the restroom. I swear, I've heard the strangest tales in nightclub restrooms."

"Crom, I know exactly what you mean. But—" She paused at Ray's upraised hand.

"One question. What is a Crom?"

"Oh, right. When my sons were young, their school was death on swearing. But kids, right?" Rona shrugged. "The kids and I talked it over and started swearing by a different god—from *Conan the Barbarian*. They still use it too."

"Love it! I tend to swear by Lovecraft's elder gods myself." *This is a very cool woman.* "Okay, I'm sorry I interrupted. Go on?"

"Ah... oh, I was going to say neither Simon nor Drake are the kind of men to share sad stories. You might get snippets, here and there."

"Snippets, huh."

"Eventually, you'll hear the whole of it." Rona smiled, her gaze on Drake. "Because he cares for you. A lot."

Ray...eventually...managed to close her mouth.

Tightening the belt on her wrap-around dress, Ray stepped into the rapidly filling elevator. The ballroom floor button was already lit, so she tucked herself into a back corner.

From the number of people obviously wearing street clothing over fetwear, the awards presentations must be over. As the door shut, she tried not to feel guilty for bailing out of attending the evening's big event.

But after a day of workshops and classes, she'd returned to the hotel room exhausted and stressed-out from the crowds and noise.

Other than that, the day had been a good one. Great workshops. Spending time off and on with three women she really liked.

With Hope, it was as if they'd never been apart, and it was wonderful to have someone to share old memories with.

Her new friend MacKensie was amazing. The scary-smart veterinarian was a crazy science fiction and fantasy fan, and since

Ray adored every genre ever created, she could *frakking* talk *Battlestar Galactica* with her.

And Mac was keen on bare-handed spankings. She was open about it—said so right out in the vendor room.

I shouldn't have commented on how I felt, not where Alex could hear. He wouldn't tell Drake...would he?

Rona was the third woman she'd spent time with. Maybe ten or more years older and an incredibly compassionate person. And submissive like Ray. Although...when Rona's hospital-administrator personality took over, she sounded almost dominant. But when Simon was around, the two of them were a prime example of living D/s, and so hot together, they could melt ice.

Watching the three women with their partners provided a good idea of how it would be to live with a Dom.

As the elevator stopped at another floor, and more people entered, Ray squeezed tighter into her corner. Thank goodness she'd had some time to restore her equilibrium...although she still felt like a loser, unable to deal with people and noise.

Drake had seen how stressed she was, hugged her, and ordered her to stay and relax in the room until time to meet him outside the dungeon.

Gods, how could such a bossy person be so...nice. He'd tucked her into the oversized bathtub with a charcuterie tray to nibble on while she soaked. After fondling her breasts for a moment—and she'd seen his erection bulging his pants—he kissed her. "I need to leave and go do Official Convention Stuff."

All aroused, she figured she'd rub one out as soon as he left. Only after studying her for a moment, he'd said, "Aralia, I intend to enjoy your body in the dungeon tonight. You will save your orgasms for me, am I clear?" The look in his dark eyes was a warning and a promise.

She'd almost melted into the water.

Damn the man. The Dom. Whatever.

The elevator door opened to the ballroom floor, and everyone flowed out. Along with the others, she passed through security, walked around the screens, and left her dress at the "coat" check. Heh, it should be called the *clothing* check.

As she moved into the socializing area outside the dungeon, a het couple walked past, both giving her appreciative glances. She glanced down, still a little shocked at the sight of her body in the black leather corset. Her waist was tiny, and her breasts were pushed up into prominent mounds. The bottom half had only thigh-high fishnet stockings held up by the attached garters and a tiny black brief.

Talk about feeling almost naked. Reminded her of the nightmares where she'd show up for a gallery opening in only her underwear.

At least, her corset wasn't too tight, since there'd been no one around to tighten the laces in back. When she'd zipped the front, she realized the fit was from the vendor room when she tried it on over her clothing.

Looser was *fine,* considering she was already short of breath from anticipation of what the evening might hold.

A group of Doms saw her, and she caught their approving smiles. *Well then.* Her pulse started a trippy rhythm. *Will Drake be pleased with my outfit?*

The pre-function and foyer areas outside the dungeon were even busier than last night. A group from one club was showing off their purchases of fetwear and toys from the vendor room. The sitting areas were filled with people, some full of energy and others exhausted, their clothing damp with sweat. They'd obviously already done a scene in the dungeon.

From behind her came Drake's deep, smooth voice...speaking French. None of which she understood. Hell, was she going to have to learn the language?

Strong hands gripped her shoulders as he turned her to face him. His gaze swept over her, and his eyes darkened to pure black.

Her heart rate quickened. No one had ever looked at her the way he did.

As he examined the O-rings on the sides of her waist, his mouth curved. "*Mmm.* These will be fun to make use of...and you, *ma chérie,* will have an interesting night."

She swallowed hard. "R-right."

The sound of muted applause caught her attention. A wall screen displayed clips from the award presentations earlier. Drake was one of the presenters, all broad-shouldered perfection in his charcoal-colored suit, with his dark facial hair and white smile.

She noticed he'd switched out his onyx studs for black diamond earrings. So fucking elegant.

Even here, in his vest and white shirt, he was collecting appreciative—and flirtatious—smiles from many in the room. Of all genders.

Don't be jealous, Ray. You don't own the Dom. She made her voice light. "Don't you clean up nice, Master Drake."

"Thank you." He motioned to the screen. "Your paddles were some of the first to be gone. They were very popular."

"Really?" Her heart lifted as she watched an award recipient get applauded before moving to a table piled with fetwear, impact and sex toys, and bondage gear. The person picked up one of her paddles, weighed it, swung it, stroked it.

Yes! All those hours of sanding and glossing were worth it.

"There's a happy smile." Drake gave her a light kiss. "You'll probably see some of them in use tonight in the dungeon."

Her smile faded. "And see the submissive getting hurt from something I made?"

"Aralia." He waited until her gaze met his. "Did you forget Casper's pleasure in being paddled?"

"Oh. Oh, right." Intense pain wasn't her kink, but Casper had loved getting spanked. And her paddles were far better than any Drake had shown her.

Drake cupped her cheek, running his thumb over her chin.

"When Jasira received an award for mentoring other Dommes, Casper yelled from the audience demanding a Ray paddle. He let out a shriek of happiness when she picked one of yours."

Delight bubbled up inside Ray, and she couldn't keep from grinning. Although... "I hope he doesn't get in trouble for being pushy."

"Oh, he'll get punished." Drake chuckled. "In his case, probably making him wait a couple of days before getting to try out his new paddle."

Ray blinked, then laughed. "Right. Paddling a masochist wouldn't work as a punishment, would it?"

"Precisely. Thankfully, it will work quite well for you."

"Wait, what?"

Drake's grin flashed. Putting an arm around her waist, he guided her toward the ballroom dungeon.

"Ray!" Near the middle of the room, Hope bounced up and down, waving. Peter stood next to her along with Alex and MacKensie. Hope wore her new corset and looked fantastic, although her mascara was smeared and her hair in tangles.

"I think someone had a good time," Ray whispered to Drake.

He chuckled. "A submissive who finds crying to be a release will usually have a Dom who finds the sight of her smeared makeup rewarding."

Huh, who would've thought? Maybe I'll wear more makeup next time.

As they got closer, Hope pursed her lips and studied Ray's attire. "The corset is perfect for you."

Peter's gaze was on the O-rings, and he grinned at Drake. "And for you also."

"My sentiments exactly," Drake murmured.

Having been half-hidden behind Peter, Theodore stepped forward. "Ray! What are you wearing? You can't..."

Oh Gods, what could she even say? "Theodore—"

Drake made a chiding sound. "You do not have permission to speak, *bébé*."

What? When had he said she had to be silent?

His stern expression made her quail...until she caught the tiny quirk of his lip.

Ohhhhh. He was removing the pressure of dealing with Theodore. Refused permission to speak, she snuggled closer to convey her gratitude.

Peter frowned and turned to Theodore, saying in a barely audible voice, "Criticizing a Dominant's choice of clothing for his submissive is considered rude. As is making anyone, submissive or Dominant, uncomfortable."

Theodore reddened slightly. He glanced at Ray, then Drake. "Please excuse me."

After regarding Theodore's disgruntled expression for a moment, Alex smiled slightly and wiggled his eyebrows. "You're getting lax, Drake. Withholding permission to speak is good. However, letting her touch you when she wants?"

Wait, Drake hadn't said anything about that either. MacKensie's Dom was not only making a point to Theodore but...also goading Ray into misbehaving? To get her in trouble?

Then again, I might get a kick out of being in trouble.

Lifting her chin, she deliberately hugged Drake's arm, rubbing her cheek against his hard bicep. *So there.*

She could feel his ribs shake with his silent laugh before he tightened his arm around her. "It appears a naughty submissive needs to be punished."

Punished? A flash of heat vied with pure worry.

"It's best to keep them in line," Alex agreed. "There's a pommel horse in the dungeon. Or did you see the old-fashioned caning table with wooden restraints shaped like a pillory?"

"*Mmm, oui.* That has potential." She could feel Drake focus on her. "Kneel, please."

Here? Now? Hope and Mac were on their feet.

Master Drake's silence carried a dangerous weight.

A flush warmed Ray's face as she dropped to her knees. Back straight, hands on thighs, gaze down.

"Very nice." The approval in his voice filled her with a disconcerting happiness. "For tonight, you will wear this."

Something cool wrapped around her neck. His fingers touched her skin as he buckled on a...collar. A collar, gods help her.

Yet there was a sense of satisfaction, of pleasure, in feeling his hands on her, of wearing his—his mark of ownership, even if it was for only one night.

"Look at me."

She lifted her head and met his dark focused gaze. Saw the flash of his teeth. "So we both enjoy you wearing my collar."

There was no answer she could give. Or was permitted to give. And yet...and yet...it filled her with contentment to have all the words taken away.

He bent, his warm hand under her chin. "Punishment means I am going to restrain you and hurt you. And then take you. I will stay within the bounds of your limit list. Do you wish to negotiate anything?"

Her world narrowed to his eyes, so steady on hers. "I trust you."

The lines beside his eyes crinkled with his smile. "Then let us begin." He gripped her waist and lifted her to her feet.

Drake had to admit he enjoyed the feeling of a soft, naked woman more than anything else, but a submissive in a tightly laced corset was almost as fine.

And Aralia in a leather bondage corset was about the sexiest sight he'd ever seen. Her curly hair danced along her shoulders, wild and free, a contrast with the ruthless constraints on the rest of her body. The black corset set off her pale skin—and freckles. He bent to kiss the top of one speckled shoulder, inhaling the light apricot scent that lingered from her bubble bath.

She smelled edible.

He nipped her velvety skin, enjoying how she never smelled the same way twice. So intriguing.

Nodding a greeting at a couple of Dominants, he headed for the bondage-pillory hybrid table. Ah, there it was. Not only empty but also close to the center of the room. Quite public.

Excellent.

He set his bag on a nearby stand and considered the table. Nice modifications. Pillory-style, wooden wrist restraints at the head of the table. Hinged wooden boards resembling stocks sat at the base of the table legs.

"Step here." He opened the box-like contraption for ankles. "Legs wide." Obviously, the table designer preferred a submissive's legs to be widely separated when shackled.

Ray's expression held worry, but she obediently set her feet by the box's semi-circles next to each table leg.

He closed the box, trapping her ankles within the precut holes. "Bend forward on the table. Arms above your head."

He fit her wrists in the half-circle holes and closed the hinged board over the top. "You should be grateful this design secures only your arms and not your head as a true pillory would."

"I'm not sure it's an improvement," she muttered, making him laugh.

"I notice your corset is looser than it should be." And how could a Dom resist? He tightened the laces of the corset before securing the O-rings on each side of her waist to the grommets on the table's edge.

Now...would any of her fears of bondage come to the surface?

He watched her try to move.

The color rose in her face as she learned even her torso was restrained. But she displayed no distress.

Stepping back, he looked her over. Bent over the length of the table, arms outstretched and secured. Waist secured. Legs apart with ankles secured. She was tall enough the table ended at her pelvis, leaving her mound easily touchable.

"This will do quite nicely. Except for this covering." Scissors were in the outside pocket of his bag—readily available—and he used them to cut off her briefs from under the black corset. The corset's leather garters held up black fishnet stockings and beautifully framed her white ass. "*Tu es si belle.*"

He brushed his fingertips over her, hearing her breath catch. Her legs were the perfect distance apart to let him see her glistening pussy.

Oui, they'd both enjoy what was to come.

But first... Alex had mentioned she'd shown interest in bare-handed spanking. Might she prefer it to paddles? "Although this kind of table is designed for caning, tonight, I will use my hand."

He could see her swallow. Her expression held worry, desire. No fear. He caressed her, playing with the garters, her buttocks, moving closer and away from her pussy. A few light swats pinkened her skin in preparation for what was to come.

"You were deliberately disobedient in the foyer." The next swat was harder, the sound satisfying. "The consequence is this spanking.

And they would find out if the consequences were punishment —or reward.

Ow, ow, ow. Master Drake had a hard hand—and she couldn't move out of range. Couldn't shield her butt with her hands, couldn't even wiggle. Talk about being forced to submit.

His next three spanks hit the undercurve of her buttocks —*owww*. Why was *there* so much more sensitive?

A serious burn set in, and a whine escaped. The corset was restricting her stomach, her chest— breathing—and made everything more intense.

And the feel of his hand—his warm, bare hand—was somehow incredibly different than a wooden paddle. More direct or personal or intimate or something.

Two more spanks, then more spanks. Oh, it burned; tears filled her eyes, even as a slow, molten throbbing woke a hunger low in her abdomen.

He stroked over her stockings, her inner bare thighs, and touched her pussy. Just like with the paddles, she was wet.

His fingers circled her clit, massaged her folds, teased her entrance. Leaning against her, he rubbed his hard erection against her so-very-painful butt and made her hiss.

Made her want desperately to be filled.

He dipped his hands into her corset to cup her breasts, to squeeze them and pinch the nipples.

She couldn't *move*. Couldn't do anything to slow the pleasure, the pain.

His breath touched her ear, his voice a dark murmur. "Soon, soon, I will take you. Push inside your tight little asshole and enjoy how it feels around me as you come."

She froze for a moment, a flashback flitting through her mind, and then he was stroking her hair. His voice softened. "Aralia, you are safe, always. Tell me your safeword, *ma chérie*."

Her answer was only a whisper. "Red."

"*Oui*." He ran his hands up and down her upstretched arms. "What color are you right now?"

The memories had disappeared. He'd restrained her, hurt her —carefully—and if she used her safeword, he'd stop. It felt as if she was falling forward into a giant leafy pile of trust.

No, more than trust.

Arousal was rising, turning into open need. "I'm green, Sir." She paused. "Is there a color that says *more, more, more*. Or... *take me?*"

His seductive laugh sent shivers through her. "Perhaps we need one—purple."

Purple. Yes. A big, huge, royalty-laden purple. "Purple!"

He was still laughing, even as he rolled her nipples firmly, slowly, until pleasure and pain made her toes curl.

Pulling back, he ran his hand down her body to her bottom and pulled her cheeks apart. The cool lube on her heated rim would've had her squirming...if she could move. He teased the rim, slid on a glove, and inserted a finger. The penetration there, in such a private place, made her feel somewhere between being a dirty girl and being...possessed.

"Good girl," he murmured, adding another finger. He would be bigger—much bigger. Anxiety tensed her around him, even as excitement raced through her blood in fizzy bubbles.

She heard his pants zipper, the sound of a condom wrapper. He pressed against her, *oh, so big*. "Push out, *bébé*."

As she did, he steadily slid in. Oh, the burn, the stretch. Too wide. She tensed. Suddenly, the head was in.

She was panting. So full, she was so full.

More lubricant, wet and cool. He pushed in farther, and she was making funny sounds, *uh, uh, uh,* not quite whimpering as he penetrated her.

Slowly, mercilessly, he filled her completely. His hard body pressed against her burning ass.

"Mmm, you feel magnificent. Tonight, rather than being silent, you will make noise. I want to hear you." When he leaned forward, the angle of his cock changed, making her gasp.

He laughed. "Not nearly loud enough. After all, there might be others watching who'd enjoy the sounds of a little submissive being taken. Orgasming."

What—wait, watching? Not Theodore or the person with the bone-chilling voice from the class yesterday or Drake's mean ex or... *No, Master Drake is here. I'm safe.*

Yet there were so many other people around, ones she'd met this weekend and tons she hadn't met, and she could almost feel the pressure of their gazes. On her.

They would see her bent over, his hands on her breasts. Her heart beat harder as excitement rose. They would see him thrusting.

Gods.

Although, taking her...there. Well, there was no way she'd get off, which was good, really. Coming in public was, maybe, too intimate, too—

He made that French-sounding *pffft*. "You are thinking, *ma douce*. Let's put a stop to that." Pulling out, he spanked her, one cheek, the other, over and over.

Her bottom burned, stung, hurt. Nothing else mattered.

Until he drove in again, the burning rim stretching around him, and her cry ringing in her ears.

He reached around her, his fingers sliding over her clit, one side and the other, so very knowledgeable. The pleasure was overwhelming.

She tried to move—couldn't. Could barely breathe. Every muscle in her body tightened, as everything spiraled down to his fingers and...

His cock. Withdrawing, pressing in, slow and steady.

Oh Gods, I'm going to come. No, not here. She tried to shake her head.

But he took hold of her hair in a hard grip, pulling her head up as he drove in. Hard. Taking her as she'd asked.

No, going much further than she'd asked. Taking complete control—and the feeling crashed over her, throwing her into an unstoppable, hard orgasm.

She panted through it—silently—and lay limp.

He slowed. And laughed. "Stubborn submissive." He released her hair with a playful tug, running his hands down her back, squeezing her tender ass cheeks and making her squeak. "It appears you need another."

Her eyes went wide. He was still thick and long inside her. She'd gotten off; he hadn't.

A buzzing sounded right before something pressed against her clit. The surge of pleasure was shocking. The vibrator didn't use any weird random patterns, just got right down to business with serious, heavy throbbing that drove her upward relentlessly.

He straightened—added more lube—and set to a steady, hard rhythm.

She was helpless against his will. Couldn't move, impaled on his shaft, and the vibrations on her clit were inescapable.

She hovered on the threshold of coming.

And then he slowed. The vibe moved away. Damn him. She opened her mouth to curse him out.

No, not smart.

The vibrator returned. His speed increased. Almost... almost...

He did it again!

"Oh, please, *pleeeeze*, Master Drake. *Pleeeeze*."

"But of course, *ma chérie*."

The next thrust was hard and deep and so, so satisfying. The vibe settled firmly right. *On. Top. Of her clit.*

He threaded the fingers of one hand into the laces of her corset, anchoring himself, and tightening it at the same time. She couldn't move, could barely breathe. And being controlled, unable to take a deep breath, swept her away.

Too many sensations.

Everything flashed white. She tried to arch—and couldn't—and the pleasure was overwhelming. "Aaaah, ahh, ahh!"

Drake grinned at the beautiful sound of a submissive coming. Of *this* submissive.

Panting, flushing red, thrashing as best she could despite the restraints and corset. He could feel the spasms, squeezing him so tightly.

His dick demanded a faster pace.

He held off long enough to loosen the corset ties to ensure she could breathe.

Merde, she felt good. He gripped her waist to add emphasis as he hammered into her, feeling a burn ignite low in his spine. Heat seared through his balls and into his cock. He pressed deep, deeper as pleasure coursed outward in hard, fast jerks.

Ahh, *parfait*. Leaning forward, he ran his hands up her body. "Do you feel adequately punished—and taken—*ma petite Ray*? Or should we begin again?"

She giggled so hard he could feel it in his dick.

"Ooooh, I can breathe again." Standing upright, Ray inhaled deeply, almost shocked at feeling her lungs able to freely expand.

Drake dropped her corset onto his toybag, covering her stockings, which he'd already stripped off her. Smiling slightly, he ran his hands over the ridges left on her skin.

Still a bit fuzzy and weak-kneed, she rested her forehead against his shoulder. And felt...funny. Too open and vulnerable, all her emotions swirling around like being in a cruel blender. Tears clogged her throat and made her breathing hitch.

"*Bébé*." He pulled her closer, enclosing her in his arms, and simply talked to her, sometimes in French, sometimes in English. Telling her how well she'd done. How proud he was.

Until the feeling of being defenseless faded away. She could feel the softness of his shirt under her cheek, against her breasts. Feel his warm hands stroking over her back. His breath ruffling her hair.

She was all right. "Thank you, Sir."

Releasing her, he kissed the top of her head. "My pleasure."

As her damp skin cooled, she shivered.

"Wait." He draped a soft, thin blanket around her shoulders. "You will sit down there while I clean the equipment."

"I should do it. Isn't it a submissive's job?"

"*Pfft*, not always. Sometimes all a submissive can do is sit and quiver, especially after a good session with impact toys." His teeth flashed in his tanned face.

"Oh." Being a masochist must be rough. "I'm okay now, really. Where's the cleaning stuff? Um, Sir."

He tilted his head, eyes narrowing slightly in a very Dominant expression. A wicked glint lit his dark eyes. "Paper towels and spray are in the stand by the wall."

When she returned, he had his bag packed up. He held out his hand. "Blanket, please."

Her corset was strapped to the side of his bag. "But..."

His chin rose fractionally.

And just like that she was handing him the blanket. In movies, drill sergeants were always shouting. They should take lessons. A Dom didn't even have to speak to get instant obedience.

A waft of coolness brushed over her body—her very naked body. She opened her mouth to say...something, but Master Drake merely smiled and motioned to the table.

Right, right, get on with it.

To her delight, he took a paper towel and wiped down the other side of the table. When everything was pristine, she hesitated and trudged over to return the cleaning supplies.

Naked.

She went past a male Dom, then a female one. Tried not to see the smiles. A submissive who was clothed, the lucky dog, winked at her sympathetically.

When she returned, Drake had the bag slung over his shoulder and...dammit, the blanket tucked away.

"You're going to make me walk out there with no clothes on?" Her voice actually squeaked at the end.

"*Oui*." A corner of his mouth tilted up. "No one may touch, but I enjoy sharing your beauty."

She glared. "What if I don't— Ow!" Her tender bottom burned again from his swift swat.

Rather than filling the air with explanations or calling her names, he stood, hands clasped behind his back, waiting for her to catch up mentally.

Because...she'd misstepped. This was a power exchange. A consenting one. Even if it meant she would be naked. "Sorry, Sir," she said grudgingly.

"Are you, Aralia?"

She opened her mouth to snap—and stopped. That was twice he'd called her on her attitude. Oddly enough, it felt right. Satisfying. Because he *was* in charge—and he knew her and liked her and still wouldn't let her get away with anything.

A knot inside her loosened. She didn't have to deal with...life. Not right now. The world was his problem.

She sighed and met his gaze. "Really, I'm sorry. And thank you."

His smile held approval. He put his free arm around her waist, keeping her close as they walked across the foyer. "So...*bébé*, should we go to a quiet aftercare room or would you prefer to stay out here, have something to eat and drink, and talk with people."

Um. Huh. She'd been a little off right at the end of their scene, all her defenses gone. But he'd hugged her and talked to her, and then she'd been back to normal.

"An aftercare room...now...would be boring. You did everything I needed already."

He nodded. "Such was my impression of how you were feeling." He looked around and then headed them over to a group of people. All dressed in various kinds of fetwear. "I will enjoy playing with my submissive's breasts while I talk."

And she realized...again...she was naked.

Dammit, I didn't think this one through.

CHAPTER SIXTEEN

The next morning, in the hotel dining room, Ray eyed the remaining piece of apple-pecan coffee cake on the platter. After cutting it, she handed a third to MacKensie, a third to Hope, and scarfed down the last piece herself. *So yummy.*

At her contented sigh, Drake looked away from his conversation with Peter and Alex and smiled at her.

Gods, he is gorgeous when he smiles. All the sternness gone. Laugh lines and the sunlines beside his eyes deepening.

Was he smiling more than he had when she met him?

She sure was. Unable to help herself, she leaned sideways, resting her shoulder against his. Just to touch him.

In answer, he rested his hand on her thigh.

Since last night, she'd felt different. Almost euphoric. As if the world had wrapped her in fuzzy cuddles. Every time Drake touched her—and he was doing that a lot more too—the feelings increased.

This is love. Of course it is.

She wasn't an idiot. It wouldn't last. At least, not with this intensity. It was like hiking in the Olympic mountains. The view from Hurricane Ridge was super-stunning, but a person couldn't live on a mountain peak.

She'd have to descend from the heights of love sometime, but for today... *I'm gonna revel in it.*

Hope rose to her feet. "I'm going to the ladies' room before we head out." She frowned at the sugar caked on her fingers. "I can't touch anything until I do."

"Me too." Ray stood and catching Drake's look, bent and kissed his cheek. She held up her hands. "Although it's a shame to wash off all the yummy sugar."

Smiling, Drake lifted Ray's hand and closed his mouth over her fingertips. His lips were soft, teeth administering a tiny nip, before he sucked lightly.

Flashes of heat ran through her. So much heat.

Releasing her, he licked his lips. "You are as sweet as I thought, *mon amour*. Off you go."

She tried to frown at him—for making her want to drag him back to bed, if nothing else. For knowing exactly what he did to her. "You're a splinter under my nail," she muttered.

"Ah, *bébé*, you don't enjoy a good...splintering?" His dark eyes were filled with wicked amusement.

Sputtering with laughter, she couldn't even summon a good scowl. *Flee, flee while you can.* "Let's go, Hope."

As they left the room and crossed to the restrooms, they both collected smiles, invitations to join different tables—usually men, occasionally others.

Returning from the restroom, they ran into the same. "We're totally running the gauntlet," Ray told Hope.

"Only you're getting hit with invitations instead of sticks."

"Ha, yes. I'm glad we did a team run to the bathroom."

"I guess it's single people's last chance to find someone with kinky interests to date." Hope turned when someone called her name. "Let me say a quick hi—I haven't seen Mercedes since the last con. I'll be quick."

Ray stayed a few feet away, out of hearing but close enough she didn't look alone. It'd sure been a lovely weekend—full of surprises and new experiences. Helping with workshops, sitting next to people in classes, she'd met some great people. And—

"Ah, it's Chains' new submissive volunteer."

Ray jumped slightly at the smooth tenor intruding into her thoughts.

The man in front of her was clean shaven, brown hair in a business cut, a line between his brows. Probably a bit older than Master Drake. Familiar-looking.

He smiled at her blank look. "I'm Blaize. Let's see, I met you at the Bainbridge coffee shop and then at Chains."

"Oh, right." She rolled her eyes. "I've met so many people, I'm forgetting my own name. I remember you. You were with the—" She hastily closed her mouth before labeling his ditch-pig friend a jerk. "Um, it's good to see you again."

"Is it now." His smile grew. "Then perhaps you should see more of me. I'd love to take you out for dinner and drinks...maybe next Friday?"

Holy kraken, he was hitting on her. Didn't he know she was dating Drake?

She eyed the way his mouth held a tilt much like a smirk. Yeah, he knew and was asking anyway. Trying to one-up Drake?

Sometimes men were real wankstains. "Sorry, but I'm afraid I'm not available."

He tilted his head. "A shame. We could have had some fun. Have a good day then." With another of his charming smiles, he strolled away.

And minute later, Hope joined her. "Sorry, sorry, I couldn't simply say hi and leave without chatting a bit."

"As if this is a surprise?" Ray snorted. "Girl, you can't even say good morning to a stray dog without stopping to chat."

"Oh, insults." Hope scowled, her lips twitching. "Twatwaffle."

"Really? Here?" Ray looked down her nose. "You're still the size of a crotch-goblin."

"You dare insult my height?" Hope's voice rose. "You crusty-ass excuse for a spunk-stain."

Apparently, Hope hadn't noticed they were close to their table. She gulped when Peter turned to regard his sweet wife with raised eyebrows.

Unable to resist, Ray said, "Wow, they let you teach school with that mouth?"

The back of Hope's hand hit her right in the gut. *Ouch.* Then again, she was already half-bent over laughing her...crusty ass off.

As was every person at the table.

Still sputtering with giggles, Ray dropped into her chair beside Drake. And enjoyed how nice laughter looked on his chiseled face.

Even better, she'd be seeing him again. Soon.

The convention was closing with this brunch. Drake planned to take Simon and Rona to his Bainbridge house for a couple of days and wanted her to join them.

She would—tomorrow. Today, she needed to go home, unwind, and spend time with Max. Although her bed was going to feel way too empty tonight. *I'm going to miss him.*

Odd. When she fell for Theodore, her feelings sure hadn't been so...so immense. When they broke up, she hadn't missed him.

"Ray. I've been looking for you."

She looked over her shoulder at the sound of her name. *Huh, speak of the devil...* Why did he keep turning up?

As Theodore approached, she turned in her chair to face him.

His expression scrunched down like one of those dried apple heads. Bad mood much?

Yikes, maybe I should stand up. "Is there a problem, Theodore?"

"Yes, there is. I know I've said this before, but today you're going to actually listen. You need to come back to me. We were good together."

Jeez, he's doing this in front of everyone? Was this a lawyer thing—public scenes?

His expression grew even angrier.

Whups, focus, Ray. "Uh, no, we weren't good together." And he accused her of not listening? "One more time: We. Are. Done." She put a hand on Drake's shoulder. "I have—"

"Now that I know what you want, what you need, I'll help you get past being over-emotional and a drama queen. And keep you happy in bed. I know you're not especially interested in sex—"

The explosion of laughter from the others at the table startled him. He frowned. "It's not funny."

"She's not interested in sex?" Hope was giggling her head off. "Sure didn't sound that way last night."

" '*Oh, please, pleeeeze, Master,*' " MacKensie said in a high voice.

"For freaking sake, I didn't sound like that," Ray snapped.

Alex tapped a finger on his chin and said in a judicious tone, "Actually, you did."

"When he finally let you get off, you deafened everyone in the area," Peter added oh-so-helpfully.

She shot him a scorching glare.

"She—she did?" Theodore looked as if he'd been zapped with a cattle prod. She'd never known people used cattle prods as a kind of weird sex toy, but last night, a Top had been using one on — *Focus, Ray.*

She'd been silent too long.

Drake had a hand over his mouth, and his shoulders were shaking.

Her face was probably the color of the strawberries left on her plate...and he was laughing. *Damn Dom.* She jammed her elbow into his ribs.

The bastard broke into deep, hearty laughter.

"But, but, Ray. I can help you." Theodore looked so confused.

She smothered a sigh. With other men, he seemed to be a good person, but when it came to her—or maybe women in general—he was a jerk. After all, it was what straight, white males were taught.

Still, this wasn't the eighteen hundreds, and if men in this century didn't make an effort to pull their heads out of their asses, then the blame was *theirs*.

"Theodore. I want you to truly listen for once." She pulled in a breath. "From what you've said, you want a partner who will enjoy you taking charge. You also—"

"You need a—"

"I am submissive, yes. Let. Me. Finish."

When Theodore opened his mouth to speak over her, Drake said in his Master-of-the-dungeon voice, "A competent Dominant opens his ears when a submissive needs to speak."

Dammit. Seems she really *could* love him even more.

She squeezed his hand in an unspoken thank you. "Theodore, you *also* want your lover to have a quiet...a *subdued*...personality. Which is absolutely fine. What *isn't* fine is trying to..." She gestured air quotes. "...improve... someone with a personality that is—"

"Loud," Theodore interjected, making her wince. "Ray, no one wants a drama queen."

"Your idea of drama is what I call vibrant and fun, and I love it." Drake's words washed away the hurt and melted her heart. "She's also..." He opened his hand to invite everyone into the conversation.

"Vivid. Sparkling," Mac added without a pause, "Even better than champagne." She grinned when Ray choked on a laugh.

"Exciting and energetic and brave." Hope glared at Theodore.

"Dazzling," Alex said thoughtfully. "Colorful and creative."

Despite being Theodore's friend and associate, even Peter jumped in. "Brilliantly vivacious."

Right now, her ex totally resembled the person he wanted in his life—subdued.

Time to finish this up. "Obviously, I'm not the right person for you." She shook her head at him. "It's wrong to try to change a lover's personality to fit your needs. Go find a submissive with a quiet nature. And make sure she appreciates who you are and won't try to change *you*."

"Well said," Drake murmured, but it was loud enough for Theodore to hear.

This time, maybe due to all the support, her words got through. Theodore's expression changed from angry determination to resignation. Even sadness. "I...I get it." His gaze swept the table. "Sorry to have interrupted your brunch."

He walked away. Dignified, polite, a nice man if he thought he was dealing with equals.

She sighed. "That right there is why I started going with him. But when it comes to women, if cluelessness was a sport, he'd be in the Olympics."

Drake put his arm over her shoulders, pulling her against his side. "*Mon cœur*, you are far better with me." He raised his voice. "*Oui*, my friends?"

And got a rousing chorus of agreement.

Ray pulled a shirt from her suitcase and tossed it into the laundry basket.

"*Mew, mew, mew.*" Perched on the bed, Max had a lot to say. *You were gone too long. The two-legger who came in didn't fix my food right. How can I sleep without a warm body to curl up against at night? I didn't get nearly enough tidbits to nibble on. Mew, mew, mew.*

Ray grinned as she listened. Unlike George's cat Yuki, who'd sulk for days after an absence, Max had greeted her with enthusiasm. With head-butts and cheek-rubs to mark her as his property.

And complaints.

She bent and gave him a cheek-rub of her own. "I missed you, too, my sweet fuzzbutt. Drake makes a wonderful sleep companion but doesn't purr worth a damn."

Head and tail high, Max jumped into the empty suitcase, made a circle, and lay down...purring extra loud.

Ray put away her new fetwear in the growing section of her closet. "If I'm ever involved in a criminal case, the cops will see this stuff, and I'll automatically become a person of interest. A lot of men figure a woman who enjoys kinky sex is obviously a criminal."

Max's ears perked up. *Mew. Two-legger men are stupid.*

"True that. Except for Master Drake, of course." Ray plucked Max out of the suitcase so she could put it away. "But it sure seems as if lots of guys get angry if a woman understands her own needs. Maybe they're afraid we'll expect a lover to do more than jump on and pump away?"

Max yawned and strolled out of the bedroom.

"Yeah, yeah, I know...sex doesn't interest you, Mr. I've-been-neutered." She followed the cat downstairs to the kitchen. "The vets insist neutered boy cats are healthier and more loving and less liable to get into trouble. Do you suppose it'd work for overly aggressive human males?"

She poured herself some apple juice. "We should put a bill into Congress. Instant birth control."

Max delivered a cynical cat stare.

"I know, I know. Rich, old, white men rule the country. They'd never go for it." She made a face. "If there weren't men like Drake and George—and Max, the human you were named for—I'd be in favor of killing off all the males in the country, leaving no more than a few alive for stud services."

Huh, I should be a writer. What a great dystopian story.

The doorbell derailed her train of thought and sent her to the door. "Hey, Marisol, what's up? Did your mom get my text that I'm home?"

"She did. Since I'm on my way back to the university, she wanted me to drop off a batch of cookies."

Ray laughed and pried off the container lid. The scent of ginger and molasses drifted up. The crinkled/cracked tops of the big amber-brown cookies glistened with sugar. "Ginger cookies?"

"Good guess. Do you like—" Marisol laughed. "Guess you do."

The *mmm-mmm-mmm* sounds Ray was making were a total giveaway. Soft, chewy cookies. She swallowed and barely managed not to reach for another. *Be polite, Ray.* "Tell your mama she's my favorite person. And how are you doing? How is school?"

Marisol glanced at the time on her phone. Missing a ferry never made anyone happy. "School is good, although summer classes are intense. But..." Her lips curved up in a happy smile.

"But...but what? Spill!"

"I met a guy...a Dom as cool as your Drake. *Dios*, Master Atlas is hot. Even his name is hot." Marisol fanned herself. "We're going to play this weekend."

"Play... BDSM play?" Observing the way Marisol was eyeing the cookies, Ray moved them out of reach. Because there was undoubtedly a box of goodies in the car. Consuela showed her love with baked goods.

"Yes. I can't wait!"

At the worry tightening her gut, Ray sighed. Marisol was over eighteen. Not a child. But still... "Did you meet Master Atlas through the BDSM club?"

"Uh-huh. He's one of the organizers, I guess."

Guess that meant he knew what he was doing, right? But damn, why did it have to be the BDSM club on campus. "What's his major?"

"Oh, he's not a student. He teaches law. Not tenured yet, though."

"He's a teacher?" Ray frowned. He'd have to have a PhD, which meant he'd be over thirty. Marisol wasn't yet twenty-one.

Okay, a ten-year age gap wasn't rare. Look at her and Drake. He was a decade or so older. Still... An older teacher and an undergraduate seemed sketchy.

"Aren't there rules about teachers dating students?" Jeez, now she sounded like Miss Judgy McJudgyFace.

"Stupid rules." Marisol grumbled and averted her gaze. "We can't let it get around. But Master Atlas said everyone who'll be at the play party on Friday is really discreet. They won't say anything."

A chill ran through Ray as little red flags started waving in her mind. A party was where she'd been assaulted. "Marisol, I... Um, it kinda doesn't feel as if he's...honest. Um, honorable. Not if he's breaking the rules and hiding his actions."

Marisol took a step back.

Ray hurried to get the next words out. "And a play party on campus—your campus. Remember I heard those rumors?"

"Oh, please. *Rumors*. You worry more'n Mamá."

"Going to a club would be safer, okay? A good one with dungeon monitors and rules. Please? You'll be twenty-one in a month and can get into a club, and you'll know this man better by then." Tears burned Ray's eyes.

"*Madre de Dios*, you really *are* upset. Don't cry, okay? I'll talk Master Atlas into waiting and going to a club."

Blinking hard, Ray hugged her. "Thank you. I'm sorry, but... yes, it means a lot to me."

"Fine, fine." Marisol glanced at her phone. "I gotta go. See you in a couple of weeks when my laundry runs out."

"Hey, I'll be in Seattle on Friday. I have a bunch of carvings and trinkets to deliver to the Pike Place gallery. I know it's not a party, but how about I buy you dinner at the Pink Door to make up for being a worrier?"

"Oooh, yes. Must be nice to be able to get reservations with only a week's notice."

Ray buffed her fingernails on her shirt. "What can I say? My artwork is in their outdoor area, and they love it."

"Everyone loves your artwork. But I love Italian. Text me a time, and I'll see you then!" Waving a hand over her head, Marisol was out the door and trotting to her car.

Heaving a relieved sigh, Ray closed the door and sagged against it. Her heart was going way too fast. *Dammit, I will not have a panic attack.*

One party circumvented. During dinner next week, she'd get more details from Marisol about her new boyfriend and the current BDSM club on campus. *It's probably fine, just fine.*

The ones who'd assaulted her wouldn't still be around. The club would have fixed their problems. Because she'd called them after her disastrous party. She'd talked to the club president anonymously and shared what'd happened.

No, the offenders would be long gone.

Right?

CHAPTER SEVENTEEN

Drake's deck was made for parties, Ray decided as she sat cross-legged on one of the loveseats and watched the ferry crossing the Sound to Seattle. It moved slower than a turtle on a wide highway.

It was a shame Hope and Peter wouldn't be able to join them until later, but she was enjoying the time with Mac and Rona. She tipped her face to the noon sun as she listened to the two women debate the merits of various protocols.

Mac rolled her eyes. "Alex sometimes goes for strict protocol when we're in the club or at a party. It bothered me at first, but I must admit it does push me into a submissive headspace."

"So how did you meet Alex?" Ray waggled her eyebrows. "Maybe at the club where he told you to kneel or something?"

"I wish. Alex and I had a dreadful introduction," Mac glanced at the open door. The rumble of men's voices came from the kitchen where they were preparing lunch.

"You seem to have overcome a rough beginning," Sitting on the facing loveseat, Rona smiled at Mac.

"A dreadful intro? Now, we really need to hear how you met. C'mon, Rona, aren't you curious too?" Ray leaned forward.

Rona laughed. "Crom, yes. Can you share, MacKensie?"

MacKensie's face went slightly pink. "Well, let me start by saying an abusive foster home left me with a couple of neuroses. Since one of the punishments there was to lock us in a tiny closet, I can't stand locked doors. I even carry lock picks."

"That is abuse." Rona's expression was furious. "Let me tell Simon their name. He'll—"

"I'll go after them," Ray said at the same time. "They'll never—"

"You two," Mac interrupted. "It's okay. The foster mom had her license taken away years ago. Anyway, I wanted to move away from the Midwest, but funds were tight, so I went through an agency to do house and dog sitting. My first job was here in Seattle. For Alex."

Whoa, this was...was better than a book. Ray bounced on the couch. "Go on."

"Well." Mac had a rueful smile. "There was a locked door, and... Locked doors are bad things. So, my bad, I opened it."

"You didn't know Alex at all?" Ray asked.

"Nope. He'd mailed me the house key. Circumstances forced him to cancel his trip. He came back and found me testing out"—her face turned red—"the spanking bench in his dungeon room."

Ray started snickering and couldn't stop.

Even unflappable Rona was grinning.

"I know. What a beginning. It gets worse. Foster care left me with another problem...and Alex figured it out." Mac sighed. "I had the unshakeable belief that being spanked means you're loved."

"What?" Rona set her glass down with a thud.

That was way wrong, Ray thought. *Wait...wait...wait.* "I get it, I think. I was in foster care too. No real punishment, not like yours—thank you, universe—but the foster mom's pampered prince and the foster boys got all the attention. Us girls were pretty much ignored. I bet your foster mother had a child who got spanked, right?"

Mac pointed her finger at Ray. "You nailed it."

Rona leaned over and set a hand over Mac's. "Alex must have helped you with this, or you wouldn't even talk about it. Did you get counseling?"

"You bet. Master Alex insisted, the bossy butt."

"I heard that," came from behind, and Ray jumped.

Pitcher of iced tea in hand, Alex refilled their drinks, then leaned over and kissed MacKensie. "Just so you know, it won't be *my* butt burning later." Without waiting for an answer, he strolled back to the kitchen.

"Guess that means he loves you, huh," Ray said in a low voice.

Mac laughed. "We've been together a while now. It's not always smooth sailing, but I know he loves me."

"How about you, Ray? Drake said this morning your relationship is new?" Rona asked. Ray knew it wasn't from curiosity but more like her being big sisterly. The woman cared about people.

"Only about a month. We're still learning about each other, but it's good, at least when we're alone. I do worry about..." Her voice faded. "Never mind." Complaining would make her sound petty.

"Friends here, girl," Mac said. "Let us help."

"I don't think you can."

But they waited, and she sighed. "It's just... I don't fit in with the other members of the club. Or not some of them, anyway. And I don't know what to do."

Mac's eyes narrowed. "I bet Justine is riling people up."

"Justine?" Rona asked.

"A submissive Drake was with for a few months last winter. He broke it off, but recently, she decided she wants him back. Only... he's gotten involved with Ray."

Ray sighed. "Loud, forgetful, impulsive, socially inept Ray. I'm sure people see me and can't believe he's really interested."

"I know how you feel. I'm not a gorgeous twenty-something." Rona cupped her breasts. "Things aren't perky; other parts are soft rather than toned. I get the same kind of disbelieving looks."

Ray's mouth dropped open. "But you're amazing; you and Simon are perfect together."

"Why, thank you. Simon's friends agree. The ones who don't can be problems." Rona smiled at Mac. "What do you see when you look at Ray and Drake?"

"He adores her; it's obvious." Mac pursed her lips. "But it's more. He's more...him...when she's around. More awake, more interested in life, laughing. Happier."

"There you go, sweetie," Rona said to Ray. "His friends know what's important."

Ray stared at Mac. And felt pure contentment. Drake was happier...because of her. Then she huffed. "If only I didn't have to deal with club members. Maybe we could live on an island?"

Mac snickered. "You do live on an island."

"I meant a tropical—"

Laughing, Rona interrupted. "Ray, you're stronger than you know. I saw you in action with the aggressive flogger in class and with your ex. You were firm without being mean or vindictive. You'll take care of this Justine when the right time comes."

Mac nodded her agreement. "I got your back—and so will Hope."

Ray blew out a breath. She sure didn't feel strong. Then she straightened her spine. But she was a tough, smart person. Her friends were right. *I can and will deal with Justine if she keeps pushing.* "So, let's go see if the men have managed to make us lunch."

"I think I missed out on a lot of fun, having a foster father who disliked visitors," Ray said to Hope and Rona as they went into

Drake's kitchen that evening. She started uncovering the pies she'd brought.

"You really did," Hope said. She and Peter had come over on the ferry for a late supper. "This was fun—and Drake is sure a great cook."

"That was yummy shrimp fettucine alfredo," Rona agreed.

Even better, everyone had pitched in to make the Caesar salad and garlic bread.

Dessert would be equally simple. Rona was already getting the vanilla ice cream out of the freezer. Hope grabbed plates.

Ray smiled at them. "You guys are the best."

"We know." Hope grinned and motioned for Ray to lead the way out.

The rest of the group were still seated around the big dining room table. Drake, Simon, Peter, Alex, and Mac.

As they all turned to look, Ray held up the two pies. "It's blueberry season, so I brought blueberry pie and vanilla ice cream as my contribution."

And she grinned at the enthusiastic comments as she dished up servings. It really had been a great day.

She'd learned more about how BDSM worked outside of the club from watching the couples interact. Hope was very submissive to Peter, even occasionally calling him Master and kneeling when he was sitting. Were they a 24/7 relationship?

MacKensie didn't seem to be as...as submissive. But when Alex gave her an order, she obeyed without even thinking about it.

Rona and Simon didn't do any D/s stuff, though their scenes in the convention dungeon had been really intense. Rona said their play was mostly in the bedroom or clubs.

What kind of D/s relationship do I want with Drake? During the day, she'd felt him studying her, but he didn't order her to do anything.

Earlier, she'd tried kneeling at his feet and calling him Master.

She shook her head. It didn't feel natural. Not at a casual gathering.

All the same, when he asked something of her or even held his hand out, everything inside her responded with happiness. With a need to please him. When his chin lifted slightly, and his quiet voice got that deep, implacable tone, she didn't even hesitate. If she'd been a dog, she'd have gone belly-up to offer her neck.

So... Her reaction made her think she wanted more than dominance being confined to the bedroom and club.

With a grunt of exasperation, she called herself back to her task. Everyone was served. She took her plate and resumed her seat beside Drake at the table.

He put his arm around her. "*Ma chérie,* what has you unhappy?" His voice was soft enough no one else heard. In the low lighting, she could see concern in his eyes.

"I was trying to...to...label what's between us. You said Justine didn't want a power exchange outside the bedroom, and you want more than club and bedroom, but not a Master/slave relationship. But...what are we?"

When his chuckle was echoed by others, she realized she hadn't lowered her voice. *Dammit, Ray, you idiot.*

Cupping her face, he kissed her, light and quick. "We are something between. No label needed. We'll explore what we want. Any time you're uncomfortable or if you decide you need more of something, we'll talk and work it out."

The knot of worry in her chest relaxed at his utter confidence. When he pulled her chair closer and put an arm around her shoulders, she leaned into his side. Her heart felt full. Yes, somehow, they'd work out what they each needed.

And eventually, she'd manage to tell him how much she loved him.

After they'd polished off dessert, everyone helped with cleaning up.

Everyone. And it was nice none of the men sat around, expecting to be served.

Huh. How weird was this? *I do love pleasing Drake.* But if he took her service for granted and expected it all the time...no, she wouldn't be happy. Although there were lots of slaves and submissives who were.

Then again, sitting around and being served would probably drive Drake nuts. He had almost as much energy as she did.

Finished with clean-up, the Doms went to look at something in Drake's garage while the women took their drinks to the deck. Drake's big deck overlooked the Sound. A table and chairs at one end, the other end had four love seats grouped around an oval oak coffee table.

They'd been discussing variations on negotiations before a scene. "I don't think I understand the difference between inclusive and exclusive," Ray said.

"With inclusive, the Top will do only the specific things you agree upon. Maybe they'd say, there'll be spanking up to level five..." Hope grinned. "...and a blowjob."

"Okay. And exclusive is..."

"You have a limits list." Rona held up an imaginary list. "The Top can and will do anything as long as it's not on the limit list."

"Ooooh."

"It's not a bad thing," MacKensie said in a judicious tone. "It's probably better, especially with newer Tops and or newer bottoms to be pretty specific at first."

"Although a lot of us enjoy the added trepidation of being unsure what our evil Doms will come up with." Hope grinned when both Rona and Mac raised their glasses in agreement.

Interesting. She hadn't realized at the time, but Drake had been inclusive in the beginning and was now moving to exclusive.

With a wry smile, she raised her glass, joining the others, and they all laughed.

"Then there's some kinksters who voluntarily give up their safewords. Or are into consensual non-consent." Hope looked at MacKensie. "Steel still feels bad about scaring you so badly."

Ray raised her eyebrows. "Someone scared you?"

Mac scowled. "Alex had a kind of stalker ex who told Steel I wanted a rape-play scene. Gave him a safeword and all that...only I was so new, I didn't even know what a safeword was. He grabbed me as I was coming back from the bathroom. Thankfully, Alex showed up before Steel got further than grabbing me."

Ray stared, feeling her mouth go dry. Talk about scary.

It roused her worry about Marisol. Again.

Ray eyed the women. All submissives, all college grads. "I don't suppose any of you went to UW?"

"Nope," Mac said. "I got my vet degree in Iowa."

Hope raised her hand. "UCLA. Dad was based in San Diego those years." Right. Hope's father was a naval officer, which was why she'd been in Bremerton to begin with.

"Not me either." Rona smiled at Hope. "I'm another California grad. I got my Master's in health care management from USC in LA."

"Damn," Ray muttered.

"Do you have questions about UW?" Hope asked. "Peter and I know some of the professors. Some students too."

"My questions are..." She fidgeted with the ring on her pointer finger, turning it around and around. How much of her past did she want to share? "A friend is an undergrad there and started dating a Dom in the campus BDSM club."

Rona took a sip of her wine and considered Ray. "If she's interested in BDSM, I don't see a problem. But you're shaking."

Oh hell, she wasn't handling this well. *Dammit*. Now they were all frowning at her.

And apparently giving off worried signals since a second later,

Drake sat down beside her so closely her hips and shoulders were against his solidness. "Aralia, what is wrong?" He took her hand, and the warmth of his fingers showed how cold she was.

"She said she has a friend with a Dom boyfriend who belongs to the UW BDSM club," Hope told him.

And now, the other three Doms were joining the group.

Ray wanted to crawl under the love seat and pull the cushions over herself. Instead, she forced herself to stay still. What could she say? Did she want to spill everything? Would it send her into a panic attack?

Drake curved his fingers around her chin, turning her face to him. Forcing her to meet his concerned gaze. "Is this related to what happened to you before?"

"Freaking hell, why do you have to be so perceptive?"

A snort of amusement came from one of the other Doms.

Drake's lips twitched. "Since this incident still bothers you, perhaps it is time to share. Let us help." He moved his hand to her shoulder, rubbing gently.

In the facing seat, Hope was holding hands with Peter, expression concerned.

Leaning on Alex, Mac gave Ray a half-smile. Her eyes held an unexpected sympathy, as if she knew how it felt to be so exposed.

Rona simply looked warm and encouraging. Standing behind her, Simon rested his hands on her shoulders, his gaze on Ray.

All the Doms were watching her, in fact. Not like prey but more like...someone they needed to protect.

Great, she'd flipped the Dominant FIND OUT WHAT'S WRONG AND FIX IT button.

In her head, C3PO was saying, *"There'll be no escape for the princess this time."*

She sighed, caving in, and Drake knew. He kissed her fingers, then held her hand in his big one. Strong and warm.

How could something so simple make her feel safe?

"Okay. My third year at the University of Washington. I...I

met a man who claimed he was a Dom—and I was"—the feeling of humiliation welled inside her—"thrilled. Obsessed with him and obsessed with trying *everything*."

"Oh, I remember that time," Mac said. "Discovering the needs and cravings we feel has a name, then wanting a man who can satisfy those needs? A lot of us went through that. And you were all of, what, twenty-two?"

"Twenty-one," Ray whispered.

"A puppy, full of hormones and emotions and no experience," Simon said.

The others nodded.

Hope murmured, "Oh yeah, *those* days."

Huh, maybe her behavior hadn't been completely stupid.

Rona leaned forward. "Frenzy"—she used air-quotes around the word—"is very common with newbies. And becomes a problem when they ignore safety in their need to explore. Too many get into trouble."

"As you did," Drake prompted. Because he knew.

"As I did. The Dom—he used the name Crypto—took me to a play party given by the campus BDSM club. It was in a big house with portable equipment, and everyone wore masks. I tried stuff. Impact stuff. Floggers and crops. Purely having fun, you know? Until it got late, and I realized people were leaving."

She bit her lip, turning away from Simon's darkening gaze, and pressed her face against Drake's shoulder. He pulled her closer, and his chest rose and fell with his slow, steady breathing. As emotions stormed through her, he felt like an age-old oak, rooted deep, unwavering.

"What did he do?" Hope blurted out the question. "Did he hurt you? I'll kill him, kill him dead."

Ray choked on a hysterical laugh. Damn, she loved her friend.

Drake squeezed her hand. "One step at a time, *ma chérie*. What happened next?"

"He brought me a drink after a light flogging, and I sucked it down. Then I felt funny. Dropped into this weird space where I absolutely loved everyone, especially him. He sat down with me and kissed me and said all the Doms adored me. It made me feel special, and I wanted to hug and kiss them all."

She pulled away from Drake, wringing her hands together. "That's not me. Way not me."

"Might have been ecstasy—MDMA. The emergency room sees a fair amount of it." Rona shook her head. "There's a loss of inhibition along with a feeling of trusting everyone. You can't give informed consent after taking a mood-altering substance."

"I..." Despite what Rona said, she still felt shame. "I let them touch me; I remember that much, but then I saw I was the only woman still there. Just me and some men, all wearing masks."

"Damn them," Alex muttered almost inaudibly.

"I tried to get up and leave, demanded my clothes. One man said he'd get them and said go ahead and get hydrated while he looked for them. Somebody handed me another drink, and I was so thirsty, I drank it. I think." Her skin felt as if it was crawling. "My memory is all messed up after that. Only bits and pieces, sounds and feelings."

Drake made a growling sound, stopped. Then his voice was calm and smooth. "Did you end up in an emergency room?"

"Uh-uh. I woke up outside my little duplex, half lying against the front door. Dressed. And sticky and everything was sore. I had"—she pulled in a breath—"bite marks and whip marks."

"Fuck," Peter said under his breath.

Suddenly, Hope shoved onto the loveseat, crowding her, hugging her. And crying. "No, it's not right, not fair. You're one of the nicest people ever, and no!" She was shaking Ray and yelling and—

Ray blinked against the tears, sobbed. Drake lifted her onto his lap, arms around her, and Hope was holding her hands while Ray bawled like a baby.

"It's fucking messed up," Peter was saying. "Ecstasy to make her think she wanted it, and afterward something, maybe ketamine, to keep her from fighting and mess with her memory."

Alex scrubbed his face with his hands. "If she reported it to the police, the Dom could say he left when she started flirting with others. And—it was a BDSM party."

"Which rules out any sympathy from law enforcement," Mac muttered. She realized Ray was listening. "Did you go to the police?"

"No. For exactly the reasons you said. What could I tell them? My memory was messed up, especially at first. Parts came back weeks later...along with flashbacks." *So many flashbacks. The feeling of hands. Of pain. Of being held down.*

She shivered—and Drake's voice was a smooth croon. "*Non, non*, you are safe here, *bébé*. Safe with me."

Yes. She leaned into him and managed to look at the others. "I couldn't do *nothing*. So I called the number for the BDSM club and talked to the president. Told him what had happened, about Crypto. The president sounded angry and promised they'd investigate and put a stop to the abuse. I figured it was the best I could do to keep another woman from the same kind of...of assault."

Drake kissed her cheek. "It's more than many would have done."

"Everyone wore masks. Hell, I guess you wouldn't recognize anyone afterward? Did you see Crypto again or—" Peter had apparently put on his lawyer hat.

"No. I...I started having panic attacks. Depression." Ray sighed—and Hope wrapped her arms around Ray's upper arm. Anchoring her. "I dropped out. Went back to Faj. Living in the woods, in his house, it was the only place I felt safe."

"Of course," Drake murmured.

"I couldn't tell Faj what happened, but he pushed me into getting counseling. And then took me to Europe." His way of bribing her to help her leave the house.

I miss you so much, Faj.

But as Drake hugged her and kissed the top of her head, the same feeling was there: *I'll protect you from anyone and anything that threatens you.*

And because of it, the fear crumbled into shreds, and she could breathe again.

Hope had an excellent idea, Drake thought. Killing Crypto sounded about right. Actually, murdering them all wouldn't be amiss. What had happened to Ray was rape, pure and simple.

To hear a *rapist calling himself a Dominant* had set up a young college student, led her on and drugged her... Dominants cared for and defended submissives.

Yes, he might well kill the man. The others as well.

He'd killed before, after all—and not for such a good reason. Drake sighed and hugged Ray closer. Although the Mafia was the most famous, most countries, including France, had organized crime. Despite Maman's objections, Papa forced Drake to follow him in as soon as his teenaged body had developed some muscle. The few he'd killed for the mob had deserved death. That knowledge didn't stave off his nightmares.

But the monster who would prey on an innocent college girl... He could handle another nightmare if it would remove the bastard from the world.

He laid his cheek against Ray's soft hair. Normally, she almost hummed with energy, but reliving this kind of trauma exhausted her.

Tears finished, she sagged against him, half-asleep.

Oui, he needed to kill the man.

"Drake." Rona rose. "Hand her over so we can get some fluids in her and put her to bed."

He eyed the women, all compassionate and kind. Although he'd rather help her himself, tonight he'd relinquish the right. Because he did come with a dick.

When she could think clearly again, he hoped she'd remember he also came with a heart.

He nodded to Rona. "Be gentle with her. If she asks, tell her to sleep, and I'll join her in a while."

As the women helped Ray to the master bedroom, his friends turned to him with grim expressions.

Alex set his drink down with a thud. "I'm ashamed of my gender."

"Did you catch the debate over whether a woman would rather encounter a man or a bear when hiking in the forest?" Peter said.

Simon's jaw tightened. "Yes. I was surprised most choose the bear. Then Rona showed me the reasoning on the internet. If a bear attacked a woman, no one would ask her if she led the bear on, or what she was wearing, or if she drank too much."

Alex pitched his voice higher. "The bear would only kill me, not tell me to enjoy it. The bear wouldn't pretend to be my friend —or brag to his friends."

The lawyer scowled. "One response really bothered me—that no one would question if a *bear* attack really happened."

Drake barely kept his hands from forming fists. This was why Ray hadn't even tried to go to the police.

He breathed out and added his own. "The worst one to me: 'If it's a bear and I scream, someone might help me.' So, my friends, let us prove ourselves better than a bear. How do we discover if there is still a problem at our university?"

They traded ideas and suggestions.

As the women returned down the stairs, Simon turned to Drake. "Although Rona and I leave for Canada in the morning, call if you need help before we get back. We can return early." He smiled slightly. "Keep in mind, I have a software expert who enjoys...*mmm*, sidestepping privacy regulations."

"Thank you, Simon." Drake rose, gaze on the approaching women.

Rona stopped in front of him. "She's tucked in and half asleep. Honestly, there are a lot of men who I'd not say this to, but I think she'd find your presence comforting." A dimple appeared in her cheek. "She said she feels safe when you're with her."

"Best compliment ever," Alex murmured from behind him.

Drake agreed. "Thank you for your care." He half turned. "I'll leave you all now, but please stay as long as you wish. You know where the guest rooms are if you wish to overnight here."

Murmured good nights came from the others.

Upstairs, he found his exhausted submissive curled into a ball, her face barely visible. After cleaning up, he stripped, slid under the covers, and wrapped around her.

She stirred, still half asleep.

"*Mon cœur,* it's me. Go back to sleep."

Instead, she didn't hesitate to turn and curl up against him. And his heart melted. To be able to trust him after what she'd endured... He would do his best to be worthy.

"I'm sorry," she whispered, her face pressed into his shoulder. "I didn't mean to ruin the party."

"Aralia," he said, ensuring he had her attention. "Did I not ask you to share the story?"

"Well, yes, but I didn't have to have a meltdown. To be...dramatic."

Ah, the wounds from her father and her fool of an ex. "You have feelings—and everyone expresses feelings differently. Your way is not wrong." He kissed the top of her head and hugged her closer. "Truly, I am impressed by your courage."

He hadn't realized she'd tensed awaiting his answer until she went limp. "Oh." A minute later, he heard an almost inaudible, "I love you so much."

His heart expanded with the feeling her words gave him. Her love and her trust were everything he'd been missing. "Do you now?"

She stiffened. "Oh freaking hell, did I say that out loud?"

He almost laughed. So he didn't have to wait to tell her his feelings, after all. "I'm pleased you did—because I feel the same. *Je t'aime*, Aralia Lanigan."

Sometime during the night, Drake woke with a start, realizing Ray was murmuring to him and stroking her hand over his chest. "It's okay. You're dreaming, Drake. You're all right."

"*Bordel de merde.*" He pulled in a breath. "Sorry, *ma chérie*. A nightmare—old memories."

"Poor Master." With a sympathetic sound, she crawled on top of him. Warm, soft, snuggly. Tonight's fragrance—an earthy sandalwood and cedar mix—made him feel as if he'd caught himself a nature spirit.

"Thank you for waking me. But it is not yet dawn," he murmured, rubbing his cheek on her hair. "You should sleep."

"Mmm." She stacked her hands on his chest and propped her chin on them. "You seemed to think talking about trauma can help. So will telling me about whatever left you with nightmares help you?"

"*Non.*" Then he stopped and thought. Oftentimes sharing did help. And she should know something about his gory past. "*Oui*, perhaps it will. It is ugly though."

"I'm tough." She moved up long enough to rub her cheek against his, then kiss him. "Tell me."

"My father was a member of *Le Milieu*. There are various names, but for simplicity we'll call it the French mob. He was a *beaux voyous*—an enforcer. He forced me to follow him as soon as I had some muscle on me. Took me with him on beatings, cripplings, killings." It was difficult to speak when his jaw was this tight. "I killed my first man when I was fourteen."

In the faint light, he could see her eyes widen. "You were only a baby."

Not a baby, more like a monster. One of them had begged for mercy. "At first, the people deserved death. I checked. But..."

He heard her sigh. "They didn't care—or were testing you?"

"*Oui*. I was ordered to cripple an old man—a shopkeeper who wouldn't pay protection money. I...refused."

"Oh no." On top of him, her body went tense. "What happened?"

"I received a...painful...lesson." They'd called in one of the biggest enforcers. *Merde*, it had hurt. "My father helped beat me. *Maman* was furious."

"Damn him. Did your mom grab you and run?"

"She...loved him. Hated the life, hated what he planned for me, but..." But not enough to leave. "*Pas assez pour me sauver.* Not enough to save me." The realization still hurt.

"With Papa's permission, she sent me to her aunt in Paris until I could recover." His eyes had been swollen shut, fingers, nose, ribs broken. Unable to even walk. "While I was in Paris, there was a...bloody reshuffling of the organization. Almost everyone on my father's side of the family was murdered." He had to pause to keep his voice even. "Including my parents."

"Oh, Drake." She hugged him hard, and he could feel the trickle of tears on his bare chest. She was crying...for him? The wonder silenced him.

"And it happened when you were mad at them."

She'd pinpointed the heart of his misery. "*Oui*. Any chance of reconciliation was lost."

"And you loved them, despite everything." She sniffed. "I'm so sorry. For all of it."

"My aunt..." He shook his head, remembering her white face. Her fear. "She was afraid the organization would also come after me, so she sent me to my uncle here in the States." He stroked his hand over Ray's silky hair.

"I'm so glad you had him." She pushed up slightly to kiss him again. "No wonder you have nightmares."

"Thank you, *mon amour*." He actually felt his heart lighten. "Talking to you did help. *Je t'aime*."

"But you said you go back to France once or twice a year. Aren't you worried someone might still come after you?"

"*Non*, the organization's leadership has turned over. No one is interested in me."

"There's a relief."

He frowned. Her body was still tense. Had this brought up her own past? Did she worry her own monsters were still out there?

The thought was infuriating. As he kissed her, he made himself a vow: He would do everything in his power to ensure she never had to fear for her safety.

CHAPTER EIGHTEEN

He loves me. He said so. More than once last night, in French and in English.

It sure sounded incredible in French though.

And now, her heart was full, as if her chest was expanding with all the emotions inside.

He loves me.

She couldn't stop smiling as she toweled off and pulled on jeans and a T-shirt. Honestly, it felt as if she was starting the day for a second time.

Laughing under her breath, she walked downstairs to a quiet house.

Alex and MacKensie hadn't spent the night since Mac had early vet appointments. Everyone else though had been here for breakfast. Then, after Peter and Hope left for the ferry, Simon and Rona headed out, planning to tour Victoria in Canada.

Everyone had been understanding about her meltdown the night before.

And brilliant, wonderful Hope deduced why Ray asked if they'd attended the university. She and Mac had written out a list of submissive women they knew who were or had been in classes there.

Now if I can only figure out how to ask strangers some rather personal questions.

Stopping in the kitchen, she looked around. Smiling a little. After everyone had left, she and Drake cleaned the kitchen, and somehow, her clothing got unbuttoned and unzipped. Stripping her bare, he'd bent her over the back of the couch and taken her. And he'd used his fingers so very skillfully, she'd come twice before he finished.

There was nothing like having to shower twice before lunch.

But, damn, what a way to start the day. *Stop grinning, Ray.*

I love him. He loves me.

But where was he?

Noise came from the great room. "Hey, Drake, I need to get back home and to work. I have projects to finish, and Max is going to think I don't love him anymore."

Sitting on the couch, he looked over his shoulder at her and smiled.

Dammit, did the man have to be quite so sexy?

"We can't have Maximillian doubting your love." Drake pursed his lips. "Bring him with you tonight. He seems quite adaptable, and I'd enjoy having him here."

Awww. It was amazing he loved cats as much as she did. "Okay, we'll give it a shot."

"Good. Now come and see what I have here."

After walking around the couch, Ray stopped. And stared.

The coffee table was covered with floggers and crops. Apparently, Drake was doing whatever Doms did to keep their impact toys conditioned, and the rich scent of leather hung in the air.

She eyed the array of *painful* toys. "Are you trying to intimidate me?"

"Is it working?" His grin flashed. "Pick one or two to try this weekend at Chains. We'll see what you like."

"Like isn't the word I'd use."

His amusement showed way too clearly. "The pain from the paddles—and being spanked—enhanced your arousal, *oui*?"

"*Maaaybe*. It still hurt."

"I think you'll enjoy being flogged even more. Truly."

His cell phone rang, and he frowned at his greasy hands. "Hey, Google, answer the call and turn on speaker phone."

When the ringing stopped, he said, "Good morning, Blaize."

"Did you manage to sleep in? It's lunchtime. If you've got a minute, I want your take on how the new tax laws might affect downtown businesses. I'm giving an evening seminar on the subject next week."

Boring. Even worse, the conversation sounded as if it would take a while. Ray scrunched up her face. Getting Drake's attention, she mimed packing her stuff and pointed to the front door.

Drake put on a sad expression but nodded. He knew she had to work. And once she left, he'd probably be back in his own office doing the same.

A few minutes later, she carried her packed overnight bag downstairs.

Blaize was still talking on speaker phone as Drake worked on a flogger.

She bent and gave Drake a quick, silent kiss.

From the phone came a crashing noise. Dishes breaking. A woman's high voice blurted out apologies. "Sorry, Master, I'm so sorry. I tripped and—"

"Jesus Christ!" Blaize shouted. "You dismal fuckface slave. All you're good for is—"

Ray jerked back so fast she lost her balance and fell on her butt...and scrambled backward like an upside-down crab. Pure panic surrounded her. Darkened the room.

Get away, away!

Drake said something, then he was lifting her. Putting her in a chair.

"Ray." His voice deepened, filled with authority. "Aralia, look at me. At my face."

She blinked, tried to see through the haze. Dark eyes. A clean, citrusy whiff of aftershave. "Drake. Oh gods, Drake. His voice... He was there."

Drake held Ray's arms gently. His little submissive was so white the freckles stood out starkly on her face. Her voice was high, broken.

But she was pulling herself together, coming out of the panic attack. Her courage awed him.

He needed to know what had set her off. "Was there—where?"

"At the BDSM party. At the university. When...when I...they drugged me."

An icy hand closed around his spine. He kept his tone soft, reassuring. "Whose voice, *bébé*?"

"His." She gripped his forearms, tried to shake him. "The man on the phone."

"You mean Blaize?" He glanced at the couch where the phone lay. When Ray panicked, he'd ended the call.

He carefully considered his next words, trying for clarity. "Are you thinking Blaize was one of the Doms who assaulted you when you were at the university?"

She froze, her fingers cold on his arms. "You don't believe me."

"*Mon cœur*, it's not a matter of belief. I simply want to be certain. Blaize has been a member of Chains for years and is a respected Dom." Over and over in his life, he'd seen too many disasters caused from hasty assumptions and accusations. Like what Faylee had done to Ghost years ago.

He needed all the facts. Although if Blaize had done this...

Fighting down fury, Drake took Ray's hands. "Last night, you suffered through a traumatic re-telling of what happened back then. It wouldn't be unusual for the past to be too vivid in your thoughts for a few days. It's possible *any* angry man might set you off."

"You don't believe me," she whispered again.

"You've spoken to Blaize before, Ray, and not had this reaction." After a second, he realized she hadn't even heard what he said. Well, this wasn't the time for logic.

Right now, he needed to take care of her. "Let me bring you some tea, and we'll talk more when you're calmer."

Before he went into the kitchen, he took the fluffy blanket off the back of the couch and wrapped it around her. The way she shivered broke his heart. "There, *bébé*. Once you're warmed up, you'll feel better."

The electric kettle took only a few minutes to boil water. He chose a chamomile-peppermint mix, added sugar, and carried the cup around the corner into the great room.

And stopped.

The chair was empty. The blanket lay on the couch.

And her overnight bag and purse were gone.

He doesn't believe me.

Ray's hands tightened on the steering wheel as she drove south, through the green tunnels made by overarching trees on each side of the road.

Today the feeling of being in the forest was claustrophobic.

He doesn't believe me. The knowledge hurt so bad, so deeply, even her bones ached.

She'd sat there, panicking, telling him she'd identified one of her attackers. And he'd been so calm. So logical. And made her feel deranged.

Because *Blaize* was a valued member of the BDSM community, a Dom. She growled under her breath. A rich white, older male, no less. And Drake's friend.

"And what AM I then?" *Well duh.* "You, girl, are merely the submissive he was fucking."

A drama queen. One obviously prone to lying, probably to get attention, right?

"I hate him," she whispered, then shouted the words, "I. HATE. HIM." He'd made her love him. Made her think they had a chance. A real relationship.

Made her think he believed in her. But why should he, really? Pa never had. And more than once, Theodore had accused her of lying—for drama.

The sight of home was such a relief she almost burst into tears.

But...I can't stay.

She parked, hurried into the house, and almost tripped over the happy furball. "We're going on a road trip, Max." She swallowed hard. "I don't think he'll come here—not for a lying, overemotional submissive—but we won't take the chance. Not until I get my head on straight and settle down."

Because she couldn't face him. Which meant she needed to leave her sanctuary for a few days.

She tossed extra changes of clothes into her go-bag. What with earthquakes and the increasing dryness of Washington's forests, Faj insisted on having go-bags for humans and cats. So all the food, equipment, and records in the oversized, pet travel crate were ready to go. The crate went into the cargo area.

The front seat got comfort munchies, drinks, and water. When she buckled the smaller cat carrier in the back seat, Max gave her a pleased mew from inside. He was the first cat she'd met to actually enjoy car travel.

"You're going to enjoy smelling the ocean, promise." She frowned, considering. "La Push or Ocean Shores? Hmm." Her mouth tightened as the sadness welled up inside. "He obviously thinks I'm all drama now...so we'll go to La Push and have drama.

When I can think better, I'll figure out what to say. Although he's probably already written me off."

He didn't believe her.

Wanting to cry, she picked up the phone and blocked him.

CHAPTER NINETEEN

"You look grim," Peter said as he walked into Drake's office. "She's still blocking you?"

"She is." At the desk, Drake leaned back and glanced out the windows. His corner office, near the top of the building, had a picture-perfect view of Seattle from one angle and the Sound and Bainbridge to the west. "I stopped by her house at noon. As far as I can tell, she hasn't been home at all."

"From what you said about your discussion, well..." Peter rested a hip on the desk. "From my lawyerly viewpoint, you were reasonable. But to Ray? You might have sounded as if you were blowing her off."

Drake walked over to the windows and stared out. *Non, you can't punch Peter for speaking the truth.* "I arrived at that conclusion the moment I saw she was gone."

"Sorry. I thought maybe you needed help figuring her out."

"*Non.* She even said exactly what she thought. '*You don't believe me*'. Trying to be reasonable, I tore open the wounds left by her father and undoubtedly by others who accused her of making up stories for attention." Drake turned to Peter. "The blind fools. She's all emotion, but not to get attention. And she doesn't lie."

"So... you don't need me for help with Ray."

"I need help to establish whether Blaize is guilty." He ran his hand through his hair. "When we talk, I'll make sure Ray knows I didn't disbelieve her."

"*If* you get a chance to talk."

"*Merde.*" He didn't need discouraging words. "I left a note each time I stopped at her place. She isn't unreasonable—I have to believe she'll read them."

He moved to the coffee stand in the corner. "This probably wouldn't have been more than a moment of anger if we'd been together longer."

"Ah." Peter motioned to the coffee with a nod to indicate he wanted a cup, then settled into a chair in the sitting area. "It does take time to be certain a new lover isn't an asshole like the previous ones. Hope and I had some stormy upsets in the beginning."

"Exactly." Drake poured two coffees, handed one over, and took a chair across from Peter. "If Ray did recognize Blaize's voice from that night, it means we have an abuser in Chains. Possibly more in the Seattle community."

"Hell. It sure sounded as if the group had done it before. What if they're still operating?" Peter leaned forward. "Hope and Mac gave Ray a list of names of submissive women at UW. Let's see about talking with those women."

Drake nodded. "We can start there."

CHAPTER TWENTY

It's Thursday. Time to deal with what happened.
On Tuesday and Wednesday, Ray had walked the first two beaches at La Push, handing off her distress to the waves rolling in and out. Breathing in the sea air, watching the sunsets. Exploring tide pools for sea stars, anemones, and crabs. Watching the surf froth around the sea stacks. Trees grew on top of the rocks—and she took heart from their rugged endurance.

Now, after a hike through the rain forest, she'd come down to beach three—the most isolated one. Her mind was quiet, her emotions settled. It was time to think.

Close to the surf's edge, she settled onto on a massive, bleached log. The fog had disappeared, leaving the sky a deep blue with white cloud fluffs. The end of August was a fine time for the shore.

Watching the waves roll in, she considered her reaction to the voice on the phone and what had happened with Drake.

The first thing that came to mind was Drake's question: Why hadn't Blaize's voice set her off before? She'd spoken with him in the coffee shop with Marisol and, again, at the club. He'd been polite, charming even, and possessed a cultured tenor.

But.

What she heard over the speaker phone on Monday sure hadn't been a smooth tenor. When he lost his temper, he'd been loud and rough. And foul.

Memories flitted through her mind in gray remnants of fog. Filmy, impossible to capture. However, during the assault, *someone* had called her a 'dismal fuckface' in exactly that tone and voice.

Maybe others would think there was room for doubt.

Her lip curled, baring her teeth. *I recognized your voice; I know it was you.*

Come to think of it... When Blaize asked her out, there'd been something unsettling in his expression. In his smile. She'd thought he was trying to one-up Drake.

But what if Blaize's smirk was because he remembered her? If he'd been one of the men who assaulted her... She shuddered. What if it suited his warped nature to do it again?

Clammy sweat rose on her skin, and her stomach turned over. Yes, he'd been there that night.

Even worse, he probably hadn't changed. Was still hurting young women.

Oh gods of the universe.

She hunched over, resting her forehead on her knees. *What should I do?*

I have to do something.

Breathing hard, she wrapped her arms around her legs. *Think, Ray.*

She could hardly point a finger at Mr. Well-respected Blaize and expect anyone to believe her. So perhaps the first step would be talking with the submissives on the list Mac and Hope had given her. Find out if the campus BDSM club was still active.

An ugly feeling tightened her chest. She'd reported the incident to the club president and assumed he'd investigate. Report the problem. Had he? Or was he part of it?

There was nothing she could do until she got back.

She pulled in a slow breath and straightened up.

For a few minutes, she listened to the waves, the low rumble, the hissing on the sand. Light glittered on the water. Sandpipers were running about on the beach. A white-haired man and woman nodded at her as they strolled past. Holding hands.

So sweet.

Back to thinking, Ray. The next question in her heart was a tough one. What about Drake?

She hadn't been able to deal with what had happened. But in every quiet moment, she'd relived their time together. And her brain had shied away from the last horrible morning. Time to unpack what had happened.

She went into the great room and heard Blaize's voice.

Had a panic attack.

Drake talked her down.

Then her accusation.

His response.

She frowned. *He didn't actually say I was lying. He offered possible reasons for my panic—and still didn't say I was full of shit, even though I basically accused his friend of rape.*

She scowled, squinting at the light dancing on the waves.

If a friend of mine insisted Hope was a murderer, would I immediately agree? Or would I be shocked and then start asking questions to get at the full story.

Drake's reaction had been understandable, hadn't it? She dug her shoe into the sand. All the times she'd been accused of lying—by Pa, by teachers, by Theodore—had left her...sensitive. Naturally, she figured Drake assumed she was lying when he didn't immediately agree with her.

Frigging hell. I really did overreact. And then essentially ghosted him.

He'd always been reasonable, concerned for her, caring. What a deplorable way to treat someone she'd said she loved. And she still loved him.

Guilt swept over her, and she tried to force it back. Her behavior was...was understandable. And Drake could have reassured her better. She scrunched up her face—because he would have been more careful if he'd realized how she was taking his questions.

I messed up. And I ran. Dammit, I promised myself I'd stop running from interpersonal altercations.

Fancy words, Ray. Just say you're a coward when it comes to dealing with people.

She'd work on it; she would.

Only it might be too late. *He might not love me any longer.* The thought...hurt way down deep. She had to blink hard to keep the tears at bay.

But there were things to do. Predators to deal with.

And Master Drake to face.

Rising, she turned and set out on the hike back to her cabin.

CHAPTER TWENTY-ONE

Friday morning, Drake considered the cell phone in his hand. Last night on his way home when he'd detoured—again—to check Ray's place, the lights in her house had been on. She'd returned. Was alive and safe at home. The relief had been indescribable.

Unfortunately, it'd been dark and far too late to knock on her door. Too much like a stalker, *oui?* No woman who lived alone would appreciate such behavior.

This morning, he'd had to check on construction of a new complex and then talk with his team of lawyers. He couldn't stall them longer.

In the past couple of days, he'd been investigating the university BDSM club, the members—and the probable victims. Peter, Bob, and Alex had helped. Bear had abandoned his sheep ranch to spend time here, as well.

The picture they were uncovering was ugly.

Now for the next step. He wanted to meet with Blaize before seeing Ray.

With a grim smile, he pulled out his cell phone, selected Blaize from his contact list, and heard the ringing.

"Hey, Drake. Good to hear from you. Did you have more to add to what you told me Tuesday?"

Drake's eyebrows rose. He hadn't thought about the taxes they'd discussed...at all. Yet it would be an excellent reason to get together. "*Oui*, I do have a few other concerns to address. Perhaps dinner tonight?"

"Damn, not tonight. I'm meeting another professor at eight at the Pink Door. But—are you spending the night at your condo? If my meeting doesn't run late, I'll give you a call, and we can have a drink together. Slave-girl will wait up if we run too late."

Drake shook his head. He'd been willing to delay seeing Ray for a few hours; not for an entire evening. "I'm returning to Bainbridge before dark." So he could swing by Ray's. "Perhaps tomorrow at noon? Same place?"

"You're on."

As Drake pocketed his phone, his admin popped in. "Sir, your meeting starts in five minutes."

He nodded and reluctantly switched his phone to silent, complying with his own orders for company meetings. "Thank you, Ms. Guldner."

Two hours later, Drake walked back into his office. The meeting had felt interminable. At least now, he could check his calls and texts.

And there it was—a text from Ray. His fingers gripped the phone almost painfully as he opened her message.

Drake.

I want to apologize right off the bat—for thinking you were accusing me of lying, for storming out of your house, for blocking you. You were being reasonable. And...

I'm sorry.

I have gallery deliveries to make today and then dinner with Marisol in Seattle, but could we talk later tonight? Wherever and whenever you want.

I'm really, really, really sorry.

Drake felt as if a boulder had lifted off his chest. Hope washed through him in a warm tsunami. She hadn't given up on them.

Oui, they would certainly talk. Both of them. They'd apologize to each other, then talk. And talk some more.

She would have read his apologies that he'd left on her porch. Nonetheless, he could say everything again.

I am also sorry for not being clear. I have never doubted your honesty.

So. We will both strive to communicate better.

Since you will be in Seattle, tonight at the condo. Whenever you can make it, I will be waiting.

I love you, Aralia Lanigan.

It was a shame he didn't have the meeting with Blaize to tell her about. Still, he would be meeting with the other Doms to discuss the latest from their investigations. Simon and Rona were back and might have ideas, as well.

After he and Ray had their talk, he'd have some plans to share with her. If the stars lined up correctly, she'd be in his arms, before, during, and after all the talking.

And all the years to follow.

Ray hauled her box of woodworking art pieces up another flight of stairs in Pike Place Market and had to step off before the next set to take a break. Guess she wasn't in as good a shape as she'd thought. Damn.

Around her, the noise from the market was as chaotic as usual, but she'd been here often enough she'd learned to adapt. And enjoy. She smiled at how the briny scent of the Sound mingled with the fishy market smells, the aroma of freshly brewed coffee, and the best of fragrances, chocolate.

Her taste buds nudged her. Maybe she should swing by indi chocolate for a truffle treat.

Stay on task, squirrel-brain. Finish the delivery to the gallery.

She'd reward herself with bagels from her favorite stall and buy some fresh produce—because why not when at the Market? And, fine, her taste buds deserved chocolate too. The cooler in her car would keep everything fresh.

Then dinner with Marisol. It was tough. *I want to see Drake sooo badly.* The need was pulling at her heart like a tugboat. But if a dinner bribe was what it took to keep Marisol away from the campus BDSM party, then fine. Hopefully, she'd find out soon if the club had changed. Was safe.

After the dinner... Tension simmered in her belly. She'd finally see Drake.

He wasn't angry. Was that a miracle or what? The notes she'd found on her doorstep were sweet and loving. He'd apologized for not being more careful with her. Realizing later he hadn't openly said he didn't think she was lying.

He'd even been investigating the campus BDSM club and wanted to share the information with her.

In each note and in his text, he said he loved her.

She sighed, rubbed the ache over her heart. *I love you too.*

Much later, walking down the Post Alley Walkway, Ray glanced at her watch with a sense of satisfaction. Her gallery delivery had been fun; the owner shared all the market gossip. Shopping was finished—including chocolate—and packed into her car in the parking garage.

And look, right on time to meet Marisol at the Pink Door. Ray grinned, remembering how Marisol used to be half an hour late for everything, but nursing school had turned her punctual.

She wasn't waiting outside though. Maybe inside? Ray pulled out her phone to text.

There was a message icon on the display screen. The hubbub of the market must have drowned out the sound.

It was from Marisol.

Ray, sry, but canceling dinner. Master Atlas was pissed off. Says I have to trust him or it's all off. I'm sure the party will be safe. Anyway, that guy you know—Blaze or something—he's supposed to be there, so I'll know someone besides my Dom. All good and TTYT.

Oh, no. No, no, no. Ray sagged against the restaurant's outside wall.

Instead of respecting Marisol's caution, the so-called fart-fucking Dom gave her an ultimatum.

Coldness engulfed Ray, making her shiver. And bringing back ugly memories of when she'd worried about not knowing anyone at a BDSM party, Crypto had reacted much the same way as this penis-fungus, Master Atlas.

And as an inexperienced, young submissive, I might as well have had "prey" tattooed across my chest.

Ray texted back: *I just read your text. Where is your party?*

No answer.

She phoned and listened to the ringing. Got voicemail. Ended the call, rang again. And again. And again.

Dammit. Of course, Marisol didn't want to have to defend her choice. To get scolded. Or maybe, she'd turned her cell off entirely.

With the next call, Ray left a message on voicemail asking Marisol to call right away, no matter what time. She texted the same message.

"Now what?" Chills ran up and down her arms. She wanted to jump in her car and cruise the streets, looking for the party. As if she'd know where to go. Crypto had said the club rented a different house for each monthly party.

It hadn't seemed suspicious at the time. Now... Was this one way they used to keep from getting caught?

Gods, what if Marisol was already there?

She stared at her phone, frozen in indecision. *Get my car and go...where?*

A cluster of tourists made her look up and... There was Drake's brilliant tower, the windows sparkling in the setting sun.

Drake. So close.

Before she could think it through, she'd headed straight there and then inside into the lobby. A middle-aged guard at the desk lifted his bushy eyebrows.

Ignoring him, she touched Drake's number on her phone.

"*Ma chérie.* I'm so happy you called." His warm voice was so welcome she almost burst out crying.

"D-Drake. I need help. I mean, I—" Her voice shook; her hand shook. She was shaking all over.

"Whatever you need, Aralia. Where are you?"

"Downstairs." She blinked hard at his instant readiness to help. "I mean, your building's lobby."

"*Bon.* I'll be there in an instant."

Ignoring the guard at the desk, she stood and watched the elevators, tensing more with each passing moment.

And there he was, black hair pulled back, dark eyes intent on her. He crossed to her with his smooth stride, and when she started to apologize, pulled her into his arms. "*Mon Dieu*, I have missed you."

His arms tightened around her, setting the world back in order. The feeling of being cared for...loved...filled her.

He held her until her trembling stopped, and the tight bands around her lungs loosened. Then he moved her back far enough to see her face. "How can I help? What is the problem?"

"Marisol. My friend who started dating a member of the University of Washington BDSM club. I talked her into holding off on going to a play party. But"—she showed him the text—"she's going anyway."

"*Merde*," Drake said under his breath.

Ray froze. *Oh no—what have I done?* Drake might've apologized for not being clear he didn't think she was lying, but still, Marisol's text mentioned Blaize. And Drake probably didn't—

"We have been investigating the university club. What we've found doesn't look good, and I don't like the way your friend's Dom manipulated her. The others are upstairs now. Let's see what we can figure out."

They were...investigating?

He waved at the guard, drew her into the elevator, and they were on the way to his condo.

Drake smiled at Ray's expression when the wave of greeting broke over her. Hope's squeal made him glad he'd gone for quality soundproofing in the building. MacKensie and Rona grabbed her for hugs.

Alex, Peter, and Simon were grinning, and Bear slapped Drake on the back. Drake had shared what had happened with Ray—and they'd been concerned.

He had been, as well. Downstairs, he needed her in his arms before he could relax. She really was here. With him.

Now for her young friend...

He raised his voice. "I fear we have a problem to deal with tonight." Once he had everyone's attention, he explained, then Ray read Marisol's text aloud.

"Call the police?" Bear asked.

After a moment, Peter shook his head. "We have no knowledge of an actual crime being committed. Even worse, the club rents a different house each month, and we don't know where tonight's party will be."

Ray's mouth dropped open. "You really are investigating."

"Well, yeah." Hope bumped Ray's shoulder, then her smile faded. "We started with the list of submissives who attended the university. From them, we got more people to talk with."

"It's a *frakking* mess, Ray." MacKensie pulled Ray over to the table to show her all the papers and explain what they'd uncovered.

Drake's mouth tightened. There was not only a pattern of violence and abuse. But the perpetrators were clever. Victims were drugged on ecstasy, reducing inhibitions. When they wised up to the gang rape, they were given another drug. Rohypnol or ketamine to destroy their ability to fight back. To fragment their memories. Due to the ecstasy, most of them wondered if they'd asked for what had been done to them.

Over the years, the very few who'd reported to the police had learned there wasn't enough evidence. Traumatized, some dropped out of school. Some left the area, even the country. Too often here in the US, a woman wasn't believed. Or law enforcement would act as if she'd probably asked for it.

Unacceptable.

Drake's jaw tightened. How could a man consider himself honorable if he didn't protect those who couldn't defend themselves?

At the table, MacKensie was explaining what they'd learned about what happened at some of the BDSM club parties. At the end, most left, but a few Doms would stay to clean up and close down the house. None of the regular members thought it was unusual since the equipment belonged to the Dominants.

The targeted submissives were always new to BDSM and the club. They only knew the so-called Dom who brought them. There were several "recruiters." The past members said there were often newbies getting drunk and becoming overly affectionate with the Doms. No one paid much attention.

But they did report Blaize was often there.

Drake handed Ray a glass of juice and put an arm around her. "My friends. How are we going to find Marisol? Anyone have an idea?"

They all shook their heads.

"Not all of the club members are criminals. Unfortunately, as a result of everyone wearing masks, we're not positive who the bad ones are." Peter grimaced. "We wouldn't even be sure of Blaize except he has a distinctive scar bisecting one eyebrow—and it shows above a mask."

The knowledge still stung. Blaize was in this up to his neck.

Ray frowned. "I don't remember anyone having a scar." Drake could see she was thinking she might have been wrong.

"You wouldn't have seen it. The scar happened around three years ago," Alex said. "Whips can be dangerous if a Dom loses focus."

"He cut *himself?*" Ray snorted.

Drake grinned at Alex.

"*Frak*," MacKensie said as she pocketed her phone. She'd been calling the few people who they knew were current members. "No one is answering."

"They probably don't have their phones with them. Crypto made me leave my cell in the car that night," Ray said. "Club rules."

Unsurprising. Most BDSM clubs and groups were vigorous about privacy.

"What about Blaize?" Hope tapped her chin. "Didn't the women say he usually arrives late—near the end of the party?"

Drake tilted his head. "Perhaps we could follow him to the party location?"

"Tailing a car at night is more difficult than you'd think," Simon said. "And Seattle has insane traffic patterns."

"He might not be planning to go," MacKensie pointed out. "People said his attendance at the parties is sporadic."

"Wait..." Leaning against Drake, Ray fidgeted with her rings before she looked up at him. "Calling Blaize wouldn't work—he'd be super suspicious—but if I saw him, I bet I could get him to take me."

Drake frowned. Why did she sound so certain? "As it happens, I know where he'll be"—he glanced at his watch—"right about now. Now explain this plan to me."

"He, ah... At the convention." Her voice carried brittle anger. "He...he asked me out on a date." She shook her head. "I turned him down...but what if he thought I changed my mind?"

Turned him down. Of course she had. Ray's loyalty was as fierce as a lioness with a cub. Drake pulled her closer.

She pulled in a breath. "So, if I accidentally ran into him, he might take me to the party."

Merde. Appalled, Drake gripped her shoulders, forcing her to face him. "Absolutely *not*."

This is not the smartest thing I've ever done. Drake was right to be worried.

Downstairs in the lobby of Drake's building, Ray sat on one of the long benches with Peter keeping her company.

Simon and Rona were having drinks at the Pink Door and watching Blaize. It made her feel weird. If Marisol hadn't canceled, they'd have been at the same restaurant with Blaize.

Waiting for a signal and location, Drake was in one car nearby, and he planned to pick up Simon if possible. In another vehicle were Alex and Bear.

If Blaize took Ray with him, both cars would follow. Peter would remain at the condo to send the cops and/or provide bail money if things went wrong.

No one could agree on exactly what to do. As Simon had said, the situation was fluid. They might call the police if needed. Admittedly, at a party, it might be difficult to prove who drugged a drink. Also, for this kind of crime, the victims were usually the ones to suffer. A nursing student sure didn't need her reputation destroyed.

So the plan was she'd go with Blaize and hopefully find Marisol. The guys would provide backup if she had trouble getting Marisol out. After that, the Doms might stay and...chat... with the club members and or the offenders if it was obvious who they were.

If nothing else, Blaize was going to be in a world of hurt.

But first, she had to get Blaize to take her to the party. Would he still be interested in her? What if he had other plans for tonight?

No, no, it would work. *We're coming, Marisol. Hang in there.*

She was as prepared as the others could make her. All their phones were connected with an app to allow the others to track her cell...as if she were a teenager.

Ray carried the tiny cell phone Simon insisted Rona carry for a backup. From the rueful smile on Rona's face, Doms who ran security companies were *excessively* overprotective.

Drake had called a private investigator he knew who'd sped over to drop off the mini video and audio camstick Ray had tucked into the jacket she wore.

Her jeans pocket held her wallet and keys. Down in her sock was a lockpick set from MacKensie. The vet always carried a set.

Ray shook her head, remembering Mac's solemn voice last Monday as she told everyone, "*Locked doors are bad things.*"

Everyone had their own traumas, didn't they?

As Ray sat with Peter in the lobby, the minutes ticked by.

"For heaven's sake, how long does it take to eat a meal?" Ray whined under her breath. "It's after 10 o'clock."

Peter patted her arm. "Blaize likes to hear himself talk."

Finally, her phone dinged with a text from Simon. *"He's walking out now."*

She rose.

Peter gave her a nod and disappeared. It wouldn't do to have Blaize see him.

But she was on her own now. *Gods.* Fear shook her, and she stuffed it down. *I can do this. For Marisol and all the others.*

Giving herself a firm nod, she crossed the lobby and spotted Blaize strolling down the sidewalk under the building lights.

Girl, find your angry face. Hauling anger up from her gut, she stomped past the guard and shoved the door open with all her might. "Goddamn fucking stupid Dom," she spat out in a loud voice.

From the corner of her eye, she saw Blaize pause. Pretending she hadn't seen him, she turned and kicked the building. "I hate you."

"Sounds as if you're having a very bad night," Blaize said from behind her.

Letting out a squeal, she jumped back and put a hand on her chest. "You—oh, it's you. You scared me to death."

"Sorry, subbie-girl." He set a hand on her shoulder, totally infringing on her personal space.

Don't cringe.

He glanced between the huge building and her. "Did you and Drake have a fight?"

"He's a complete butthead, thinks he's *all that*, and I'm done with his shit. Just done." She crossed her arms over her breasts, pressing them upward—and he definitely noticed.

She summoned her cutest pout. "He can keep his stupid club too. I'm never going back *there* again."

"Oh, baby, I'm sorry you're unhappy." He wore a perfectly tailored dark suit. Clean shaven with his light brown hair carefully swept off his brow, he was a good looking man...and utterly gave her the creeps. "Let me make it better."

She lifted her eyebrows. "Now how would you do that?"

He chuckled. "If you don't like Chains, you should go to a BDSM play party with me. You'd have fun. Promise."

It took everything she had not to run. To tilt her head and look intrigued. "A party? Really?" She frowned slightly. "I dunno. I went to one years ago, and it was bad, and afterward, I had nightmares *forevah*."

His eyes took on a cruel gleam. His charming smile turned almost sharklike before his mask slipped back in place. He savored the knowledge he'd given her nightmares. "Now that's just sad. But this one will be fun."

Taking her hand, he pulled her to his side. "Don't worry. I'll take good care of you."

"The traffic is picking up." Drake tightened his grip on the steering wheel. "Why did the *imbécile* have to take Highway 99?" They were passing T-Mobile Park and... "*Merde*. The Mariners must have a game tonight—and it's just let out."

Seattle loved its sports teams, including the major league baseball team. But with all the cars flowing onto the highway, there was no way to close the distance to Blaize's vehicle.

In the passenger seat beside him, Rona flinched as a pickup veered across three lanes and horns sounded. "*Crom*. I think every driver on the road is drunk."

Drake had to agree. "I can't catch up." In the darkness, he could barely tell which vehicle was Blaize's. "Is that his car taking the West Seattle exit?"

The vehicle increased in speed.

"Yes, it's him," Simon confirmed.

Drake followed onto the exit. Not that the traffic improved, and he couldn't spot Blaize's car any longer. "Is Ray's phone still showing on the tracking app?"

"It is, but they're making better time than we are." Tension edged Simon's steady voice. "I wish we'd had time to pick up better equipment." The owner of an international security company loved all the techy stuff.

"It was good you could equip her with a mini-phone and the camstick." A flashy Mustang darted in front of the car. Drake slammed on the brakes.

Simon's phone dinged with a text, then another. "I asked Alex where they are. According to the map, they're even farther behind than we are."

Drake scowled. Drivers hated the congestion on the West Seattle Bridge, and it was worse at night. "Hopefully, the traffic will ease up and I can—"

Ahead of them, brakes squealed followed by the ear-splitting sound of a collision. Metal shrieked. And from the sound of it, more cars crashed. Ahead and around them, brake lights flickered on like an all-red fireworks display...and traffic slowed to a crawl. A multi-car accident on the West Seattle Bridge was *not* what they needed.

Drake clamped his jaw to keep from spitting out curses.

Their highway had just turned into a parking lot.

Masks. I hate masks. Saying everyone at the party had to wear a mask, Blaize insisted Ray put on a medical-style blue spangled cloth. As she walked with him up the sidewalk toward a house, the cloth over her mouth fluttered and left her feeling as if she couldn't get a whole breath.

Blaize had on the kind of mask worn by criminals and ICE agents—a stretchy black, face-covering gaiter drawn up over his nose and extending to his collarbone.

I don't want to do this. She hugged herself as she looked around the rundown neighborhood. The house on the left was condemned. The one on the right had no lights showing.

She glanced over her shoulder, and her stomach sank. There were no car headlights showing from down the street.

The accident on West Seattle Bridge had been close behind Blaize's car. When the bridge was congested, clearing away wrecked cars took a long time. Drake and the others were probably still stuck there.

I have no rescue anytime soon.

Blaize looked down at her. "To keep everything confidential, no one uses real names here...and submissives don't get names at all. I'll call you slave."

"No." She spat out the rejection without thinking and saw anger flash in his eyes. "Sorry! It's just...the word *slave* makes my skin crawl. Can we, please, use something else, maybe. Sir?" She almost gagged on the placating words.

But they worked. His eyes smiled at her. "All right. Subbie-girl will work."

Ugh. I am not submissive to you, you lying rapist. She forced a smile behind the mask. "Great! Thank you."

"Hey. Didn't think you were coming today." The deeply tan man at the door had a shaved head and a gaiter mask with a graphic of bared teeth. "Who're you tonight? It's hero night. I'm Conan."

Ray stopped, unable to move forward. She'd had so many nightmares where everyone wore masks.

"Conan. Good choice. I'll be Wick." A couple of inches

shorter than the big man, Blaize clapped him on the arm. "I hadn't planned on attending, but my slave has been annoying as shit."

He had a slave. Was she who he'd called fuckface on the phone? Was he cheating on his slave, bringing Ray to a party? Yeah, he really was a douchenozzle.

"Besides I knew subbie-girl here would enjoy our party."

She nodded enthusiastically. And heard the faint sneer as he said subbie-girl. To these guys, a submissive was...a nothing. She was nothing.

"Oh yeah?" Conan's gaze ran over her in a sexual appraisal that made her skin crawl. "Yeah, I can see why. *Niiiice*. Welcome, subbie-girl. Did you leave your phone in the car?"

She wet her dry lips and found her voice. "Um, yes, uh, Sir." It'd been distressing to leave her cell on the front seat. Involuntarily, she bumped her ankle against her other leg to reassure herself she still had Rona's tiny phone.

I have a phone. I'm not completely out of touch.

"She's a very good girl." Blaize put an arm around her and guided her into a big living room.

It was, indeed, a different house from where she'd been before. With an open floor plan, the living room separated from the kitchen by a tile-topped island. Bottles of alcohol and glasses were lined up along the top.

If she'd known more about BDSM back then, she'd have seen the way they pushed alcohol on her before playing as a red flag.

Focus, Ray. Find Marisol and get her out of here.

Hey, maybe she'd get lucky, and Marisol wouldn't be drugged or anything. But the nursing student was exactly what these animals preferred—a sweet, eager-to-please newbie who didn't know anyone in the group. And the way her Dom pushed to get her here? Really suspicious.

In the living area were two beat-up couches facing each other along with several more overstuffed chairs. A small TV on top of wall shelves played loud music videos. Curtains on the side and front windows were drawn.

The members appeared mostly heterosexual with more female submissives. The male Dominants were in their twenties to late thirties, all with masks.

Some of the submissives appeared to have lost their masks along with much of their clothing.

None of them was Marisol. Where could she be? *I can't leave unless I know for sure she's not here.*

Portable BDSM equipment was scattered through the room with different scenes playing out. A gagged woman on a St. Andrew's cross getting lightly flogged. A man caning a woman on a spanking bench. Wax play on a compact massage table.

Memories of her assault kept sideswiping her, until she had to clench her hands to keep from screaming and running as fast and far as she could. Thankfully, the lights were low enough Blaize didn't notice how terrified she was.

Although Master Drake certainly would have. Blaize wasn't very perceptive, was he?

She bit her lip and glanced at a woman getting flogged. *Please be close by, Drake.*

Surely he was. All of them.

But she felt awfully alone.

Nonetheless, it was time to act.

"Wow, it's pretty warm in here." She pulled off her jacket, looked around, and...*there*. The TV was on a head-high empty bookcase against the right wall Perfect. "Let me put this out of the way."

Walking away from Blaize with her hands hidden in the fabric, she turned on the camstick, clipped the device to a fold with the camera pointing outward, and rolled the jacket up. The roll fit neatly on top of the bookshelf, camera barely poking out, and should give a good view of the room.

Returning to Blaize, she leaned against him. "What's with the scene names? I don't understand."

"We pick a theme and use new names each party."

That was new. A shiver ran up her spine. It would make identification even more difficult.

"Oh." *C'mon, Ray. Keep the man buttered up.* "And you picked Wick." She smiled up at him. "I could see you as a legendary hitman."

Ha, he stood a little straighter. "Let me show you around, not that there's much to see. Kitchen, of course."

At the back of the room, he pointed to the hallway. "Bathroom is on the right."

"Always good to know."

"St. Andrew's cross. Spanking bench." As Blaize led her in a circle around the living space, the predatory eyes on her made her skin crawl.

An over-muscled one muttered to the other, "It's a twofer night, is it? This'll be fun."

Blaize stopped in back of one of the couches. "You're wearing too many clothes." After pulling off her shirt and bra—and permitting her to keep her pants on—Blaize fondled her.

She suppressed her gag reflex and let him. When he pulled cuffs out of his toybag, she shook her head. "Please, Sir, I have nightmares about being restrained except at clubs. It scares me too much."

Amusement glinted in his eyes again. "Then you'll have to hold very still. I'll start with a light caning. Pull your pants down. And count for me."

Trying to show enthusiasm, she complied and bent over the back of the couch. "One, two..." She yelped when the blows progressed quickly past light to almost savage. *Gods, it hurt.* Tears rolled down her cheeks. "I...I lost count."

Delight showed in his gaze as he pulled her mask right off and kissed her cheeks. "Poor subbie-girl. I'll get you something to drink, and you'll feel better. Maybe a rum and coke?"

"Yes, please." She pulled her pants up over her burning butt.

He turned and called, "Bartender. What's your name tonight?"

At the island dividing the kitchen from the rest of the open space was a big man with receding sandy hair and cold blue eyes. "Savage. You?"

"Wick. Bring over a rum and coke for the girl."

"Coming right up." Savage pulled out a coke from the fridge.

"Hey, subbie-girl, check out the spanking over there." Blaize pointed to a scene across the room. Was he was trying to keep her attention away from the bartender?

Might as well cooperate. "Oh, he's hitting her hard." The poor woman was crying. The Dom was a total jerk, taunting her in a sneering voice.

Bastard. He had shaggy brown hair. Average height but a huge chest. Tattoo sleeves peeked out from under the cuff of his long-sleeved tee.

Avoid him for sure.

"He seems kinda mean." As Blaize watched the scene, Ray twisted far enough to keep an eye on Savage.

She blinked when he carried her drink into the hallway and turned to the right. Into the bathroom.

What in the world?

Before Blaize noticed where her attention was, she focused on the spanking. "Ouch, she's not going to be able to sit down for a week." Wiggling, she added, "I'm going to have problems too. Thanks for that, Sir."

"Sir is good." Blaize gripped her hair painfully hard. "I prefer Master."

"Uh... Yes, Master Wick." *Master Slime-sucking Guttertrash.*

"Much better." He turned. "Ah, here's your drink." He sounded so disgustingly smug her hand itched to slap him.

Instead, she accepted her undoubtedly drugged drink from

Savage. Holding it to her mouth, she wet her lips and pretended to swallow.

The satisfied gleam in Blaize's eyes nauseated her.

Her hand trembled so much she almost spilled the drink. *I have to*—have to—*get rid of this.*

No convenient flower pot. However, the carpet was a variegated brown shag—and ugly.

"Oh, look, the spanking is done." She tried to sound disappointed.

Blaize followed her gaze across the room.

Now. She bent and set the glass on the floor beside her foot, sloshing the liquid onto the carpet beneath the couch.

Straightening, she put her hands on her lower back and arched with a groan. "I tell you, woodworking for a living is sure hard on the back."

Her breasts captured his attention, and he ran his hands over them. *Again.* "I admire your industry, subbie-girl."

Gag me.

She giggled, as if the alcohol—and drugs—were hitting. "You're so funny."

Picking up her glass, she pretended to drink again, before flopping over his knees. "Maybe you should swat *me* a couple of times too."

This time, while wiggling and waving her ass in the air to keep his attention, she spilled the last of the drink beside his foot. With her hand wrapped around the bottom of the glass, she pretended to finish it off. "All done. Spank away."

He hit her, fairly hard—but at least her jeans made it less painful. Still, she yelped and played it up.

At the front of the room, the innocent club members were starting to leave. Several offered to help with the clean-up and equipment takedown.

Holding the door open, a Dom with dark red hair laughed and said, "We got this. But thanks for offering."

A harder swat to her sore bottom made Ray half-scream.

"There, that should keep you in line." Laughing, Blaize helped her sit up.

Damn him. Unlike the spanking with Drake, this one simply *hurt*. Hurt a lot.

Blaize wiped her face with her shirt. "You're a real crybaby, aren't you?"

What a tool. She half-lowered her eyes, whispering, "Sorry, sorry, Master." *How did I act when I was drugged before?* From what the other victims reported, the same drugs were used each time, starting out with ecstasy. Rona had told her how it affected people. Time for some acting.

She sniffled, then giggled a little. "I don't know why I'm crying; I feel so good!" She giggled more. "All full of energy—and you're so nice to me." She flung her arms around Blaize, hugging him hard and slurring her words. "You're just *amaishing*. So much more commanding than Drake."

"Yes, I am." He was so arrogant, she wanted to plant her knee in his balls. "Now let's—"

Before he could come up with something painful, she squeaked and bounced on the cushions. "Oh, oh, I gotta pee. Before we do anything else. Bathroom first, please, Master?"

Blaize helped her stand, chuckling when she staggered. "First room on the right."

"Thank you, Mashter."

The hallway had two doors past the bathroom. She glanced over her shoulder and saw Blaize joining the Doms at the front door. They were sending off the regular club members.

No one was watching her. *Marisol, where are you, dammit?* She turned the handle on the first door. Unlocked. An empty bedroom.

The door at the end of the hallway was locked. Ha, not a problem. How many doors had she unlocked as a teen when helping Pa in his handyman business?

She even had lock picks to use. *Thank you, MacKensie.* She reached into her left sock and pulled out the lock picks.

Old building, interior door lock. Easy peasy lemon squeezy. After tucking the lockpicks back in her sock, she silently eased the door open. The dim light from the hallway spilled into the tiny bedroom—and over the woman on the bed. Tied-up, gagged, eyes closed.

Marisol. Ray barely kept from shouting. She glanced around and behind to ensure none of the assholes were around, then hurried inside.

A dark, swelling bruise on Marisol's cheek sent anger flaring through Ray's blood. Someone had slapped the girl. Hard. She'd probably wanted to leave, and they decided to drug her and lock her up for later. But thank all the gods, she was still fully dressed.

Ray bent and whispered in her ear, "Hey, Marisol, wake up." No movement.

A shaking didn't help much.

"Mmm, mmmh." Eyes opened, gaze unfocused, and pupils so dilated her brown eyes were black.

Damn, damn, damn. Ray's worst fears. Drugged. And already falling back asleep. Shallow breathing.

Call 911? No, if Blaize and the other Doms heard sirens, who knew what they'd do to keep an obviously drugged woman from being found? One with restraint marks on her body.

Ray glanced around the room. One narrow window with a bush in front of it. *I could get through it with some scratches—but not hauling a limp body.* Not quietly.

And then what? *If I don't go back in the living room real soon, Blaize will come looking. Find they're missing Marisol, and they'd come after us. I wouldn't get far trying to carry her.*

Marisol might be short, but she was solidly built, and she wasn't a lightweight.

Bending, Ray whispered in her ear, "I can't rescue you. But others can—and they're coming. Hang on. Just hang on."

Tears burned her eyes as she slipped out of the room, relocking the door behind her. Leaving her friend behind.

Lips pressed together to keep from sobbing, Ray walked into the bathroom, closed and locked the door.

Now what? What can I do? Gods, there were too many bad guys here. Simon or Drake would have to take Marisol to the hospital—or maybe both would leave if she woke up confused or needed medical care on the way. And there were too many belligerent assholes here for only one man to handle. What if Alex and Bear couldn't get out of the traffic jam for...for hours?

Her internal voice felt as if it was shrieking. *I'll be here. Alone.*

Fear swept over her, and she started to shake. *If they catch me, they'll do it to me too.* Drugged, tied up, assaulted. Again.

I can't do this. She eyed the window. *Get out of here and run. Can't. Have to get Marisol out.*

Breathing hard, she took a moment. Then dropped her pants and sat on the toilet. And was still so scared it was even difficult to pee. While sitting, she worked the mini phone out of the hem pocket Hope had sewn into her jeans.

Such a tiny thing. *I can call Drake.* Everything inside her *needed* to hear his voice.

No. Can't risk the sound. She blew out a breath, checked the sound was off, and texted Simon—the only phone number in the directory.

93515 Hazelwood M in locked back bedroom north side of house. Drugged—pulse weak. Needs hospital. How soon can you get her free?

She stared at the tiny display. *Please, please, come soon.*

Us-approx fifteen minutes. Will break into back bedroom. Z&A-unsure.

. . .

She calculated distances in her head. Drake and Simon must have gotten through the traffic pileup and were getting off the bridge. Bear and Alex must be stuck farther back.

Stupid bridge.

She bit her lip. If there was trouble, they needed Bear and Alex. Because... A couple of the Doms looked really aggressive.

Hell. Okay, girl, play it by ear. It'll work out.

Her laugh came out bitter. *Sure it would.*

After replacing the phone in the hem pocket, she washed her hands and...frowned.

Why did the bartender bring my drink in here? How about I make like a detective and search the joint.

The medicine cabinet and counter drawers were empty.

But! Beneath the sink was one of those fireproof safe boxes. Small enough to be portable. *I bet they take this to all their "club" party houses.*

It was locked, of course.

Hoorah, I'm a master of locks. It only took her a few seconds to get the safe open. Inside the padded box were corked vials. Some labeled MDMA, which was ecstasy. Two vials were empty. Yeah, probably from going into her and Marisol's drinks. *Damn them.*

Three were labeled R, probably for Rohypnol. One empty one. *The one they used for Marisol?*

It kinda seemed a shame for perfectly good drugs to go unused.

No, don't do it, Ray.

But... The boys would simply *lurve* to try out their own drugs, right?

Gotta. Just gotta.

She already had her keys and wallet in her tight jeans. The two Rohypnol vials barely fit.

As she walked out, the cool air in the hall wafted over her bare skin, making her far too aware of being half dressed. *I hate this.*

But—no choice. She needed to keep the men's attention on her until Simon and Drake or someone got Marisol free. Less than fifteen minutes until help would arrive. Hopefully.

I mustn't give up yet.

Her mouth was so dry she couldn't even swallow.

As she entered the living room, Blaize and the remaining Doms were on the front steps with a couple of persistently flirtatious submissives who didn't want to leave.

Yes! Elder Gods, bless those horny women.

Now how to use these vials?

In the kitchen area, Ray opened the fridge and found ready-to-drink cocktails, including Cutwater tequila margaritas. *Score.* She set up four glasses, rimmed them with salt, emptied the vials into two of them, swiping some of the salt off to mark them. The canned cocktails went in last.

I better have something to drink to look authentic. She poured a lemon-lime soda for herself and moved it to one side.

The men walked back in. All male Doms, no submissives. Blaize paused to lock the door, having to push his shoulder against it to get the deadbolt to work. "Get a newer house next time, Savage."

"Noted."

As they headed straight for her, she counted. Seven of them.

They included Conan. And Savage, the bartender. Her heart sank.

One pulled off his shirt, showing tats from wrist to shoulders. Her stomach dropped as she recognized the cruel shaggy-haired sadist.

She sure didn't have enough drugged drinks. Gods help her. Hastily, she made three more drinks. Without drugs. *Dammit.*

Okay, get your acting hat on. From behind the island—as if it would protect her—she beamed at them all. Perhaps it was good she wasn't wearing a mask. Made it easier to appear to be drugged to the gills.

Why hadn't she brought a gun or something?

"I made you drinkshs!" She leaned over the island and held out an undrugged drink. "For you, Master Wick." *Seeing as you don't look as rough as the others, Master Creeper.*

He pulled his mask down as did the others. Seeing their faces didn't help her fear at all.

Gods.

Before she could move, a pale, lanky blond called Bourne grabbed a drink from her tray. One of the drugged ones.

Damn him. She'd wanted the drugged drinks to go to the most dangerous men.

Pulling the tray closer to her, she handed a plain one to Savage, the icy blue-eyed, overweight bartender. She couldn't take the chance he'd recognize the taste of Rohypnol.

"Here you go, Sir." The other roofied drink went to a bodybuilder type with bulging muscles and mean eyes. Definitely someone who needed to be knocked out.

Moving sideways, she pretended to stagger, and they all laughed.

Conan, the big skinhead who'd guarded the door, sauntered around the island. Ignoring her attempt to give him a drink, he grabbed her and squeezed her breasts hard enough to make her grit her teeth.

Can't hit him. Not yet. Instead, she hugged him, preventing him from getting more handsy. "You're so nice! Want a drink?"

On the other side of the island, the mean-looking bodybuilder held up his drink and snorted. "Here, Hellboy. You like this shit." He handed the glass to a stocky bearded man with dark red hair who took a taste and nodded approval.

Damn. So much for taking the dangerous ones out of the picture.

"Let's get the party started." Blaize took out his phone and propped it on the island, facing the living room space.

Savage took out his own phone and put it by the television—again facing the couches.

They recorded their assaults? An unnerving thought made her stiffen. Did they have a video of her from the past?

I'm going to throw up.

No, no, keep going. They weren't the only ones recording the events tonight.

Sliding out of Conan's grip, she hurried to Blaize and wrapped around him. She rubbed her breasts against his arm.

"You're pretty cute, subbie-girl." He rubbed his crotch against her.

Don't puke.

Blond Bourne and bearded Hellboy were sipping moderately. How long would it be before they were incapacitated?

Stall some more. Hey, she was hyper and crazy, obviously put on this earth to distract these hedge-pigs. *Go, me!*

"Hey, I'sh beed learning dance an' rapic-pactic...Ack, pr-ac-ti-cing," she said slowly. "Imma show you."

Swinging her hips like an over-sized metronome, she headed over to the phone beside the speaker box and scrolled the playlist. *Yeah, this one.* The Eurythmics' cynical lyrics of "Sweet Dreams (Are Made of This)" blasted out.

Upping the volume, she started dancing in the center of the sitting area. A few occasional staggers added veracity.

The men moved into a circle around her. Watching her with a nauseating lust in their eyes.

When Annie Lennox got to the "some of them want" list, she cupped her breasts and mouthed the words, "abuse you."

Bartender Savage drained his drink and took a step forward.

And then Bourne dropped down onto the couch as if his legs had given out.

Ray's heart rate kicked up a notch. *Don't figure it out, please!*

She smiled at the men, tilting her head in a drunken way, eyes half-closed. "Whatcha planning to do with me?" She blinked and frowned as if noticing the number of men. "There's a lot of you."

"Bitch, we're gonna fuck you so hard you won't be able to walk tomorrow," the door guard Conan said.

Savage nodded. "Start with her, then bring out the other one."

By "other one," the bastard meant Marisol. *Oh, you need a foot to the crotch. I can kick you in the jewels so hard—*

Brain, stay focused. This is being recorded. She asked loudly, "All seven of you?"

"Yeah, fuckmeat, all of us," Blaize said loudly.

Time to register non-consent. Loudly and verbally—although even being drugged should be enough. But if and when they got arrested, she'd be able to say—and show on the recording—she had refused. She held her hands up, palms out, shook her head, and retreated several steps. "No. I don't want any of you. I do *not* want to have sex with you. I'm going to go home now."

"The fuck you will." Rambo, the mean-eyed bodybuilder who hadn't gotten a drugged drink stalked forward and grabbed her arm. Yanked her to him. "You and Conan's bitch are our fuckmeat for tonight."

Conan's bitch. Was Conan the same person as Marisol's Master Atlas? Gods, she wanted to hurt him so bad.

"You..." Even as he twisted her arm and made her yelp, Rambo was looking her over. "Wick's right. You're older, but I remember you from before."

Ice ran up her spine.

"Yeah, before. She gotta great scream," Hellboy slurred.

"Hold off, Rambo," Savage said. "Roofie her first. Don't want her remembering anything tomorrow."

"What?" Frowning, blond Bourne looked up from where he sat on the couch. "I thought you said the girls were into consensual non-consent play. But drugging her... That's not the same thing. An' she doesn't look like she wants it."

"You're new, right? Relax, we've all done this lots of times." The tattooed sadist grinned.

"Yeah, this shit works great. You'll see. Makes great vids too." Bartender Savage pulled out a key and headed down the hall.

Uh-oh. Even half-frozen with fear, Ray yanked her arm out of Rambo's grip and stepped away from him.

Savage's angry shout sounded from down the hall. "Hey, two of the vials are gone."

"What?" Conan yelled back.

With a moan, the stocky, red-bearded man staggered backward. His eyelids were at half-mast, his chin sagging. Near the front window, he sank down to the floor and toppled sideways.

"What the fuck, Hellboy." Conan walked over and nudged the limp man with a boot. No reaction. "You're actin' like a roofied bitch."

"I feel funny," the blond Bourne whined.

Oh, damn, damn, damn. Ray glanced at the front door. How was she ever going to get out of here?

"Someone jimmied open the safe box." Savage stomped across the living room. He stared at Hellboy, who lay on the floor. At the half-conscious blond. His eyes widened. "Someone roofied *our* drinks. This a joke?"

"Sure ain't one of us," the sadist snapped.

Blaize's eyes narrowed at her. "*She* went to the bathroom."

They all turned to stare at her.

She took two more steps back.

"Yeah, she did it. The bitch drugged their drinks." Conan's cursing was so foul her skin crawled.

"I gave mine to Hellboy." Rambo stalked toward her. "Oh, bitch, you're gonna be sorry I didn't drink any." The bodybuilder's grin was full of malice. "I'm going to enjoy making you scream."

Gods, I'm going to die. Her fear spiked impossibly higher.

She sucked in a breath and deliberately closed her hands into fists. Time to fight. *I want to live—I will live.*

He lunged at her.

A scream escaped her as she dodged.

CHAPTER TWENTY-TWO

Quel désastre. Outside the so-called "party" house, Drake watched as the dark shadow of his car sped down the street into the night. His mouth tightened.

A few minutes ago, they'd silently broken through the window into the bedroom and found Marisol. The girl had been stuporous until they moved her, then she turned into a wildcat. A half-conscious one. She'd finally quieted when they got her outside, and she saw and heard Rona.

So Simon had driven the car with Rona to take her to the ER. The hospital wasn't far, and Simon would drop them off and return immediately.

Alex and Bear were still stuck in traffic.

At the moment, Ray's rescue party consisted of Drake by himself.

He eased around the side of the house toward a front window. His knee hit something hard. *Merde.* Ah, he'd run into a thigh-high, concrete garden gnome set in a weed-filled flowerbed.

At least it wasn't a guard dog.

He glanced at the front door. Ray was in there, and everything inside him demanded he act. Maybe he should pound on the door and demand they send her out.

Chance of success? Slim. If Blaize saw him, he'd know Drake would do everything possible to have them all arrested.

According to the members they'd interviewed, there would be at least five or more men inside. Drake was a competent fighter, *oui*, but he wasn't a superman.

Would the bastards kill to keep from getting caught? Kill Ray?

He couldn't take the chance. It would be best to wait until Alex and Bear arrived, and he could get her out safely.

Leaning his head against the window, he tried to understand what was going on inside.

There were several voices—all male. The sound of Ray's voice lifted his heart. She was there. Alive. Able to speak. She sounded calm.

A man shouted, sounding pissed off. Had they discovered Marisol was gone? More shouting—and the words, "The bitch drugged their drinks."

Clever, sneaky woman. He grinned, then fear crawled into his gut. Obviously, not all of them were drugged. This wouldn't end well.

Shouting erupted inside. A scream.

Merde. Drake flung the garden gnome through the window. Glass shattered, the sound drowned out by yelling. He jumped through the window and tripped over a bearded man out cold on the floor.

In the center of the room, two couches and several chairs made a large circular sitting area. Blaize and three men stood inside the circle. A blond man sprawled on one couch, eyes half-closed, oblivious to the noise.

Four bastards to fight, no...five. Across the room, an over-muscled man shoved a bondage table out of his way to get at Ray.

Before Drake could move, she turned to face Muscles-On-

Steroids and, with a smooth sidestep, grabbed his leading arm, spun, and flung him into the wall.

He hit hard, staggered, and fell. Scrambled to his feet. "Stinking cunt, you're going to die for that."

Ray had already run, and at the front door was struggling to turn the deadbolt. "Out, out, out, gotta get out."

Blaize yelled, "Get her!"

Yelling, three of the men from the center of the room ran toward her.

Drake charged in to intercept them.

One noticed. "Fuck! Intruder!" The motherfucker was at least six-three and the size of a truck. He turned and swung at Drake. Another with tats joined him.

The other man, shaved bald, kept going toward Ray.

Frantic to keep her from getting hurt, Drake punched the motherfucker who staggered back with a shout of pain.

The man with tattoo sleeves lunged.

Moving offline, Drake snapped a sidekick into the man's ribs. Felt them break.

Turning, he checked Ray.

Turn, you stupid deadbolt! Footsteps pounded closer. *No!* Ray whirled. Conan was almost on her. Her punch to his gut wasn't the strongest, then she powered up from her hips, shooting out her palm straight to his nose. He made a squeaking sound, stopping short, eyes wide.

And legs apart.

Total invitation, right? Her foot came up fast, kicking him between the legs so hard she felt his testicles flatten. He collapsed, hands between his legs, puking.

"Fucking slut." Like a football player, Blaize charged in and crushed her against the wall with his heavy body. Her head thumped the wood.

One hand on her throat, choking her, he pulled back, his other hand raised.

Can't breathe. Her head spun from knocking into the wall, from lack of air. Then muscle memory kicked in from Tomo's lessons. Twisting, she struck at the inside of his wrist with all her might, bashing his hand away from her throat.

His weight unbalanced, he leaned forward to catch himself.

She completed her turn with an elbow strike to the side of his head, then another strike, even harder. Wrapping her arm around his neck, she rammed his head into the wall. His legs started to give.

"Don't let your attacker recover. It's called insurance." Tomo's voice sounded in her head.

Insurance. She kicked the side of his knee so hard it made a crunching sound. "Fuck you, Blaize."

Knees weren't meant to bend sideways. He let out a high-pitched scream. And dropped.

"And fuck the horse you rode in on."

Halfway across the room to her, Drake stopped, stared, and nodded. Two down. *Ms. Lanigan has fine moves.*

"You bitch! Eat lead." Muscles-On-Steroids stood near the bookshelves. He pointed a pistol at Ray.

Non! Drake dove at Ray, taking her down. Even as the gun fired loudly, they were sliding over the wood floor, ending behind the couch. Concealment but not protection.

The pistol sounded again.

The bullet went through the couch. He felt the thud against his arm. A second later, burning pain fire tore across his deltoid. *Merde.* He clenched his jaw.

"Drake. You're *here*." She stared at him with wide eyes. Then obviously recalled the shooter. Scowling, she started to pull her feet under her. Probably planning to jump out.

Bad plan. The man was too far away—and had good aim.

"Diversion, first," Drake whispered. He needed... There, a big pillow lay on the floor beside them. "Throw that at the far wall when I say."

"Stand up and get over here, or I'll fill you full of holes," Muscles bellowed.

"What the fuck! Watch where you're aiming," one of the assholes yelled.

Drake edged to the other side of the couch and eyed the small wooden end table. He crouched. "Now."

Ray grabbed the cushion. No argument, no crying. She flung the pillow, hard and fast.

It flew across the room. A shooter would instinctively track any moving object with their pistol.

Springing to his feet, Drake hauled up the end table and threw it at the man.

It slammed into the shooter's chest, knocking him back into the bookshelves.

Charging, Drake tackled him before he could fire again. They hit the floor, Drake on top. Rolling off, on hands and knees, Drake back-kicked the man in the head.

The bastard's eyes rolled up, and he went limp.

One kick, one knock-out. *Bon.* He stood and used his foot to sweep the pistol under the couch. Three men down. But he hadn't incapacitated the two who'd attacked when he came in.

And even as he thought it, a blow across his back drove him to his knees.

"No!" Ray saw Drake fall, and panic hit. She sprinted across the room, and suddenly the tattooed sadist stepped in front of her. Before she could react, he backhanded her to the floor.

Pain seared along her jaw. Gods, she was already dizzy from

hitting the wall, now her head really spun. *Don't throw up. Need to stand. Need.*

"Hey, tats. Try me instead." Was the smooth voice Simon's? He stepped between her and the sadist.

Then there was a grunt, another. Blood splattered across the floor.

A body hit the floor near her. Bare chest, tattooed arms. The sadist.

Blinking tear-filled eyes, she managed to look up.

Simon winked at her and turned to survey the room.

The front door slammed open with a crashing sound. Bear and Alex piled in.

Across the room, Drake had regained his feet, even as Savage swung the chair at him again. Drake sidestepped, then grinned. "Here, *mon ami*, a toy for you." He shoved the gorilla-sized man toward Alex

"Thanks." With a cold laugh, Alex punched Savage in the gut and followed with a right hook.

The huge man hit the floor and didn't move.

Ray pulled in a breath. Her head had stopped spinning. Drake was all right. The others were here.

A yelp made her jump and look toward the front door.

"Stay down, asshole." Crowbar raised, Bear stood over Conan whose shaved head now had a bleeding welt.

Drake knelt beside her. "*Ma chérie*, where are you hurt?" He had her shirt in his hand.

And suddenly, there was nothing more she wanted than to have it on. To not be half-naked in this...this place. She frantically pulled it on. And heaved a sigh. "Thank you. It—I needed clothes."

"But of course." Then his eyes darkened. He gently tilted her chin, his gaze on her very-sore jaw. "I will kill him."

"Okay." When he started to rise, she grabbed his arm. "No, wait." *I don't think my brain is working quite right yet.* "No killing.

Maybe...a hug instead? For me, not him."

"*Zut*. That I can do." After a quick glance at the room, he sat down and wrapped his strong arms around her. "For me, I badly need to hold you. This—this was far too close."

Hearing his unspoken words—*you almost died*—she started to shake. She had—and so had he. Far, far too close.

She melted into his embrace, his hard, solid body against hers, his arms iron bands around her. *Safe. I'm safe.* And along with the relief was surprise.

Because, this time, she'd been *saved*. Drake had come for her. So had the others.

The men who'd assaulted her that night weren't all powerful. They *weren't*. She'd fought back. And others had come to help.

We won.

"I was so scared," she whispered, pressing her face against his neck. "I saw the traffic accident behind us. I didn't think you'd make it out. Not in time.

"We were terrified for you." He ran his hands up and down her back, soothing her.

"Hell, got a runner!" Bear yelled.

Ray twisted and saw the tattooed sadist dash through the kitchen to...a back door? "Oh no, he'll get away."

Bear chased after him.

With a slam of the door, the sadist disappeared outside. There was a yell of pain.

A woman shouted, "Ha, got you!"

Bear reached the back door as MacKensie and Hope walked through it. They dragged the sadist behind them. By the feet.

He appeared only half-conscious.

Ray stared at them, confused, as the two women got applause and whistles.

Simon asked, "Has someone called the police?"

Alex held up his phone. "They're on the way. I also called the chief of investigations and explained this mess. She said she'll be sure we get the right detectives."

Thank goodness.

Seeing Ray, Hope charged across the room and dropped to her knees. "Ray, are you hurt? Are you okay? Did we get here in time?"

"What—what are you doing here? You and Mac are supposed to be at the condo."

"*Ha.* As if we'd let you and the men take all the risk." Hope leaned forward, half-pulling her out of Drake's arms to hug her.

"Whoa, whoa, I can't breathe."

"Are you *hurt*?" Hope eased back and looked Ray over. "I cannot *believe* you came in here even knowing we got stuck in traffic, and you'd have no backup."

Ray actually grinned. "I cannot *believe* you and MacKensie were out there in the dark, staking out the back door. Good job!" She high-fived Hope.

MacKensie kicked the tattooed sadist on her way past to get her own high-five and lean down for a hug. "It felt really good to hit one of them."

Standing nearby, Alex nodded approval of his violent woman. *Okay then.*

Ray leaned against Drake again, heard the pleased rumble he made, then asked, "Is Marisol okay? At the hospital?"

"Yes and yes," Simon said.

"I'm so glad." Ray sagged in relief. Marisol was safe. *I got her out before...anything. I didn't escape before, but with this attack...* It was almost as if she'd saved her younger self. "Was she conscious?"

"Confused and fighting off and on. It's why I had to help Rona get her to the hospital rather than stay with Drake." Simon went down on one knee to talk. "Rona stayed at the hospital with her. But she texted the girl will be all right but will be in the hospital overnight."

"Rona was *here*?"

Simon's mouth twitched in a smile. "She voiced the same sentiments as Hope and MacKensie about remaining behind. Perhaps slightly politer."

Oh, I bet. Ray couldn't believe she actually felt like laughing at this point. But she *soooo* wished to have seen the argument. Three stubborn submissives, three overprotective Doms.

And they all came here. To help.

Her eyes burned with tears. "Thank you," she said. "Thank you all."

"You're welcome, lass. And you did very well." Turning to Drake, Simon frowned. "Is your sleeve wet...or bloody?"

Ray pulled away and stared at his dark shirt. "Rambo shot at us. The bullet *hit* you?"

Holding out his arm, Drake fingered the rip in his shirt. "*Pfft*, merely a graze. The bleeding has almost stopped." He pulled her back against him.

With a tsking sound, Simon pulled a tie from his pants pocket and bound it around Drake's arm.

"Glad you're all right, girl," Bear murmured as he joined them. He jerked his chin toward the two she'd drugged. "What happened to them? Too much alcohol?"

"I found their date-rape drugs in a safe box and made them *special* drinks." She eyed the others who were fighting the zip ties Alex and Simon had used. "It's a shame there aren't more vials to give the rest a good time too."

"A woman after my own heart." The corners of Drake's eyes crinkled.

Simon and Bear laughed...and then sirens sounded.

The police procedures seemed to take forever, but finally there was a scene she'd never forget.

The seven dregs of humanity arrested. In handcuffs.

Hellboy and Bourne, the two she'd drugged, were awake and able to stagger out. Obviously the doses were calculated for smaller women.

Walking bow-legged—so gratifying—Conan had a broken nose, and his shaved head sported a swollen welt.

Rambo, now conscious, sported a purple swollen area on his head where Drake had kicked him.

The tattooed sadist couldn't stand up straight. She was guessing broken ribs.

Savage also had an arm across his ribs as well as pulped lips.

Best of all, Mr. Impeccably Dressed Blaize was a scruffy, bloody mess and still not able to walk.

Most of the pond scum would need to be seen at a hospital. And then...then they'd go to jail.

In the future, when the nightmares returned, she'd present her memory with this picture.

Hours later, they returned to Drake's condo and settled down with drinks and finger foods. Unfortunately, her jaw was so sore, it was hard to eat. Rona had made a sympathetic sound and made up a cloth-wrapped plastic bag of ice to help the swelling.

As she relaxed, she was discovering all sorts of sore spots. Her throat, the back of her head, her hands and knees from landing on the floor. Drake had seen her pull up her pant legs to poke at her knees and chuckled. "We'll both be moving stiffly tomorrow."

She could only imagine. His poor back from being hit by the chair. His knuckles were swollen too.

Although the rest of the group was enjoying beers and wine, Ray hadn't wanted any alcohol, just pure water. Her mouth was dry from having repeated her story so many times for the police.

The whole night had been purely horrible, especially Drake getting shot. But now, she leaned against him, taking comfort from the feeling of his warm, hard body against hers, from his slow inhalations, even from his clean woodsy scent. It all wove around her in a feeling of security, of caring.

Drake was such a protector. Her heart was growing too full to contain all her feelings for him. He'd thrown himself in front of a *gun* to keep her safe.

From the way his arm tightened around her at intervals, he bore his own moments of remembering how close to death they'd been.

Blaize and Savage hadn't ended their phones' recordings, and she'd pointed them out to the police. Talk about damning themselves on film.

A minute before the police arrived, Alex had retrieved Ray's phone from Blaize's car—and it reminded her of Simon's camstick. She'd put on her jacket and tucked it into her pocket. Their own record of what happened.

In the safety of Drake's condo, the group watched the recording. She got approving comments of her acting ability. Cheers when Hellboy passed out.

When Rambo started shooting, she started to shiver...until Bear's football commentator critique of Drake's tackle reduced her to giggles.

Mac and Hope thoroughly enjoyed watching themselves drag in the sadist.

With a sigh, Peter shook his head at Hope. "Way to take ten years off my life." He turned the video off and shook his head. "Their own words eliminate any doubt they've done this before."

"From what they said, the idiots recorded their other assaults." Drake smiled slightly. "The detective plans to get a search warrant and find those recordings. On the way here, I called in a favor with a judge to get the warrant expedited. She takes a hard line on sexual assault."

"This would've been a mess if all we had was he said/she said." Bear sprawled in an armchair, legs up on an ottoman. "They'd say they didn't know anything about drugs. Would say you asked for it. Would drag you through the court system—especially since you drugged a couple of them."

"And Marisol wouldn't remember enough to be a valid witness," Hope added in a grim voice.

"You did a great job tonight, Ray." Rona shook her head. "You made it clear you were saying no and even got them mentioning previous assaults with drugs."

"Without the recordings..." Drake's arm around her tightened. "...there would be several ways they'd get this thrown out in court."

"To be honest, if there wasn't enough evidence, I was of the mind to do something to get them off the street," Bear said. "My daughters will be in college in three years."

"I know what you mean. I might have been able to monitor them to some extent, but it certainly wouldn't have been twenty-four/seven." Simon's gaze was hard. "Killing them would eliminate the problem."

Ray straightened. "Whoa, too far."

Bear laughed. "My solution was less final. You know what we do to ram lambs if they're not good enough to keep for breeding?"

"You mean neutering or...no, it's called castrating?" Simon raised his eyebrows.

"Yep." The sheep rancher glanced toward the street. "As it happens, I even had the right tool in the truck. Was a shame I didn't get to use it."

Ray felt her eyes widen. Talk about bloodthirsty males. Although tempting... "I guess it's good we have plenty of documentation."

She turned to Rona. "And Marisol?"

"The hospital's keeping her overnight to make sure there are no complications. She's still not tracking too well. But her mother is with her."

"I didn't think to ask you, Rona. Did you tell anyone where you found her?" Peter asked.

"No. I said I got lost on my way back from a restaurant, and she staggered out in front of me and collapsed." Rona assumed an angelic expression. "Her shirt was half-ripped off, and she's even younger than my children. Being a mom, I couldn't drive away and leave her there."

Ray smiled. In all reality, the caring, determined woman would do the same if she *had* seen a young woman in Marisol's condition on the street. "You are awesome."

Rona dimpled. "Back at you, Wonder Woman."

"I love how you drugged two of them—and damn, you can fight," MacKensie said.

Hope grinned. "My kickass buddy. You go, girl!"

Hitting the bastards—especially Blaize—had been seriously rewarding. *And huh, I did kick some ass.*

In fact, after this, facing off against other submissives should be a piece of cake.

The disaster was averted, the talking was done, and now Drake had his woman in his arms, all soft and sleepy.

"I missed you," he murmured, brushing his lips over her hair.

"Me, too, you." She pulled in a breath, snuggling closer.

Her bare skin was smooth and silky, with an intriguing woodsy-lemon scent. She'd obviously discovered his present in the bathroom—a basket from Pike Place Market with bath soap samples in different fragrances.

Because she loved matching a scent to her mood.

"What soap did you choose? Why this one?" Someday, perhaps, he'd be able to tell if she was sad or happy from her scent.

"It's a hinoki-based soap. Um, Japanese cypress. It kind of made me feel like I was home."

Of course, she would love a scent that reminded her of George and WoodSong. She'd been a lost teenager finding safety and acceptance for the first time.

He stroked her arm. "I hope someday you'll find the same comfort with me."

"I do." Raising up enough to kiss him, she smiled. "And vice versa. Your childhood was worse than mine in a lot of ways." She sighed and wrinkled her nose. "I'm still sorry about running away to the beach."

"It is in the past. And next time we stumble over triggers, we'll know to talk it out."

She sighed. "When I help Marisol find a counselor, I think I'll find one for me too. I know the criticism from Pa and Theodore and others makes me over-react sometimes. And I have trouble facing someone in confrontation stuff. I just kinda...run."

"Understandable." And something he'd have to be careful about. "It's a reflex you'll overcome now you are aware of it."

"I guess. This time I'll talk to the counselor about my childhood. And try to be open about the BDSM part of my assault back then."

He hugged her, giving her a physical reward for her courage. "*Tres bien*. If you want me to join you for some sessions, I will."

Her eyes popped open. "Really?"

"*Oui*. Bear in mind, *ma chérie*, since the counselor must have all the information she needs to help you, if you aren't open about what happened, I will discipline you until you are."

She froze, even her breathing stopping.

And he studied her, waiting for her to process his pushing her in this way. Usurping a bit of her independence for her own good. It was what some submissives refused and others craved.

"You're such a Dom." Her tone was cranky, even as she melted against him. And whispered, "Thank you."

CHAPTER TWENTY-THREE

On Sunday morning, Ray answered the door. "Finally!" She grabbed Marisol in hug tight enough to make her friend squeak. "It's been a week, and I've been worried. Texting isn't the same as seeing you."

"Sorry, sorry. I just...needed a bit of time." Marisol squeezed back.

"S'okay. You're here now." Stepping back, Ray waved her into the house. "So have—"

"Wait." Marisol sniffed the air. "What smells so good?"

"Beignets. When Drake was growing up, his mom made them on Sundays—and he was feeling nostalgic." And he'd wanted to make Ray feel better. She'd been making difficult phone calls, then had a nightmare about Blaize and woken up feeling guilty and angry and still terrified.

Sugar wasn't supposed to fix emotions, was it? Yet the pastries and lots of Drake's hugs had her feeling better.

She'd finally thought of a way to show her gratitude. Or her love. Both? And she'd be spending time in the workshop to get it made.

Because he totally deserved it. He was so amazing. They'd

been together all their free moments—and she kept falling deeper in love.

"He made a whole batch of beignets this morning. We both ate too many." Ray patted her stomach. "Which is why he's gone jogging."

"You know, I'm working the evening shift, and there'll be lots of walking..." Marisol said hopefully.

Marisol must have returned to her part-time job as a student nurse tech at Harborview. Ray grinned as her spirits lifted. Things were getting back to normal.

Hope and Peter, actually *everyone*, had gone back to work. Simon and Rona had returned to San Francisco a few days ago. *I'm already missing Rona.*

But she had friends here. Like Marisol.

"Well, we can't have you wasting away," Ray said lightly and brought out a plateful of powdered sugar-covered pastries and a glass of milk. "Eat and tell me how you've been. More than text emojis."

"Really, not too bad. It took a couple of days to get back into studying. Thursday, I had my first visit with the counselor you found for me. She's really nice." Marisol took a bite of beignet and chewed it. "It helps a lot she isn't weirded out by kink or BDSM."

"I'm glad you're able to be honest with her." MacKensie had provided a list of kink-friendly counselors, including the one Ray started with yesterday. "When I got counseling the first time, the therapist was strait-laced, so I wasn't completely honest with her." She snorted. "Now I get to work through everything I covered up."

Knowing Drake would ask and hold her accountable had helped when she wanted to evade being honest.

Marisol wrinkled her nose. "I wanna think I'd go ahead and shock a judgy one, but yeah, being open sucks. I can see why you didn't tell all."

From nearby, a thud sounded. A few seconds later, a furry head poked up high enough to check out the food on the coffee table. "*Mew.*"

"Sorry, Max. No sweets for kitties." Ray moved the plate out of paw's reach.

The feline glare was ferocious in the little furry face.

"Oooh, no purrs in your future." Marisol snickered.

"Can't blame him. Beignets smell so tasty." Ray eyed the pastries, so pretty and round and tempting. *No, no, don't do it. Just one more. Promise.* She chose one and took a happy bite with a hand beneath in a useless effort to catch the fall of powdered sugar. And left it to Marisol to choose what to talk about.

"So..." Marisol eyed Ray. "I still don't remember everything about last weekend. I know I went to the party with Master Atlas, but all the Doms called each other weird names. He told me to call him Conan."

Ray choked on her bite of beignet. She'd been right. Conan, the door guard, was the jerk who'd manipulated Marisol into attending the party so he and his twisted buddies could assault her. *You're going to jail for a long time, you bastard.* "Was that the last you remember?"

"No." Marisol frowned. "I was drinking and feeling great, and feeling as if I loved him so much, and we were making out, only then another guy came over. I wasn't down with it, and Master Atlas said okay, no problem, and he got me something to drink. But after I had a couple sips, I remembered what you said, and I didn't finish it. Only then it all gets foggy."

No wonder Marisol hadn't been totally out of it, and they'd had to restrain her in the back bedroom. In fact, Rona said Marisol had punched Simon right in the gut. "It's scary to have messed up memories and not be sure what really happened."

Ray picked up Max and set him on Marisol's lap. A purring cat was the best of comforters.

"It really is." Marisol stroked Max until his purr was loud and happy. "Anyway, I do remember some stuff. Being carried out a back window. A car ride. Where there was a woman. One of the men had a French accent. It's odd my memories don't match what the woman who picked me up told the nurses."

Dammit, Drake. You should have stayed silent. "Huh, interesting. Well, no matter how it happened, I'm glad you got out of there."

Marisol had a funny expression on her face. "It's also kind of strange your texts from that night stopped all of a sudden, and yet, you showed up at the hospital the next morning. Even though Mamá says she didn't call you, and hospitals don't give out information."

Ray flinched. *Oops, hadn't thought that one through.*

"Is your face feeling better?" Marisol traced a finger down her own jawline. "Must be embarrassing to hit your face on a workbench."

Okay, so it wasn't the best of excuses. She wasn't about to tell Marisol she got backhanded by a sadist. At Marisol's party. "It is so embarrassing. How will people ever trust me with their work if I can't even keep my own face safe?"

Marisol's expression was...odd. "You know what's more interesting? Master Atlas didn't show up at his classes."

"Huh. Good riddance, right?"

"Oh yeah. Only I really wanted to punch him." Marisol scowled. "So, at the party, I exchanged numbers with a woman there, cuz I thought it'd be cool to have other submissives to talk with."

Ray blinked. Conan must have missed seeing that.

"Anyway, on Monday I texted her I'd been roofied at the party and ended up in the hospital. She was already freaked since the police had been talking to all the BDSM club members. About the parties and especially what they remember about Master Atlas and some others, including that smooth dude from your Chains club."

"Holy cryptids. I guess the bad guys got outed." Ray

scrunched up her face. "I'm glad you got out of the party before anything worse happened."

"Oh boy, yeah." Marisol shook her head. "I guess the BDSM club is discussing everything—and plans to make a rule so only students can be members. No older guys or faculty."

"Not a bad idea."

"For me, I'm going to concentrate on school. Maybe try kink again later. Much later." Marisol finished her beignet and rose. She gave Ray a hug and whispered, "You and Drake? Thank you from all my heart."

At the door, Ray waved her off, both of them smiling.

CHAPTER TWENTY-FOUR

"I know, it's so hard. But it was wonderful seeing the cops push them out of the house in handcuffs." In the front seat of her car, Ray held the phone to her ear. She'd curled into a ball as if it would help her endure the conversation.

It had been a rough two weeks since the night they rescued Marisol.

The search warrants had come through; the police had searched the men's houses and found videos of previous assaults.

Law enforcement located and interviewed the other survivors. Like Ray, the women didn't want to be dragged through months of trials, let alone appeals.

The prosecuting attorney was surprisingly understanding, and although all the processes would undoubtedly drag out for a long time, he thought the perpetrators would accept plea negotiation. Because a jury trial would probably give them a lifetime in jail, notoriety that would affect their families...and possibly decrease their chance of surviving prison.

Inmates often targeted prisoners convicted of crimes against women and children. *Go, jailhouse justice.*

The prosecutor said he had such a strong case, he wouldn't

offer the bastards anything other than a reduced sentence. They'd have to plead guilty to the felonies. Would serve time—a lot of time—and be registered as sexual offenders.

When resourceful Simon provided Ray with the other survivors' information, she reached out to them. The women hadn't been told much more than the "alleged" criminals had been arrested, and Ray shared what had happened. Because, for her, it'd been so very healing to see her rapists arrested. To know they'd go to jail.

She ended up talking to her sister-survivors. A lot.

On the phone, Celeste burst into choked sobs. "I'm sorry I'm being such a wuss."

Making comforting sounds, Ray wiped tears from her face. *Why is this so hard?* Probably because the calls usually ended up with her having her own meltdown sooner or later.

"You're no wuss, and it's okay to cry," Ray said into the phone. "I spent years crying and having panic attacks. It helps me to know the bastards have been identified and will end up behind bars."

There was a moment of silence.

Then Celeste burst out with a loud, "Yes. It does help. I'm having a tough time now, but eventually, I'm gonna sleep a whole lot better." There was a pause, then, "Ray, thank you. And please give my thanks to your crew who helped take them down. And bruised them up before the police arrived."

My crew. Ray smiled. "Our pleasure."

Celeste half-laughed. "I'll call y'all The Avengers in my head and hum the theme song whenever I get scared."

Which meant Ray was grinning as she finished the call.

Sitting up, Ray wiped her wet face and straightened her clothing. The Chains' parking lot wasn't where she'd wanted to have this kind of conversation, but when Celeste returned her call, Ray couldn't refuse to answer. Even though she'd talked to another victim earlier.

Drake wouldn't be happy with her.

A few days ago, after talking to three women in one day, she'd had a total meltdown and couldn't sleep. So he put on his Dominant hat; they talked, and she agreed to only one call every couple of days.

He wanted her to be healthy. Happy.

Gods, she loved him so much.

But now she was late in meeting him in the club.

Yikes, he'd already texted. I am way late.

She replied to let him know she'd arrived—and admitted she'd been talking to the last survivor.

He didn't answer.

Oh, not a good sign.

Unlike Pa, who lost his temper immediately, Drake would wait until he considered the problem from all sides. He'd decide how he felt and what he wanted to happen. His control over himself was awe inspiring and a little scary.

No reply now meant he was...thinking.

A couple of minutes later, she was inside. Time to change into fetwear.

The club's universal locker room was a cheerful place with rainbow-colored lockers. Above the lockers, wall murals showed various Pride and kink parades.

At a sink in the so-called wet area, she scrubbed her face and... thinking of a comment Drake made, applied mascara and eyeliner and lip gloss. Good enough. Even better, it hid the fact she'd been crying.

In one of the private changing rooms, she pulled out the fetwear she'd bought after getting Alex's payment for the custom shelving. A Dom's money should totally go for fetwear, right? Even if he wasn't *her* Dom.

She pulled on the dress, exhaled hard, and squirmed to zip up the back. The dress was made of black wet-look vinyl. The hem ended thigh-high in front and draped lower in back. Skintight around the waist. The bra-like bodice was made of see-through lace. A lace flower was strategically positioned over each nipple—but still didn't hide much.

No underwear.

Drake's smile had been wicked when he said he wouldn't tell her what to wear but reserved the right to tell her what *not* to wear. She so couldn't wait for him to run his hands under her skirt to check.

Bad girl, Ray.

A pair of sparkly, silver-sequined, leopard-print ballet flats completed the outfit—cuz heels were a no-go for her.

Finished, she packed up, used a locker to stow her bag, and headed into the club.

Drake smiled at the little submissive tucked against his side. He'd been talking to one of his dungeon monitors when she quietly joined him. A bit on the pale side, eyes slightly reddened, although the makeup covered up any reddening of her eyelids.

She'd been crying.

But she slowly relaxed against him and soon joined the conversation. When her laugh rang out, he knew she'd found her balance. The woman had incredible resilience.

He took his time crossing the room, stopping to speak with different members.

It wasn't yet time to address the issue of her talking to more than one assault survivor today, let alone doing it in the parking lot where she had no support from anyone. During each call, she would share each woman's pain, cry with them, and give them a chance for catharsis. Her kindness and courage awed him.

Eventually, when she looked back to normal...and as if she was thinking she'd escaped the consequences, he stopped.

"Let's get you a soda or water." He squeezed her shoulders lightly. "You need fortification for the evening to come."

She stumbled. "Wait, *what?*"

Chuckling, he chose a table near the dance floor, snuggled his worried submissive against his side, and fed her some trail mix and apple juice.

As she nibbled and watched the dancers, she answered his questions about her phone conversation. "And that was it. I think she'll be all right." She stirred the trail mix with her finger.

"Looking for another chocolate chip? I noticed you ate all of them before starting on the nuts."

"Well, duh."

Yes, he really did love this woman. Grinning, he lifted her hand and kissed her fingers. "Since you're finished, it's time for the dungeon."

"Uh...right." She rose slowly, her muscles tense.

Ah, very nice. He did enjoy seeing a submissive beginning to worry about what an unhappy Dom might have planned for her.

He *was* displeased, and he did have plans. Actually, more for her sake than the sake of discipline.

After more than one call, she often ended up with anxiety and nightmares. With too many voices playing in her head and feeling too many emotions.

Tonight he'd do his best to ensure her head—and her emotions—were emptied out.

Even if she had to sleep on her side for a few nights.

"Come, *ma chérie*." Smiling, Master Drake bent and kissed Ray's forehead. But somehow, his affection didn't calm her nerves at all.

Because he was leading her straight to the stairs. *No postponement for me.*

Dammit!

With each step down into the dungeon, her anxiety rose, like a giant balloon inside her, pressing on her stomach, compressing her lungs.

At the foot of the stairs, he stopped. "Aralia."

What was he planning?

"*Aralia.*"

"Oh, right, yes, Sir?"

"Did I mention how delightful your dress is?" His dark gaze swept over her, head to toes, so very warm. "You look lovely."

"Thank you."

"However, since you were disobedient earlier, I must ascertain if you have been defiant in other ways."

"What?"

His lips tilted up. "Did you remember you are not permitted underwear in the dungeon?" Before she could answer, he put an arm around her waist and drew her close. His other hand slid under her short skirt and between her thighs before cupping her pussy. "Ah, very good."

His warm, calloused palm stayed pressed against her bare pubes.

At the foot of the stairs, in plain sight of everyone, he had his hand under her skirt. She felt her face heating, turning red.

His cheek creased with a smile. "For someone who enjoys being taken in front of others, you are remarkably modest." He tapped her cheek, smiling slightly. "Pink is a good color on you."

Whap, whap, whap. In a mesmerizingly rhythmic fashion, the flogger struck Ray's back like pattering rain. A while back, the floor beneath her bare feet had turned all soft and mushy. Or was *she* soft and mushy? It was good her arms were secured over her head since she was turning into a melted ice cream puddle

Her thoughts kept drifting away. Except for...

Something hit her back differently. Master Drake had switched to his mean, stinging flogger. It hurt. "Owwww."

With his whole body, he pressed against her from behind, his clothing cool against her hot, tenderized skin. Arms around her, he squeezed her breasts and murmured in her ear. "You're being punished so you remember to keep your promises or call me right away if you cannot."

Oh, right. He'd said that before. More than once. The puffy fog was lifting from her brain.

He paused and squeezed her breasts to the point of pain. "Aralia, why are you being flogged?"

"So I..." *Um, um...* "Remember to keep promises. Or call." *There was more...* "Right away."

"Very good." His approval wrapped around her, even more reassuring than his arms around her. "I think you have it."

So... Drake couldn't have been more pleased. His little submissive enjoyed flogging if he kept her aroused. He did enjoy wielding a flogger. Keeping the pain at the level where it increased her excitement was a tightrope that put him right into Dom space.

And rather than being furious at being flogged, each time he'd told her the next blow was punishment so she would remember and do better next time, he'd seen the melting expression in her face. She wasn't a slave, wouldn't obey him mindlessly. But in this case, when she knew his dominance was in her best interests, she not only accepted the pain, but it sent her deep into a submissive headspace.

Smiling, he moved his well-tenderized submissive to the adjacent bondage table. Back when they'd discussed limits, she wanted to see if painful reinforcement might work for her. In a few days, after she processed this scene, he'd see what she thought.

Being able to help her in this way would be gratifying. And the next part of what he'd planned would be enjoyable for them both.

As she lay on her back, he massaged her shoulders before securing her arms over her head to the top of the table. A slow kiss kept her focus on him.

He did love kissing her. And fondling her breasts, teasing the nipples. No clamps tonight since he preferred the feel of bare breasts.

The table height was already adjusted for convenient fucking. Now he tugged her all the way down to the end of the table. Her arms straightened. A strap went over her pelvis to keep her immobile. Bending her legs, he restrained her knees outward, opening her.

Perfect.

When he opened his electrostim box, she was far enough out of subspace, and alarm filled her eyes. Indeed, the contents *were* rather intimidating.

It was difficult to suppress his smile. She had wanted to try erotic electrostimulation—and insisted she liked surprises if the kink came from her approved list.

Now she was naked, bound, and spread open. Totally at his mercy. And she realized it.

He fastened the electrode sticky pads to her labia on each side of her clit.

She wet her lips. "M-Master Drake? Is this still punishment?"

"No, *bébé*." He pressed down on the adhesive pads, ensuring the contact was good. "This is going to be fun for both of us."

He winked at her...and inserted a well-lubed butt plug. A good-sized one.

Ray's breathing stopped. The anal plug felt good, but elder gods help her.... She'd caught a glimpse of a wire connecting it to some box.

It was another electro-something device and was in her *butt*.

Oh gods, had she ever worried she'd get bored with sex? It'd never happen with him. And the chain station and bondage table were right in the center of the room. Where everyone walked past.

For fuck's sake, she should've been more worried about heart attacks from pure nervousness.

"Aralia." He ran his warm hands over her inner thighs, up her waist. His eyes were dark. Serious. "I'll start low, and you tell me what you're feeling, *oui*?"

She swallowed hard. "Yes, Sir."

He reached over to his case, fiddling with something she couldn't see. His gaze was on her face.

Nothing was happening. Maybe it was broken? Such a relief. He'd surely—

A tingle ran over her labia, but different from a vibrator. It grew stronger, more intense, until it was pulsing...across her clit.

"Look at those wide eyes," he murmured. "This is a good setting for now."

He watched her, smiling slightly, undoubtedly seeing the tingling sensation was getting to her...but it wasn't enough to get off. It soon became as frustrating as being licked too lightly. Really, really maddening.

Imma gonna hit him. She pulled at her arms. No give.

Ohhhhh, the need increased, made worse by the butt plug where the fullness reminded her of how empty her pussy was. "Masterrrrr..."

Chuckling, he ran his hands up and down her body, fondled her breasts, and returned to looking at the boxes again.

The thing in her butt began to tingle too. She tried to lift her ass, but he had her securely restrained.

"Mmm, I'm pleased with this setting for you. Not hurting or stinging?"

"No. Uh, no, Sir." As the tingling grew more intense, her muscles tightened around the plug.

"Now...let's play." He opened his pants and sheathed himself in a condom.

"Here? You're going to fuck me here? In the club in front of *everybody*? Again?"

He burst out laughing—"*Oui, bébé,* I've seen how much you enjoy being watched"—and he pressed in, unstoppable, until he was in to the hilt. The fullness, especially with the anal plug, took her breath away. Her body throbbed around him and around the plug in uncontrollable pulses of pleasure.

Way, way, way fuller than when he'd used an anal plug before. *Whoa.*

He pulled back slowly, slid in, and her eyes almost crossed. *So good.* And she still couldn't come. Her hips wanted to lift.

Couldn't.

She couldn't move *anything*, could only let him take her. And take her he did. His cock penetrated her, in and out, in a devastatingly relentless rhythm.

So many sensations yet none quite enough. The edge of coming grew excruciating. Her moan of frustration turned into a growl.

"*Zut*, such impatience." He reached sideways to the box and turned something.

The tingles in her butt turned intense, and suddenly, her muscles clenched around it, over and over. It wasn't pain—not quite.

Then he reached down and pulled the plug half-way out, and the sensations grew so, so much, almost hurting, and then he pushed it back in.

She spasmed violently around it. "Oh, oh, oh."

He laughed. And did it again and again in merciless erotic torment. Her whole world narrowed to her lower body, to the shuddering pleasure.

Leaving the plug fully inside her, he started to thrust, his shaft thick and long, hitting her g-spot in a way that made her toes curl.

Her neck arched, everything inside her pulling tight.

"I can feel you clenching back there," he murmured. "Let us make everything clench." He slid his fingers through the wetness around his shaft and rubbed her clit.

Right. There.

Everything inside her broke loose, as if she'd burst out of a cocoon into the bright white of day. And the entire world was all pure pleasure. Each tingle, each throb, each thrust, sent her higher and higher as she screamed and shook and—

Came and came and came.

"Did I destroy your dexterity for all time?" While finishing the cleaning, Drake was trying his best not to laugh at his exhausted submissive's fumble-fingered—determined—attempts to get dressed.

She ignored him.

"So stubborn." The wipes to clean off and the arnica gel had left her skin damp, so there was no way she'd get back into her tight vinyl dress. He plucked the dress from her, rolled it into a ball and put it into his bag.

"Hey!" Fluffed-up hair, a glare. She looked like a pissed off kitten.

"This will be more comfortable, *mon amour*." He dressed her in one of his old, oversized hoodies. A faded blue, washed-to-softness, and long enough to reach mid-thigh.

With a soft sigh, she buried her face in it. Her words came out muffled. "It smells like you."

He chuckled. "Do you want the quiet aftercare room or to join friends upstairs."

"Friends. Please?"

"But of course."

Upstairs, Ray could feel Drake looking down at her. His arm around her waist was firm...as if he wasn't sure she was capable of walking.

The Dom needed to realize she recovered faster than his previous wussy women. "I'm good. Look." She pulled away, did a quick whirl, and...feeling the breeze on abused girl-bits, winced. No underwear.

No twirling, you fool.

Master Dom MacDomFace was grinning.

"Shut up," she grumped at him, pulling the bottom of the hoodie down as far as it would go. "You know if you were a few inches taller, this would be longer on me."

His smile widened slightly, black eyes dancing. "*Bébé*, I was just regretting not being a few inches shorter. Then the hem would end about"—he slid his hand under the cloth and traced a line along the crease between her buttocks and thighs—"about here."

"Ooooh, keep it up, Master Drake. I'll loosen all the screws in your bed so every time we make love, your neighbors will complain."

Gods, she loved the sound of his laughter. "Mouthy submissive." He pulled her close enough to squeeze her bottom and make her squeak. "You obviously need something to occupy your mouth. Either fetch drinks for us both, or I'll use your mouth for other things."

She could feel heat rush up her neck into her face. He would put her on her knees and fill her mouth with his cock. Right here. "Oh, my beloved Sir, I'd be thrilled to fetch drinks."

"What a shame. I'll wait over there." He motioned toward a back corner. At a table were Hope and Peter, Alex and Mac, Lynn and Bob...and Bear by himself.

Drake waited for her reply, and—not being completely an idiot— she kept her mouth shut and simply nodded.

He grinned and planted a quick kiss on her lips.

She hurried across the room. In a hoodie—and no pants!—rather than fetwear, she was way underdressed, so chose a spot at the end of the bar, rather than near the center. Claudia was bartending and gave her a nod that she'd been seen.

Leaning an arm on the bar top, Ray catalogued the messages from her body. Her back and butt felt like a bad sunburn, even though Drake had gone easy on her. Imagine how a hard flogging would feel afterward.

Her pussy and asshole still had odd tingles—as well as feeling really well used.

Gods, that had been a great orgasm.

As she sighed, she heard a loud woman's voice from farther down the bar. "Hey, did you see—Master Drake is here tonight. Mmm, he's looking fine."

Ray rolled her eyes. Was there any moment in time when Drake *didn't* look fine?

"Over there? Oh, yeah." Another woman raised her voice. "Hey, Justine, Drake's here. Gonna make a move and get your man back?"

Excuse me, what? Ray stiffened.

"Absolutely." The Boston accent made Justine easily identifiable. "He must be getting tired of that loud and bitchy drama queen by now."

"For sure. How long since she stole him from you—months, right?"

Months? Ray wrinkled her nose. Maybe a month and a half. Or seven weeks?

And what was this "*steal him*" stuff?

"Yes, months," Justine said. "That snarky beeotch took advantage of the troubles we were having last winter."

Anger rose, hot and heart-pounding. Justine's name-calling was bad enough, but lying? Ray's hands fisted.

Then she took a step back. A confrontation, here? *No, uh-uh.* Even the thought made her stomach churn.

But...

Why is it so hard to defend myself. Dammit, I'd confront someone if they called Hope nasty names, let alone lied about her.

She pulled in a breath. Hadn't she promised herself she'd stop running? Yet, after taking several steps in that direction, her feet stopped and refused to go farther.

"Ray." Tess, Bear's submissive, stood at the bar. "You got this."

"Sure." *Nope, I really don't.*

"Chin up and get in there, girl."

Ray sighed. Nodded.

Hey, you bastard Elder Gods, is this supposed to be a test? I don't want it.

But...I faced down six rapists. One obnoxious—jealous—woman? I can do this.

Ray straightened and strode with firm steps to the group of women. *The WBA lightweight champion enters the ring; the crowd goes wild!*

The fetwear-clad women were in a cluster near the center of the bar.

Not in the group, farther down was slender Faylee, the cookie-loving little who'd filled swag bags with Ray. Faylee glanced between Ray and Justine, frowned, and without a word, walked away.

Ouch. Guess we're not going to be friends. Ray tried to shrug off the blow.

So, four women and Justine. Not the greatest of odds.

But oops, I can't simply punch them out. Use your words, Lanigan.

Back to Ray, Justine hadn't seen her, although one woman did, and her eyes widened.

"I hear Ray-Ray gets off on stealing men who are in relationships. It's her thing," Justine said.

"Simply disgusting," a brunette in red Fetwear said.

"And I hear Justine is a liar," Ray said loudly.

The women turned—as did several others nearby.

Justine flushed—then sneered. "Oh, if it isn't the noisy skank."

"You know, Justine, I don't know you, but I heard you say I'm loud and a drama-queen. And a snarky beeotch. It hurts to have someone calling me names, especially since everyone else here has been really welcoming."

Justine blinked. "You should—"

"Along with name-calling, you're lying about me." Ray's heart seemed to be pressing against her lungs, making it difficult to breathe.

Justine's face reddened, and she drew herself up. "I don't lie."

"You're telling people I stole Drake from you and caused your breakup last winter."

The women around her all nodded, looking angry.

"That'd be difficult since I was in Indiana all winter for college and didn't return here until I graduated in May."

Mouths dropped open.

Justine's eyes widened. "That's not—"

"I didn't meet Drake until the end of July when Hope and MacKensie invited me to Chains because George, my foster-father, was a woodworker and made some of the equipment here. The pretty spiderweb?"

There were surprised looks and low comments from people.

"When they said he was into BDSM"—Ray half-smiled at the memory—"I didn't believe them, and so I came here to see the equipment."

"I knew George." The brunette in red fetwear gave Ray a sympathetic smile. "I'm sorry for your loss."

"Thank you." Ray blinked the moisture from her eyes before narrowing her eyes at Justine. "Anyway, stop lying about me. Your losing Drake had nothing to do with me. Drake says you broke up due to the fact you want an only-in-the-bedroom Dom, and he didn't want those limits. That dating you was worth a try but didn't work for him."

"It could have." Justine's voice rose. "If he'd tried harder." She slapped her hand on the bar top and screeched, "If he loved me more, he could have made it work."

Gods, the woman was deluded. Pitiful and deluded. Was she even going to listen? "Justine, honesty is required between a Dom and submissive. It's also needed in a BDSM community, any community, and you are outright *lying* to the club members."

The woman glared at Ray. "You fucking bitch, I am going to—"

"*Excusez-moi.*" Drake's smooth voice stopped all conversation. He moved forward through the onlookers.

Oh wonderful, her perfectly good catfight interrupted by the king of the pride.

Behind Master Drake, Faylee winked at Ray with a half-smile.

Ooooh, *she'd* fetched him.

And his eyes were snapping with anger.

Justine took a step forward. "Um, Master Drake, we were just talking. Girl-talk, you know." Her voice was so soft and sweet she didn't sound like the same person.

"I believe I heard most of your *girl talk*."

Ray almost choked. He had? And, knowing Drake, he would have wanted to intervene. But he hadn't. *He let me stand up to Justine.*

And I did. Go, me! Ms. Rocky raises her hands over her head in victory.

But now, the Dom was unleashed. Drake crossed his arms over his chest. Cold, terrifyingly unapproachable. "I told you last winter: I don't love you. I enjoyed being with you—at first—but neither of us spoke of love."

Breathing hard, Justine clenched her fists, then her expression changed. Turned sweet, her eyes soft. "But Drake..." She motioned to Ray. "That woman... Ray got between us. It's *her* fault."

"Hardly. I stopped seeing you last winter. I met Ray in July. You know this." He looked entirely unmoved. "It appears you deliberately lied about another member to cause her harm."

Justine's face was turning pale.

"I am placing your membership on hold. I will consider reinstating you if you meet two conditions. First, you will get counseling, and your counselor must confirm you have discussed how you lied to yourself and others about breaking up. After that, you will provide me with an essay of how you will deal with breakups in the future."

"You-you..." Justine's voice rose. "That's not fair! You're only punishing me because we broke up."

"Actually." Faylee stepped forward to stand beside Ray. "When I slandered someone in the club, Master Drake insisted on talking to my counselor before he let me return. Later he helped me make a video to apologize to the Dom I wronged." She flipped her hand in a dismissive gesture. "You're not so special, Justine. Get over yourself. And get help."

With their shoulders bumping, Ray could feel Faylee trembling. How much courage did it take to revive old, ugly memories? She put her arm around Faylee's waist and felt the woman lean in.

"Thank you, Faylee," Master Drake said softly, then beckoned to a stocky man in a dungeon monitor vest. "Shawn, please escort Justine to clear out her locker and to her car."

"Yes, Master Drake." Shawn motioned to Justine.

"But...but..." Justine looked at the other members. There were no sympathetic faces. Her friends turned away. Shoulders slumping, she walked over to Shawn, and the two headed for the restroom.

Ray bit her lip. This had escalated past what she'd wanted.

"You were really brave," Faylee whispered.

As the woman stepped away, a tall man took her hand, pulling her into an encompassing hug. "You did good, baby girl. I'm proud of you."

Aww, Faylee had a really cool Daddy Dom.

"You did good as well," Drake murmured to Ray. His expression was soft, his black eyes holding hers. He held out his hand. "Come, *mon cœur*."

Ray took a step forward, and he gently but firmly pulled her against his side.

As they walked away, she heard the women whispering behind her.

"What did he call her?"

"*My heart.* Sooo romantic."

"Lordie, do I feel stupid," said a third. "Do you realize Justine lied to us about *everything?*"

· · ·

Drake kept his arm around Ray as he fought his anger. Being a CEO, owning a BDSM club, and simply being a Dom meant he had a fair amount of tolerance for emotional upsets and shouting matches.

Not for this kind of misbehavior. People in the lifestyle often felt on the outskirts of society; they needed connection with others. But slander struck at the heart of the BDSM community.

"Now, *ma chérie*. Are you all right?"

"Oh, sure." She looked up at him ruefully. "Sorry about the drama."

"*Zut*, you simply defended yourself from her lies. I'm proud of you for standing up for yourself." It had been difficult not to step in sooner. But she had stood up for herself most admirably.

"Huh. I'm proud of me, too, I guess." Her lips curved. "Hey, do I get gold stickers?"

So adorable. Grinning, he bent down for a quick kiss.

· · ·

Ray's lips were still tingling as Master Drake guided her to the table with the others. "Hey, everyone. Sorry for the delay." She sat down beside Drake.

Tess dropped down in a chair beside Bear. "Here, I grabbed drinks from Claudia for you two." She handed Drake a sparkling water and Ray a Gatorade.

"It is appreciated." Drake smiled at Tess as he opened the bottle for Ray.

"Thanks, Tess." Ray drank a good portion of the bottle. "The sadist here made me drink one downstairs—and yet, I'm still dry."

"All that panting...and coming," Drake murmured. When she glared at him, he grinned.

Snickering, Mac added, "And screaming. Don't forget the screaming."

Oh gods, she *had* screamed. Loudly. And begged. Loudly. And...huffing out a breath, Ray straightened her shoulders. Straightened her spine. Because, dammit, this was who she was.

And Master Drake wasn't complaining. Instead, he lifted her hand, kissing her fingers in that way he had, smiling at her. "The screaming was as magnificent as the begging."

She blinked.

Across the table, Bob gave Lynn a noisy kiss. "It took you a couple of years before you felt comfortable enough to let loose with a good scream."

Lynn laughed and told Ray, "I do envy you, how open you are with what you say. I'm sure it gets you into trouble, but some of us are so repressed we've forgotten how to share our emotions and thoughts. Don't let the world muzzle you."

Ray blinked, seeing Mac and Hope nod agreement—and the men as well.

"*Oui*," Drake squeezed her shoulder. "I love you just the way you are."

With a happy sigh, Ray sipped her drink. After a few minutes of conversation, she noticed Hope was staring and lifting her eyebrows in the way that meant Ray'd missed something.

Oh! She almost forgotten the present for Drake. For Chains.

The pieces she'd made for the Elfame room were wonderful, of course, but were to finish what Faj had started. In honor of him.

But this one... Drake hadn't asked for it, but the place behind the bar where the SAFE, SANE, & CONSENSUAL painting had been needed to be filled. She'd been working on this project since last week.

Would he like it? She squirmed. If he didn't, he'd be kind, of course he would, but she'd see it in his eyes. And it would hurt. A lot.

"*Ma douce,* what has you worried?"

"I...um." *Okay, it was time.* Her gaze shot to Hope, who motioned with her chin and looked down at the table. Right, under the table.

Ray bent and pulled out the long, flat box covered in wrapping paper. "I made something. For you. For the club. I think it'll...um, but you don't have to, and if it's not right, you can..."

He touched her cheek, his gaze soft. "I would cherish anything you make for me, even if you weren't a superb artist. But you are. May I open this here?"

Unable to speak after what he'd said, she pushed the box into his lap.

Across the table, Hope was already bouncing. "Open, open, let's see it."

Drake carefully ripped off the paper and went motionless as he looked at what was inside. Then at the empty space behind the bar. "*C'est parfait.*"

"Show us, oh Master of the club," Alex said.

Smiling, Drake removed the piece from the box.

The oval-shaped carved wood gleamed under the lights. The letters she'd worked on so carefully were easy to read. Then, to her shock, he rose to his feet. He waved at the DJ, catching his attention, and made a cutting motion across his throat.

The music stopped.

"Your attention, please." Conversations stopped. Everyone turned to watch Drake.

His deep voice was exactly loud enough to fill the room. "My friends. You have seen the empty space on the wall behind the bar. And you know the foundation of BDSM—and the central tenet of Chains—is consent. Many of you are here after suffering from your trust being broken. You have found this a safe space because we honor consent, *oui?*"

Everyone yelled their answers, from "yes" to "aye" to "*oui.*"

"Ray here has also suffered and fought back from a dark place. Being as talented as our beloved George, she has created something to fill the space and to remind us all of the basis of our practice. *Consent.*"

He held up the carved wood, turning in a circle so all could see. The arc of CONSENT across the top. The word IS in the center with EVERYTHING curving up from the bottom.

"Consent is everything. A perfect reminder for what we believe and how we practice." Drake bent and kissed her. "Thank you, *mon amour.*"

Around the room, people were applauding, cheering. And some—some of them had tears in their eyes as they nodded and smiled at her. One mouthed, "Yes. Thank you."

Smiling, Drake handed the piece to a dungeon monitor who immediately hung it in the empty space. The screw had already been there and since she'd done her measurements, it fit perfectly.

She beamed. It looked perfect.

"You could have given me nothing finer," he murmured in her ear. Pulling her chair closer, he tucked her against his side.

A few minutes later, Ray heard a buzzing sound, and Drake

pulled out his cell phone. He was one of the few allowed a phone in the club.

Reading the message, Master Drake chuckled—then handed her the phone.

It was from Max Drago. A bittersweet feeling welled up, the memory of being a rescued homeless teenager and how much she'd wished she had someone like Max in her life someday.

Then she smiled. *Look, Max, I found him.*

She looked down at the text he wrote.

Got your email about Ray. WTF! But I'm glad you all dealt with the bastards—and I'm glad you're there for her. You're one of the finest men and Doms I know.

However.

If you don't treat her well, you'll be dealing with me.

Her mouth dropped open. "He threatened you?"

"You mean a lot to him, *bébé*. Of course he did."

There was the burble of a new message, and the text appeared while she was still holding the phone.

I can't believe Ray got a cat that pisses all over her house and named it after me!!!

What? Her cat didn't pee anywhere except in the litter box. Breaking into laughter, she showed Drake the text. "You lied to Max the cop about Max the cat? Shame on you."

When his grin flashed, she started laughing again.

. . .

Texting back:

This is Ray. Drake lied. My Max is charming and supportive and wonderful. Just like you.

His reply: "*Whew.*"

And then he added:

Drake's proud of how brave you were last weekend—and so am I. You've come a long way, little burglar.
And I knew you'd find your someone. Never had a doubt.

Years ago, he'd said he knew that—because she was very lovable.
A sob crawled up her throat. *Dammit, I already bawled my head off in the parking lot. Again?*
Making a comforting sound low in his throat, Drake pulled her against his shoulder and let her cry.
When she lifted her head, she saw all the concerned faces around the table. And she smiled at them.
Not homeless. Not unloved. I have amazing friends.
And Drake.
Turning, she captured his face between her hands. "I love you so very much. So much!" Her words rang out, free and loud.
So loud, actually, that *everyone* heard.
As raucous cheers and whistles filled the room, Drake's smile lit his stern face. "*Je t'aime, mon cœur.*" He put his hand behind her head and kissed her, long and slow.
Her heart was singing. *Here...here is my home.*

AUTHOR'S NOTE

The books I write are fiction, not reality, and as in most romantic fiction, the romance is compressed into a very, very short time period.

You, my darlings, live in the real world, and I want you to take a little more time in your relationships. Good Doms don't grow on trees, and there are some strange people out there. So while you're looking for that special Dom, please, be careful.

When you find him, realize he can't read your mind. Yes, frightening as it might be, you're going to have to open up and talk to him. And you listen to him, in return. Share your hopes and fears, what you want from him, what scares you spitless. Okay, he may try to push your boundaries a little—he's a Dom, after all—but you will have your safe word. You will have a safe word, am I clear? Use protection. Have a back-up person. Communicate.

Remember: safe, sane, and consensual.

Know that I'm hoping you find that special, loving person who will understand your needs and hold you close.

And while you're looking or even if you have already found your dearheart, come and hang out with the Masters.

Love,
Cherise

ABOUT THE AUTHOR

Cherise Sinclair is a *New York Times* and *USA Today* bestselling author of emotional, suspenseful romance. She loves to match up devastatingly powerful males with heroines who can hold their own against the subtle—and not-so-subtle—alpha male pressure.

Fledglings having flown the nest, Cherise, her beloved husband, an eighty-pound lap-puppy, and one fussy feline live in the Pacific Northwest where nothing is cozier than a rainy day spent writing.

www.ingramcontent.com/pod-product-compliance
Lightning Source LLC
LaVergne TN
LVHW012340210126
830370LV00043B/1228